Also by Mildred Gail Digby:

Phoenix
Perfect Match, Book One
Perfect Match, Book Two
Stay
Uncovered

Bloodring

Mildred Gail Digby

Mystic Books
by Regal Crest

ISBN 978-1-61929-444-8

First Edition 2020

9 8 7 6 5 4 3 2 1

Cover design by AcornGraphics

Published by:

Regal Crest Enterprises

Find us on the World Wide Web at
http://www.regalcrest.biz

Published in the United States of America

Acknowledgments

First of all, a big thank you to everyone at Regal Crest for their unending support. Cathy, for taking a chance on me starting with *Phoenix*, Patty and Staci the editing team of awesomeness, and finally experienced authors who help me (and other writers who, like me, are fairly new to the writing/ publishing scene) with advice and positive interactions.

Finally, many thanks to readers who support lesfic by reading and reviewing.

Dedication

For Masa

Chapter One

A CRASH ECHOED through the yard, followed closely by a scrambling bunch of chickens. They fled in a flurry of feathers and scurried under the porch steps of the stout homestead. Another crash and a burst of bad words punctuated the chickens' exclamations.

Lark coughed on the cloud of dust that rose from the hole in the side of the barn. Jagged splinters were all that was left of the solid oak door. She shook her golden mane out of her face before she leaned over to bat at her dust-covered clothing, a dress-like shirt over loose, calf-length trousers. Both were unadorned and dun-colored, as all children's clothing was. Her sturdy boots stood her in good stead as she stomped out a sullenly smoking piece of the door frame.

The door of the homestead burst open and Lark's mother, Dillah, appeared from within. She had an apron on over her homespun tunic and long skirts. Her footsteps rang against the boards of the porch before she dashed down the two steps to the ground. The chickens sheltering under the porch scurried back into the yard, looking ruffled and harried.

Dillah threw herself between the wrecked barn door and her daughter. For an instant, Lark stood still and her heart thudded. Her mother didn't look angry. The only expression on her face was fear. Almost as if it had never been, the flash of emotion vanished and Dillah was once again her usual, matriarchal self.

"Lark! Larkspur Greenpool! What did you just do to that door?"

Guiltily, Lark rose to her full height and rubbed a sun-browned hand through her hair.

"Aw dags," Lark muttered before she stuffed her hands into the pockets of her long shirt. "Sorry, Mah. I just—well, I was just trying to fix the Lock. The fool thing stuck again."

"For once I wish you were telling me a falsehood. Don't you remember what your dah and I told you? You are never to try and fix Metal. Ever! What do you have to say for yourself, young lady?"

Lark didn't have an explanation. With a regretful sigh, she tried to grin at the woman across from herself but was only rewarded with another stern look.

A stranger looking at the two of them would never guess they were mother and daughter. Where Lark was long and gawky like a newborn foal, Dillah was solid. Instead of Lark's explosion of golden hair that fell down her back and hung into her amber eyes, Dillah was all shades of brown, and her red-cheeked face was usually wreathed in smiles—which were notably absent at that moment.

Lark summoned her courage and said, "I know I should have left well enough alone. But it just seemed like I could feel something from it. You know?"

"No, I do not know," Dillah said. "Step away from there at once. You'd best be leaving things such as that to others who know better than you. If I've told your dah once, I've told him a hundred times it's not up-and-up to be having Metal things around where there's curious young people. But no, he says. It's perfectly safe, says he. But I know better. These Metal things look after themselves and *do* step away from there this instant. I do not want to disturb the peace but if you provoke me once more, young lady, I do believe I may have to use somewhat offensive means on you. And that means I get out my wooden spoon!"

"I'm stepping," Lark said. She raised both hands and moved away.

"That's better. Now where is your wand?"

Lark looked down at her empty hands in surprise. Her head swiveled as she scanned the area. "It just kind of flew off over there."

"Well, you'd best be going over *there* and getting it. Toot toot and post haste! You've got to practice your tasks before you go to Jean Elliott's for your examinations."

Not fazed by the scolding, Lark threw a grin over her shoulder at her mother and loped into the bushes that surrounded the yard. The morning sunlight streamed through the trees above Lark's head. It cast diamonds of light down over her. She bent down and rummaged around in the brush before she picked up her wand, a sturdy staff of polished maple wood, easily the length of a pitchfork handle. It had a cheerful lanyard threaded through a knothole in one end and tied securely around the other. Lark ducked her head and whirled the wand over her shoulder in a motion as natural as breathing. It settled against her back like an old friend with the lanyard snug over her chest.

A chicken cautiously came over and pecked at one of the berries dislodged by Lark's venture into the bushes before it retreated to the safety of the chicken corral, urged by Dillah clicking her tongue.

"I don't know what's gotten into you these days, dabbling in Metal, which you know you shouldn't," Dillah said from her post at the gate to the chicken corral. She slammed the gate closed with more force than necessary, eliciting a cacophony of clucking from within. Dillah frowned and placed her hands on her generous hips. "And don't think I don't know you were up until the wee hours last night scrying with Merton."

Lark emerged from the bushes in a ruffled state. "We were only talking."

Dillah's stern expression relaxed. "There's no need to feel shy, my child. If I had a fivepiece for every late night your father and I spent scrying while we were courting I could buy us a new cart and a fine white horse to pull it."

In the fenced-in enclosure nearby, the donkey raised his head from his oats and gave a heehaw as if he understood.

"Just joking there, Brownie," Dillah said. With a jovial overarm throw, she tossed the donkey one of the yams from her apron pocket. "There's no mare or stallion fitter to pull our little buggy than you."

Lark froze. One hand clutched her wand. "Courting? You think I'd court with Merton?" She moved her mouth around the words as if they were a prickly chestnut. "Good thunder, woman. I wouldn't court Merton if he were the last living being on this green earth."

"Don't you 'woman' me! I'm your mah and you are still a fortnight away from your sixteenth birthday so don't even try and get away with sassing back to your elders. And what's wrong with young Mister Appleton? His mah and dah are good people and raised a solid, hardworking young man. You could do a lot worse than a lad like him."

Lark didn't reply. She made a sour face as Dillah turned and hustled back into the homestead. Lark wished there were some-one other than Merton who she could talk to. He didn't really understand her, but at least he treated her as an equal and not as an oddity. Lark didn't really have any female friends. She always felt more comfortable with the village boys. The talk of pretty trinkets and future suitors never interested Lark the way it did the other girls her age. Although, if more of them were like her teacher, Lark wouldn't mind at all having them as friends.

The schoolhouse had been closed for a month now, as the harvest was due, so Lark couldn't even take refuge in lessons. Not that she was a particularly brilliant student, but she liked making their teacher give her that warm, gentle smile when she made a good effort. Lark sighed. When the schoolhouse reopened after the harvest, it would be Lark's last term there before she said goodbye to it and Miss Beccah Goldwheat as well.

Lark felt a strange kind of emptiness. When Goodman River-bottom was the schoolmaster, Lark never looked forward to les-sons starting up again after the harvest and spring planting breaks. Maybe she was getting smart from eating fish. Her father always told her the fat trouts he brought home were brain food. Maybe it was true.

Lark loped across the yard and into the house. Still not used to her height, she nearly whacked her head on the rows of brass pots hanging from the rafters. She ducked and muttered not-polite words under her breath as she slouched into the kitchen. A nice smell wafted from the little potbellied stove and Lark went over to investigate.

"Now don't be getting into the yam bake," Dillah said from her perch on the stool in the corner. She had a sheaf of paper opened over her lap and glasses on her nose. "That's for the vil-lage meeting tonight."

"Tonight? I forgot about that."

"That's why I've been telling you to get in your practice now. There'll be lots to keep you busy tonight. Why don't you offer to help with the young ones?"

"No, not kid-herding," Lark moaned. Automatically, she took off her wand and propped it up against the table before she fell into one of the solid, wooden chairs. "I'll do anything else. I'll be on latrine duty, I'll cut the town square grass with my teeth. I'll personally pick up manure from every goat in the village but don't make me be in charge of all those whiny, annoying kids."

"Don't know what you've got against younguns." Dillah rustled the paper in her lap, which displayed the title *Poplar Valley Times*. "You'll change your mind soon enough when you've got a few of your own."

"Oh no, never." Lark gritted her teeth.

At that, Lark's father poked his head in the window. "Never what?" he asked.

"Just Lark being ornery," Dillah sighed. She folded the newsletter and fixed him with a stern look. "Well, you're back early, my good husband. Was there anything good at the market?"

"Not too much, but I did get a basket of rutabagas from Earlton Ploughright that look mighty nice." Walfer produced a wicker basket and passed it through the opened window into the little kitchen. His cheerful, bearded face disappeared from the window and soon he popped in through the front door and clomped into the kitchen. He stuck his hands into his worn overalls that he wore with a plain homespun shirt. The front pocket held a compact leather-bound book. The corners were soft and rounded from decades of use.

"What do you think?" Walfer asked. He paused beside his wife to drop a kiss to her cheek, which elicited a twinkle in her eyes and a slight flush.

Dillah peered at the rutabagas. "They are rather nice, Walfer. They'll make good pickles."

"Morning, Lark," Walfer said. He sat down at the table next to Lark and tousled her hair. "You're up early for someone who was up half the night. How is young sir Appleton anyhoo?"

"We're not courting." Lark dropped her head into her hands. "Dah!"

Unfazed, her father rocked back in his chair, beaming through a bushy and incorrigible beard. "Of course not."

"We're not. We really aren't." Lark crossed her arms over her chest. She said, "Besides, I can't see the Appletons wanting their well-brought up Crystalgazing son matched up with someone like me."

"Now don't say things like that." Walfer's smile vanished. "The Appletons are fine people and you can use crystals just as well as the next person. Doesn't matter where you came from, nobody with a lick of sense would take issue with that." His demeanor changed and just as quickly his broad grin was back. "Say honey bunch, how are you doing with that slice of agate you picked up at the last fair? If I recall correctly, none of the others in your age group have anything like that. Takes a person of some merit to handle an agate, let me tell you."

Proudly Lark reached into her shirt and summoned the polished rock from the pouch hanging from her neck. It nestled into her hand without balking and she held it up to the light. "Not too bad. I think it likes me. Probably going to be a good directional marker. Maybe even a navigation stone."

"There you are," Dillah said. She patted her daughter on the arm. "You'll be a fine match for whoever you choose. But first, the porridge is ready. Give us a hand there, would you?"

Lark obligingly accepted a tray containing a trio of bowls filled with generous ladles of porridge. She placed them around the squat wooden table before she dropped into her accustomed chair. Lark clasped hands with her parents and bowed her head while her mother gave a brief blessing. As soon as she was released, she attacked her breakfast.

"Good porridge," Lark said. She swallowed the last mouthful and held her bowl out for another helping from her father, who was in front of the stove tending to the yam bake.

"By the by, Walfer," Dillah said, "You need to get the carpenter down here to fix that barn door. Lark's done gone and blown up the Lock on it."

Lark's father choked on the spoonful of yam he was tasting. He pounded himself on the chest and looked through watery eyes at Lark. "You didn't now, did you? After we told you to stay away from it."

"I told Mah I thought I could fix it. That Lock always sticks." Lark finished her porridge and put the empty bowl down on the solid oak table. "I looked at it and something about it called to me. I just *knew* what was wrong with it. I was getting the pieces lined up and suddenly it blew up. I'm sorry for wrecking it."

She nearly missed the alarmed look that passed between her parents. What was suddenly so bad about her messing up the Lock? The fearful way they reacted hinted Lark's transgression was more than just the fact that since the Great Division, Metal items were irreplaceable. They should be angry, but they were afraid. Lark got an uncomfortable chill. She hunched her shoulders in shame.

"Come now, don't fret yourself," Walfer said in a gentle voice, perhaps in response to his daughter's sudden withdrawal. "I'll call Goodman Goldwheat up. Hopefully he can come by today. I'd like to have that door fixed afore the meeting. Don't want the goats getting loose and eating all the seed apples again."

Lark's breath caught in her throat. The village carpenter Rowell Goldwheat was Miss Becca's father. Maybe there was a small chance she would see her teacher before school started. Lark's heart pounded. Her body tingled in a way she had no explanation for.

"Better get word out right away, then," Dillah said. She rose and went over to the stone sink with their empty bowls in her hands. "Lark, be a good girl and get the big scrying crystal from the sitting room."

"Yes ma'am."

Still tingling, Lark ran the three steps from the warm kitchen into the little cubby they called the sitting room. Opposite from their comfortably sagging couch, it housed a wooden chest filled with their winter shoes and cloaks which was covered by a woolen blanket and piled with hand-stitched cushions. Two of the more lopsided cushions had been done painstakingly and most reluctantly by Lark.

Behind the chest, built into the wall were a number of shelves. All but the top one held the family's collection of books. Besides the well-worn and formidable family Almanac, they had titles like: *Cooking Naturally with Whole Grains*; *Home Remedies for Most Illnesses*; and *Family Planning for the Married Woman*. The last one Lark, on occasion, snuck down from her loft at night and perched furtively on the bench, thumbing through the soft pages with only a single crystal for light. She never found satisfaction between those yellowed pages, and always put the book back with more questions than answers.

She didn't have time to read anything that day. Lark kicked off her boots and jumped up onto the bench where she was at eye-level with their large scrying crystal. She got a sudden surge of pride. For the first time in her life, Lark was tall enough to reach the top shelf without stretching.

She reached out and carefully lifted the box. It had shiny brass corners and was heavy and firm in her hands. Lark balanced it on one knee before she hopped down into her boots. With her prize held carefully in both hands, she returned to the kitchen.

"Thank ye." Her father put the box down on a clear spot on the table and opened it, revealing a polished sphere of fine pink quartz, shot through with veins of white. It was about the size of a muskmelon and sat in a nest of blue velvet that was worn at the folds. The box lid was lined with reflective silver, not shiny enough to be a mirror, but caught the light and lent a glow to the depths of the crystal. At the moment, the only thing visible in the sphere was an upside-down version of Walfer's scruffy beard.

His work-worn hands combed through his whiskers. "Heh, might want to get a bit more seemly when calling up the local schoolmarm's family, eh?" He looked up and caught Lark's eye.

Lark tried to seem nonchalant, but a wild surge of giggles bubbled up from her chest. She pretended to be busy reorganizing the line of preserves on the counter before her mother came and shooed her off.

Serious again, Walfer took his hands out of his beard and rested them lightly on the tabletop. He stared at the sphere and it glowed slightly in response. Soon blurry shapes could be seen moving around in the crystal. One became clearer and Lark peered furtively over her father's broad shoulder. She made out the image of Gillie Goldwheat, the youngest of the numerous Goldwheat daughters.

"Hiya Goodman Greenpool," Gillie said. "Wanna talk to my dah?"

"Sure do little lady," he said merrily. "Or your mah, whoever's handy."

Gillie's face faded into the background and was soon replaced by a man who was smiling broadly through his own fine beard. "How's the weather over there, Walfer?"

"Not bad, not bad at all Rowell. Yourself?"

"Good here too. Looks like the corn's going to be comin' in early this year."

"Yep. Bumper crop of apples too. Come winter there's gonna be a lot of cider parties around these parts, I reckon."

"Keep some of the best of the lot back for the spring." Rowell's cheerful face became even more so. "There just may be an event of some importance coming up then. My oldest, Beccah's got herself a young man who's been coming round quite a bit these days. Daisy and I are just waiting for him to come up and formally ask permission."

"How about that!" Walfer chuckled broadly. "Might have to do just that, seeing as there could be a handfasting coming up."

"Men, never getting to the point," Dillah huffed. She clattered the dishes in a meaningful way.

"Uh, anyways, before we get too far off topic," Walfer coughed sheepishly into his beard, "I just wanted to see if you were free to do a bit of a job for us out here. See, we had a small incident with the barn door and it looks like we'll be needing a new one."

"Small is an understatement." Dillah snapped the dishtowel at Lark, who stood mute in the middle of the kitchen. Lark was not bothered by the towel snapping. She was busy being bothered by something else entirely. Energy filled her. She couldn't stand still. Lark grabbed up her wand and ran out of the homestead, into the vegetable garden where she paced back and forth in front of the compost box. Her nerves were on fire.

Why should she be bothered if her teacher was getting handfasted? What did it matter to her? Their lessons wouldn't suffer and unless nature sped up the ceremony by way of necessity, Miss Beccah wouldn't quit the school to bring up young ones until Lark was finished there anyway. She desperately wanted to scry up Merton and tell him the news to see what he thought about it, but didn't think she would be able to put words to what she was feeling. Miss Beccah was pretty and cheerful, capable and calm. She would make a good wife and if she headed a household the way she did her schoolroom, her family would be well-taken care of and well-trained. Lark should be happy for her, but her chest felt like someone had shoveled it empty.

With a sigh that came from the sole of her boots, Lark studied the clouds. She leaned back against the tall wooden box until her wand stuck into her shoulder.

"Aw, what the hey." She stuck her hand down the front of her shirt and dug out the little leather bag again. It was heavy and comforting in her hands. She pried the drawstring open and upended it over her hand. The crystals inside settled but didn't fall out until Lark focused on the one she wanted. Obediently, the sphere tumbled into her hand. She automatically stuffed the pouch back into her shirt and tucked it into her undershirt.

Lark calmed her breathing and let her gaze soften. In her mind, the sun-speckled yard became diffuse. The ground fell away from her, the trees became green tufts in the distance. The crystal in her palm warmed. Her vision narrowed to a simple homestead much like her own, with two squat and well-kept barns flanking it.

She stopped just outside the walls and silently asked for permission. Lark waited until a golden glow opened before her. A warm, sunlight-filled loft room, not unlike her own filled the crystal and expanded in her mind. A boy's round, pleasant face appeared.

"Hey, what's the weather like there?"

"Same as usual." Lark had no patience for the normal greetings. "Merton, I want to talk to you about something I just heard."

"Is it important?" Merton's affable face wasn't able to make a sour expression very well, but he tried. "I'm just having a rest before I go to help Mah with the pies for tonight's village meeting."

"Yes it's important, Good Grass, man. I wrecked the barn door."

"So? You wreck things all the time."

"Okay, yes I do. Anyway Dah called Rowell Goldwheat to come over and fix it and I listened."

At once, Merton sat up, alert. The crumpled quilt behind him abruptly changed to the wooden boards of his bedroom wall. "Did he say anything about Miss Beccah?"

"Yeah, big news. Looks like Miss Beccah's got herself a fellow." Lark forced her face into a smile. "Lucky tucker, eh?"

"No!"

"Oh come on, Merton. It's not the end of the world." Lark was more objective once it was not just her own reaction she had to deal with. "We should be happy for her."

Merton's face crumpled. Like most Crystalgazers, he tended to be emotional and dramatic. Lark waited until he had fished out his handkerchief and calmed down somewhat.

"You okay there Mert?" Lark asked.

"Yeah, fine." Merton blew his nose into his handkerchief. "I bet it's Bertie Millerhouse from over the hill. He's got three new goats recently and Mah said he was talking to old Bartholomew Waterington about renting out his old fallow field next spring. Bet it's Bertie."

"Whoever it is, we'll keep an eye on them," Lark said. "If he treats her wrong, we'll get after him and keep him in line."

"Yeah! If we don't find out anything at the meeting today, I'll listen in when Mah's talking to the planting group. They always know everything. Dah's fishing friends too."

"Okay, that's settled. Now we just have to get that door fixed. Hold your horses, I think I see the Goldwheats' cart coming over the hill. Nice of them to come the same day."

"Your family's always done good by them, so no surprise there," Merton said. "Let me know if there's any news, eh?"

"Will do," Lark said. She closed her hand over the crystal. It grew cold against her skin. She slipped it back into the leather pouch around her neck. She narrowed her eyes to better study the approaching caravan. It looked like both of the Goldwheats, matriarch and patriarch were in the front of the cart. Several tow-headed young ones ran around the wagon with tools in their hands. "Fertile as a newly-sown field," Lark's mother was wont to say to her husband over the dinner dishes when she thought Lark was asleep in her loft. Only one of the little bobbing heads was dark.

A short and cheerfully freckled young woman also came into view, striding beside the wagon.

"Tall Trees and Green Grass," Lark whispered. Beccah Goldwheat herself had come over to help oversee the fixing of the Greenpool barn door. She wore her long blonde hair in a plait that hung down her back instead of the severe bun Lark was used to in the schoolhouse. Since Beccah was unmarried, she didn't yet wear the lace shawl over her shoulders, but her clothing was that of an adult. Her long skirts swept the close-cropped grass of the Greenpool homestead as she walked. Her tunic and skirt were a delicate green color with embroidery at the cuffs and neckline, the front-lacing bodice was pulled tight over the swell of her breasts.

Lark was at once very aware of her own childish clothes, the ones that both boys and girls wore with very little variation, just as much as she was extremely aware of the tousled beauty of the other young woman's hair and the feminine curves under her clothing. Beccah looked radiant as she oversaw her many sisters.

A strange heat flickered into life just under Lark's belt. She was struck by the compulsion to run over and do something brash and heroic in front of the lovely young schoolmistress. At the same time, her feet were stuck to the spot as if her heavy round boots had suddenly grown roots into the ground. She knew Merton would tease her about it later, but Lark stood mute and still while the Goldwheats dismounted and the repairs began.

The front door slammed and Dillah came hurrying onto the porch and out to the yard. She'd hastily thrown on her shawl from the disheveled looks of things. No amount of wrapping with the supple white cloth that all women wore could contain her matronly bosom, Lark mused, not at all in the same way she'd been thinking about Beccah Goldwheat's lush form.

"There you are," Dillah said. "I was wondering if you'd run off someplace."

"I was just keeping out of the way," Lark said. "I don't want to break anything else."

"I daresay with everything you manage to break, it would be a sight more convenient if you could do so when there's a carpenting family here to fix it." Her eyes crinkled up at the corners, belying the strictness of her words. "I just came over to say I've invited the Goldwheats over for lunch once the repairs are finished and then we'll all go down to the village meeting together. I'm organizing the girls in dragging out our picnic tables and such, and your dah's going to need your help getting the pies and preserves out. Green Trees knows how he's always falling off the step-stair."

"Yes ma'am."

"You go now, shoo!"

Lark took off for the kitchen. Her heart pounded. She wondered if she'd manage to swallow anything while sitting at the same table as the lovely Beccah Goldwheat.

Chapter Two

"AN' MAH MADE three pies and Dah said I could help stir the punch," Jackie, the third youngest of the Goldwheat girls said into Lark's ear.

"Is that so?" Lark replied in a preoccupied way. "Make sure you don't let any leaves and bugs get into it like young Ellis Fallowfield did last time."

"He did that on purpose," Jackie announced to the table at large. "Cause he's a spoiled brat and a donkey. Just like Gillie."

"I'm not!" Gillie looked up from the pile of mashed potatoes on her plate with tears in her eyes. "You're a donkey Jackie-whacky!"

Lark sighed. She removed her plate from the table and hitched her knobby stool away from the argument. In only two more weeks, she'd be of age. Why did she still have to be relegated to the children's table at gatherings? She stole an envious glance at the adults' table, where Beccah paid delicate attention to the current discussion, which revolved around goat feed.

Lark moodily dreaded the town meeting even more. She resolved to volunteer for any kind of duty that didn't involve children. Meanwhile, the two dueling sisters launched themselves from the table and tugged at each other's hair. The remainder either shouted encouragement or started up their own whining tirades. Lark felt the beginning of a headache coming on. She scooted her stool backwards some more until she was clear of the table and its shrieking members.

"What are you doing sitting all the way back there?" Dillah appeared in front of Lark. "Here, take this basket and gather up the dishes. Your father's getting Brownie ready to go. No dawdling, toot toot!"

Lark heaved a sigh and looked at the laden table, surrounded by squawking, whining little girls. "I'd rather help with Brownie," she said.

"How about if I give you a hand?" Beccah came over with a stack of cups in her hands.

Lark leapt into action at once. She grabbed at all the dishes, grinning wildly. "That's right kind of you, Miss Beccah. Here, let me get those for you. Don't want to get blueberry on your nice sleeve there." Lark spoke quickly, her face was hot and her heart pounded.

"You're very helpful," Beccah said.

"Doing my best," Lark said. The end of her wand caught on the tablecloth and caused a stack of dishes to tumble off the corner of the table. "Aw dags! I mean, uh, oh dear."

"Larkspur," Dillah called from the kitchen window. "Watch your language, young lady."

"Ears of a bat, that one," Lark muttered. She jumped guiltily. "Uh, of course with only the best intentions in mind."

"Of course," Beccah replied with a conspiratorial smile that warmed Lark to the depths of her soul. "My mah and dah have the best ears and eyes in the world when there's naughtiness around."

"Can't think they'd have any trouble with you," Lark said. She couldn't look away from her teacher's deep eyes. She felt like she was drowning in their hazel depths. In the background, three of the medium-sized Goldwheat sisters were in the midst of a heated discussion about who would get to sit in the front seat of the cart but Lark tuned out everything other than Beccah's voice.

Beccah laughed. "I'm sure I gave them my fare share of worries, I have to say. Although being the oldest does have some benefits. I didn't have anyone around older than me to spar with. And speaking of older siblings, how's Yarrow doing these days? I heard he got himself a place out near Miller's Hill."

"Big bro's fine," Lark said. Her mind whirled with the effort to be coherent. She was having a real adult-like conversation with Miss Beccah. Merton would be so jealous. Lark hooked her thumbs into her belt and said, "He's settling into his new place pretty well. Mah and Dah gave him a bunch of sprouts from our orchard and he's got a good start on his own now. He also went and got himself some livestock from old Gorram Maywind last I heard. By next year's harvest he'll have a full operation going, looks like."

"That's wonderful. Good luck to him." Beccah's final words were spoken overly-loudly in order to be heard over her younger sister, Jackie's, exclamations.

Jackie stood beside the Goldwheats' cart. She slapped at the feet of the one dark-haired sister who sat in the front seat. "No fair. You always get the front, 'Melia! You're not even one of us, you're just some stray we found in a wicker basket. You don't even belong here, just like *her!*" At this, Jackie's finger stuck out and pointed directly at Lark.

Their mother, Daisy, rushed over in a flurry of skirts. She yanked at Jackie's arm, her usually smiling face was dark with anger.

"Jacinda! For shame," Daisy said. "I don't remember bringing up such an insensitive boor of a child as you. It doesn't matter how or from where any of you came to be here, you're all our dear precious children. For your untoward comment you'll have no pudding tonight."

"Aw Mah," Jackie whined. She kicked at the dirt and stuck her lower lip out in a pout. "We should just send her back where she came from."

"None of that. For your unkind words, I'm sending you home with your sister Beccah this instant. Go now."

Lark turned away from the scene. Her face burned. Something tugged on her sleeve and Lark looked down. Amelia clung to her, eyes damp. In the distance, Beccah called out a brief farewell before she took her whining and squirming sister away by the arm. Lark's previous good mood evaporated into the golden afternoon air. Around her, everyone bustled about, business as usual. In the middle of the fuss, Lark and Amelia stood without speaking. Lark gently removed her sleeve from Amelia's grasp and patted the girl's head awkwardly. Lark chewed her lip and wracked her brain for something to say, but nothing inspirational came to mind.

"There's sure to be a lot of nice tarts and things at the meeting tonight," Lark said.

Amelia nodded. She looked down at her shoes.

Lark swallowed hard. She felt different enough without Jackie pointing it out. For her entire life, she felt like she didn't belong, like something was fundamentally different about her. Lark wanted to believe the only cause was her birthright.

Accordingly, the new barn door was finished, the donkeys were hitched to the carts and the assembled people were ready to move out. The Greenpool cart had a few of the younger Gold-

wheat sisters in it plus a box of yam tarts and bottles of something which wouldn't surface until after the meeting's business
was finished. Rowell came over to where Lark and Amelia were.
He bent down and hoisted the child in his arms.

"Ready to go to the village meeting, sweet pea?"

Amelia threw her arms around her father's neck and giggled
into his bushy beard. The icy, frozen feeling around Lark dissi-
pated. It was time to move out. Lark always felt better in motion.
She broke into long strides and loped out in front of the lead cart
on the hard-packed dirt road. The merry procession fell behind
her.

Lark's ground-devouring pace brought her over the hill and
down into a valley filled with waving grasses. Yarrow's patch of
land spread out on the east side of the road, still neither planted
nor mowed. The new addition of a rough but sturdy fence
intrigued Lark and she trotted over to inspect it. She stood on the
lower rung and peered over the fallow field. A straw hat bobbed
in the distance. Lark hopped up and down, waving and hooting.

"Hey Yarrow, over here!"

A lean figure came into view. Lark dropped her hand in surprise. It wasn't Yarrow, but Dusty Steadystream. He was slim,
dark-haired and dusky skinned. He wore close-fitting denim
trousers and a checked shirt. As he got closer, Lark noticed his
handsome leather belt with a silver and turquoise-inlaid buckle
that made Lark at once ashamed of the braided straw rope she
had tied around her waist. The unusual clothes were a testament
to Dusty's home village's vast marketplace which boasted goods
from all over, even including the world outside their protected
area. For a moment, Lark longed to have clothes like that, much
easier to move around in than the long skirt and petticoat she'd
have to wear come her sixteenth birthday.

"Well if it isn't Dusty Steadystream from Riverbend," Lark
said. "I didn't know you were back in town. You seen Yarrow
anywhere around here?"

"Sure have." Dusty took off his hat and rubbed a hand
through his hair. The black curls stood up in a halo around his
face. "He was putting some stuff away in the kitchen and I just
came out here to check the gate was closed before we head off to
the village meeting."

"Kitchen? Yarrow's kitchen?" Lark jumped down from the

fence. "Hang on a minute, you live here?"

Dusty grinned. "Sure do. With all those new fields and a new homestead, Yarrow needed an extra hand around the farm and I just happened to be looking for someplace to be. Worked out pretty well for both of us, I reckon." He hooked strong thumbs through his belt loops as he spoke.

Lark returned the grin, glad Dusty had chosen to stay. He'd first come to Poplar Valley the previous winter looking for work and helped the Greenpools out with shoveling snow and other tasks. He really hit it off with Yarrow and the two of them became fast friends.

Side by side, they worked tirelessly and could be found together every time they had a free moment. Lark liked Dusty. He didn't talk too much, but when he did it was usually some wisdom from his Farmer's Almanac or an interesting story about the people in Riverbend. He could also make more flapjacks in a tin cooking griddle than any three other people. And Lark was a big fan of flapjacks. Evidently, Yarrow was too.

Lark glanced back over her shoulder. "It was nice running into you, but I better get back on the road. Mah and Dah and the Goldwheats are coming up soon."

"I'll see you at the village meeting then. Me and Yarrow are in charge of bringing the buckets for chipfling."

"Really?" Lark perked up. "Hey, if you put in a good word for me, you think they'll let me join in the game with you adults? You know I'm a cracking flinger. The kids don't let me play with them since I put a hole in both their buckets. I wanna play with the grownup folks now. Come on, Dusty, help a gal out. I'm almost of age, you know."

"See what I can do, Miss Greenpool." Dusty put his hat back on and tipped it at a rakish angle. He winked at her before he waded back into the field.

"Thanks Dust!" Lark hollered. She ran back to the road and found the little procession coming over the crest. Lark walked with them to the clearing in the middle of the village where they parked their carts and let the donkeys off to graze.

Over to one side of the main assembly area was a small tent staffed by the travelling Wanderer healer whose yellow robes stood out from the more subdued colors worn by the Crystalgazers. He was on hand in case anyone got too much cider into them and fell over during the after-meeting festivities. While Crystal-gazers had a good amount of healing ability, nothing was better or faster at fixing bumps and bruises than a wand.

The village leader, Hayfah Wellwater, came over to the new arrivals. She beamed and clasped hands with everyone, including Lark, who puffed up with pride at being treated like an adult. Hayfah ushered the Greenpool and Goldwheat families over to a grouping of logs. Lark arranged herself on one of them and looked around at the bustling activity. Merton's father was over-seeing the punch bowl and waved at her. Lark took leave of her own parents and went over to him.

"Hey, that looks mighty good."

"It should," Jorge Appleton said. "Got our farm's gooseber-ries in it. Oh, and don't drink from that bucket over yonder. I saw some of the village boys slipping some cider into it a tad back."

"Got it," Lark said. She glanced over at the bucket in ques-tion. She wondered if she could sneak a mugful later on when everyone was busy with other things.

"Oh there's our boy now," he said. "Over here, son."

Merton trotted over with a washtub filled with mugs.

"Hey Lark. Saw your folks over yonder with Brownie and the Goldwheats. Did Miss Beccah come with?"

"Nah, she had to take little Jackie home 'cause she was being a gosling," Lark said.

"Figures. Nothing lucky ever happens to me."

"Toot toot!" Merton's father called out from his station by the punch bowl. "Those mugs ain't going to set themselves out now, are they?"

"No sir," the two young people replied.

They got busy digging out mugs. They had a silent, intense battle about who could put out the most mugs before they ran out with Lark in the lead. A small crowd assembled and soon a num-ber of mugs were filled and passed around.

Lark dipped her own cup into the non-cidered bucket before she wandered around with it at her mouth. She avoided a clot of giggling, chatting girls who did nothing more than annoy her before she found a perch on a pile of rocks somewhat removed from the main meeting area.

The village leader rang the meeting bell. At the clanking sound, the people who were standing found a seat and the people who were talking hushed down. Lark tried to pay attention, but her mind wandered. She could only listen to so much discussion about where to put the new footbridge and if they should paint the village hall blue or green before she started getting sleepy. Nice smells wafted over from the big cooking pots and griddles at the fire pits and she wondered how much longer the meeting was going to last.

The meeting meandered on. Lark put her feet up on her rock and looked up at the sky. The clouds covered the sky in little puffs, predicting rain in a day or so. She came back to reality when someone tugged at her sleeve. Expecting little Amelia Goldwheat again, she recoiled when she saw Reuel Bucketsworth crouching by her side.

In the warm afternoon light, he looked even more disreputable than usual. His scraggly blackish hair hung into his face, which was creased and stubbly. Puffy bags bloated the skin under his watery eyes. She'd seen him often enough, skulking around the dry goods shop his family ran, but never really had the urge to talk to him. He never spoke to her either, but always seemed to stare directly at her without blinking.

Lark was ill-at-ease around Reuel. He wasn't like the other villagers. Reuel liked to make himself capes and long shawls out of the black canvas bags people kept their winter potatoes in to wear over his plain homespun shirt and overalls. He didn't go to any of the socials or dances the young men and women of the nearby villages liked to have. He didn't shave either, and cultivated a scraggly-looking ring of whiskers around his mouth like a newly married man working on his first beard. He was scruffy and stooped. He was just thirty and already he looked like life had worn him down like the back of an old shoe.

Lark swallowed her nervousness and tried to be polite. "Hi there Goodman Bucketsworth. Nice to see you at the village meeting. Have you got yourself some punch? It's pretty good."

"Goodman Bucketsworth is my father," he snarled. "I'd prefer you addressed me as an equal."

As odd as it was for her, Lark forced herself to say, "Uh, okay, Reuel."

"Come with me." Reuel's sinewy fingers clamped onto her arm and half dragged, half pulled Lark away from the assembly. Lark was too alarmed at the turn of events to wonder why he was wearing sturdy gardening gloves.

"Wait, I probably shouldn't leave in the middle of the meeting. My mah will be —"

"Never mind those hayseeds. I have something to show you."

Lark dearly hoped it wasn't anything unseemly. She steeled herself, ready to whip her wand into her hand and use it if necessary. They stopped under a big willow tree by the road. The heavy branches drooped nearly to the ground, creating a patch of shadow and an uncomfortable privacy. Reuel let go of Lark in favor of rummaging around in the disreputable canvas bag he always dragged around with him.

"Only you would understand this," he said. His hair fell down over his face, making a jagged white part on his head. "Nobody else listens. You need to see this."

Lark shifted her weight from one foot to the other while she waited. Reuel drew a clot of canvas from his bag. He shook a pair of scissors into one hand and thrust it under her nose. They were made of tarnished silver, black, and dark red in places. The blades were long and too thin to be of any practical use. Some kind of engraving was scratched over the surface, impossibly tiny and delicate in an inhuman way. They were unlike any scissors Lark had ever seen. Automatically she curled her fingers into protective fists, as if the blades would reach out and snip them off.

The sky above seemed to dim, the wind picked up and threw a spray of stones at them.

"What's that?" Lark asked.

"It's an artifact." His thin, creepy voice was soft. The way Reuel was hunched over the item, turning it over in his gloved hands using only his fingertips made Lark want to be somewhere else. He took a step closer to her and Lark swore the scissors twitched in his hands. He made a soft shushing sound, as if calming a fussy infant. Tenderly, he wrapped the scissors up in the canvas and tucked it into his bag.

"Blue Skies," Lark breathed.

"It is one of *their* artifacts," Reuel said. "They cannot be destroyed, only hidden. The Great Division couldn't kill them. They need to live. They want to. This little one called to me, and every day I hear more. I yearn to find them, reclaim them from their solitary confinement. They are made of pure power. You know what this is. You must feel it calling to you too."

"I don't know anything about those." Lark took a step back. "Why would I? That sure is one creepy-looking thing though. Can't fathom where you got it, but maybe it'd be best to put it back there?"

Reuel peered up at her. His bloodshot eyes narrowed into watery slits. "I've been watching you all these years. I've seen how you hold yourself differently, even from the other foundlings. I see how you don't concern yourself with silly fripperies and even sillier ideas of romance like the other girls. You are not like them. You are destined for more than marriage to some foolish village boy and being bred like a sow."

A shot of panic hit Lark. She shook her head. "Stop this," Lark said. Her voice was a sickly croak.

"Listen to me, Larkspur," Reuel said. The way he mouthed over her name sent curdles of disgust down Lark's back. "You don't belong here, burrowing in the dirt until you drop dead. You belong with me, releasing these beautiful items from their prison." He held out a hand. Lark instinctively took a step back. Her heart pounded, her entire body trembled with the urge to flee. Reuel said, "Join me and leave this pile of sticks behind."

"Never," Lark said. She cleared her throat. Lark grabbed her wand with a shaking hand and pointed it at Reuel. "I don't want to have to use this on you, but you're being strange and I don't like it."

Reuel didn't flinch, as if he didn't register the fact that he had a wand trained on him. His eyes didn't leave Lark's face as he said, "You have powers that I do not. You can take me to them. You can help me find more artifacts. We can help each other."

Lark had heard enough.

"This conversation is over," she snapped. Lark didn't care if he was her elder, he'd asked to be treated as an equal so he would be. With a sweeping motion she called forth an arc of red energy and released it on the hunched man. It bowled him over and sent his flailing body sprawling onto the dirt road. His bag rolled in the other direction.

Lark left Reuel fumbling around in the dust for his dropped items and charged back to the village square. Her eyes stung. Every step felt heavier. Lark grabbed at her chest, but the comforting feeling from holding her crystal pouch didn't come. She stopped and pressed the palms of her hands against her eyes, trying to shut out the nagging memory of Reuel's words.

You are not like them.

Lark didn't want to think about that. So what if she wasn't a typical village girl? Who gave a dried up donkeyturd about romance and marriage anyway? It wasn't as if Lark never felt the need, she just never felt it in the proper direction. A bitter taste swam into her mouth and Lark spat on the ground.

She found her parents and shoved herself between them.

"Are you all right, sweetie pie?" her mother asked.

"Yeah, just annoyed," Lark answered. She was finished being disgusted and scared. Now she was just plain angry. Lark scowled to herself. Reuel Bucketsworth didn't know what he was talking about. His mind was addled by those horrible scissors.

As the meeting droned on around her, Lark reviewed what little she knew about Reuel. He was always trying to set up a table in his family's dry goods store to sell his change purses and things he'd made or found, but this was the first time he'd ever come up with something dangerous. Lark had no idea how he'd come across that artifact. Nobody traded with Ringsworn anymore. The Great Division put an end to that. A few years ago rumors circulated about a group of cloaked and hooded people who slipped through the market at Riverbend at dusk and paid for their potatoes and leftover pies with polished gems and tarnished silver coins, but they hadn't been seen for a while.

While a small number of enterprising Wanderers known as "vultures" picked up and sold items left behind as Ringsworn families died out or moved off somewhere, they knew better than to touch anything dangerous, specializing in furniture and the like. Apart from Lark's family, a bunch of the villagers had old Locks that were Ringsworn-made, left over from before the Great Division, and one family had a bucket that never spilled which was rumored to be so as well. No Rings, though. Even if they could get one, nobody was stupid enough to mess with it. Lark certainly hoped Reuel wasn't going to try.

The remainder of the village meeting passed without further incident and Lark managed to put the conversation with Reuel Bucketsworth out of her head even though she felt the crawling sensation of someone's eyes on her more than once.

Chapter Three

IT WAS STILL dark when Lark woke up the next morning. Her loft was silent and cool. She rolled over on her low pallet and eased the brown paper blind open with a slow pull. The wan pre-dawn light filtered in. The air was heavy, the clouds overhead low and foreboding. Lark bit back a sigh. Of all days, this one would be stormy. The night before, her father thumbed through the family Almanac and proclaimed it wasn't the season for that kind of weather. The rolling black clouds on the horizon proved his prediction wrong. It was the first time Lark had ever known the Almanac to be mistaken.

She swallowed the nagging worry that welled up from the Almanac's misinformation. Lark wondered if she'd be able to get a coach with a roof. She didn't feel like wielding an umbrella while trying to stay in her seat.

Her stomach growled. Lark rolled off her pallet and got up. Somehow her sleeping shift had gotten twisted up around her armpits and she impatiently tugged it down. Her crystal pouch had also come off during the night. She habitually slept with it around her neck and its absence worried her. Another bad omen on a day where Lark needed good ones more than ever. Lark fumbled in her haste as she dug her wand out from between the wall and her pallet. She waved it around, making streaks of light that illuminated the room long enough for her to find her crystal pouch. As the room returned to its original darkness, she shook out a large, clear quartz and activated it with a thought. The room filled with soft, golden light. She left the crystal to float up around the rafters.

Lark guided the paper blind closed once again and shed her nightclothes in an untidy pile on the floor. She jumped into her unbleached muslin drawers, then rummaged around until she found the length of supple binding fabric. Starting under her arm, she wrapped the cloth around her chest, pressing down her breasts until she made the typical gentle curve that fit well under the dun-colored children's clothing she pulled from her clothing box. Underneath them, three sets of long tunics and skirts waited. Lark gazed at them with mixed feelings.

When she came of age she'd wear the new clothing she and her parents made over the past several months. Lark would graduate from earth-tones and dull grays to colors and patterns, go from the relative freedom of the calf-length trousers to hampering skirts. She had a small, guilty thought that once she was of age, she'd be more worthy of notice to certain people like Miss Beccah Goldwheat. What would that notice yield? Lark wasn't yet able to finish the thought.

Careful to not make any noise, she crept downstairs and went to visit Brownie. The donkey was nibbling on some grass near his shed and hee-hawed when he saw her.

"At least *you* aren't turning strange and creepy." Lark rubbed Brownie's head, chafing the spiky hairs of his mane under her hands. "Not like a certain someone who rucked up the village meeting yesterday."

While she knew she'd miss her parents and her familiar room, Lark was glad the visit to her mentor put a good distance between herself and a certain member of the Bucketsworth family. She didn't want to think about what he said about her being...*different*. He was mistaken. He had to be. Reuel was a shut-in with no friends and strange ideas. There was no way anything he said about her could in any way be correct. She'd barely seen him before and had never spoken to him at all before that day. He was just being off his head. Maybe it was a side-effect from spending too much time on his own.

Lark stayed with the donkey until a good, oaty smell lured her back inside. Her father was in the kitchen, stirring a pot of porridge that bubbled merrily on the stove.

"Morning, sweets. Here, grab a bowl. The porridge's ready."

After a quick, mumbled blessing, Lark stirred a dollop of honey into her porridge and blew on the hot spoonful. Suddenly ravenous, she shoveled porridge into her mouth.

"Hey now, nobody's gonna steal your bowl," Walfer said. He patted Lark on the shoulder. "You can slow down. Chew your food, girl."

"Yessir," Lark said. She busied herself with her porridge until she scraped the last bit from her bowl.

"Don't make too much noise, y'hear now," Walfer said.

"Your mah had a bit too much of that good cider last night and I think we'd best let her be for the time being. I'll put something together for your lunch bucket. You got anything you need to do before going to the coach station? Got your things packed?"

"I'll go check, but I think I'm all ready." Lark crept up the stairs. Her wand bumped against her back. She found her satchel and rummaged through it to check the contents. She always kept it filled with her most useful things: her favorite books, some extra socks, a bunch of marbles, her prized deck of Magic Squares cards, and a handful of rubber bands which were great for flicking at people or tying things into bunches as she saw fit. Satisfied, she knotted the drawstring and slung her bag over her shoulder. She forgot to be quiet on her way back down the stairs.

"What did I say about not making too much noise?" Walfer poked his head out of the kitchen with a disapproving look.

"Sorry Dah."

"Don't worry yourself, your mah's out like a bear in winter so no harm done. Here's your lunch bucket. I know Jean Elliott's gonna want to feed y'all when you get there, but do your old dah a favor and take this with. I put in the leftover tarts from the meeting and some of your mah's good wheat bread as well as a bunch of other things you like."

"Thanks." Lark took the basket her father handed her. Her parents didn't trust her mentor's cooking, but Lark managed to survive on it until that point. True, Jean didn't have much in the way of gourmet ability, but she was able to keep her students fed when they were over at her place. It didn't hurt that Lark wasn't picky when it came to her meals. She could survive on a bucket of boiled eggs and a handful of salt if she had to.

"Your mah's probably not gonna be seeing the light of day today," Walfer said. "I'll say your goodbyes for you. You'd best head down to the coach station pretty soon. There should be someone stopping by about ten o'clock. Don't want to be late for your last mentoring, now do you?"

"No sir," Lark said. Her heart sped up. She would be taking her final exams in a few days' time. If she passed, she'd be able to apply to be apprenticed to an experienced Wanderer and complete more specialized training than what mentoring offered. Lark nursed a hankering to be a coach driver, but first of all she had to pass her exams. If she failed, she always had the option to break her wand and give up her Wanderer heritage to live the rest of her life as a Crystalgazer. While the idea of staying in one place for the rest of life galled Lark, her parents would be pleased to have her help Yarrow carry on looking after their orchard and fields when they got too old to do so. Lark felt something heavy in her throat as she looked down at the wand in her hands.

"Give us a call when you get to Miss Elliott's, y'hear?"

"Sure thing." She hugged her father goodbye and scrambled outside.

Lark took one last look over her shoulder at the homestead before she set off down the road. Overhead, flocks of birds chirped in the trees. Her shadow was long in the morning light. Lark peered up at the sky. If she was lucky, the rain would hold off until the afternoon.

As Lark walked, she hummed tunelessly. The coach station was several fields' walk away, but Lark was used to trekking and made good time. After she passed her final exams, she'd be allowed to use levitation to make her own coach, but until then, Lark had to walk the earth. Not that she minded. She liked the feel of the road under her feet. She was a true Wanderer, a born traveler. It was a fact Lark always held on to.

Lark's inner musings were interrupted by a subliminal hum from her crystal pouch. In the space of a heartbeat the pink crystal sphere was in her hand. Merton's placid face appeared in it, glowing and distended.

"Get your snout away from the crystal," Lark said by way of greeting. "You look like you've got a fish for a face. You always shove your smeller too close when you scry me up."

"Are you going to your mentor's?" he asked. He drew back enough so his face became more normal in scale.

"Yup," Lark replied. "I'll be there until the end of the month. Final exams, you know."

"Lucky you. I got to stay here and Mah's volunteered me for tree planting. Hey, you walking?"

"What do you think?"

"No need to get tetchy. You said you could rise things, that's all."

"After my exam," Lark huffed. "I could do it now, but then Mentor Elliott would have my hide when I got to her place. She always does a back-runner on our wands when we come to training and is a complete hard-hand about it too."

Merton laughed. "At least you don't moon over her like you do Miss Goldwheat. Even if you were a fellow, you wouldn't have a chance with her."

Lark stopped walking. The cloud of dust that followed her caught up to her and billowed around her legs. When Lark spoke, her voice was low and quiet, with barely contained anger. "What on this Good Green Earth are you talking about, boy?"

"Nothing. Forget it." Merton never could hold his own in a fight.

"No, I will not forget," she hollered at her crystal, but it had already gone dark. "Dags and mildew!"

Lark hurled the little sphere into the dust and stomped on it. Bad-naturedly, she yanked her wand around and sent a spiral of energy through it, making a tiny dust-devil in the middle of the road. She let the wind pick up the crystal and whirl it towards her. When it got close enough, she snatched it out of the air and shoved it back into the little pouch around her neck.

Spurred by the passage of time, Lark picked up the pace. She left her confused anger behind her as she walked. She wished coach drivers had scrying crystals so she could call ahead and ask them to wait for her. Lark broke into a ground-devouring lope. The energy from her verbal sparring match with Merton fueled her run. Her wand bounced against one shoulder as she crested the final hill. With relief, she noted the sign for the ten o'clock coach was still up. The coach station itself was a simple wooden platform made by the villagers, who used the coaches when travel by buggy was too slow for their purposes.

Lark slung herself down at the side of the station and dug around in her bag for her canteen. She gulped down a good measure and left water spots in the dirt around her feet. She lowered her canteen with a sigh and gazed into the sky. With time to think, she remembered Merton and his words.

What did he mean by saying she mooned over their teacher? Lark was both angry and confused and more than a little uncomfortable. How could he know the things she dreamt about? The dreams that left her hot and gasping with a tingling urge between her thighs that could only be quieted, but not completely satisfied, by herself. She never breathed a word about that to anyone.

A shadow fell over her, and Lark stood, shading her eyes. A

large wooden structure hovered over the platform. The coach driver leaned over the side with a cheerful wave and a smile on her sun-browned face.

"Hello there Miss Lark Greenpool. Nice to see you here again."

"Hey right back at you, Coach-Driver Cassie MacLean." Lark grabbed her bag and hauled it over one shoulder.

"I'm running late. Got an extra pickup over in Pineville," Cassie shouted down at her. "Would you mind if I just threw down the ladder for you?"

"That's fine, I'm great at clambering up ladders."

A rope ladder tumbled over the side and Lark scrambled up. Cassie helped her onto the coach with a strong arm and cheerful encouragements.

"I upgraded my coach. What do you think?" Cassie asked as Lark and her basket got settled.

"Very nice," Lark said. "It's a real beauty."

Lark wasn't exaggerating. The coach was made out of a huge overturned table with ropes tied between three of the legs that held heavy burgundy velvet curtains. They had acquired a fine mist of road dust, but were still rich and elegant. The red cloak signifying Cassie's profession hung from one of the legs like a cheerful flag.

Cassie beamed. "I got it cheap at an estate auction. A Ring-sworn family up north pulled chalks and made off for wherever they go to nowadays. I even got benches." Cassie gestured to a line of black boxes nailed to the floor. "The auction master threw those in for free. Used to be silverware-containers. They got belts somewhere around them. Buckle up and hang on. Next stop, Pineville, and then onto Pinecone Cottage!"

Lark barely had time to grab onto the leather strap before the gigantic banquet table-turned-coach shot into the air. As Poplar Valley sank into the distance, Lark leaned back and enjoyed the breeze.

The coach ride to her mentor's cottage was short and fun. A group of three Wanderers wearing the brown cloaks of tradespeople got on at Pineville. They amused Lark by telling boastful stories of their travels around the Protected Isles.

As the sturdy homestead and outbuildings of Pinecone Cottage came into view, Lark slipped her pink scrying crystal into her hand and quickly called her father. While Lark was never ashamed of her crystals, she keenly felt the glances her study mates sent her way whenever she used them. By the time she stowed her pouch under her wraps, they were slowing down.

"Okay, here we are," Cassie dropped the coach through the trees and brought it to a low hover over the picnic table in the yard. Lark waved at the other Wanderer students who pelted across the mossy grass towards them. Elsie was already of age and looked pretty and put-together in her long skirts and fine tunic.

"Hey Dwight! Hey Elsie!" Lark called out. She looked down at the third student, a boy of about eight years old with a blonde bowl of hair on his round head. He stared back, calm and only slightly sticky-looking. "Hey new kid," Lark said. "Haven't seen you around here before."

"I'm Howie," the new kid said. He wiped his nose on his sleeve. "I'm not doing mentoring yet. I'm just here to see what it's like."

"Oh great," Lark said. Cassie helpfully threw her bag over the side of the coach and tumbled the ladder down after it. Lark dug around in her pocket and found the folded paper with her coach fare in it, from her parents' small stash. "Thanks Cassie."

"Anytime, hon. Take care now and good luck on your final examinations."

With a theatrical groan, Lark scampered down the ladder. The basket full of goodies her father packed hung from one arm. She joined the other trainees on the grass as the coach soared off.

"You should have been here for breakfast," Dwight said. "Medina made the best potato cakes ever. I ate four of them."

"I ate four too," Howie added proudly, hooking his little thumbs through his overall straps.

"Who's Medina?" Lark asked. "Is she apprenticing with Mentor Elliott?"

"No. And you'll find out who she is soon enough," Elsie said with a smirk. "But first, did you bring your Magic Squares cards with you?"

"As if I'd forget," Lark said. "If I remember correctly, I'm beating both of you by five games."

"That's cause they're your cards," Dwight said. "They like you better than us."

"Can I help it if I'm nicer and cuter than you?"

"You're not cuter than me," Elsie said. She pulled her long jet-black braid over one shoulder and batted her eyes at Lark.

"That's true," Lark said. "They don't come any cuter than you."

Elsie preened. "See Dwight, that's the way you have to talk to a girl to get her to fancy you."

"Noted," Dwight said and rolled his eyes. "Anyway, let's go up to the house. You have to meet Medina."

"She's nice," Howie said.

"Yeah, and Mentor Elliott's been in a really good mood," Elsie said. "Lucky for us with our test coming up. I was sure she'd be super hard on us."

"She will be anyway," Dwight moaned. "She'll just be smiling when she squashes us like bugs."

"I'm glad I'm only going on nine," Howie said. "It sounds like a lot of trouble being older."

"Yeah, but we're a lot smarter and better than you," Lark said.

The boy shrugged.

"There they are now," Elsie said. She pointed a finger at the couple coming across the lawn toward them.

Jean Elliott was tall and sturdy with close-cropped graying hair. Instead of dresses, she favored Outsider-made clothing of a practical nature. She was in loose dungarees and a plaid shirt. The first time Lark met her at age ten, she felt a certain kinship with the older woman which didn't change even through her years of mentoring. Before becoming a mentor, Jean was a Guardian and fought during the war that preceed the Great Division, although she never spoke of it. Lark often wondered if that was how Jean had sustained the injury that took her ability to walk well, but it wasn't her place to ask. Even though Jean listed heavily to one side and used a gnarled walking staff, it didn't slow her down.

Jean carried a basket much like the one Lark had brought with her. Behind her another woman walked with long Wanderer's strides. In contrast to Jean's short, spiky hair she had a head full of curls of a bewitching chestnut color. She'd tied them up in a kerchief but a number of them had escaped, making pretty ringlets around her face. She nodded at them in greeting and Lark grinned back.

"You must be Medina," Lark said.

"And you must be Miss Larkspur Greenpool. I'm Medina Edgewright and it's nice to meet you." The woman looked to be about thirty, and had a singsong accent Lark wasn't familiar with. She held out her hand to Lark, just as if she was a grown-up. Pleased, Lark shook the other woman's hand energetically.

"Nice to meet you too Miss Edgewright."

"Just Medina is fine. After all, Jean's told me you've only got a few days before you're of age."

"More than a few," Lark told her modestly. "Almost two weeks, actually."

"I'll be of age in seven years, three months and seventeen days," Howie said.

"We don't care," Elsie replied.

Ignoring Elsie and Howie, who were slapping at each other, Lark focused her attention on Medina. "Whereabouts are you from?"

"Craven Port," she said.

"I'm from Applegrove Island," Howie piped up.

"We know," Elsie said. "You've told us all that before. You see what we have to deal with? They should raise the starting age." She gave Howie a shove with her elbow. His indignant "Hey!" was overlapped by Jean clearing her throat and giving them a stern look.

"How about some lunch, then?" Jean asked. She took the brightly colored cloth off her basket and spread it on the grass. In a chivalrous fashion, Dwight rushed over to help. Elsie nonchalantly poked her wand out from where she'd tucked it under her arm and sent a mini-zapper snaking across the grass. Dwight tripped and landed sprawled and tangled in the cloth, inches from the food basket.

"Careful there, son," Jean said with a concerned look on her face.

"Have a nice trip Dwight?" Elsie snickered. "See you next fall."

"Why did I have to be in your training group?" Dwight moaned. "Why?" He sat up and made a quick inspection. "That was close. I could'a squashed the breads. Ooh, look at the nice pies in there. Is that a roast I see? Wow, Mentor Elliott, your cooking's really improved."

"Blah blah blah," Elsie said

"That's Medina's doing," Jean told them. "I take credit for
the cabbage rolls."

"So that's what those things are," Elsie said. She leaned over
to peer into the basket. "I was wondering."

"I bet they taste great all the same," Lark said. She threw herself down in a leggy pile on the picnic blanket and brandished her
basket. "I brought some good stuff too. Some sandwiches and
yam tarts. My dah made them."

"Don't stand too close to the fire after eating those tarts,"
Dwight whispered to Howie. "You'll burn the place down."

Howie nodded solemnly. He took a basket of rolls from Jean
and placed it in the middle of the picnic blanket. Not wasting a
second, Elsie moved it closer to herself and grabbed a raisin bun.
She picked at the sugar on the top and scooted over to Medina,
who poured out cups of hot tea from a large flask.

"Are you here to take care of Mentor Elliott?" Lark asked
through half a ham sandwich.

For some reason, Medina found that funny and hid her
laughter behind the lid of the cabbage rolls. Elsie hooted without
reservation. Medina said, "I guess you could say that."

"What are you two going on about so coyly? This fine lady is
my bride." Jean stretched across the blanket and grabbed Medina
in a hug. "Though for the life of me I can't figure out why she'd
pick a grounded Wanderer like me to shack up with."

Suddenly awkward, Lark focused on the half-eaten sandwich
in her hand. Now she understood why there had never been any
rumors of gentlemen callers coming round Pinecone Cottage.
Lark wasn't used to blatant displays of affection between any two
people and seeing her mentor involved in a full-on woman-on-
woman hug, with an exhibition containing kisses on the cheek by
Jean made her feel strangely electrified. Something deep inside
her belly fluttered and awoke, and it wasn't the ham sandwich.
At least she hoped it wasn't.

At fifteen years of age, she and three other village girls born
in the same year had undergone the standard women's education
with a female Healer the Wanderers sent for that purpose, so Lark
was familiar with the mechanics of what occurred within a marriage, the proper names for things and basically everything there

was to know. Or so she thought. It never occurred to Lark until that moment there was an alternative. Her face must have shown her utter confusion because Elsie grabbed a wooden spoon from the potato salad and waved it at the amorous couple.

"Simmer down you two," she said. "You're forgetting Lark's a hayseed. They're uptight and backward when it comes to stuff like that. Look, you're putting her off her food. I bet it's never occurred to her that there's more to do than the thing that results in babies."

"Sorry about that," Medina said without looking the slightest bit contrite. Still, she removed Jean's hands from around her waist and put a chaste distance between them.

"Newlyweds," Dwight sighed. "Potato salad?" He passed over a plate. Grateful for the distraction, Lark dove at the food.

After the meal, Jean took the three older students over to the barn where they had most of their practical sessions. She checked their wands and collected a short writing assignment before they started their practice. Lark liked the open feeling of the barn. The wooden floor was smooth from generations of students and large windows let in the abundant sunlight. A number of barrels lined the wall, ready to be used as practice targets. Hay bales were stacked at the end of the room and served as a crash-landing zone. Lark had ended up in them more than once during her time with Jean.

That day they were scheduled to work on levitation. Lark practiced by herself for a while before a crash brought her back to the present.

"Aw turnip roots." Dwight hung his head. He stood between two barrels that lay haphazardly on the floor. "One thing is okay, but more than that and I get all confused."

"Keep your gaze unfocused," Jean said from her perch on another barrel. She gestured with her wand and sent a burst of energy through the gnarled wood. The barrels rose into the air and held steady. "If you need to, try and move them closer together. You'll get points taken off for that, of course, but less than if they drop."

Lark looked over at Elsie and, as one, they leapt into the air and each landed perched on a barrel.

"Hey now you two," Jean said. "I'm trying to teach something here. Your final test is only two days away."

"Yeah, so anything we don't already know we're not gonna get in time," Elsie pointed out from her barrel. The barrel gave a lurch and she shrieked. Her long braid flew out as she righted herself. "Mentor Elliott! You did that on purpose. I nearly dropped my wand."

"You don't want to do that," Jean said.

"We know," Elsie replied. "So I wasn't gonna. I just said I nearly did."

"Glad to hear that. Now you two get your butts off our barrels. Dwight and I are practicing."

"Yeah!" Dwight said. He held his wand in his hands. Like most wands, it was a spoon-shaped piece of white birch half the length of his arm, delicately curved with a slim knothole in the very middle of it. He said, "You two had better get some of that practicing done too if you know what's good for you."

"And no more comments from you." Their mentor leveled her steely gaze to Dwight. He snapped to attention. Jean addressed the girls, "And you two get back to your practicing. I want to see results when I've finished looking at Dwight's performance."

"Yes, Ma'am." Elsie leaped from her barrel and landed lightly on the hay bales. Lark tried to follow suit but the toe of her boot caught on the barrel and she tumbled into the hay. For a while Elsie and Dwight ignored their tasks and became busy throwing things at Lark and zapping her with their wands. Their mentor silently hung her head and sighed.

THE DAY PASSED into evening. The rain that threatened didn't fall, however black clouds blotted out the sun far before nightfall. After dinner, as she walked back to her loft, Lark got out her agate and consulted it, but only got hazy, unsettled resonance from it. An odd kind of electricity hung in the sluggish air.

She let herself into the loft, where the four youngsters passed the time until lights-out, quietly absorbed in a furious game of cards while they crunched on roasted peas from a bag Dwight produced. Howie kept up with them fairly well, then his little bowl-head started nodding over his cards and eventually they rolled his sleeping body onto his pallet on the boys' side.

"Okay, now that the little runt is out, we can finally get out the good stuff." Dwight rummaged in his satchel and came out with a covered glass jar. "I got some flaming whammies from my big bro."

"And so many!" Elsie pounced. "We only ever get one each and that's at Midwinter festival when it's too cold and damp to properly enjoy them. Come on, let's take them outside and set them off."

"But what if Mentor Elliott sees us?" Lark asked. "We'll get our butts handed to us on a spatula."

"No way, that's the old Mentor Elliott," Elsie told her. "Now she's got better things to do at night than keep tabs on us. And no I'm not going to explain it in more detail than that. That's what older siblings and the back section of the library are for."

"Huh, you don't say." Lark made a mental note to venture into the murkiest depths of the travelling library wagon that came around every month. So far she'd only found various reference books and the Amelia Strawberry Girls' Adventure Series. Maybe there was something better that she'd missed, although she had to admit having a great fondness for Amelia Strawberry and the many wonderful and exciting things she did.

"Let's go." Dwight gathered up a last handful of roasted peas and shoved them into his mouth. He grabbed his wand and the three of them tromped outside. The woods surrounding Pinecone Cottage thrummed with crickets. The air still kept a hint of the autumn sun's heat, but the wind was cool. Lark felt it ruffle the ends of her tunic and for a moment wished for a warmer wrapper. Then Elsie pried the lid off the jar and shook out the shining contents and Lark forgot about being cold.

"You go first," Dwight said. "It takes me a while to get mine hot enough."

"Okay, stand back." Elsie slipped her wand from her sleeve. It wasn't as compact as Dwight's but it still fit inside her sleeve. It was a gently curving blade of sleek cherry wood, sanded and polished by years of handling. She used her wand to roll one of the glistening balls away from the rest. "Don't want to set them all off at once," she muttered. She put both hands on her wand. A shining light appeared at the tip. It illuminated the little clearing in a warm yellow-orange shimmer. The flaming whammy started to vibrate and Lark thought she heard a high-pitched whistle coming from it.

"All right, you're doing it!" Dwight crowed. Elsie shot him a stern look and he quickly put both hands over his mouth. "Sorry," he whispered.

Suddenly the whammy ignited and the three of them forgot about being quiet and hollered in glee as threads of fire began spinning off from the little gleaming jewel-like ball. It shot into the air and the threads became burning ropes that snaked over the grass and through the air. The three of them grabbed their wands and had great fun battling off the spitting, whipping tentacles.

"Good one." Lark blew a few strands of hair out of her mouth. "You really set that one off well. It nearly got my foot and I think it singed my sleeve. Very nice!"

"You next." Elsie pointed at the pile of remaining flaming whammies. "Take that big red one there. It looks like it'd go off nicely. I'm going levitate that rock over there and escape that way. Hang on a minute and let me go get it."

Lark grabbed her wand with both hands and carefully separated the whammy she'd been eyeing, getting a feel for it. She drew energy from her core and breathed it through the wooden veins. The whammy vibrated, then glowed a fierce red-gold.

Elsie came back, hovering on her rock. "Okay, I'm ready. You can set it off now."

Before Lark could send the activating pulse thorough her wand, the clearing was illuminated in a sudden blinding light and the air cracked in two. The three of them dove to the ground, hands over their ears and eyes wide.

"What the heck did you do to that whammy?" Dwight wavered, his face was ghostly white in the sudden blackness that followed the explosion.

"I didn't do anything," Lark said. "Green Trees and Blue Sky, look at the cottage."

A red, roiling cloud gathered over the cottage and spat lightning bolts at the roof. Shingles tumbled off and fell like rain to the grass below. With another deafening thunderclap, all of the windows exploded outward and two figures burst from the ruined building. Jean had one hand clutching Medina's arm as they ran a few steps away from the cottage and stopped out of range of the falling shingles. They stood together, shoulder to shoulder.

Lark got her first glimpse of full-fledged Wanderers unleashing their trained fighting ability on a common enemy.

It was a stunning display of grace and power. The air around them sparkled a deadly blue. A wave of static shot through Lark as the combined energy of the two women was set loose upon the heaving cloud. They breathed and moved as one. Lark couldn't see where one ended and the other began. They were a perfect match, complementing one another and becoming much more than the sum of their abilities. The wave hit the cloud in a blue arrow of pure power and succeeded in driving it back a ways but it didn't dissipate. The attack took its toll and the two Wanderers fell to their knees. Jean grabbed for her staff and tried to struggle to her feet.

The lighting crashed down again. The cloud drifted toward the barn where the trainees' loft was.

"We have to go over there and help," Lark shouted into the wind. "Howie's in there and he's probably scared stiff."

Lark took off across the grass with Dwight and Elsie close behind her.

"What do we do?" Dwight asked.

"We'll blast them just like Mentor Elliott and Medina tried," Lark said. She twitched her wand over her shoulder and into her hand. Elsie and Dwight also brandished their wands on either side of her. "There's three of us so we've got an advantage. I'll do the levitating. Dwight, I need you to give them a quick burst with as much energy you can summon. Elsie, you do the shielding until we can get them into position. Got it?"

"Got it," they said in unison.

She grabbed her wand in both hands and levitated three boulders. Lark kept her focus on the boulders and held them steady. At her signal, Dwight primed them with a sudden volley of energy that Lark could never duplicate no matter how hard she tried, and Elsie cast her glowing yellow shield over them. Lark stood still and concentrated on the task with all her might. The boulders touched the edge of the storm.

"Almost there," Lark gritted. Her arms shook but she just dug her heels into the ground and held on. She fought against the whirling clouds and nudged the boulders into the mass. Once she couldn't push any further, Lark shouted, "Now, Elsie!"

The shield flicked out. The boulders detonated in a wave of fire that blazed crimson from the core of the clouds. Raw energy pierced the clouds from inside, shining out like swords of light. For a minute it looked as if the wild, dark clouds would win the fight. They reformed and thickened. Another bolt of blue energy came from Jean and Medina. It flew like a dragon into the cloud and erupted into a searing inferno. In an instant the black, sickly billowing clouds became no more than puffs of smoke. Thick dust rained down on them and the three trainees danced around, busy shaking the nasty stuff out of their hair and clothes.

"Went down my shirt," Lark said. She yanked off her belt and flapped her clothing about herself.

Jean and Medina came over to them at a dead run. Medina was the first to reach them. She grabbed a very surprised Lark in a fierce hug. Jean patted her down all over. Howie stumbled out of the loft and clung to Jean's sleeve. He looked very small in his frog-print pajamas.

"Are any of you hurt?" Jean asked. She was pale and looked exhausted.

"No, we're okay," Elsie said. She didn't look much better than Jean. Her hair had fallen out of its usually sleek braid and was standing up all over, still crackling with static and somewhat dusty. "What the heck was that thing?"

Jean said, "It's called a hungry squall. I haven't seen one since the Great Division. I don't know how, but someone must have found one of the forbidden Bloodring caches."

Lark got a sudden chill. She remembered Reuel Bucketsworth and his dreadful treasure. Did he have something to do with this?

"What's a squall? What's a Bloodring?" Howie flapped around.

Medina pressed her lips together and shook her head. "A Bloodring is incredibly powerful and incredibly evil. It's not like a regular Ring, which only affects the wearer, it can be used on others. Even without their consent."

"That's not good." Howie whimpered.

"It isn't," Medina said. "And a hungry squall is the destructive energy that gets released when a Bloodring is touched by someone who is not the imprinted bearer. We have to get word to the Guardians as soon as possible. If I take our coach right now, I'll get to Shadowmoor by dawn."

"No, you're drained and I need you here," Jean said. She placed a hand on Medina's arm.

"There's no other way."

"There has to be a way." Jean crossed her arms and scowled at the scuffed grass beneath her feet. She snapped her fingers. "Lark, I need your help."

"Sure," Lark said. "What can I do?"

Jean looked at her for a long moment. "You aren't tired at all?"

"Nope," Lark said. She glanced over to Dwight and Elsie. Both of them were on the grass. Dwight knelt while Elsie sprawled onto her back. Both of them looked exhausted. Lark quelled her burst of unease with a grin she didn't feel. "Must be the stubborn hayseed in me."

Jean studied Lark for a heartbeat longer, then looked back toward the cottage with her brow furrowed.

"I'll take care of the students," Medina said. "You go with Lark."

Jean nodded and started walking back to the cottage at a good clip. Lark followed. A hundred questions buzzed into her mind, but she kept quiet until Jean sat her down at the long kitchen table in the cottage. The night wind blew through the room. Lark was used to noisy, fun mealtimes in the cottage and the silent darkness of the room had her on edge.

"Careful of the broken glass," Jean said. She folded her hands on the table and said, "Lark, get out your scrying crystal. I need you to call the Guardian's council. They've got a crystal in their meeting room and someone's usually around, even at this time of night."

Lark grabbed reflexively at her crystal pouch. "Medina said it would take all night to reach there. I've got to be out of range."

"No you're not," Jean said in a low, commanding voice. "I know you Lark. I've trained you for nearly four years. If you go slow and steady, you can do this."

Lark nodded. If Jean believed she could reach Shadowmoor using only her small crystal, then perhaps Lark actually could. At any rate, she had to try. She got out her pink scrying crystal and cupped her hands around it. Behind her, she heard the door close and then footsteps. Lark focused on her crystal, only peripherally aware of Medina who stood behind Jean with one arm protectively around her.

"Which direction is Shadowmoor?" Lark asked.

"East," Jean said softly. "It's on the other side of the Deep Forest and then south. It's quite close to the Border."

Lark focused on her crystal. She had never tried to call a place so far away. Slowly her consciousness extended and the vision swam before her eyes. Underneath her, the land spun away. She travelled faster than any coach, fast as thought.

"Yes, you're almost there," Jean said. Her voice was tight with excitement. "You're doing it, Lark!"

Lark was aware of a sprawling, black mass of buildings in a clearing. She had no idea how large it was, but she felt the hum of life, stronger and denser than her own village. Jean's whispered directions led her to a large building and Lark felt the call of the scrying crystal resonate through her. The lid of the box opened and Lark stared into a man's face. He was young and tousled, in a black cloak. Behind him, Lark could just make out rich wallpaper and a large table surrounded by chairs.

"Hello there," he said in a surprised voice. "What can I do for you, young lady?"

"Why, if it isn't Calvin Johnson," Jean said. She leaned closer to Lark and peered into the crystal. "Can you hear me?"

"Sure can," he said. "Mentor Elliott, is there something wrong?"

Jean pressed her lips together. "Is Head Guardian Williams around? I need to speak to him urgently."

"All right, hang on."

The young man's face vanished.

"Are you all right?" Jean asked Lark in a quiet voice.

"Yeah, I'm good," Lark said. She felt the energy flowing through her like it always did, pulled from somewhere below her feet and seeming without end. She focused on the crystal and soon a second man came into view. He was older and radiated authority.

"What is it?" he asked without pleasantries.

"Head Guardian Williams," Jean said. "I need to report a hungry squall visited us tonight."

"Are you certain?"

"Yes, I am. I've seen enough of them in my day. My three students banished it," Jean said the last bit with a hint of pride.

Williams' eyebrows went up. "Completely?"

"That's right," Jean said. "I don't know if it was an isolated incident, but I thought you should know as soon as possible."

"We will look into it," Williams said. "Thank you for the prompt information." He started to say something, then stopped and looked directly at Lark, who felt at once gawky and out of place. "Is this one of your students who fought the squall?"

"Yes, she's Larkspur Greenpool from Poplar Valley," Jean said. "She's one of us, but Crystalgazer-raised."

"A double," Williams said, more to himself than anyone. He straightened up. "I will not keep you and your student any longer. If you are not in need of assistance?"

"No, we're fine here," Jean said.

"Good to hear. Expect a visit tomorrow."

With that, the crystal went dark. Lark slumped into her chair and breathed again.

"You heard the man," Jean said. She heaved herself to her feet and stood beside Medina. "We're having company tomorrow, so we'd best hit the hay early tonight. Good work, Lark. I'm proud of you."

Lark was certain she outshone the moon with her grin.

AT DAWN, A coach arrived. It was sleek and black, a wooden ship with no sails. The driver didn't shout out greetings or sing like the coach drivers and tithe-collectors Lark was used to. The passengers didn't clamber down makeshift ladders or slide down a pole but stepped down properly on a compact wooden staircase the driver flipped over the side with a wave of his wand. Lark stood silently with the other students, cowed and shy as four black-cloaked figures descended from the coach. Lark knew about the Guardians from her studies, even though she'd never seen one in person. One of them was Patroller-rank, with a double set of gold lines on the hood and around the hem of his cloak while the rest were Trackers with rows of silver lines.

One figure was smaller than the others. When the four visitors removed their hoods, Lark discovered the Guardian was a young woman only a few years older than herself. She was very pretty, with clear blue eyes and full pink lips. Lark looked longer than she knew was polite, but she couldn't help it. She felt like the sun had frozen in the sky and the birds stopped in mid-flight. That's how pretty the girl was. She had masses of jet-black curls that made her flawless skin look even more pale and lovely next to it. She'd tied up most of her hair in a silver clip with a few loose ringlets framing her heart-shaped face.

The girl must have felt Lark's gaze on her because she turned her head slightly and smiled right at her. Lark's face bloomed into a stupid, beaming grin. She felt like she'd swallowed a golden ball of happiness.

With conscious effort, Lark turned her attention to the other three black-robed visitors. The senior Guardian was an older man who had a spider web-like pattern of scars across his face and down his neck as far as his collar revealed. A woman of about the same age walked beside him, her steps crisp and quick as they crossed the distance from the coach. A young man with a long ponytail stood off by himself a ways. He looked sullen, as if he would rather be somewhere else.

Jean and Medina bolted out of Pinecone Cottage a little later than the trainees. Jean was still yanking her formal cloak around her shoulders. Unlike the guests, hers was dark green and looked pleasant next to Medina's warm brown one.

Jean and the older man clasped hands like old friends. She said, "If it isn't Leonard Brenner, back from the slow life. What, retirement too boring for you?"

"I wish it were that simple," Leonard said, his face grim. "I think it would be prudent to discuss this under the shelter of your roof. I believe your wards are still in place even after last night?"

"They are." Suddenly all business, Jean said, "Come this way, please." She moved across the lawn, leaning on her crutch but still moving at a good pace. Jean looked back over her shoulder and called out to Lark and the other students. "You four as well. After what nearly happened to us all last night, I think you all are entitled to hear this."

Lark was both apprehensive and pleased as she followed the group into the cottage. The girl who smiled at her earlier walked ahead, her strides were long and matched those of the young man beside her.

Leonard spoke to Jean as they walked across the dew-damp grass. "And while we're here on official business, I must offer my sincere congratulations on your handfasting. It seems like just yesterday I was officiating at young Medina's final exam. Best displacing techniques I ever did see."

"You were certainly strict enough about making us do it until we fell down exhausted," Medina told him, although she didn't seem too upset.

"I'm sorry you didn't join the Guardians, but I can see you've got a better destiny than that. Oh and by-the-way, you know my son, Theodore," Leonard said. The young man nodded, flicking his ponytail out of his folded-back hood as he did so. "And this is Justine Brightgrove. I believe you may have met once before at one of our gatherings?"

"It's good to see you, Jean," Justine said. "I only wish it could be under more fortuitous circumstances."

"As do I."

"And here is the shining star of our team," Leonard gestured to the young woman. Lark's heart gave a funny jump. "I'm very pleased to introduce Rosalie Jordan. She's Yannis and Helen's girl. Fastest training in the history of the Guardians and our most recent addition. Without her we'd never have been able to do half the things we've done. If only she'd been around in the time of the Great Division, things may have turned out much differently."

"Come on, Leonard," the young woman spoke in a casual way even to the high-ranking Guardian. Lark basked in the beauty of her voice, a bright soprano with sweet, clear intonation. "You make it seem like I'm some kind of hero. I'm just a regular girl."

"You've certainly helped us out of a lot of tight spots in the short time you've been with us."

They reached the cottage and the group filed inside, the robed Guardians took their places around the big kitchen table. Lark and the rest stood off to the side. Without glass in the windows, there was nothing to stop the chilly breeze. The cheerful and homey kitchen felt cold. Medina got busy at the stove and soon everybody had mugs of hot spiced tea in front of them.

A basket of sweet buns sat on the sideboard. Lark grabbed a couple buns and passed them to her fellow students, who, like her, hadn't yet eaten due to the excitement of preparing for the Guardians. If Lark's rumbling stomach disturbed that very solemn meeting she'd never live it down.

First, Jean gave a short summary of the events of the night before. When she talked about how her three students helped defeat the squall, she looked most proud. Lark watched Rosalie intently, fascinated by the way she twirled her wand between her fingers.

It was a perfectly straight wand of pure white, as long as her forearm. The smooth wood swelled out gently over the knothole about a third of the way down from where Rosalie held it. Lark suddenly felt her own wand with its cheerful lanyard tied through the knothole at the end was ungainly and childish.

"Thanks to your warning, we were able to investigate what happened before the evidence vanished. Our monitors picked up the last vestiges of the disturbance last night. It was indeed a hungry squall," Leonard said. "We received reports of possibly two others in the past several days, but were unable to confirm."

"We'll find out who is responsible," Justine said. "We've got all our available teams working on it. Hopefully we can locate the source before the trail goes dark."

"This is not going to be the last one, I'm sure of it," Theodore said. "I'm trying to tell you, the Ringsworn have been planning something underhanded for ages. They've been too quiet. We've seen them moving out in droves and going somewhere, but that's just a front to make us think they've been beaten and are moving on. They're gathering and plotting something, I just know it. We didn't finish them well enough before so now they think they can take us on again."

His father held up a hand that showed traces of scars, stilling the flow of accusations. "We need to gather evidence before making such a judgment, Theo. It's not a foregone conclusion that this is the malicious work of a Ringsworn. I should think they've suffered an ample enough defeat already without the need to add to it. There could be any number of explanations." He paused, "And they, like us, have fifteen years of peace to grow soft and forgetful."

"But this type of squall is from one of their Bloodrings. No Wanderer would touch such a thing and don't tell me that Crystalgazers could unleash that kind of power. The only things they're good at is chasing chickens and shoveling manure."

Lark scowled. Shoveling manure indeed. True, she did that a lot but it was an important part of keeping up the farm. She glared at Theo before she could help herself.

Theo got to his feet and threw his hands out. "It must be the

Ringsworn. If they want a fight, we'll give it to them all right."

"Sit down, son," Leonard commanded. "We can discuss this another time. Now we have to decide what to do in the short term and if these people here need our help. Or on the contrary, can give us some."

"We've got the place secured pretty well," Jean said. "What these three did last night is enough to set my mind at ease. With them around, nothing's going to get though our defenses, and even if it does, we can take care of it."

"Good to hear it," Leonard said.

The talk went on for a while, but Lark was too jumpy and excited to listen properly. She preferred to sneak sideways glances at Rosalie. Under her black robe, the young woman wore the usual front-lacing tunic and long skirt Lark was used to, but something about it was different. She'd left the ties of it loosely laced and, standing somewhat behind her, Lark was at a perfect angle to see into the front of it well enough to understand Rosalie wasn't wearing a binding cloth.

Instead, her breasts made two separate mounds under her clothing, the white, inner curves just visible through the opened fastenings. Lark had a more than an educational glance as she helped collect the empty mugs at one point in the discussion. The lacy garment was the most delicate thing Lark had ever seen. An odd, burning feeling started deep within her belly. Lark gulped and suddenly became very interested in the stray tea leaves swirling around the bottom of her mug. She knew she shouldn't have looked and mentally scolded herself.

Green Grass, she wasn't able to concentrate at all. What was wrong with her? Lark didn't know a whole lot, but she knew she wanted to get to know this young Guardian better. For the first time in her life, Lark was certain she'd never be a Crystalgazer. She often wondered what would happen to her after she came of age, and now she knew. She would be a Guardian. She would apply to become Jean Elliott's apprentice. She'd swear to protect and uphold the laws of the Wanderers and fight for the good of society. And Rosalie. They hadn't even spoken a single word to each other, but Lark already knew she would do anything the young woman asked her. And she wished to be asked.

"That does seem all we can do for now, but do keep your eyes and ears open, all of you. Report anything unusual, however small." Leonard stood and drew his hood over his head.

The meeting was over. Lark hurriedly jumped out of the way. She didn't want to look like a donkey in front of the Guardians. Especially in front of Rosalie.

Lark walked behind the group as Jean saw the four Guardians to the middle of the yard again. They boarded the black coach and left just as silently as they arrived.

The trainees returned to their chores. Lark couldn't help but twirl around between rounds of chopping kindling. She felt light and giddy.

"Lark's full of beans today," Jean said to Medina as they washed the dishes in the kitchen. Through the glassless window, Lark could hear their words clearly. She dropped the axe and stood still.

"Probably excited seeing Guardians up close," Medina's soft, lilting voice replied. "They don't come out this way very often."

"We'll be seeing more of them before long," Jean said. Her tone was low and worried. Lark moved so she could see into the cottage. Jean rubbed a hand through her salt-and-pepper hair. Her face was grim. She said, "We can only pray this isn't the start of another war. I don't think I could go through that again."

"If it is, it is." Medina drew close to Jean. She put the bowl she was holding on the table. "If it isn't, it isn't. There's nothing we can do except be ready. And you won't be facing this alone. I'll be by your side and if they want to take us on, they have to take us both. Together as one."

Closing the distance between them, Medina took the older woman into her arms. It was a private moment, but Lark couldn't look away. She felt suddenly very alone. She thought of Rosalie and knew she wasn't alone. Not anymore.

"Together as one," Lark repeated the words under her breath. Yes, that was the way it would be.

Chapter Four

Two years later

"I'LL GET OUT and walk from here," Lark said to the coach driver. The flying rowboat lowered to the ground and hovered while she jumped out. She stood with her feet planted firmly on the dusty road and waved to the boat's driver as it zoomed off.

Lark took a deep breath and looked around. In the two years she'd been away, the road hadn't changed, but she had. Anyone standing behind her would first notice the several long, ropy plaits she had tied up at the back of her head that fell to her waist. The rest of her hair was short and shaggy, the whole of it a brilliant blonde which glowed like golden fire in the late afternoon sunlight, resembling the dried grasses left-over from winter on either side of the road.

She turned and began walking down the road in long, ground-devouring strides, unhampered by long skirts and petticoats. Her legs were encased in thick black trousers that ended in wide cuffs just below the knees, decorated with jaunty buckles. They matched the black shirt that hugged her body, with long sleeves that came down to the middle of her hands. Over the black shirt, she wore another one, sleeveless and dappled green and yellow with brown patches. It looked like she could blend into the surrounding shimmering trees if she wanted to.

Her feet were in tall boots that laced up the front and she had a long black cloak draped over one shoulder. Around her waist, she wore a short skirt made of well-worked strips of deep green leather, fashioned into pockets, that were lashed together and hung from a sturdy belt, slung low over her hips. Leather strips hung from her belt and swayed as she walked, weighted at the ends by silver beads. While it wasn't like Dusty's silver and turquoise buckled one she admired ages ago, Lark was quite satisfied with her own belt.

Lark skimmed one hand through the tall grass while she walked. A worn khaki canvas bag swung from the other. She felt good. Free and strong and powerful. She hummed to herself as she turned into the neatly-kept garden outside her familiar homestead.

"Lark! We weren't expecting you until tomorrow." Dillah came running down the few steps from the porch.

"My schedule's been moved up and I've got to report to Shadowmoor Outpost tomorrow. They've got a coach coming for me at—owf!" Lark staggered back a step as her mother hit her with a big hug. "I brought you and Dah some presents. Hope you like Wanderer-spun towels. Got a bunch at the last fair. I got some for Yarrow too that I can give him tonight, if he's not too busy to come over."

"It would take more than a few chores to keep Yarrow away from his darling little sister—and my good roast ham." Dillah reached out and tousled Lark's hair. "I can't say I've gotten used to those tails of yours, but they are growing on me."

"I hope so," Lark told her. "Because they're certainly growing on me."

Her mother sighed at the attempt at humor. "And where ever did you get those strange clothes? I have to say, they look mighty fetching, though."

"These are Outsider fashion," Lark said. She kicked out one booted foot. "Mentor Elliott took me to the big market in Riverbend and they had so many tables of this kind of thing. I picked out this whole outfit myself."

"Blue Sky, well I reckon if you like it, that's the main thing. You never were a big one for dresses." Dillah fixed Lark with a sharp look. "Don't tell me that's your Guardian cloak you've got hanging off your shoulder. Honestly, after all the trouble you went through to get it."

Lark grinned crookedly and continued her trek to the homestead. Her father nearly fell off the porch swing when Lark came striding confidently across the yard.

"Well, I'll be!" Walfer rubbed a hand through his thinning hair. "Looks like we'll need to put another measure of water into the kettle for tea. How've you been keeping yourself, honey bunch?"

"Busy." Lark flopped down onto the swing beside her father and unfurled her long legs out in front of herself. "I'm only here for the night, though. The new fledglings officially start training tomorrow. Hopefully I'll get my rank up soon. I've got a hankering to go out on patrol and see all over the Protected Isles for myself."

"Dangerous out there," Walfer said. "Are they sure you young folks are ready?"

"She's not a youngun anymore, love," Dillah poked her head out of the window to inform them. She had a potato in her hands and was busy peeling it. "Her eighteenth birthday came and went last month already. Besides, if she wasn't ready, there's no way Jean would have even let her take the test. And here she is, Guardian Greenpool."

"Mah, I'm not anything yet," Lark said. Still, she flushed with pride at hearing her mother address her in Wanderer manner, by her chosen profession, for the first time. "Mind if I go take a bath before dinner? I've got travel-dust all over me."

"Heh, funny thing for a Wanderer to mind," her father joked.

"I'm a Crystalgazer when I'm here." Lark paused in yanking off her waist pocket. "Must be something in the air."

Dillah's smile was gentle. "All right, you go over and wash up. You know where everything is."

"Yup, I sure do."

Lark ran into the homestead to grab some towels and a change of clothes. She burst out of the back door and clambered down the steps, pausing only to greet Brownie and give the donkey a quick scratch about the ears on her way to the bathhouse.

Inside the bathhouse, Lark reached up to lightly brush the crystal above her head with a finger, setting it aglow with a casual thought. She stripped off her travel-stiff clothes before she stepped into the washing-room with her scrubber, a handful of loosely-woven cloth, in her hand. Next to the wooden tub was a small washing-up area with a stool and a bucket. A large pink crystal bowl was set in one wall of the bath. Water tumbled down from a spout above it, pooling inside before it spilled into the tub below.

Lark ignored the stool. She knelt down and grabbed the bucket. She dipped it into the big tub and poured cascades of water over herself. With her scrubber, she chased the dust from her skin. She rinsed her long tails and rubbed them briskly with a towel before she tied them up on top of her head. Water overflowed from the bath as she got in. In the embrace of the hot water, Lark tried to forget the urgency that hung over her head.

The hungry squall that visited her mentor's cottage a little over two years ago was only the beginning. Since then, more storms blew up, each one worse than the last. The storms set off a ripple effect that was felt throughout the Protected Isles. Nothing was safe. Lark forced herself to put aside the rumors of wells gone to acid and the surge of misborn livestock. For just a moment, Lark was back in her childhood home, in a time before the storms wrecked entire fields and the coming of winter wasn't looked on with dread.

When Lark was thoroughly pink, she hauled herself out. She pulled clean underclothes from the bundle she brought with her, then got into the long skirt, petticoat, and tunic. She shook out her tails, liking the way they whipped around her back, and trotted into to the homestead where she was ambushed by her brother. He was shorter than Lark, but strong and stocky like their parents.

"Hey there stranger." Yarrow rose from the sofa and hugged Lark. He held her at arm's length. "They been feeding you enough over there at Pinecone Cottage? You look scrawny."

"Shut it Yarrow." Lark punched her brother in the arm and he collapsed back into the sofa cushions. He pretended to be wounded and sprawled ungracefully over the other occupant of the sofa. Dusty didn't look annoyed at the sudden invasion of his personal space. He just patted Yarrow on the head.

Dusty grinned up at Lark. "Warn me next time you're sending Yarrow on a trip, eh?"

"Sorry Dusty," Lark said. "My big bro isn't all that tough, it seems."

"No problem," Dusty said. "I punch him enough anyway. He should be used to it by now."

"That's called domestic violence," Yarrow pointed out.

Unconcerned, Dusty freed himself from Yarrow's outflung limbs and wandered over to the table. As if it was the most natural thing in the world, he chatted with Dillah about the yam harvest while he helped haul platters and baskets from the kitchen nook to the table. Lark took over Dusty's place on the sofa. She basked in the normalcy of the scene. She needed to believe some things hadn't changed.

Walfer trotted into the room. "Just came back from the

Appletons' and they're coming over for dinner. Jorge smoked a ham joint and he said he'd bring it over with some of Columbah's good gooseberry wine."

"How nice," Dillah said. "It's been ages since we've had the Appletons over here. Although we did have a good time at their bonfire last week. It's nice to be able to return the favor."

"And I won the chipfling," Walfer told the assembled group. "In three straight sets too."

"Yes, yes, we know. Now would you be a dear and set out the wine cups? Thank you love."

"Hey Lark."

Merton stood in the doorway. He was still as stolid and tow-headed as ever, but not quite as round-faced as she remembered.

"Hey Merton." Lark strode over, surprised to find herself still taller than him. He hadn't grown much in the time she'd been away. "How's things been with you?"

"Not bad. My parents have given me their east field and I've got some good-looking corn on the way. What the storms haven't smashed, anyway."

"Glad to hear that." For the first time, Lark felt awkward around her childhood friend. Something in the way his eyes were fixed on her made her antsy.

"Jorge! Columbah!" Walfer's cheerful greeting to Merton's parents broke the strained mood. He ushered the three guests to their seats around the rough-hewn table. Lark used the bustle of activity to escape to her own place, strategically far away from Merton.

Once they were seated, Dillah asked, "Jorge, would you lead us in the prayer?"

"I would be honored," he said.

Lark took the hands of her mother and brother on either side of her and bowed her head.

Jorge took a deep breath and spoke in an unearthly groan. "Dear Great Provider of all good things, we do thank You for the seasons which pass the year. We thank You for the spring, with its new lambs and nourishing rains. Its overflowing rivers and cool nights. The reawakening of the ground and the seedlings bringing life anew. We thank You for the summer, with its hot days and clear, dry skies. The golden sheen of the sun on the lake and the happy shouts of our children playing in the pools."

A quick squeeze from Yarrow brought Lark's head up a fraction. He wrinkled his nose at her and she responded with a pained look. The prayer dragged on. Lark sighed. She gazed at the pile of mashed yams in front of her. A basket of cut apple pieces next to a fat jar of pickles caught Lark's eye, then she was mesmerized by a big pyramid of nut breads that were not getting any fresher as the prayer dragged on. Jorge finished listing the seasons and went on about "Praise for the poems of nature" and other abstract concepts that Lark didn't really care about. Her stomach rumbled. She shifted her weight on the rough-hewn chair.

"Protect us all," Jorge said at last. Lark tightened her grip on the hands holding her own. "Protect our people and our livelihood from these storms. Let the sun shine through them and let them pass away from here and leave us be. Amen!"

The meal proceeded normally for a Greenpool affair, with Lark and Yarrow getting into a mostly friendly arm-wrestling competition at the table with Dusty refereeing. Dillah had a long and involved discussion with anyone who would listen to her about the state of the village's trees and what to do with them. Walfer bustled around, carrying his plate over people's heads as he made sure everyone had enough to eat and drink. He toted the bread basket around in the crook of his arm and dealt out buns liberally.

"Shame about the Bucketsworth boy," Jorge said. Lark's ears perked up. She lost her concentration just long enough for Yarrow to get the upper hand and steal the last piece of stewed pumpkin. Gloating, he chewed loudly, mouth open.

"Yarrow, please!" Dillah rapped on the table. "Remember we have company."

"S'rry. Mph."

Jorge continued as if nothing happened. "I heard his father's given up that he'll come back. I was just down at the Bucketsworth Dry Goods store the other day and a couple people were talking about it. Brought back the memory. Real shame it is, that family."

"What happened?" Lark asked. She forgot about her dinner and leaned over her plate.

Jorge put down his fork and said, "You know my dear, young Reuel's never been real sociable, but he managed to get along pretty well until a couple years ago. You were away then, so I guess you may'n't have gotten wind of it. Oh, don't mind if I do." Jorge accepted a slice of pie from Dillah. He focused on Lark once more. "It was about that time when he started going a bit, well, for lack of a better word, odd."

"He was always kind of odd," Lark muttered.

"It seems like one time he picked up something he shouldn't have. A lot of things, actually," Jorge paused to take a bite of pie. "Mm! Wonderful pie there, Dillah."

"Why thank you." She beamed. "Although I can't take credit for it. Dusty and Yarrow brought it over. Dusty takes such good care of our boy, sometimes I think it'll be a shame when Yarrow brings home a bride."

"Maaaaaah," Yarrow said in a pained voice. "I don't have time for that nonsense. Not with winter coming and a chicken barn with still half a roof on it."

"Well a mother worries about her children and their futures."

"Don't worry Goodwife Greenpool," Dusty piped up. "Your son's in good hands with me."

"I can see that," she said, spooning thick cream liberally over his pie. "And I am grateful for you, Dusty. I hope you don't get tired of Yarrow's bumpkin ways."

"Not a bumpkin," mouth full, Yarrow protested. "Just hungry, is all."

"Goodman Appleton, mind if I ask what Reuel Bucketsworth had?" Lark didn't want the conversation to drift to other topics.

"I don't want to say exactly," Jorge said in a conspiratorial tone. "Never saw for myself, and can't trust hearsay. Nonetheless, there was a point where a bunch of people's old Keys were going missing and it came to light that young Reuel was the most likely culprit. Clytie Winterpastures thought she saw someone rummaging in her shed and she was well shook up about it. Her Key went that night, but she couldn't rightly remember anything. Strange thing, that. Nobody got the chance to ask 'cause he just lit out and nobody's seen hair nor hide of him since. His poor mah and dah were the only ones who really took it hard. Don't know what the fool boy thought he'd be able to do with a bunch of Keys, though. Most people took offence 'cause there's no replacing them nowadays. The Goldwheats had a busy time of it, helping people get into their barns, breaking the doors and making new ones after there weren't no other way to open their Locks."

"Our old Key went missing too," Walfer added. "That one didn't even have a Lock anymore. Kept it on a hook in the chicken barn with the rest of the tools and one day it was gone. Whoever took it left the gate open and me and my good wife spent half the day chasing our chooks around creation. Couple of them got all the way down to the Wellwater ranch over yonder. Old Cormick brought them 'round in his wheelbarrow."

"Well, that is a shame," Columbah said. "Some folks have got no decency. I bet if he had just asked, you'd have given it to him."

"Sure woulda." Walfer nodded. "Got no use for a Key with no Lock."

So Reuel Bucketsworth was gone. Lark wasn't sure if she should be relieved or worried.

"No matter how many times I met that young feller on the road, he never said so much as a 'How's the weather.'" Jorge shook his finger at Lark, as if she was the one to forgo proper greetings. "I always said there's no good coming from a young man who can't give a decent greeting. Didn't I, Columbah?"

"You certainly did, my husband," she said, nodding grimly.

Jorge continued in a severe tone, "Tell you what, though, we're better off without, I say. Strange ill-mannered young man and those unnatural Ringsworn-made relics both. Neither did anybody a lick of good and I can't say I'm sorry to see our village without them."

Through the discussion, Merton picked at his ham and potatoes with a sour look on his face.

"Something not agreeing with you, son?" Walfer asked. Above his beard, his face was a jolly red.

Without answering, Merton threw his spoon down on the table and pushed back his chair. "Lark, could I have a word with you in the garden?"

"Okay, but only for a minute. I heard there's gooseberry wine coming."

The garden was bathed in golden-red light from the sinking sun. The days were already getting shorter, soon the leaves would be turning red. The wind carried the scent of harvest with it. Merton didn't say anything. He walked over to the fence around Brownie's paddock. The donkey was munching on some oats in his trough and swiveled one ear towards them.

"What did you want to talk about?" Lark asked. She leaned back on the fence and propped one foot up against it.

"You know I got my own field now. I'm going to make it into a proper farm. Enough for a stall in the marketplace."

"Good for you. It's what you always wanted."

"I can provide a good home and living. Dah and I were talking, and he said he'd help me make a proposal to the village council to build me a homestead out on the east field. It'd be done probably in a year or so."

"Sound nice." Lark stifled a yawn. Brownie came over to investigate and bumped Lark on the shoulder. She absently reached out to give the donkey a pat on the head.

"I can wait until I get my homestead built, but not much longer than that." Merton turned to look at her directly for the first time. Lark got a very odd feeling that she'd missed something.

"Wait for what?"

"Wait for you to finish whatever business you've got with the Wanderers, of course. A good woman needs an education and a trade if she's going to be responsible for bringing up the young ones properly."

"Huh? Who's bringing up what?"

"You. Our children."

Lark's world tilted. She fell off the fence and landed on her backside in a cloud of dust. "Hang on, what's this about—what in the Wide Blue Sky are you going on about, boy?"

Merton shoved himself away from the fence. He stomped his foot and turned to glare down at Lark. "Haven't you been listening to anything I've said? I'm talking about giving you a secure future and a chance to have a home of your own. It's coming time for me to settle down and some of the village girls are of age and looking for a good match, but I figure you'd do well enough."

"You are off your head." Lark got to her feet and slapped at the dust on her skirt. "If I find out Yarrow's put you up to this as a joke, I'll dropkick him like a ripe pumpkin."

"It's not a joke." Merton's nostrils billowed. He shoved his hands deep into his overall pockets. "It's your only chance for a respectable life. Who'd else have you? I don't aim to ask twice." He kicked a rock into Brownie's pen. "Why are you being so obstinate? If you're shy, don't be. While you were off doing whatever it is you people do at Jean Elliott's, I took Healer Drew's marital preparation course. I have confidence I could be a good husband to you. When I approached them, your parents welcomed the idea. They should, after all. You haven't got any other prospects and they must be worried about who'll look after you when they're gone."

Lark backed away. She shook her head, which set her plaits flying. She was at that uncomfortable point between laughing and shouting. "You've got manure where your brains should be if you think I'd jump at you."

"Why not? If there's a reason, out with it."

Lark's head came up and their eyes met in a fierce, breathless instant. Merton dared her to speak. In the silence, Lark felt as if she was swaying on the edge of a precipice. After a long, tense moment, the spell broke with a rough, ill-humored laugh from Lark.

"For Green Earth's sake," Lark said. "We used to play in the mud together and stay up all night practicing duck calls."

"What's that got to do with this?"

"I've whipped your sorry butt in a fight more times than I can count. Whatever gave you the idea I'd have you?"

Merton punched the fence. His hand bounced off the supple bough. He sucked in a breath and rubbed his knuckles against his overalls.

Lark wasn't finished. She shouted, "And what possessed you to go behind my back, applying to my parents? You know me, right? You *have* met me, right? If you have half a logical thought in that round melon on your shoulders then you should have known it'll be a frigid day in midsummer before I ever even *think* of laying down with you."

"You don't have to put it so insultingly," Merton snapped. He turned away. "Fine. I don't care. Enjoy your life alone, never written into anybody's family Almanac. That's the last time I try and do something nice for you. You—you ungrateful wall-eyed catfish!" He broke into a full run and took off in the direction of his family's house.

"Ignorant butt-sniffing rooster!" Lark hollered back. She turned so she didn't have to watch her old friend running away from her. Lark felt very alone at that moment. A sick wave of guilt washed over her. Lark wanted to blame Merton for seeing something where there was nothing, but she couldn't. Lark was at fault. Anybody else would have welcomed the proposal, she was certain of that. But Lark couldn't. Something wasn't right with her and she couldn't pretend otherwise.

Lark headed back to the house. She followed the cheerful sounds of bottles being opened and full glasses clinking. She wanted nothing more than to quiet the itching worry by drowning it in wine.

LARK AWOKE TO bright sunlight in her face. Mouth parched, she rolled off her bed and tumbled down the stairs, still in her sleeping clothes. After drinking half a bucket of water, she wandered blearily out to the porch, where her father lay on the swing. He held a bowl of dried persimmons in his hand. He shook the bowl in her direction and Lark helped herself to a couple pieces of fruit.

"That'll cure what ails ya. And a bit of this," he said. He dug into his crystal pouch and took out an amethyst. He held it to his head. "Better. How about I get you too?"

Lark leaned forward and allowed her father to banish her headache with his crystal, something he hadn't done since she was very small and didn't have the means to do it herself. Her headache stilled, but the pleasant bleariness remained, which she didn't mind. She dozed on the sunny front steps. As if from a great distance, she heard her father's voice.

"What time's your coach?"

"Umm....about three."

"You all packed and everything?"

"Yup. I didn't bother unpacking last night."

"Good plan, that. Wouldn't want to have you forget anything and have to do without until your first leave."

"That's all right, I don't need much," she said. "I guess Mah's still asleep?"

"You know how she is, sleeping off her drink without any trouble. That gooseberry wine Columbah brought round sure was tasty." He chuckled and clasped his hands over his middle.

Lark fought the urge to ask her father how he could have welcomed Merton's petition to propose marriage to her. Surely both he and her mother knew she'd made her decision and there would be no homestead for her for many years, maybe not ever.

Lark tried not to think about any other reason she had for refusing the earnest young man.

After a leisurely morning and lunch about the house, Lark went up to her room and dressed herself for the road. She decided on a long skirt and tunic to save her Outside clothes from travel dust. In the middle of changing, Lark let her binding cloth fall and cupped her hands over her breasts. They were warm and firm against her palms, not much more than a handful. The soft swells were paler than her sun-bronzed hands, the nubs darker still.

Her mind went back two years, the first time she met Rosalie and that scandalous glimpse Lark stole. She thought about how Rosalie got hers to be that way, both separated and lifted. She studied her reflection and tried to make the shape with her hands. It felt nice, thinking about Rosalie with her hands warming herself. Lark ran her fingers over her softness, then stroked her nipples. The dark areolas pebbled under her thumbs, the hard nubs stood at attention. A wonderful feeling zinged through her body and settled between her legs. She sucked in a breath and closed her eyes.

She was a Guardian now. They both were. A low, sultry heat started in her belly. Suddenly self-conscious, Lark dropped her hands and turned away. She yanked her wraps around her chest with more force than necessary. While she couldn't bind herself to the nearly flat shape she had in her younger days, the result Lark ended up with was tight enough to squash the lingering hum of excitement in her chest. The warm tension between her thighs didn't let up and Lark forced herself to ignore it.

A quick glance out the window showed Lark the sun was high overhead. The coach was going to arrive soon. It wouldn't do for her to be late for her private pickup. She grabbed up her canvas bag and did a quick check of the room. She wouldn't see the spare, warm space again for a long time. She slung her wand across her back and thundered down the stairs.

Her parents waited for her on the porch. Her father with his hands in his overall pockets and her mother with hers wringing her apron. Wordlessly, Dillah gave Lark a long hug, holding her tighter than she ever had before.

"Do take care of yourself," Dillah said with a catch in her voice. "Don't be in a hurry to strike out on your own, now."

"Hey, I'll be okay," Lark said once she was released and could breathe again.

"A mother worries," she said. Dillah turned and hurried into the kitchen where she dabbed at her eyes with the edge of her apron.

Walfer cleared his throat. "Don't forget where you came from. You've always got a home here. No matter what."

"Thanks Dah," Lark said. Her voice came out rough with emotion. She had left home so many times before, she thought that time wouldn't be any different. But it was. Lark dredged up a grin and clasped her father's outstretched hand. "I'll make you and Mah proud of me."

"You already do. Every day." Walfer patted her on the shoulder. "Now get going there, wouldn't want to be late for your private pickup."

Lark couldn't speak past the lump in her throat. She nodded and turned quickly. Her skirts flapped and her unadorned black cloak billowed out in an impressive way behind her as Lark strode away from her childhood home, toward the biggest adventure of her life.

By the time Lark got to the landing platform, she was calm once more. To her relief, it wasn't the official Guardian's coach that awaited her but Cassie MacLean's cheerful overturned table. In addition to the heavy curtains, streamers hung from the table legs and fluttered in the wind.

"Ready to move out?" Cassie's freckled, cheerful face poked over the side. She hadn't changed in the years Lark had known her, save to become even frecklier and more cheerful.

"Sure am." Lark grabbed the end of the rope ladder that fell down toward her and clambered up. She accepted Cassie's invitation to sit up front beside her. Poplar Valley fell away from them, but Lark only had eyes for the way ahead.

"We're not as good as you Crystalgazers about keeping in touch with each other," Cassie said. "But we sure do like to gossip when we do meet up. Let me tell you the news. You heard about Elsie Mason, right?"

"No, I haven't," Lark said. She was eager to hear about her long-ago training-mate. During the final year of her apprenticeship, a newly-married Dwight returned once in order to introduce his new bride, a pretty and outspoken Wanderer from the next village over who, while she obviously doted on her husband, never failed to put him in his place if the situation called for it. Lark swallowed a bittersweet pang as she'd offered up her heart-felt congratulations. An odd, removed sense came over her. Lark couldn't imagine herself being some fellow's wife. It was an alien idea. Cassie's words brought Lark back to the present.

"She apprenticed with Dale Lyon and got her accounting cer-tificate."

"That's great news," Lark said. "Elsie has a real knack for numbers. She was always steadier than any of us too. Go on then Cassie, where's she practicing?"

"I don't wanna give it away," Cassie said. She nudged Lark on the arm, "But you may be seeing her around Shadowmoor one of these days. I dropped her off at the main intake post in North-wood yesterday, but you know how they move around once they're official."

"Huh. How about that?" Lark said. Only the best accountants got assigned to intake duty. Dealing with the collection and allo-cation of the tithes from the many villages wasn't a job for just anyone.

"Good head on her shoulders, that girl," Cassie said.

"Agreed," Lark said. She drew back the curtain from between the upturned table legs and watched the scenery zipping by below.

The trees below gave way to rippling fields of deep green and gold, spotted with little cottages and the occasional village. That in turn gave way to more forest, wilder and deeper than Lark was used to. Under their flying table, the trees became darker and bramblier and the air eerily silent. They passed over rivers and long, silent stretches of sea that separated their cluster of islands.

They didn't speak until Shadowmoor came into view, and then only a few words. Lark was tongue-tied by the sight. She only saw the briefest glimpse of Shadowmoor in that long-ago night when she scryed up their meeting room. For the first time, she understood the sheer size of the outpost. Shadowmoor was a village in itself. A number of large buildings were clustered in the middle of a clearing with medium-sized ones in various group-ings scattered around, some connected to each other by path-ways. The smallest ones were the most numerous, set back into the forest, away from the main area. The forest itself was thick and stately, filled with ancient trees that dwarfed even the largest building.

One of those buildings had half of its roof charred and burned off. A few black-cloaked figures could be seen swarming around to put a sturdy brown tarp over it and secure it with little flashes from their wands.

"Looks like someone lost control of their energy beam again," Cassie said. "I'm just gonna circle around the back. There's a nice landing stage there, just outside the main hangar. Built last year by a bunch of fledglings and works like a charm."

As Cassie concentrated on driving, Lark took that opportunity to gather up her scattered possessions and shoulder her bag. Her hands fumbled more than usual. Her heart pounded under her too-tight binding cloth. Lark was breathless and felt light-headed. The glance she took of the compound had revealed a large number of people, some wearing black cloaks, others in Healer's yellow or the grey of accountants plus a few brown ones here and there, and others without cloaks. It was more people than she had ever seen at one time, even at their village meetings. For the first time, Lark regretted choosing her mentor's familiar home for her apprenticeship instead of trying for a place where she could have gotten more practice meeting new people. Lark gulped.

How would she remember everyone's names? What if she accidentally slighted one of her seniors? Would she find anyone to be friends with, or would they all look at her like the manure-smelling hayseed she was? Crystalgazer-raised Wanderers were in the vast minority when it came to those assigned to the outposts, and even fewer chose to join the ranks of the Guardians.

Lark didn't reply to Cassie's next few questions. She didn't hear them and even if she did, she didn't have the breath to speak. Her chest felt unbearably tight, straining against her wraps and Lark wished there was a way to loosen the material strangling her without shedding her entire outfit onto the floor of the coach.

"You'll be okay, hon." Cassie patted Lark on one knee. Below, a few people came over to welcome the coach with shouts and waves. Cassie waved back but Lark could only stare.

The coach settled onto the padded supports of the landing stage and Lark jumped to her feet. She had to properly greet the people who she would be working with for the rest of her life. Her vision buzzed and black stars exploded around her eyes. Her knees buckled before she could finish the movement and she grabbed desperately at the curtain beside her. She only yanked it from the table leg and brought the whole wall of it down over her as blackness claimed her.

Chapter Five

"SHE'S WAKING UP, stand back people."

"Get that ice pack from the table over there Alice, just in case we need it."

"It's melted."

"Just give it a zap there."

"I would, but the last time I tried it the whole thing went up in smoke."

"Get someone to zap it for you if you can't do it yourself."

"Here, let me do it."

"Thanks Murray."

"Hey Jake, you seen that bag she had with her?"

"I don't know, but I think I saw Healer Andrews chuck it somewhere over there when they hauled her in. Poor thing looked scared half to death before she hit the dirt."

Behind her heavy lids, Lark struggled to surface. She heard the sound of chair legs scraping against the floor and the rustle of someone sitting down next to her.

"What d'you think's wrong with her?" a young male voice asked.

"Altitude sickness," a bright female voice declared. "Either that or the coach driver flew through a cursed cloud."

"Shut your opinion-maker there, Alice! I've been flying coaches since before you were a twinkle in your daddy's eye and there's no way I'd be dumb enough to fly through something like that."

"Just pointing out the possibility. No need to get all upset."

"In addition to that," a calm, cool voice said, "Coach-driver MacLean would be equally affected. No, this is simply the case of nerves overcoming sense. Happens to the best of us. Now, if you would all please stand back a little, I think our patient is waking up."

Blinking into the sudden light, Lark took a deep breath and sat up. Somehow the pressure on her chest had eased. Her binding cloth was gone. Had it gone flying off on its own, or had someone liberated her of it? Both ideas were equally disturbing. She felt foolish and extremely shy.

The eldest of the people clustered around her was a Healer. She wore a light yellow robe draped over her daily clothes. Cassie hovered over Lark with a concerned expression. Behind her were three more people, two young men, and a young woman who smiled encouragingly at her. The room itself was long and open. A row of unoccupied beds were placed at intervals down one wall, and the air was bright with sunlight streaming in from the large windows.

Cassie patted Lark awkwardly on the shoulder.

"You keeled over just as we landed. You remember anything after that?"

"Not really," Lark said. Still uneasy about her missing binding cloth, she yanked the sheets up to her chin. "Sorry about all the fuss. I'm fine now."

"Glad to hear that. I'd hate to have to break the news to your folks that my driving finally killed someone."

"You heard Miss Greenpool. She's fine, no need to worry. Go back to your duties." The Healer stood and began shooing the assembled people out the door. When they were gone, she turned back to Lark. "Glad to see you're back to your regular self. In the future, just remember not to bind too tightly, but it's nothing that can't be fixed with a little bit of care, anyway. Here, I've brought another wrap for you to try. It's a bit softer than the ones you're used to, but still strong enough to keep your modesty intact."

"Thanks." Lark tried to smile and not feel mortified. She took the bundle of white cloth the Healer handed over. It felt smooth in her hands. "I didn't mean to do that. I just, you know, I just wanted to make a good impression." She laughed in a false way that sounded a lot like a donkey. She stopped.

Healer Andrews smiled knowingly and said, "No harm done. And you made one of the more memorable entrances in our little outpost's history."

"Glad I could brighten everyone's day," Lark said with an internal wince.

"Just so you know, all of the Guardians are having a meeting to introduce everyone in about an hour. I'll have Alice come up to fetch you in a few minutes and she can show you around and get you settled in."

After the Healer left, Lark jumped up and put the gifted wrap to good use. It was nice and held her in a different way than the usual one had. Quickly, Lark laced herself back into her tunic. It was her best one that she saved for the auspicious occasion—dark green Wanderer-spun linen with a border of white stitching around the hem of her long skirt and cuffs. She was glad it wasn't too dusty from her trip. Lark found her pocket-belt on the small table beside the bed and strapped it around her waist. Just as she finished putting herself back in order, someone knocked on the door and Lark hurried to open it. The smiling young woman from before was back.

"Hi there. That was quite a tumble you took. Are you okay?" she asked.

"Body is fine," Lark said. "Dignity slightly rumpled."

"Don't worry about it. We all get nervous on our first day."

"You must be Alice, then."

"Yup. Alisson Chance actually. But you can call me Alice. I'm a fledgling too, passed the test last month. I came up from Boulder Ridge and I've been here a week."

"Nice to meet you, and I'm Lark Greenpool."

Lark's unease lessened in the face of the other young woman's friendly manner. Besides Elsie and Dwight, She hadn't met too many Wanderer-born-and-raised people before, but if they were like Alice, Lark wasn't going to have any trouble.

Alice was short and cute. She had a mischievous-looking face and her sunny blonde hair was tied up into two messy tails. She wasn't wearing her black cloak, just a white tunic and red skirt. She'd tucked the hem of her skirt up into her belt so it was about at mid-calf level, intentionally showing off the shorter striped underskirt, as Lark later learned most Wanderer women did when they were in the mood to move fast.

Lark swept up her cloak and held it in her hands, undecided if she should put it on or not.

"Only Healers have to wear their colors all the time, most of the rest of us don't bother," Alice said, with a friendly nod at the bundle in Lark's hands. "Once I get my first Tracker's stripe, now that's a different story."

"Same here," Lark said.

"Anyway, Healer Andrews said I'm to show you around. Are you okay to walk?"

"Yup, I'm fine," Lark said. "By the way, sorry about the dramatic entrance. Really, I'm just a calm country-girl."

"That's good to know," Alice said. "Come on down this way and I'll show you the place. It's not much, but it'll be a good home until we get our stripes and can hit the skies."

Lark didn't have the chance to reply before Alice grabbed her by the wrist and ran down the long wooden hallway.

"This building's the Wellness Center. They've got private rooms upstairs and Healer Andrews or one of her assistants are always around if you need them."

Lark looked around with wide eyes. She'd never been inside such a large building. Even her village's meeting hall was dwarfed beside it. The lanterns hanging from the ceiling were brightly polished silver and crystal-like glass. The blue flames in them burned low, waiting for dusk. Lark was used to the small one her mentor had in her kitchen. A wave of a wand would swell the flame into warm yellow brightness. The old lantern that hung in the main room of Lark's own house was a tin bucket with holes cut in the sides, lit by a tallow candle.

They left the building and burst into the main compound.

"That's our main practice hall," Alice said, pointing to the long tarp-covered building. "It's usually much nicer and we can go inside, but this morning we were practicing deflections and Nora accidentally blew half the roof off. You should have seen Outpost Head Weinberg! I thought he'd blow the rest of it off with his hollering." She giggled and covered her mouth with one hand.

"You won't have to worry about me blowing anything up," Lark said. "I'm more of a slow-and-steady kind of person."

"Glad to hear it."

They came to a pair of wide, three-storied buildings.

Alice said, "The one on the left is the girls' dormitory and the boys are on the right. The first floor has our common room where we can gather and play games or just relax. Us fledglings all share the second floor. The third floor is just a loft. Everybody else mostly stays in the cottages but some of the junior accountants live over the office. I like dorm life pretty well so far. I hear we can have a bonfire in the middle here if we want. You can see the burn-mark. I hope you know lots of songs."

"Sure do. We like bonfires back home too."

"Great! We've got to hurry if we want to be in time for the introduction meeting so I'll just give you the mini-tour now and you can ask me about anything else later," Alice said as they trotted through the compound.

In quick succession, Lark saw the council-house where the Guardians met for important business, the meal hall which doubled as a general assembly area, and the library. Lark was used to the book-lending wagon that came around her village once a month and stood, transfixed, in front of the towering red-brick edifice until Alice tugged her away. On their way back to the meal hall, they passed in front of a building with a red and white awning.

"Here's the commissary," Alice said. "If you have coins, you can use them here to buy stuff or just have the clerk put everything on your account."

"My account?" Lark knit her brow.

Alice smacked herself on the forehead. "Of course, you didn't have time to get your ledger. Come on, I'll take you to get it now. My friend Bethanie's an accountant here. We mentored together and she's really nice."

Alice hurried off with Lark in close pursuit. Without even hesitating, Alice pushed open the double doors to the accounting building. The large central room was filled with neat rows of desks with earnestly-working people behind them. Most people had their grey cloaks draped over the backs of their chairs. A long counter separated the sea of desks from the entrance and Alice trotted up to it. She leaned both elbows on the desk.

"May I help you?" a scholarly-looking fellow came over to them.

"Yes, I just wanted to help my friend get her ledger," Alice said. Lark, who was tongue-tied at the scale of the room, was grateful for Alice's forthrightness. "Is Bethanie Miller free?"

"Just a moment."

The man looked over his shoulder and beckoned to a slim, freckly redhead. She abandoned her task and bounded up to them.

"Hi Alice," she said as she looked Lark up and down. "Who do you have here?"

"One of the new fledglings," Alice said. She quickly introduced the two of them.

"So you need your ledger, right?" Bethanie asked. Lark nod-ded. "Show me your registration parchment and I'll get it right out for you."

Lark dug the square of folded parchment out of her pocket and passed it over. It was the first time anybody asked to see it. Her name and her parents' names were on it, along with the date that the Village Head guessed was her birth date. Bethanie stuck the tip of her tongue out in a thoughtful way as she filled out a small form and then dashed off. She returned with a slim, blue-covered book which she passed to Lark.

"Just check your name and everything's okay and you're good to go," Bethanie said.

Lark flipped through the first few pages. Her name and rank were written in the front, as well as the small stipend allocated for her rank. "Looks fine," Lark said. She quickly slipped it and her parchment into the pocket on her belt she reserved for her most important things.

"Thanks for dropping by, don't be a stranger," Bethanie said. She grinned at both of them before she whirled and pattered back to her desk.

Alice glanced at the sand-clock on the wall. "Do you want to drop your stuff in the dorm before the meeting?"

"Sure," Lark said.

The long room on the second floor housed a row of beds, each with a wooden box at the foot to hold their worldly posses-sions. Folding screens stood between them for a small amount of privacy. Lark found the one assigned to her and unceremoniously dumped her satchel and cloak into the box. She hooked her thumbs through her belt and looked around at the place she would live until she earned her stripe and would be free to go wherever the wind took her.

A bell rang outside and Alice peeked around the screen into Lark's domain.

"That's the meeting bell. Let's go."

They dashed into the meal hall that was full of Guardians, plus a few people in aprons who handed out mugs of tea.

The bell rang again and everyone grabbed chairs and sat down with scraping sounds. Enos Weinberg, who took care of the administrative aspects and daily running of the outpost, got up on the dais at the front of the room and gave a short welcoming speech, then Healer Andrews gave an address complete with some advice to prevent burnout from overzealous wand practice. The newly promoted Guardians as well as the new intake were introduced, but Lark didn't hear a word. Behind them, a slim, dark-haired young woman stood in with the other Patrollers. In two years, she'd been promoted and was now the youngest Guardian to earn that rank. Lark felt the gold stripe on her cloak glowed with the warmth of the sun. Rosalie stood with casual grace, her light, river-blue eyes regarded the assembly calmly.

"That's Rosalie Jordan," Alice elbowed Lark and hissed in a whisper.

"I know," Lark elbowed her back.

The meeting ended and Lark joined everyone in milling around. Alice suddenly tugged at her sleeve. "She's coming over, Rosalie's actually coming over. Who are you, Miss Lark Greenpool?"

"Nobody," Lark said.

"Well if it isn't the little Crystalgazer from Jean Elliott's group," Rosalie said. Her lovely eyes danced. She tossed back a wave of curls over her shoulder and smiled. "I was wondering if I would ever see you again."

"Yeah, I decided to become a Guardian like you," Lark said.

Instantly, she wanted to take the foolish words back, but Rosalie just pursed her rosebud lips and looked so pretty Lark could barely breathe. Rosalie hummed to herself and said, "Just so you know, I've been asked to help out with getting you people into shape. I'm here to make sure you've got what it takes to go out in the field with us and face what's messing up our skies and fields."

"I'm ready," Lark said with a conviction she had to fake.

"Glad to hear that," Rosalie said. She smiled and Lark melted. "I think you'll be a valuable addition to the Guardians." She held out her hand and Lark stared at it for a heartbeat before she reached out and took it in both of hers. It wasn't a handshake. Their fingers curled around each other. She held Rosalie's hand in hers for a long, delicious moment before Rosalie stepped back and ended the contact. Lark struggled to calm her breathing as Rosalie turned and drifted away.

Lark got herself back under control when the fledglings were called over to assemble in front of one of the Patrollers, a thin, nervous-looking man by the name of David Costas. Lark counted twenty-five of them. Most of them were young like her, but a few were older. They looked the most serious. Costas told them to form into study groups of four members each. Alice took charge and rounded up Lark, who was hugely relieved at being included. The other two were Nora Kenelm of the roof-destroying reputation and Murray Buckley who Lark vaguely remembered being in her sick-room. He looked just as nervous as Lark felt.

Once everyone was properly grouped, they were shown the duty roster which had everyone's chores that were part of the exchange for room and board at the outpost. As the lowest-ranking, the fledglings were accordingly given the most menial duties. Lark didn't mind, she liked keeping busy. Their first job was to restore the meal hall to its usual arrangement. She and the other fledglings got out the many round tables and chairs and arranged them around the large room. At the front of the room, a long, rectangular table overlooked the room on the dais. Lark assumed that was for the higher-ranking members as the overstuffed chairs were significantly more gorgeous than the simple ones on the floor. Murray was the first to receive a reprimand as he used his wand to summon a trio of chairs from across the room.

"You need to conserve your energy," Costas snapped. Murray twitched and the chairs tumbled to the floor. "If something happens, you need to be ready to act. Understood?"

"Yes sir," Murray said. He hung his head.

While the fledglings worked, the cook and his staff bustled around, setting out large tureens of soup, platters of roast chicken and potatoes, and heaping baskets of rolls. Good smells wafted through the room and Lark's stomach growled. Someone rang the bell and people started filing in. The room resounded with laughter and conversation.

The fledglings waited until the senior ranks got their meals before they filled their plates. Lark ended up at a table with Alice and Bethanie who talked enthusiastically about every subject under the sun. For the first time, Shadowmoor felt like home.

After dinner, Lark stood shoulder-to-shoulder with Murray and Alice at the long sink in the kitchen where they scrubbed out the pots and pans. As penance for blowing off the roof, instead of dish-duty, Nora's assigned task was chopping shingles behind the woodshed.

"I can't believe I already got told off," Murray said in a desolate voice. He heaved a deep sigh.

"Don't sweat it," Lark said. "We're all going to be in your shoes one of these days. You just beat us to it."

"Thanks," Murray said. He brushed a pale brown strand of hair out of his eyes using the back of one soapy hand. "My Great Auntie Pacifica always told me to be proud of getting told off because anyone who causes trouble is going places."

Alice and Lark raised their eyebrows at each other and continued their scrubbing.

"The only place I want to go is Outside," Alice said. "Just think of how exciting it would be to see a real city like Compton. I've already memorized the map for when they let us go out there."

"Why?" Murray paused in his washing to stare at her. "It just seems like a big, noisy place where you can get into lots of trouble. Plus it's filled with Outsiders, and they're just stupid brutes who don't know how to do anything. As for me, I want to see everything in the Protected Isles. Think about how amazing the Salt Cliffs of Blacksea are and the Great Forest where the trees grow so close it's always night on the ground. If you want Outsider stuff, you can get anything that catches your fancy at the market in Riverbend."

Alice waved a dismissive hand. "Yeah, we've got some pretty nice places here too, but Compton is so different and so dangerous too."

"Danger? I guess, if that's what you like." Murray shrugged. "My Great Auntie Pacifica's been there a bunch of times and always gets into some kind of trouble. Once she even got locked up overnight in an Outsider facility for bad people and had to stay with a bunch of drunkards. She stunned the guard and blasted the doors open and let everyone escape."

Alice's eyes shone.

"Don't even think about it," Lark said. "If the Council hears about you stunning people Outside you'll wish you were locked up with drunkards."

"Okay, I won't," Alice said. She sighed dreamily and grabbed a large frying pan.

THAT NIGHT, LARK lay on her assigned bed and listened to the soft sounds of the other fledglings as they slept. Her heart beat faster under her clasped hands. Along with her fellow fledglings, she would learn how to enforce the laws of their land within their Border as well as survive outside of it, and Rosalie was going to take part in training them.

Lark was glad she wouldn't have to fake being interested in Rosalie's lessons. She would probably have to fake not being too interested. She hadn't felt that excited about lessons since Miss Beccah Goldwheat offered to teach her geometry one-on-one after a series of disastrous test results. Unfortunately, Lark still didn't have any idea about geometry, but she did have a good idea of the pretty way Miss Goldwheat's hair caught the late afternoon sun. Sighing, Lark let that image go like a leaf down the river. She had a new teacher now, lots of new teachers. One of them was a lovely young woman with pretty eyes and a cute smile.

She closed her eyes, trying to will herself asleep. Outside, a breeze picked up, bringing the clean, good smells of the forest in through the open window. For once the lingering thunder in the air seemed to fade.

Chapter Six

AT THE START of her ninth month at Shadowmoor, Lark sprawled out on her bed with a book in her hands she wasn't reading. It was a hot, airless summer night, rare for their area and Lark was restless and unsettled. An unseasonable chest cough kept her from joining the rest of the fledglings on a seven-day stay in a safehouse in the Outsider city of Compton. It was part of a larger mass known as "New Brunswick" to the Outsiders. The safehouse was part of the vast network of inns where Wanderers stayed on their endless journeys. The majority of them were located in various places around the Protected Isles, along with simple, often unmanned waystations. The one in Compton was the most interesting to Alice. She talked about nothing else for weeks and Lark got caught up in the excitement until she was ordered to stay behind.

Most of the other Guardians were out on patrol due to the fact that without the fledglings present, there were no training modules that week. The compound was deserted except for a skeleton crew of Guardians in addition to the usual outpost staff and various accountants. This left Lark with not only a grumbling sense of the unfairness of life but also an unprecedented amount of free time. After she was released from her overnight stay in the Wellness Center, she went digging in the back of the library and came up with a novel called *The Right Husband for the Lady of the Coach-House* which Lark found both fascinating and unsatisfying in equal measures.

Lark didn't know if it was the weather or the book, but that night her skin felt electrified. She twitched and couldn't sit still. A flash of white light threw the room into sharp relief. Right on top of it, a boom of thunder cracked through the compound. It sounded like someone let off a depth-charge overhead. A deep creaking, groaning sound filled the room.

Lark jumped to her feet and her book tumbled to the floor. She knew the sound of a tree falling over when she heard it, but never one as huge as that. She burst from the dormitory in time to see one of the ancient trees that circled the compound keel over and smash down onto the roof of the accounting building. Flames spurted from the fallen tree. Grey-cloaked people ran from the door and congregated in a cluster some distance away, but Lark wasn't concerned with them. Her eyes were on the fallen tree. The harsh wind only fed the flames. They crawled up the massive trunk, heading inexorably to the wooden shingled roof.

"Lark, come with me!"

Lark snapped to attention as Rosalie grabbed her arm. Without hesitation, Lark pounded after her. They stopped in front of the ruined building. Already a group of Healers were converged around the accountants. Overhead, the clouds rumbled and cracked. The sky was a horrible greenish color and the air was damp with the threat of a downpour.

Rosalie looked up at the clouds with narrowed eyes. She drew her wand and said, "We don't time to wait for rain. Lark, I know your technique better than you know mine, so you're in the lead. I can support you better that way. Our first priority is get that fire out before it reaches the building and then we can worry about moving that tree."

"Got it," Lark said. Even though it was an emergency, she couldn't help the thrill that raced through her. She squared her shoulders and held her wand in both hands. She ignored the shouts of pain and fear around her and concentrated only on the task at hand. Lark didn't even have to think. The words came automatically. She said, "We'll start with standard flame-extinguishing procedures, cold-blast and then a follow-up with vacuum-shields."

"Perfect. Go ahead," Rosalie said. She got into her stance next to Lark, who had to fight to keep her mind clear. Her heart thudded.

Months of training paid off and Lark's blast erupted simultaneously with Rosalie's. Her own red beam danced along with Rosalie's steady blue and hit the burning tree. In a few moments, nothing more than smoke billowed from it.

"People are still trapped in there. We have to get the tree off," Lark said. "Do you think we can do it with just the two of us?"

Rosalie shook her head. "It's too big. We'll burn out. Wait a moment, Lark." She looked around, then darted off. She returned a moment later with two sturdy accountants in tow.

"I'm Harris," one of them said. "He's Parker."

"Nice to meet you," Lark said.

"Okay, enough pleasantries," Rosalie said. "We have work to do. Lark's in charge, so get behind her."

They fell into formation and once more Lark raised her wand. She addressed the new additions. "Follow my lead and lift that tree off as gently as you can. We'll move it away from the building and set it down somewhere. Got it?" She waited for their affirmative answer before she said, "On my count, one, two, and *go!*"

As one, they threw themselves into their task. The tree groaned and started to move. A sliver of sky appeared between it and the ruined roof. Shingles fell like rain onto the ground. More people ran out of the building. Lark prayed that Alice's friend Bethanie was safe in the chaos. Slowly, the gigantic tree rose, but caught on the jagged rafters and stopped.

"Plague and river-rot," Lark spat.

Sweat beaded at her hairline and a drop rolled down Lark's face. She gritted her teeth and dug deep within herself for more energy. Her own steady but slow stream wasn't enough. She was almost at the point of anger at her own impotence when she felt her energy source shift from under her feet to her chest. At once, Lark had more power than she knew what to do with and she let out a triumphant shout. The tree soared up, free from the wreckage.

"I see a good spot to put it," Rosalie said, her voice tight with strain. "Over behind the wash-shed."

"Got it," Lark said. Her energy waned but she gave one last burst and was rewarded by the tree obediently moving in a slow arc toward the clearing between the buildings. Lark shouted orders and they carefully set the huge trunk onto the grass. The instant the tree was down, Lark snapped off her energy and fell to her knees. For the first time in her life she was drained to the limit. She clutched at her chest and struggled to breathe. Her vision swam black. She was on the verge of passing out when a gentle but strong arm came around her shoulders and held her up.

"We did it," Rosalie said. "Lark, you're a hero."

"Huh," Lark said. She blinked twice, dropped her wand and pitched forward onto her face.

WHEN LARK WOKE up in the Wellness Center with a bad case of burnout, she learned the extent of the damage to the compound. The storm was the worst one yet and only a few buildings came through unscathed.

Sequestered in one of the private sick-rooms, Lark revisited the moment when she stood side-by-side with Rosalie in battle. It was like a dream come true, but not quite worth the day and a half Lark spent throwing up into a bucket while battling a headache that neither wands nor crystals could ease. For the first time, she understood Wanderer's reluctance to overspend their internal energy resources and vowed never to put herself in that useless and unprepared state again.

Several days after the storm, Head Guardian Williams announced during lunch that all members of the outpost were called to attend a very important meeting that afternoon. Buzzing whispers filled the hall even before the announcement was over. Propriety and the stern looks from the Head Guardian stopped most speculation over the meal.

After lunch, Lark washed the dishes with Murray, Alice, and Nora. Only then could they speak freely.

"What do you think the meeting's about?" Murray asked. "Alice, you've got the biggest ears around here, what do you think?"

"I don't know for sure, but..." Alice glanced around and made a beckoning motion with one finger. The others leaned closer, dripping sponges forgotten in their hands. "Bethanie told me last night Head Guardian Williams ordered the official seal be brought from the vault into the council-house. It's only used when a formal treaty is signed. Like, Great Division formal."

"So what does that mean?" Lark asked. She shook back her long tails as they tried to get into the dishwater.

"Something's in the works. Something big, like a secret weapon."

"I wonder what it is," Lark mused aloud.

"I bet it's a giant boomerang that turns into fire if you throw it," Alice said. "I read about it in one of the Amelia Strawberry books. The one where she goes to the island with the giant lizards."

"No way," Murray scoffed. "My Great Auntie Pacifica had one of those and she only used it to open champagne bottles. If

we have a secret weapon, I bet it's something way more dangerous."

Nora piped up, "Besides, Amelia Strawberry's not even real."

"I know Amelia Strawberry's not a real person," Alice said.
"Kinda glad too. If she were, then Amelia's mortal enemy, Elvira
Flavia duKillovsky would be real too, and I don't want to think
someone as scary as that could exist."

Lark couldn't resist. She said, "You know, I think Elvira
secretly just wants to be friends with Amelia and is too shy to
come right out and say it."

"Strange way of being friends," Alice said with her eyebrows
raised, "trying to get her killed and putting curses on her and
stuff like that. Besides, they're always arguing and saying nasty
things to each other."

"It's not what they say, it's all about what they *don't* say,"
Lark said.

They finished their duties in contemplative silence. The
heady buzz of excitement and the feeling something huge was
about to happen increased as coaches arrived with guests, including Jean and Medina. Lark could barely contain her curiosity and
made more mistakes than usual in her afternoon training session.
Finally the meeting bell clanged and Lark joined the procession
into their meal hall. The tables had been cleared and the room
was filled to bursting with attendees. By skimming along the wall
while dragging a stool, Lark managed to find a space to sit next to
Jean and Medina quite near the raised dais at the front of the
room. Alice wedged herself in behind the trio.

Williams swept into the room and took the few steps up to
the dais. He stood at the podium and motioned for silence. Immediately, a deep hush fell. He gazed out over the crowd for a
moment before he spoke.

"I'm sure you are all wondering why I called this meeting,"
Williams said. "I would like to announce the next step in our cam-
paign to neutralize the storms, which is a definitive step to recover
the artifact or artifacts that are causing them. It is time for us to
admit we cannot do this alone and thusly, I have applied for assistance. The result is a very special alliance. One that will allow us to
defeat this new foe." Williams looked over to the entrance. "Come
in, please," he called out in a commanding voice.

The doors to the hall creaked open, revealing a hooded and

cloaked figure. The figure walked with measured steps, crossing the room in a straight, purposeful line. The figure's cloak was made of some light-sucking material that made a hole of absolute darkness, darker than dark in the sunlit room. Sharp footsteps from delicate, low-heeled boots shattered the shocked silence of the room as the mysterious stranger approached the dais.

Slender, white hands emerged, pushed back the hood and threw open the cloak, revealing the stranger was female. Lark held her breath and leaned forward on her chair. She had never seen anyone as magnificent as that woman.

The newcomer's skin was milky white as if she'd never seen the sun and her hair was the color of clotted blood. The heavy braids were coiled on her head, held with jeweled combs. She had painted her eyes with black and her lips with red. Under the paint, her dark eyes were a delicate almond shape and hooded as she glowered over the assembly.

Her mouth, generously-lipped, was turned into a frown. Her long. swan-like neck was adorned with a necklace that looked more like a collar. It was of some black metal, heavily set with jewels and hung with chains. A large polished stone, red as blood, hung from it to nestle in the creamy curves of her bosom.

The woman's figure was encased in a bodice of a silky, deep red cloth, pulled tight around her slim body. Lark gulped. Her gaze settled on the vista below the necklace and her face went hot. Lark's world narrowed to the hallowed area revealed by the low, square-cut neckline of the bodice. In a way that Lark had never seen before, never even dreamed of, her breasts were exposed to almost an indecent degree, pushed up to form a round shelf of perfect mounds. She was so pale that Lark could see the blue spider web of veins running under her skin.

From her small waist, a long, full, midnight-black skirt billowed out and fell in liquid folds to the floor. Tucked against her skirt, she wore a brace of slim daggers, three on each side. She looked deadly, stone-faced and unwavering as the entire room gaped at her. She was, in short, the single most amazing creature Lark had ever seen.

"Oh my goodness, it's Elvira Flavia duKillovsky," Alice gasped from her perch behind Lark. "Where's Amelia Strawberry when you need her?"

Williams drew his cloak about himself and stepped back,

respectfully giving the floor to the visitor. She stood at the podium for a moment and surveyed the room. Lark wasn't certain, but she thought the visitor's gaze lingered on her for a moment longer than anyone else. Uncomfortably aware of her boyish Outsider clothing, Lark wondered if she should have worn something more conventional. Unconsciously, she straightened up from her casual sprawl and pulled her knees together. Then the visitor spoke and Lark forgot everything else existed.

"Greetings," she said. Her voice was low and dark, but carried to the farthest corners of the room. A shiver that wasn't quite unpleasant raced down Lark's spine. "I am Violet Ironwrought, and I come here as an ambassador of the Ringsworn as a show of cooperation and goodwill to assist in identifying and neutralizing the threat against all of our people. You will treat me with the respect due to my status or I will squash all of you like the insignificant insects you are." Over the slim bodice, she folded her hands, white and delicate and long-fingered. Lark was interested to see her nails were short and her hands were unadorned.

"Welcome to Shadowmoor Outpost." Outpost Head Weinberg rose from the bench and self-importantly brushed off his ruffled clothes. "I can assure you, everyone here is properly mannered and well-trained, and no disrespect will be shown."

"That remains to be seen," Violet replied in her soft, dangerous voice.

"You must be tired from your long journey," Weinberg said. "We've prepared a cottage for you. It is rather simple, such as we Wanderers are, however I'm sure you'll find it suitable."

"As long as it is private and dark. Sunlight in large doses pains me."

"I'll see what we can do." Weinberg's bald spot sweated. He nodded to one of the older trainees, a swarthy young man who immediately stood. "I have selected Jerome Richards to be your liaison while you are here with us. He will make sure you are properly taken care of and will be a perfect gentleman. Never let it be said that Wanderers lack for hospitality."

Jerome bowed slightly before he took a step toward the visitor and offered his arm in a courtly manner. Violet recoiled. She took a step back, her face unreadable. Her hands clutched at her cloak and wound it around her body as if shielding herself from attack.

"There is no one else?" Violet's voice was a shadow of its former bravado. "I do not wish to be alone in the presence of a male, not even one who purports to be a 'gentleman'."

Spurred by a burst of energy she couldn't quite explain, Lark stood. She addressed Weinberg, "How about asking me? I'm as good a helper as anyone here."

Rustles and whispers filled the room. Head Guardian Williams silenced them with a stern look.

Weinberg looked over at Lark with surprise written all over his face. His mouth flapped open and shut. He looked over to Williams in silent appeal.

"I know this young one, and I believe she has the ability to serve in this capacity," Williams said. He acknowledged Lark with a nod. Now it was Lark's turn to be surprised. She was certain he wouldn't remember her from the incident at Jean's. Perhaps such attention to detail made him rise to the top of the Guardians.

"Well then," Weinberg said. "It is highly irregular, however it can be done if our guest is in agreement with this change."

"I am," Violet said immediately.

"Understood." Weinberg looked over at Lark. "Very well, young fledgling. I give you the heavy task and honor of assisting our most important visitor in any way necessary. After all, hospitality is our highest priority here. Hopefully you will not become a casualty."

"Don't worry sir, I'm sure our guest is friendly," Lark said.

"No, I am not friendly," Violet intoned. She loomed up behind Weinberg which caused him to twitch violently. She fixed Lark with her unwavering stare as she continued, "It would do you all in good stead to remember that I am as evil as I look, and will rain down retribution when provoked."

"Hopefully not anytime soon," Weinberg said in a falsely-jolly voice. He backed away. "We've put you up in Primrose Cottage. It's quite near the washing-up shed and the baths. Very pleasant and convenient location."

Lark turned to Violet. She was struck by how stiffly the Ring-sworn held herself, how her eyes darted about as if looking for an escape. Lark didn't blame her, she wanted to get out of the spotlight as well. The combined scrutiny of the entire outpost made her nervous.

"Why don't we go away from all this fuss and get you settled?" Lark asked.

Violet inclined her regal head. The tension in her muscles
eased the slightest fraction. "Yes, that would be acceptable."

"By the way, I'm Larkspur Greenpool, but everybody calls
me Lark. Right this way, please."

She started walking, aware that everyone in the room was
staring at them, some with pity and others with disbelief. Violet
fell into step slightly behind her. The long skirts made lovely,
deep swishes around her legs. Along the way, they passed the
coach station and collected a small but sturdy travelling trunk.
Violet made a move as if to pick it up, but Lark stepped in with
her wand.

"That's all right, Miss Ironwrought, I've got it," Lark said.
With a flick of her wrist, the trunk rose into the air. Violet's eyes
widened in surprise. The cold mask slipped for just an instant,
showing someone younger and more human than Lark expected.

Violet stepped back. The trunk bobbed along obediently
behind them as they continued toward the guest cottage. En
route, Lark wondered which coach driver had the honor of ferry-
ing the Ringsworn to them. Perhaps the task had been allotted to
the Guardians' black barge. She couldn't quite imagine Cassie's
overturned table sitting well with the dark woman, particularly
considering where it came from.

The cottage was indeed conveniently located, but set back
away from the main compound enough so it was private and
shielded from the daily bustle by several mature trees. As usual
for Wanderers, the door was unlocked. Anything that needed to
be secure was guarded by a Ringsworn-made Lock. Wanderers
could open any latch or pick any regular lock faster than a frog
could snare a fly; they were stopped only by courtesy. To Lark's
knowledge, the only Lock in the compound was in the holding
cell in the basement of the council-house.

Lark ushered Violet inside with what she hoped was a suit-
ably gentle bow. The door clacked closed behind Lark and she
surveyed the room with satisfaction.

The cottage was small but well-furnished and looked comfortable. The single room had a big fluffy bed piled high with
handmade patchwork cushions and a matching bedspread. A
small pine dresser with a mirror was pushed against the wall.

Next to the dresser was a washstand and a small pile of soaps on the folded towel that filled the room with the scent of lilacs. The nicest feature was a three-paned window facing the forest behind the cottage, equipped with a comfortable-looking window seat. A door led off from the main room, apparently leading to the water closet. One of the ubiquitous lanterns hung from the ceiling, waiting for nightfall.

Taking great care not to jostle anything, Lark put the trunk down at the foot of the bed. Its heavy darkness clashed with the bright and airy decor.

Lark said, "It's not much, but I hope you like it here."

Violet stood in the middle of the room and looked around with a sigh. "It will do for the moment. However I need silence and darkness. Those drapes are ineffective. Replace them. Preferably with black or ruby velvet."

"Okay, I'm on it," Lark said. She glowed with the idea she could help their very important guest. "Anything else?"

"Yes. This bedspread, how anyone can fall into restful slumber with this chaotic dizziness all over, I don't know. Find me something less dazzling. I require peace and simplicity for adequate repose. I have one condition that must be met at all times," Violet said, her voice low and urgent, "Everything must be as old as possible. I do not mind how threadbare or moth-eaten, but I will accept nothing new. This is something you must never forget."

"Sure thing. Is that all, Miss Ironwrought?"

"Please call me Violet. And yes, that is all. For now. You are dismissed."

"Okay." Lark turned and was about to scamper off when Violet's voice stopped her.

"One more thing. Don't be so damned cheerful all the time."

"I'll do my best!" Lark knew she was being annoying, but she said it with a big grin and saluted jauntily before she whirled and skipped off.

Chapter Seven

LESS THAN AN hour later, Lark returned. Her arms were laden with items she rummaged up from the farthest, deepest corner of the storage shed. Without a free hand to knock, Lark stood at the door and cleared her throat.

"Miss Violet," she called out. "It's Lark. I've brought some things for you."

The door creaked open and Lark caught her breath. Violet's face was damp and free from the paint, and a slight air of lilac wafted about her. She held a towel in both hands and didn't appear happy to be seen in that state.

Lark didn't mean to stare, but she couldn't look away.

Violet's lips, instead of the artificial blood-red, were in fact a delicate but deep pink, as if she had been eating cherries. Her eyes looked softer and wider than when ringed in black. Violet had taken down her crown of plaits and her long hair hung down in a thick braid, falling below her waist. She'd also removed her necklace, offering an unobstructed view of someplace Lark knew she should not be caught staring at. With effort, Lark raised her eyes to meet Violet's deep ones.

Unbidden, Lark felt her cheeks flush under the direct gaze. She lowered her eyes and glanced over to where Violet's brace of daggers lay on the bedside table in a placid bundle.

"I didn't expect you back so quickly," Violet said. She threw her towel down and crossed her arms.

"Sorry about that, Miss Violet," Lark said. The load in her arms slipped and Lark boosted it with one knee. "If you're tired or want to be alone that's fine. I can come back later."

"No. You have prepared the items as I have asked." She opened the door fully and moved back. "Come in then, no need to be cluttering the pathway with your presence. And I believe I also asked you to drop the 'Miss'."

"Sorry about that Mi—uh, Violet." Lark grabbed at the extra cushions stacked on top of her load and followed Violet straight back into the room. In the time Lark was on her mission, it appeared that Violet had unpacked. In addition to a few bottles on the dresser, a long white gown of delicate muslin hung over the privacy screen in the corner. Lark wondered if that was what Violet slept in. Lark's mind buffeted her with a vision of the visitor curled up in the quilts, her long limbs bare under that thin dress, her body soft and relaxed. An electric tingle, not unlike an imminent lightning strike skimmed over Lark's skin. Her face grew warm again.

Discomfited, Lark dumped her armful onto the bed. She held up a thick bolt of cloth. "Here's the velvet for the drapes. There's more if this isn't enough. I hope dark blue's okay."

Violet nodded curtly and Lark beamed.

"These winter potato sacks should do for pillowcases, they're pretty soft actually, and I thought this tablecloth might do for the bedspread. We really only use it for funerals, if that's too morbid just let me know and I can find something else."

"This will do nicely," Violet said as she looked at the somber, nearly black homespun cloth. Her lips drew back to reveal a row of even white teeth in an expression that was not a smile. "I often think sleep is akin to the eternal repose of death."

"It sure seems like that sometimes, especially during harvest," Lark's own smile felt brittle. "Don't worry, everything's plenty old. Anything you don't want, I can take back."

"That's not necessary. I will accept the items. They suit me better than this...conglomeration."

Violet stood over the bed and stared down at the patchwork bedspread with a look, not of disgust as Lark expected, but almost fear. She clasped her hands together in front of herself, as if to prevent from reaching out to touch it.

"You want me to get rid of that?" Lark asked.

Violet's shoulders dropped. She let out a breath. "Yes, please do."

Lark stripped off the quilt and the pillowcases. As soon as Lark was finished, Violet shook out the tablecloth. With a quick, easy motion, she unfurled it over the plain sheets and thick woolen blanket. The potato sacks followed and Lark was relieved to see they fit the pillows perfectly. Once the bed was made, Violet placed her hand flat on the dark material and closed her eyes for a moment, as if testing for something. She removed her hand and crossed her arms under her marvelous bosom with a satisfied look.

Violet reached up and shielded her eyes with one hand. "Shall we put up the drapes as soon as possible? I am unused to so much daylight, especially at this time of year."

"No problem, all we have to do is stitch a bit of a hem and we're ready to go," Lark said.

Lark went over to the window. She pulled a handy length of twine from one of her pockets and used it to measure the window while Violet watched from behind her. When Lark finished, Violet picked up the velvet and settled down on the window seat in a billow of black skirts.

"You are welcome to sit beside me. That is, if you are not averse to sharing space with the enemy."

Lark slipped her wand over her head and propped it up against the wall before she plopped down onto the window seat. She kicked out her long legs and gave Violet a grin to cover up the flash of unease at being so close to the dark woman. "I don't mind. We're on the same side now, you know."

Violet didn't reply. She just studied Lark with an intensity that had Lark feeling somewhat flayed before her. With a few quick measurements and folds, the velvet was ready to be sewn.

Lark dug out a needle and spool of thread from her pocket. "I can do this myself. I mean, you've probably got better things to do right now. I could actually go somewhere else if you'd rather be alone."

"No, you may stay. I'd like to help. I have been well-trained in the art of needlework and it has stood me in good stead, although the ones who taught me are now gone." Her face twisted for an instant before her usual cold expression fell into place. Violet delved a hand into a slit in her skirt, where Lark assumed she kept her pocket-belt, and came up with a long, lethal-looking bone needle and her own packet of thread. "It is not even necessary for you to assist me in this. In fact, it would be better if you didn't."

"I can't let you do that. You're a guest and it's always better to share the chores." Lark gave Violet what she hoped was a reassuring smile. "This way we'll be finished in half the time and get you out of the sunlight that much faster."

Violet's expression didn't waver. "I cannot argue with that. However, realize you undertake this task at your own peril."

Lark wasn't sure how to answer that, so she picked up the

velvet and started sewing. They sat for a while, stitching in silence. At first, Lark was tense and jumpy, but relaxed into the familiar action. The dark velvet over both of their laps was actually quite warm and comfortable. After a few minutes, Lark glanced over at Violet and drew in a breath of admiration at her skill, mesmerized by the motions of her long fingers, framed by the delicate lace at her cuffs. Violet held the needle in her left hand with practiced ease. Suddenly Violet glanced up and caught Lark mid-stare.

Instead of calling her on it, Violet simply dropped her eyes to her task once more. She asked, "So what do you do here, Miss Larkspur Greenpool?"

"I'm training to be a full-fledged Guardian."

"The elite of the Wanderers," Violet said without the venom Lark expected.

"There's nothing elite about me," Lark said. Her needle slowed. She shook out her cramping hands. "I'm Crystalgazer-raised."

"Really?" The word was accompanied by an arch of one eyebrow. "Is that common?"

"Not really for Guardians, but for anyone else, it's no big deal. There are a bunch like me in my village alone."

"Somehow I doubt there are many like you." After a few more sure, even stitches Violet spoke again. "Before being summoned here, I have never met either Wanderers or Crystalgazers, and so have no basis of reference. I assume there are fundamental differences between the two groups?"

"Not really," Lark said. "We all just want the same thing, I guess. To find our place in this world and be happy."

Violet bent down and bit off the thread. She didn't look at Lark as she said, "Happiness is nothing but an infantile illusion."

The heartrending tone alone made Lark pause in her work again. She wrestled up a cheerful tone and asked, "How about you, Violet? What did you do before you came here?"

She was silent for so long, Lark wasn't sure she'd heard the question. Suddenly, Violet turned her head. She fixed Lark with a cold, guarded look. "You should only ask that question if you truly wish to know the answer."

Lark was at once aware of how close Violet was to her. For the first time she realized that Violet's eyes weren't black the way she had thought, but the deepest brown. A darker ring circled her iris and made them seem that much darker. Suddenly the window seat felt too small. After a breathless moment where Lark couldn't move, Violet stood. She backed up a step and peered at Lark and the window expectantly.

Lark tied off her own thread and stowed her sewing kit. She draped the newly-hemmed velvet over one shoulder before she quickly took off her boots, using the clever zipper at the side that saved her from having to unlace them. In her socks, Lark scrambled up onto the window seat.

"I'm going to have to take down the old curtains," Lark said. "If you don't like sunlight, you might want to go behind the dressing-screen or something."

"I will remain here." Violet got a slight glint in her eyes that was almost humorous. "A few minutes in the light will not cause me to burst into flames."

"Hope not," Lark replied with a grin. "But let me know if you start feeling a bit hot. I'll go fetch one of the fire buckets to douse you with some good old rainwater."

"Of course. That would be much appreciated," Violet said with a regal bow of her head.

Lark twisted around to give a joking reply when the padded cover slipped under her foot. The velvet curtain billowed out as Lark pitched backwards off the window seat. The world tilted. Lark braced for the impact with the floor but instead was stopped halfway by something soft but unyielding.

Violet had grabbed her.

The shout of surprise died in Lark's throat. She had never been held like that. The arms holding her were strong and circled protectively around her waist. She felt Violet's warmth, her softness pressed against Lark's back. Before Lark even had time to draw in a breath, she was released.

"I apologize for the breach of propriety," Violet said. She drew away with downcast eyes.

"No, that's okay," Lark said. Her heart pounded. "I should be saying thanks to you. I properly unbalanced there and you saved me from a nasty tumble."

"As long as you are unhurt."

"I'm right as rain," Lark said. More carefully this time, Lark clambered up once more to resume her task. She got the old curtains down and the new curtains in place and was about to step down when Violet held out a hand. Without a second thought, Lark took it. She was surprised once more at the strength of Violet's grip as she guided Lark to the floor.

"Thanks again," Lark said.

It could have been the altitude, but she was a bit lightheaded. Their fingers were still intertwined. Lark quickly let go. She bent down and zipped herself back into her long boots.

"This is much better. Well done, Lark," Violet said. She twitched back the heavy drapes so a single shaft of sunlight fell across the floor. She turned and glanced over one shoulder at Lark. Her eyes hardened. Violet leveled Lark with such a stern, piercing gaze that Lark backed up a step. "This is not your work," Violet hissed. "Do you understand? You have no investment in these curtains, no claim to their making. Swear to me you divorce them from your consciousness."

"I don't—"

"Swear it!"

The force of the words shocked Lark. She placed a hand over her heart and said, "I swear on my family's Almanac, that's your work one hundred percent."

The tension in Violet's body drained from her. "You have just saved your own life, Wanderer."

"Hey, anything for our honored guest," Lark said in a shaky voice. The tense moment passed. Her legs gave out and she slung herself down on the window seat. Lark glanced at the sand-clock on the wall. "Oh wow, it's nearly dinnertime. If you want, you can sit with me and I'll introduce you around. I usually sit with Alice and Bethanie, sometimes Nora and Murray too, and they're really nice. Or I could have a tray sent up for you if you'd rather have some privacy."

Violet's teeth worried at her lower lip. She let out a breath and said, "My presence has been requested at the head table. I am afraid it is not negotiable." She paused before speaking again. Her voice was bitter. "It's probably for the best. I'm sure your dining partners would mind one such as I in their midst. I cannot imagine it would be conductive to the appetite."

"Hey now, none of that," Lark said with an uncomfortable jolt in her belly. "We're all in this together and the sooner we get to know each other the better."

Violet didn't reply. Instead, she turned to her dressing table and picked up a heavy hairpin. She didn't look back as she said, "I must prepare for the evening meal. You are dismissed."

After the cottage door closed behind her, Lark swallowed the complex rush of emotions that rose up within herself. All she knew was she'd never met anyone like Miss Violet Ironwrought and she felt drawn to her like nobody else. Lark wanted to talk to her and get to know her better, even as her common sense warned her to stay away from such a strange and not exactly harmless person.

Chapter Eight

"WHAT'S THE SCARY new guest like?" Alice whispered to Lark that evening as they dunked the supper dishes in the washing-up hogsheads. "You know who, Elvira Flavia duKillovsky. Did you see she used her own fork and knife? I guess our cutlery's not good enough for her."

"She's all right. And her name is Violet." Lark shook excess water from a serving tray and set it in the drying rack. "I think it'd be a good idea for us to treat her as normally as possible."

"Yeah, whatever. Go right ahead. I'm going to hang out with people who actually *are* normal. And dress normally too."

"What's that supposed to mean?" Lark suddenly found the spoon she was rinsing very fascinating.

"Come on, you must have noticed," Alice said. She elbowed Lark in the ribs. "How do you think she gets her, you knows to go like that?"

"Her what do I knows?"

"Her womanly curves," Alice clarified. "Boobs, melons, bazooms, dairy orbs, milk jugs, ta-tas, big mams. Breasts." She trilled the "r" with her tongue.

"Oh." Lark's face got hot. "I don't know. I didn't even notice them. Not at all. Not even one bit."

"It looks like she's found a way around gravity. All the boys had their tongues on the floor when she took off her cloak at the meeting. It's like she's trying to make everyone go strange. And that thing she's got hanging around her neck? It looks like she's stuck her head through a garden-hose winder. She doesn't wear Rings, but that neck-thing's big and gross enough, it could be a Ring. I bet it's got some kind of malevolent power or can turn into a snake or something like that."

"That's enough Alice." Lark threw her sponge into the washing barrel. "We don't know the first thing about Ringsworn fashion and customs. I suspect Violet thinks we look strange too."

"At least my bosom is snug and safe under my wraps. And did you see, she barely ate anything? She only gulped wine all evening. Too high-born to swallow our swill, huh? What, was she waiting for someone to bring it to her on a golden platter or something? Maybe the meat was too dead for her." Alice snickered at her own words.

Lark hesitated before she spoke. She grasped the side of her barrel and leaned on her hands, deep in thought. During the meal, her attention was pulled to the dark visitor. Lark noticed a few things that weighed on her mind.

"Alice, maybe she couldn't," Lark said softly. "Did you see how her hands were shaking? It was all she could do to hang onto her cup."

"I didn't notice that." Alice at least had the decency to look contrite. "But yeah, I would probably be nervous too if I was just new here and had to sit up there with all of those high-rankers yakking away around me. I never thought about that, and I guess I was a bit spiteful before. I launched my mouth off before I engaged my thinker."

"It's okay, just give Violet a chance," Lark said. She let out a breath, suddenly infinitely lighter.

"Yeah," Alice said. She made a move to pick up the last pot but Lark stopped her.

"I've got this," Lark said. "Why don't you go ahead?"

"Really? Thanks." Alice rinsed her sponge and tidied her area. "I'm going to hang out in the common room and see if anyone wants to play cards."

"Have fun," Lark said. Alice breezed out and Lark turned back to her task with her mind full of the mysterious visitor. Something certainly had her terrified at the table. Lark wondered how she was and got an urge to go and see her. With a shake of her head, Lark squashed the thought. Violet wouldn't be interested in spending time with a backwards hayseed like herself. Still, the thought of staying away made Lark feel a brush of loss. Violet was certainly the most impressive person Lark had ever met, and she was fascinated.

Outside, the last glow of sunset was fading. Lark picked up her wand and idly looked up for the lantern overhead and froze in panic. Lanterns! Without a wand, the one in Violet's cottage was useless to her.

Lark's boots kicked up a great spray of grass as she galloped over the compound. Her loping strides brought her to Violet's cottage just in time to see the door open and the unlit lantern come sailing out. It landed in a clattering heap on the flagstone path.

Violet looked up and her eyes raked over Lark. Violet's face was white, save for two bright patches of red on her cheeks. The black paint around her eyes was smudged. She hung onto the door frame as if it were a lifeline.

Violet's eyes never left Lark's. She said, "I would rather spend my nights blind than rely on that cobbled-together piece of refuse for illumination."

Her fingers slipped from the frame and she stumbled backwards into the cottage. Instincts took over and Lark jumped forward just as Violet's heel collided with her trunk. Lark flung out a hand in an attempt to stop her fall but didn't get there in time. Her fingers closed on nothing but air. Violet's arms pinwheeled in an ungainly arc before she landed on the floor, sprawled out in a sea of black petticoats.

Violet buried her face in her hands, not fast enough to hide the bleak expression.

Even though Lark's common sense told her to run away, she couldn't leave Violet like that. The combination of hardly any food plus several cups of wine had left Violet in a perilous state. Lark came into the cottage and eased the door closed behind her. She got down on the braided rug next to Violet and rummaged in her pockets.

"I'm really sorry about that," Lark said, "Nobody was trying to make you feel bad, it was just a mistake. We don't use those lanterns either back home. Here, I've got some candles and—"

Lark's words cut off abruptly as Violet lashed out and slapped the offering from her hand.

"I have no need of either your pity or your charity. Leave me."

Lark sat back on her heels and let out a breath. Her body twitched with the warring urges to reach out to Violet and at the same time, to put as much distance between them as possible. The first urge won. She reached out and laid a hesitant hand on Violet's arm. "Hey, it's okay. I know what it's like to be alone and far away from home. I just want to be your friend."

"Friend?" Violet bared her teeth and let go with a mirthless laugh but didn't pull away. "You would be best served by replacing friendship with fear. For your own safety."

In order not to compromise Violet's dignity any more, Lark got to her feet. "If you're good here, I'll be on my way. If you need anything else, just let me know, all right? And I meant what I said, about being your friend." She held out a hand and was surprised when Violet placed cold fingers in hers and allowed Lark to help her up. This time it was Violet who let go first.

"Goodnight Violet," Lark said softly, not surprised when there was no answer.

Without another word, Lark went back to her dormitory. She ignored the cheerful shouts and laughter that spilled out from the common room.

THE NEXT DAY, Violet was sequestered with the senior Guardians in the council-house, discussing something so important and secret, they didn't even take a break for meals. Instead, Cook Brown sent over several of his staff with covered trays and baskets.

For the first time, Lark's curiosity got the better of her. She told herself it had nothing to do with worry and interest about their visitor, but the overall wellbeing of her people. She and Alice sneaked under the window of the council-house meeting room and tried to eavesdrop, but were shooed away and given extra chores for their troubles.

That evening, after everyone else had gone off to their evening pursuits, Lark finished washing up and lingered behind the meal hall with troubled thoughts clouding her mind. She detected a presence behind her and whirled around to come face-to-face with Violet. The black of her gown blended in with the soft darkness and only her face and hands could be seen. She looked much more composed than she had the night before. Lark couldn't help the grin that broke across her face. She made a move to speak, but was silenced by a small shake of Violet's head.

"I wish to apologize for my outburst last night," she said. "I was not in a proper state of mind. I just wanted to say I appreciate the candles you left and I am grateful for your forethought and kindness."

"No problem," Lark said. She leaned back against one of the rain barrels. "We have boxes of them in storage, how about I get you one right now?"

"I have enough for the time being. At any rate, that is all I came here to say. Good evening."

With a stab of regret at the abrupt end of the exchange, Lark knit her brow. Violet took a step back. She drew her skirts up in preparation to leave. A shaft of lantern light from the window fell over her face. Lark saw for the first time how pale and exhausted she looked.

Lark blurted out, "Want to get a snack?"

Violet held herself still. She tilted her head as if she hadn't heard properly.

"Nobody's in the pantry now," Lark said in a rush. "We can help ourselves to leftovers and have a midnight feast. I don't know about you, but I've got a hankering for a bit of that ham we had yesterday at lunch. Maybe some of Cook Brown's good fruit-cake too."

"That would be," Violet faltered. She looked as if she wanted to bolt. For an instant, Lark was sure she would, but Violet unclenched her hands and let out a breath. Her shoulders dropped. With a regal bow of her head, she said, "That would be most agreeable. Lead the way."

Lark couldn't stop smiling as she trotted toward the small outbuilding that served as the pantry for the kitchens. Violet followed close beside her. While the cook kept baskets of snacks and jugs of tea in the meal hall during the day, it was all packed up at night. From what little Lark had observed, she figured Violet might appreciate the peace of the deserted pantry shed. Lark couldn't help but glance at Violet as they walked. She moved with grace and stealth. Her long skirts swished with every movement.

"Watch out for that branch there," Violet's voice was low and soft in Lark's ear. The warning had the opposite effect. Lark jumped, got her feet tangled in the obstacle, and tripped. Before she could even spit out a curse, Lark's forward moment stopped. Violet grabbed her again, this time from the front. For a second Lark just stood stunned, feeling the other woman's slender strength against her. The second time affected her no less than the first. Lark's heart nearly burst through her chest. Violet let go and stepped away.

"Green Trees, I'm not usually so clumsy," Lark said. She easily regained her balance, but not her mental equilibrium. "Thanks for keeping this lumbering colt on her feet yet again. You've got great night-sight there."

"I am accustomed to moving about in darkness," Violet said.

"It's sure coming in handy tonight. Here we are, after you."

With a courtly wave, Lark ushered Violet into the pantry shed. Moonlight from the opened door filled the room. A long counter ran down one wall that was used for preparation during the day. Lark herself had spent many hours there peeling potatoes or coring apples for Cook Brown.

Lark was ready to light the lantern, but before she could, Violet dug a candle stub from her pocket and set it alight with a curious apparatus that looked like a silver box with a lid that snapped closed to douse the flame. Lark closed the door and drew close to where Violet was perched on a stool at the counter. Lark peered at the contraption, fascinated. Violet looked up at her, then held out the item for Lark to inspect.

Wordlessly, Violet opened it again, calling the flame with a quick motion of her thumb on the little wheel. With a wicked light in the depths of her eyes, Violet closed the box, only to click it open again. Deftly, she spun the item between the fingers of her left hand before she flicked the object into life once more. The flame snaked between her fingers as she continued to twirl it. Surprising Lark, Violet doused the flame with a touch. She drew back and, with a snap of her fingers, the flame returned.

"Is that Metal?" Lark asked breathlessly.

"No, it is analogue," Violet said. She snapped the box closed. "I have simply had an abundance of time in order to become proficient at handling this item."

"It's brix!" Lark said. Maybe it was a trick of the light, but she could have sworn Violet's expression wasn't as guarded as before.

The candle made a warm, homey glow and filled the narrow space with a golden light. Lark went into the back room where the dishes and icebox were to get some tea. Remembering Violet's words, Lark dug through the mugs until she found the oldest one. A patina of cracks covered the dull red surface and generations of drinks left the inside layered with striations. The mug was decorated with a mysterious symbol that looked like two golden letter W's nestled into one another, almost worn off by years of scrubbing.

"Who made this?" Violet asked when Lark presented her with the mug.

"I don't know," Lark said. "From the looks of it, it's Outsider-made. Probably churned out from a giant workshop somewhere across the sea. That's where they get a lot of their stuff, I heard."

After a moment more of consideration, Violet reached out and cupped her hands around the mug. She closed her eyes for an instant as if fighting against some kind of urge, similar to when she touched the bedcover. When she opened them again, her expression was one of relief. She lifted the mug and said, "A toast to new...friends."

Lark clunked her mug with Violet's and drank deeply. She got to her feet once more and looked over her shoulder at the full shelves of the pantry. "How about that snack, then? Anything in particular you'd like?"

Long white fingers twitched and tightened around the mug. Violet said, "Something—not so soft and fatty. I'm afraid the dishes your kind seems to favor do not sit well with me."

"No problem," Lark said. "How about some hard-boiled eggs? Cook Brown always has a bunch in the cooler."

The way Violet's eyes lit up at the mention, Lark knew she'd guessed right.

"How many days old are they?" Violet asked when Lark came over with a basket and a shaker of salt.

"Um, zero," Lark said. She tapped her egg on the counter before she peeled off the shell. "We collect them every morning."

"Pity," Violet said. She held out her unshelled egg for Lark to salt. She took a bite and briefly closed her eyes with a satisfied sigh that filled Lark with relief and joy. Suddenly Violet said, "My home was a convent, a hall of worship surrounded by the northern sea on all sides. Once the tithes ended, we had to survive on only what the sea and land around us could provide. It was my habit to climb the cliffs for seabird eggs and boil them in salt water. At five days, the consistency is like a rich, meaty pudding, and at seventeen days it is perfection."

The first glimpse into the life of the mysterious stranger intrigued Lark. She was both grateful for the small tidbit and hungry for more. She didn't want to push Violet away when she'd just taken the first step forward, so Lark refrained from asking the hundreds of questions that filled her mind.

Lark said, "Sounds like a good way to get your protein. Probably better than killing the adult birds for meat."

"Yes, we must learn to coexist to survive," Violet said. "The seabirds never attacked me. They seemed to know with that single sacrifice, the others are spared to see another sunrise. I feel somewhat akin to them at this moment as I leave behind the people I never knew for an entirely new reality. I am but one from many."

The words hit Lark in a deep place. Silently, she passed over the basket, offering another egg. As Violet's nimble fingers made short work of the shell, Lark glanced down at the richly embroidered bodice and floor-length skirts.

"I don't mean to be rude," Lark said, "But I can't imagine how anyone can climb up cliffs in all that."

The smallest tug at the corner of Violet's mouth transformed her expression into a mischievous one. "When I climb, I do so in a more practical outfit I fashioned from cast-off robes." She dropped her voice to a low purr, "And when I dive for shellfish, I wear only the hand of the goddess."

Lark's mouth fell open and she nearly lost her egg. She didn't know if Violet realized how bewitching she looked with that wicked gleam in her eyes in the candlelight. Unable to stay still, Lark jumped up and rummaged around in the back. She returned with fresh offerings in the basket, which she presented to Violet with a proud flair.

"This beats sitting at the head table, right at the front of the room surrounded by all those high-rankers I bet," Lark said. She folded a slice of ham around a hunk of cheese and thick slice of fruitcake before she shoved the whole thing into her mouth and chewed blissfully.

"Yes it does," Violet said. She looked down at the piece of cake in her hands with a wry twist of her lips. "This is much better. I was still very young when the order of Limor was disbanded. Only a single aged Abbess remained and I was forbidden to show myself to any of the travelers who passed through the convent's halls after that. As a result, I am not accustomed to dining with others."

Lark mulled over that new information. She studied Violet

and drew in a breath as she realized exactly how beautiful Violet was. More than just her physical appearance, she held herself with strength and grace even during what had to be the hardest task of her life. The memory of Violet's arms around her rose in her mind. A strange, humming feeling started in her belly.

Violet spoke again in a soft voice, "I am also not accustomed to having friends. Allow me to apologize in advance for my lack of skill."

Lark grinned widely. She said, "Don't worry about it. I don't have a lot of friends either. There's just Alice here and Merton Appleton back home." A sharp pang speared Lark in the belly and she grimaced. "But I wouldn't really call him a friend. Not anymore."

"This Mr. Merton Appleton," Violet asked in her stilted, formal way, "Is he your lover?"

The gulp of tea went down the wrong way. Lark sputtered, "Green Trees, no. He's just the boy next door. We were friends before he got some fool notion in his head I'd throw myself at him, but there's no way under the Great Blue Sky I'd ever marry that gosling. I can't imagine what he was barking at making the suggestion." Lark shook her head and attempted a laugh, very aware of Violet studying her without moving.

"Is there another you'd rather join with?"

The question punched the breath from Lark's lungs. She said, "I don't have time to think about stuff like that."

"But you will marry someday." It was not a question. The air between them was tense. Lark couldn't bring herself to meet Violet's eyes.

"I guess so," Lark said. "Everybody does. It's the natural order of things. You marry someone, build a homestead, have a few younguns to carry on after you. That's the way life goes." Lark fought the alien feeling rising up from her belly as she said those words. She couldn't imagine taking that path. The idea of lying under some fellow left her unmoved and somewhat queasy.

To lighten the mood, Lark grabbed the pitcher and sloshed more tea into their mugs with a too-bright smile on her face. She said, "That's just the way things are. Even our driving instructor, Jane Snell, who's the grouchiest person I've ever met, found someone to put up with her."

"So did Jean Elliott."

"That's different," Lark said. Her smile froze. Her heart pounded in her chest and her hands clenched on her mug. Sweat popped out on her brow. The conversation was venturing into dangerous territory and Lark couldn't let it go any further. "That's not normal." Lark flinched at her own choice of words. A long silence fell, broken only by the singing of the crickets outside.

Violet broke the frozen spell by pushing herself away from the counter. She said, "I will return to my cottage. Thank you for the excellent snack and company."

Unnerved by the sudden dismissal, Lark jumped to her feet. She swept the counter clean and quickly washed her own mug at the pump. Violet had hers in her hands and looked possessive of it. Lark aimed a grin over her shoulder at Violet, who stood in the middle of the room. Lark said, "I'm glad you liked it. You know, I'm always up for a midnight rummage. Feel free to let me know if you're in the mood for one too. I'd be happy to volunteer."

"I shall keep that in mind," Violet said. She reached over and snuffed the candle.

They walked together in the darkness until the path split and Violet silently turned and swept away.

Back in her dormitory, surrounded by a soft chorus of snores, Lark lay in her bed, awake. She clasped her hands behind her head and gazed up at the moonlit ceiling beams overhead. When she did fall into a fitful doze, her dreams left her feeling restless, her skin hot and hungry for something she couldn't name.

Chapter Nine

THE LATEST BOUT of storms left more damage than just the accounting building and the fallen tree. Everyone was called on to assist in the repairs, and Lark enthusiastically joined in. Due to the repair efforts, Lark and the other fledglings enjoyed unparalleled freedom to come and go from all the buildings and Lark got a dangerous idea. On the pretence of going up to the roof to assist in refastening the eaves trough, Lark slipped into the council-house's main meeting room and found the scrying crystal she'd used to call their outpost from Jean Elliott's kitchen.

With Violet involved, Lark's curiosity about the secret meetings that took place in the council-house was insatiable. She hungered to know everything. She had a vague feeling that she could protect Violet somehow. And the crystal was her doorway into that room. She could tap into it and spy on one of those meetings.

It was in a good place to overlook the table already, and Lark didn't have to do anything more than ease the box open a crack. She wedged a scrap of paper from one of her pockets into the hinge to keep it from closing completely. The position was such that it might come in handy for herself—Lark would only get one chance to use it and the reason would have to be worth the trouble it could get her into.

Over the next few weeks, Lark threw herself into her lessons and discussions with her fellow fledglings. While she enjoyed learning and eagerly anticipated earning her own Tracker's stripe, Lark looked forward to the late night trysts in the pantry shed more than anything. About every other night, Lark would find herself sitting next to Violet with a basket between them and cups of tea in their hands.

They drifted together after the evening chores were finished and the others were engaged in their own solitary pursuits, finding each other in the twilight that Violet seemed to prefer over daylight. Violet seemed to be more comfortable taking her meals at the head table, however neither she nor Lark mentioned that fact. Conversation and companionship gradually took priority over the actual food. More often than not their snacks were nothing more than cups of cool tea and dried fruit.

Violet rarely spoke about herself, but she paid rapt attention when Lark talked about her own life. Lark enjoyed the way Violet focused on her and spoke at length about the many things Crystalgazers did to fill their days, such as attending village meetings and their many festivals.

One night, after Lark explained their Midwinter festivities, Violet finally spoke. She said, "I remember our own Grand Solstice my convent hosted one year." She clasped her hands under her chin. Her eyes focused on some faraway scene. "There were dances and contests. Archery, knife-throwing, flame-juggling, and so much music. The courtyard rang with it and the corridors and prayer hall resounded until the rafters rang. The Sisters, the Wraiths of Limor as they were called, sang songs of praise to the goddess until I was certain She would rise from the sea and walk among us. "

Entranced, Lark said, "The way you tell it, I feel like I'm there. I wish I could have seen it."

"Maybe one day you will," Violet said with the closest thing Lark had ever seen to a smile on her sculpted lips. "I will always remember that day. The costumes and jewels were dazzling. Everyone sparkled like the sun on the ocean. I watched from my tower, I saw everything. I drank in the splendor and thought I would drown from the wonder of it. One of the Sisters snuck me a straw filled with colored sugar and I have never tasted anything so exquisite. I was eight years old and it was the last festival I ever saw. Perhaps it was the last one my people ever had. I never thought—" Abruptly Violet stopped talking and stood up. The expression on her face was so indifferent Lark was certain she was feeling anything but.

The dried apple slice Violet had been nibbling on fell to the floor. Lark felt a stab of apprehension and sorrow at the look of despair in her eyes before she turned and stalked out of the pantry shed. By the time Lark got the kitchen back into order, the door to Violet's cottage was shut and the heavy curtains pulled closed. Her quiet knocks went unanswered and Lark had no other choice but turn around and head back to the dormitory with a heavy heart.

THE NEXT DAY, Violet didn't leave her room. According to the rumor mill, their guest was feeling under the weather with an oncoming cold. Only Lark knew differently and she ached with the need to do something. Violet's absence pained her in a way nothing ever had before. She had no explanation for the almost undeniable urge to go and see Violet, speak to her in person and accept her responsibility in causing the situation in the first place. Even though Lark itched to dash across the compound immediately, she decided to wait until evening, both not to attract attention as well as let Violet have the solitude she needed.

Morning lectures and lunch dragged. Lark thought the day would never end.

That night, Lark waited until after lights out, each second felt like a hundred. She forced herself to lie still, listening until she was sure everyone was asleep before she slipped out. She left her wand hanging from its hook on the wall, but her crystal pouch hung reassuringly between her breasts. Her bare feet made no sound as she padded over the flagstones on the path to the cottages.

Summer was drawing to an end and the wind was biting. A shivering Lark wished she'd thought to grab a cardigan or something to throw over her calf-length nightshirt. She didn't particularly want to dig out her onyx. Instead she let the cold drive her down the path with only a vague idea of what awaited her at the end of it.

In front of the door to Violet's cottage, Lark was plagued with second thoughts. Why would she matter to someone of Violet's importance? Maybe the apparent offer of friendship had only been politeness. With a determined shake of her head, Lark reassured herself that someone who spoke to people the way Violet did wouldn't be particularly concerned with polite gestures. The worst that could happen was Violet would send her away with some scathing remark.

Before she even had a chance to knock, the door opened. The room was warm with the golden glow of a few candles. Violet was still in her day clothes and Lark felt distinctly underdressed in her nightshirt. An odd change came over Violet's face when Lark gave her a cheerful grin, as if she wanted to echo the expression but didn't exactly know how. Her gaze dropped to where Lark's nightshirt ended mid-calf and then snapped up again. It might have been the flickering candlelight, but Violet's cheeks were pink.

"Mind if I come in for a bit?" Lark asked. She hugged her arms to her chest and shivered. She didn't have to fake the fact that she was freezing. "I, um, want to talk to you."

"You are welcome." Violet stepped back and retreated to the bed. She settled down in the depression in the black-covered pillows where she'd apparently been before Lark disturbed her. The double "W" mug was on the bedside table and an open book rested beside her. Lark saw the cover briefly as Violet put it away in the bedside table and was intrigued to see it was a Crystalgazer-written book about astronomy.

After hesitating for only a second, Lark slung herself down over the foot of the bed and tucked her feet underneath herself. Warmth gradually seeped into her chilled limbs. Violet fixed her with a cool stare that made Lark nervous.

"About last night," Lark said in a rush. "I didn't mean to upset you or anything. Really, I didn't. I'm sorry."

"No, it is I who should ask your forgiveness," Violet said. She twisted her fingers together and Lark noticed she was trembling. "It has been so long since I let myself think of the Old Days. Remembering is dangerous for me. For those around me as well. You would be best advised to leave me be. Walk out of here and never turn back. Do not worry, I will not follow you."

Lark took that information in. Some things were becoming clear to her about Violet, while there was still so much she didn't know. Lark wondered what Violet was hiding beneath her cold and controlled exterior. While it didn't seem like Violet was afraid of touching her, there was the issue she had with touching various items. She obviously had some kind of power, hence the "secret weapon" status. Lark wondered if she'd ever find out what it was.

Lark took a breath and said, "I'm not afraid of you, Violet."

"You should be."

Lark shook her head. "I'm sorry if I make you feel things you shouldn't. But I'm your friend and I'm not going to just leave you. I know you wouldn't hurt me."

"No, I'm sorry that I put you into—" Violet met Lark's eyes. She got that odd half-smile again and said, "We seem to be saying 'sorry' a lot to one another."

"It is one of the big three," Lark said.

Tilting her head, Violet drew her brows together in a silent question.

"The big three important and difficult things to say," Lark told her.

"And the other two are?"

"Thank you, and I love you." Lark felt odd saying those words in front of Violet. They seemed weightier than when she said them any other time.

Violet half-closed her eyes and murmured, "Who would you say the last one to?"

"My folks, maybe my big bro Yarrow if he saved my butt or I wanted a big favor."

"I have no memory of my family, however I heard I have a twin brother." The words were flat. Emotionless. The old Violet was back.

"Bet he's handsome as can be," Lark gushed. "I mean, since he's your brother and you're one of the most beautiful, um." Lark closed her babbling mouth and prepared for the abrupt dismissal she'd come to expect after a topic touched a nerve with Violet. It didn't come.

Instead, Violet straightened up and said, "Family is more than a matter of biology, which I'm sure you already know quite well. I consider Sister Perpetua, the Abbess who raised me to be my true family. I even took the name Ironwrought from her; she gave it up to join the Order. And I will deny this tomorrow," she said with a light in her eyes. "However, I am beginning to consider one or two members of this compound as more than just trivial annoyances. Particularly Jean Elliott, who is honest and honorable. I consider myself fortunate for making her acquaintance. Your friend Alice as well was quite kind the other day when I asked her for directions to the storage shed. She answered promptly without running away or offering to zap me with that wand of hers."

Spurred by Violet's frank admission, Lark said, "Glad to hear it. Why don't you sit with me and Alice tomorrow morning? Even the senior Guardians are pretty relaxed at breakfast. Some of them don't even bother to sit down, just get their tea and go."

Violet cast her deep eyes down. She shifted against the pillows at her back. After a moment of inner debate, her head came up again. She said, "Very well, I will impose on you and your friend as this is the second time you've extended the invitation. Although I will not apologize for any gastric upset caused by my presence."

"That's not going to happen. I'm glad to have you," Lark said, beaming. "And I'm sure Alice will be too."

"If that is all, I will see you tomorrow," Violet said. She got to her feet and walked the few steps with Lark to the door.

"Sure thing. I'm glad I came by to see you tonight," Lark said.

"I am too," Violet answered. She looked up into Lark's face. Lark couldn't breathe. One corner of Violet's mouth quirked up and then the other. A slow smile blossomed on her face, the first real one Lark had ever seen on her. The beauty of the simple expression hit Lark square in the chest. Violet stepped back, and Lark could move again.

Lark felt as if her feet didn't touch the ground as she let herself out of the cottage. For some reason, Lark didn't feel the chill of the night air on the return leg of her journey.

WHEN BREAKFAST TIME came around, Lark perched expectantly at their table. That morning, Murray decided to join them and chatted with Alice while Lark stayed silent. She ignored the basket of muffins in front of her, instead she kept an eye on the door, turning to look every time it opened.

"What's crawling around in your drawers?" Alice asked the third time Lark swiveled in her seat. "You've been jumping at every little thing. Are you in trouble again?"

"No. Nothing like that," Lark said.

Then it came, the hush that fell over the meal hall every time Violet's dark presence appeared in the doorway. It hurt Lark to see everyone dropping their eyes to their plates, heads down as if trying to keep out of her notice, as if they needed to protect themselves from an attack. Instead of taking her usual place at the long table at the front of the room, Violet made her way across the room, her steps clipped and deliberate.

"Oh no, it's Elvira." Alice clutched at Lark. She hissed, "And she's coming right for us."

"Watch it, you nearly spilled the jam." Lark was busy rescuing the jar and didn't look up when a shadow fell across their table.

"Who is this Elvira?" a voice sounding suspiciously like it belonged to Violet asked.

"Nobody," Murray and Alice said at the same time. "Nobody at all!"

With one eyebrow cocked, Violet loomed over the table. Alice and Murray both looked like they wanted to climb into the muffin basket and vanish. Alice's friend Bethanie who was walking over to them with a mug in her hands, suddenly changed tacks and sat down with another group.

Lark allowed herself the luxury of letting her gaze drift over Violet's form. She held herself still and tall in the soft morning light, but not with the cold distain she once did. Violet had changed over the time she'd been at the compound. She no longer painted her face in ferocious colors and more often than not had her hair down in a simple, long plait. As for her heavy jewelry, she had been without it for a while now. More than that, sometimes she even looked friendly.

"Is this seat taken?" Violet asked in a low voice as eddies of shocked whispers swirled around the meal hall.

"We've been saving it for you, if you don't mind mixed company," Lark said.

"Not at all," Violet replied.

Lark jumped to her feet and pulled the chair out for Violet, who settled into it with a billow of midnight skirts. She held out her mug and Lark filled it from the pot on the table. Her chest brimmed with a glowing, effervescent feeling. "Have a muffin," Lark said and passed over the basket. "We've got some cranberry ones in there. I know you like those so I grabbed a bunch. They always go first."

"They do look very nice," Violet said. She glanced at Murray and Alice, who cowered in their chairs, clutching at each other with their faces frozen in expressions of fear. Violet leaned back into her chair with a cranberry muffin in her hands and said in a conversational tone, "Lark, our tablemates don't seem to be breathing."

"Snap out of it you two," Lark said. She sighed as she broke the top off her muffin and reached for the apple butter. "Violet's been here for over a month. You've got to be used to her by now."

Murray's Adam's apple bobbed as he gulped a few times. He mopped his forehead with his handkerchief and said, "It's nice of you to join us this most lovely morning, Miss Ironwrought."

Violet lowered the direct gaze that Lark had been on the receiving end of so many times and speared the young man with it. He blanched and shrank back against his chair. She asked, "Would you care to receive a brief explanation of an acorn?"

"Uh, sure," Murray said. His eyes darted about.

"In a nutshell," Violet intoned, "it's an oak tree."

Midway through taking a gulp from her mug, Alice gave a snort of laughter and sprayed tea all over herself. "Aw turds," she spat. She leapt to her feet and patted herself down with Murray's handkerchief.

Lark let out a peal of laughter. She sprawled her long limbs out, propping her elbows up on the table in a way that would have her mother whacking at her with her trusty wooden spoon. She fixed Violet with a long look and a warm feeling crashed over her. Murray looked at the newcomer to their table with wide eyes, as if he didn't know whether to laugh or take her seriously. Alice recovered from her tea dunking incident and helped herself to a muffin from the basket. The frozen, uncomfortable spell broke. The other people in the hall went on with their breakfasts and conversations buzzed around them.

"What is your schedule like today, Lark?" Violet asked.

"Lecture in the morning and practice in the afternoon," Lark said. She leaned back in her chair, feeling odd at how normal the scene was. "We're on the third day of a wilderness cooking module. I think today we're doing rabbits and other small game."

"That sounds quite useful and tasty," Violet said.

Alice added, "We've also got to chop kindling, help Cook Brown with the cornbread for lunch and potatoes for dinner, scrub out the baths, collect eggs and sweep out the chicken barn." She sighed dramatically. "Plus our usual dishwashing duty this evening."

"We would all have more free time," Murray said, "if you gave up trying to eavesdrop on what's going on in the council-house." His shoulders hunched. He quickly added, "Um, I mean, not like we actually are trying to spy on you or anything. Uh, it was just a joke."

"I understand your concern," Violet said. "Sometimes the

authorities are too miserly with information and that can put people who don't know in danger."

"Are we in danger?" Murray asked in a hoarse whisper.

"No more here than anywhere else," Violet said.

"That helps," Murray muttered.

Lark met Violet's eyes. She wanted to apologize for her friend's behavior, but Violet wasn't angry. She seemed amused. While her face was still the usual carefully-maintained aloof mask, Lark knew her well enough to see through it.

A FEW NIGHTS LATER, after a particularly difficult practice session, Lark sat on the big fallen tree, a favorite thinking spot of hers. The night air was cold but Lark put the discomfort from her mind. She didn't want to go inside quite yet. She raised her eyes to the horizon where the last glow of sunset lingered. She hunched her shoulders as a freezing blast of wind whipped around her.

Absently, Lark dug out her crystal pouch and took out her flat-backed onyx. She didn't even need conscious thought for warmth to spread through her, soft and gentle as a mother's touch. Lark opened her hand and looked down at the stone.

An urge came over her, one that Lark couldn't stop in time. Stretching out one hand, palm down, she placed the stone on the back of one finger. It fit perfectly. The stone was exactly the shape and size to be set in a ring. Had it been sold as such willingly, or had it been pried from a Ring whose owner had died...or been killed? Lark snatched the stone off her hand and thrust it back into the pouch. She tucked it into her shirt more roughly than necessary. The night air felt bitterly cold.

"Stargazing?" The soft voice cut into her roiling thoughts. Violet stood before Lark and gazed up at her.

"No, just woolgathering," Lark said. She extended a hand to help Violet scramble up onto the tree to sit beside her.

"Sometimes a bit of introspection is good for the soul," Violet said. The wind picked up Violet's skirts in a liquid rustle. She shivered and rubbed her arms.

Without thinking, Lark reached out and wrapped her arms around Violet's body from behind, pulling her close. At the first contact, Violet tensed, then she relaxed into the friendly embrace.

"You should have a shawl or something at this time of year. You'll catch your death," Lark said. Her heart thudded in her chest. Her own audacity shocked her, although she reasoned she was merely helping their visitor not to catch a cold. Violet shifted and leaned back against her with a sigh. Lark couldn't believe how good Violet felt in her arms. Muscles like steel under the silk of her skin, her hair fragrant and soft against Lark's cheek. They fit together so well. Lark tilted her head down. She pressed her face into Violet's thick hair, breathing in her scent.

"Why would I need a shawl," Violet asked in an amused voice, "when I have you?"

"Just making sure you're all right," Lark said. Her voice came out huskier than she planned. Violet moved again, this time her back pressed against Lark's breasts. Their bodies molded together without a single space between them. Violet's heartbeat echoed her own. Lark drew in a breath as a sultry heat started up from where they touched and stained southward. A flash of panic ripped through her. Just as suddenly as she put her arms around Violet in the first place, Lark let go.

"How about heading over to the pantry shed for a cup of tea?" Lark suggested. She didn't wait for an answer before she hopped down. She held out a hand to assist, but Violet ignored the unspoken offer and dismounted in a swirl of skirts.

"Actually," Violet said, "I was just coming to see if you'd like to share a windfall that came my way. Guardian Prior's grandmother sent up a number of gift baskets, one of which I received. I believe she's living somewhere they referred to as 'The Port' and my share is far too generous for just myself. It includes several bottles of beer and some kind of dried fish, as well as a round of cheese."

"Thanks very much, Miss Violet." Nerves prodded Lark to fall into the more formal address. She didn't miss the eyebrow-lift Violet did at the slip. Lark said, "I can't turn down an offer like that. Beer from the Port's really nice." She was grateful to have a safe topic to occupy her mind. She couldn't stop thinking about the instant she pulled Violet close.

Violet didn't say anything more, just gave Lark a little smile that made her breath catch in her throat. In comfortable silence, they walked back to Violet's cottage. Lark sat on the window seat and inspected the contents of the basket while Violet, citing the need to get out of her day clothes, slipped behind the dressing-screen.

Lark tried very hard to shut out the sound of clothing slipping over Violet's bare skin while she used her wand to cool the beers. Lark blew a piece of hair out of her face and wished she could cool herself down as well. A sheen of frost bloomed on the stout brown bottles. Violet, in her long nightdress, stepped back into the room. Lark's mouth fell open and she nearly dropped her wand at the sight of Violet with her hair fully unbound, her body soft and natural under the thin, delicate material.

"That's much better," Violet said and stretched her arms over her head in a gesture that made Lark cast her gaze frantically about the room. Not appearing to notice Lark's discomfit, Violet plopped down on the bed.

Lark's fumbling fingers managed to uncork two bottles and she held one out.

"Why don't you join me here?" Violet asked. "That way I can put the basket between us and we can both have easy access. And it isn't like we haven't shared this bed before." She dropped her voice to a low purr.

"All right, if it's not too crowded," Lark said. Her face went hot. She handed Violet one of the two chilled bottles of beer and unzipped her boots one-handed. She kicked them off and transferred herself to the bed.

Both of them bowed their heads in a silent prayer of thanks before they clunked the bottlenecks together in a toast. They both drank deeply. The beer was dark and sweet, heavy with fragrant herbs.

Lark wiped a hand over her mouth with a satisfied sigh. "Told you it was nice, didn't I?"

"You did not lie," Violet said. She picked up one of her daggers from the bedside table and cut the round of cheese into neat sections.

"What do you do all day holed up in the council-house anyway?" Lark asked. She hastily added, "I don't want to know anything secret, just how you spend the time."

"It's no secret. Now that the bulk of my negotiations are finished, most of my time is spent waiting for information from the Guardians passing through," Violet said. She paused and nibbled delicately on a dried fish. "Often the senior Guardians join them and make elaborate strategies and plans, which I take part in if the topic is to my interest. Otherwise, I am left to my own devices, which means I am free to read whatever I like from the library or practice with my blades. They have set aside a small room for me which I use as a study. I am used to passing long hours in solitary captivity and can entertain myself quite well. At any rate, everyone is probably more comfortable without my presence."

"Sounds lonely," Lark said before she could stop herself.

Violet just gave a small shrug and sipped her beer. "It is all I have ever known and solitude has always been my preferred state." She looked over at Lark and said in a low voice, "Until now."

Lark's heart gave a jolt.

"Really?" Lark breathed.

"Yes," Violet said. She didn't elaborate.

"What exactly were you negotiating?" Lark asked before the silence could go on too long. "If it's all right to ask."

"That is fine. I'm certain all Wanderers will hear of it eventually. After all, your people will be involved in carrying out the agreement." Violet cradled her beer in her hands. She looked quite comfortable. "In the Old Days, we had seven great halls, each one dedicated to one of our seven gods. They were our schools, wellness centers, and government. Every Ringsworn was obligated to make at least one pilgrimage in their lifetime where they visited all seven in turn. Now they are abandoned and lying in ruins. I am not here because the Ringsworn are overflowing with altruism. In exchange for my services, we have received permission to begin reconstruction of two of our halls. I am currently negotiating how much assistance the Wanderers are willing to give us as our numbers are not what they once were." She paused. "I am not a puppet. I am not interested in re-negotiating the Ring-making restrictions. Rebuilding the wonderful and grand parts of our world is the only part of the agreement I want. While I detest haggling over details, I wish to know those who come after me will have that much at least."

Lark sat up. A wondrous feeling blossomed in her chest. "Is yours one of those going to be rebuilt?"

"No," Violet said with a shake of her head. "My convent is dedicated to Limor, who is the goddess of darkness and death."

Violet's eyes met Lark's. Her voice was soft as she said, "And for-giveness."

Lark said, "I guess I can see why the Wanderers' Council wouldn't want that one rebuilt, but when you think about it, if we didn't have the dark then nobody would get a good night's sleep and if you can't die in the end, there's really very little point in living. It goes without saying that without forgiveness, even the smallest argument would go on forever."

"Yes," Violet breathed the word. She studied Lark for a moment longer.

"Thanks for telling me," Lark said. She scooted forward in order to help herself to a piece of cheese and ended up closer to Violet than she intended. Their knees almost brushed. Lark struggled to keep her voice even as she said, "You can tell me anything you want. I'll keep your confidence, don't worry."

"I appreciate that," Violet said. "However you are young, I don't want to plague you with a heavier burden than I already have."

"Hey, I'm going on nineteen," Lark said with her chin at a proud angle.

"And I will be thirty next May," Violet said in a low voice that sent a velvet shiver down Lark's spine. She lowered a mischievous look at Lark as she picked up the novel that rested on the bedside table. Violet waved the book in the air. "Most likely far too well-aged and mature for something of this nature, however I have to admit, your Amelia Strawberry series is quite entertaining."

"Nobody's too old for those," Lark said. "I've been reading them since I was a youngun and I still check whenever a new one comes out. They're lots of fun. Better than those boring law books I've got to slog through."

"At least now I know who Elvira is," Violet said in a carefully nonchalant tone. She looked up at Lark's gasp. Violet's lips quirked up at the corners.

"Alice didn't mean anything by that," Lark said.

"It's all right, I rather appreciate the comparison." Violet said. She leaned forward with her hands clasped under her chin and looked directly into Lark's eyes. They were so close, Lark could feel Violet's soft breath on her face. The delicate scent of chamomile enveloped her. Lark's heart gave a great jump. Violet said in a low voice, "And you remind me of Amelia."

"Me?" Lark squeaked.

"Like her, you are always observing and thinking, trying to figure things out. Both loyal and kind, capable and fun," Violet said. Her gaze held Lark's. "You have a beautiful soul. It shows in how much you care about your friends."

"Yeah, I do care about my friends," Lark said.

The moment broke when Violet looked away to help herself to another piece of cheese. They sipped their beers and the conversation moved on to more mundane topics. Lark excitedly told Violet about one of their special lectures a fun pair of double-stripe Trackers gave them the other day.

"It's called fast food," Lark said, waving her bottle. "As if Outsiders are too busy to bother with normal speed food. See, they go up to a counter and tell the person behind it what they want—and the cooks make it right then and there. Doesn't that just beat all? Can you imagine if Cook Brown had us doing that?"

Violet's lips parted slightly. "It sounds fascinating, but I can't imagine how that would work."

"How about I show you?" Lark quickly downed the last dregs of her beer, set aside her empty bottle, and stood up. "For this scenario, I'm the fast food worker. This dresser is the counter. I'll stand on this side, the side where they make the food, and you stand here in front of me. Imagine they've got a sign on the wall behind me with all the dishes and prices listed. Ready?"

Violet nodded. She rose from the bed and took her place.

"Welcome to, uh, Lark's Lightning-Fast Fast Food Restaurant. Are you ready to order, Miss?"

"Yes, I am," Violet said. She pretended to study the menu. "I would like to order a roast wildebeest, smothered in chocolate-raspberry sauce, with extra chilies and a honey-apple in its mouth. It will be accompanied by a tureen of steamed spiral mollusks in lilac garlic sauce and a horn of creamed sea urchins. Oh, and a dozen devil crabs, smashed and dusted with blueberries and black pepper."

Lark suppressed her smile and said in a crisp voice, "Okay, so lunch special number two. Would you like fries with that?"

"What are *fries*?" Violet asked. "Are they perhaps the dying embers of the excised liver of the volcano lizard? If so, I would like six of them."

"Coming right up," Lark said. "That will be twenty-seven coins. Is that for here or to go?"

"To go." Playing along admirably, Violet pretended to take a handful of coins from her pocket. She put her fingers lightly in Lark's outstretched hand and said, "My servants will carry out my order on their bronzed backs." She paused. Her fingers still rested softly on Lark's palm. "How was that?"

"Great, you're a natural. You got the hang of it better than the backwards trout I had to practice with today," Lark said. She didn't want to move in case she broke the breathless spell that was keeping Violet's hand in hers. Lark felt like she was on the peak of a mountain, bathing in the sun. She grinned and closed her fingers around Violet's for a moment before she drew away. "Do you want to switch roles and try it again?" Lark asked.

"Yes, I do," Violet said. She took her place behind the "counter" and served with cool efficiency. She kept her expression calm as she suggested dishes of such outrageous proportions that Lark had to bite her lip a few times to keep her guffaws from spilling out all over the place. Finally, Lark gave up and collapsed onto the bed in laughter.

"I can't remember a more pleasant evening," Lark declared as Violet opened a second bottle of beer for her.

"Neither can I," Violet said. She bowed her head over the basket while she selected a snack and Lark couldn't help but drink in the sensuous curve of her neck. Violet's skin glowed pale in the candlelight. Lark's fingers tingled with the need to reach out and brush the soft fall of long hair away from Violet's nape. She ached to reveal the delicate skin and press her lips to that spot. Startled, Lark clutched at her bottle.

"I should let you know I'm going out on patrol starting tomorrow," Lark said in a rush. "We're going all the way to the Border this time."

"How long will you be gone?" Violet asked in a soft voice.

"We're scheduled to be out for a week."

Violet dropped her gaze to her hands, which she clasped in her lap. "Will there be danger where you go?"

"Nah. I can't think what would bother a bunch of trainees all the way out there," Lark said. She grimaced. "We'll be roughing it, no staying over at safehouses or even a waystation. They said it's to teach us survival skills in nature."

She didn't know why her chest ached at the forlorn look on Violet's face.

"If a storm hits while you're out there..."

"We'll be all right," Lark said in a forced jolly tone. She finished her beer and stood. "Thanks for the refreshment. I guess I'll see you when I get back."

Violet stood as well. Lark was extremely aware of how close they were to each other. She knew she should step back, but she didn't. Violet took Lark's hands in hers.

"Be safe," she said. Her voice was barely more than a whisper. "I'll keep a lantern in the window for you. May the goddess guide your path and protect you from harm."

"Thanks," Lark said. Reluctantly, she eased her hands from Violet's. She opened the door to leave and glanced back with a rakish grin that Violet didn't return.

Chapter Ten

"STEADY ON THERE," Theo called over his shoulder as the coach bucked and sent his current travelling partner Neil Clements and the group of four fledglings in a tumble to the floor. "Alice, keep an even keel."

"Trying," Alice muttered from her position at the stern. She gripped her wand and shifted on the bench. The coach, a lunking boat-like monstrosity was the largest size in the fleet the Guardians kept at Shadowmoor. It cut through the sunset-tinged air like a lumbering beast that sent all of them sprawling with Alice's inexpert driving. Lark righted herelf and squashed the urge to take out her wand and give Alice a hand. It was only their first day out. Her own turn to drive would come soon enough.

Theo held up a hand in a signal to Alice. "We're almost at the Border. Land and prepare to disembark."

"Thank goodness," Murray said. He hung over the side. "I was getting seasick."

"Shut it," Alice gritted. She directed the coach into a clearing and set it down with a thump.

Everyone piled out.

Theo led them into the woods. The scenery was no different from anywhere else but something felt off. Lark could almost hear a note humming through the air. She stood still and cocked her head to listen.

"Do you hear it?" Theo asked them. "That's the Border. It's old, older than wands or Rings. Even older than crystals. Try and walk through it from this side and you'll just freeze. Do it from the other side, you'll end up walking in a circle back to where you came from without even realizing it."

While Theo wasn't Lark's favorite person due to his long-ago remark about Crystalgazers and manure, she had to admit he took his work seriously.

"Can I have a volunteer?" Theo asked.

Lark didn't even think before her hand shot up. Whatever it was, she wanted to try it and show Theo she was good at more than just shoveling the result of hay-fed farm animals.

"All right Guardian Greenpool, come to the front and stand by me."

Lark did as he asked. The hum was even stronger there. She had to be very close to the Border.

"Close your eyes and listen carefully. Try and match the note."

"Match it? Like, I have to sing?" Lark asked. For a moment, she wondered if Theo was pranking her, trying to make her look like a foolish hayseed in front of everyone.

Theo nodded. "Resonant energy. Match the note and you'll be able to pass through."

He seemed sincere. There was only way to know for sure. Lark shook back her trailing bangs and let out a breath. She closed her eyes, extremely aware of everyone else looking at her. She tried to shut them out and concentrate on listening. Slowly, the note formed in her mind. She grabbed it and hummed. Nothing. She coughed and tried again. That time, her note hit true. A shimmering sensation gripped her. She felt as if the wind on her face was from an alien, far away place. It held a tang of something she'd never experienced before. The air was heavy with some kind of smoke, laden with spices that weren't necessarily pleasant.

"That's it. You did it." Theo's voice brought her back to reality. "Okay fledglings split into pairs and practice until you've done it five times each. Go!"

Lark paired up with Alice, who nudged her on their way to a secluded practice spot.

"Nice work," she said. "Trying to impress the teacher?"

"Maybe," Lark replied. She flushed and didn't elaborate. Alice never treated her like a hayseed and she didn't want to invite it.

Alice hooted and slapped Lark on the shoulder. "I didn't think Theo was your type, but if you need someone to create a diversion so you two can get a bit of alone time, let me know."

Lark froze in her tracks. She looked at Alice in utter confusion. "What?" she barked out.

"Uh sorry, I take it that's a 'no'?"

"What on this Great Green Earth are you...oh." For a second, Lark entertained the idea of going along with Alice, playing the part of a normal girl who got dreamy-eyed over boys. But Theo? Lark couldn't contain her distain. She planted her hands on her hips and said, "That's not important. We're here to learn how to be Guardians, not...whatever you thought was going on. That's the last thing on my mind right now. And Theo? Really? You know me better than that. Don't ever bring this up again." Lark glowered at Alice. She looked entirely too pleased with herself.

"Interesting," Alice said in an enigmatic way.

Lark threw her hands into the air. "Just get on with your practice, all right?"

"Okay, sorry," Alice said. To her credit, she didn't mention it again. Lark expected at least a sly look when they reassembled to clamber onto the coach again, but Alice was admirably stoic.

"IT'S ALMOST DARK," Theo said. His long ponytail whipped around his face as he turned to address them. "How about we stop for the night soon?"

A volley of tired cheers welcomed his request. After their practice at the Border, they loaded back into the coach and continued their patrol for several hours. Their first day out was a long one. Lark was frazzled and very glad to see solid ground under the coach.

They disembarked and Theo directed Alice and Murray into the forest to look for kindling, while he and Nora started preparation for their evening meal. Lark was glad of that as the day's rations consisted only of dried goat meat and hard bread. Lark and Neil were tasked with building lean-tos in preparation for their camp.

Once darkness fell, the group of six Guardians sat around the crackling campfire with bowls of stew in their hands. Jokes and songs rang out around her, but Lark kept quiet. She gazed into the heart of the fire and wondered what Violet was doing. For the first time, the songs and stories around the campfire bored Lark. She wanted something else. Her soul hungered for it.

After everyone retired to their lean-tos, wrapped up in their cloaks, Lark couldn't keep still. She slipped from the campsite with a nod to Murray who was taking the first watch. In a tiny moonlit clearing, Lark found a fallen tree. Although it was much smaller than the behemoth back at Shadowmoor, it was still a good place to sit and think. Lark clambered up and perched upon it.

Lark gazed up at the wan crescent moon above. She bit back a deep sigh. Was Violet looking up at the same moon right now? Her chest ached. She felt empty, as if she was missing a vital part of herself. After a long while of incomplete musings, Lark returned to the campsite and slipped into her lean-to. The boughs beneath her cloak were springy and not uncomfortable. The thick cloak cradled her in warmth.

Snores and muffled mutterings filled her ears but Lark couldn't find peace. She rolled over and cupped her turquoise. It lulled her and finally Lark closed her eyes and welcomed the darkness.

BY THE THIRD day of their patrol, Lark was thoroughly tired of stew and was seriously rethinking her career choice as they skimmed along in their increasingly cramped and smelly coach. The only thing she looked forward to was taking her turn to drive, which didn't come nearly often enough. It was during one of Lark's turns when Theo shouted out, "Veer south!"

Lark did without question. The change in direction roused Neil and the other fledglings who were mostly dozing in the afternoon warmth.

"What is it?" Murray asked.

"Something's wrong. It should be here."

"What should?" Murray's hands worried at the hem of his cloak.

"The Border. It should be here and...this should not." Theo held up a hand and Lark brought the barge to a hover. She held her breath.

Something indeed was very wrong. In front of them, great swatches of trees were gone. Only cleanly cut stumps remained. The ground was red with mud, churned up as if by great, toothed ploughs. No one who lived within the Protected Isles would unleash such destruction on nature.

"Who did this?" Lark asked, sickened by the destruction.

"Outsiders," Theo said. When he turned to address them, his face was white. "There's a gap in the Border."

"We have to get out of here." Murray jumped to his feet. The coach rocked in an alarming way.

"Steady," Lark snapped. Her body jolted with nerves. Her hands shook and she gripped her wand tighter.

"Set the coach down," Theo said. He whipped out his wand. "We have to try and patch it up."

"How?" Alice asked. "I thought it was, like, automatic."

"We have to do something," Theo snapped. "It won't hold for long, but it's better than this gaping hole."

Lark set the coach down and everyone scrambled out with their wands at the ready. Lark bounced on the balls of her feet.

"Get ready, folks," Theo said. Wordlessly, Neil stood beside him and drew his wand. The fledglings fell into formation behind them. Theo brandished his wand and called forth a humming yellow force. At his gesture, Lark and the others braced themselves and one by one they added their effort to his. The shield slowly grew. Lark poured all of her energy into it. The shimmering wall started to take shape as the Guardians around Lark drained their small resources. Beside her, Murray let out a yelp and fell to his knees.

Theo didn't let up. He shouted, "Don't stop! The edges need to meet before we can finish here!"

Lark squared her shoulders. Around her, fledglings fell to the soft forest floor, their wands still out and humming. One by one, they flickered out until it was just herself and Theo. Lark's arms shook, but she stood strong and steady.

"You're holding back," he shouted over his shoulder.

"I'm giving you all I can," Lark said. She grit her teeth and held on. The shield they made got stronger and grew.

Finally, the edges of their patched-together shield met and melded. As soon as it was done, they snapped off their energy. Theo stumbled forward onto his knees. Lark looked around in a panic. She couldn't take care of the entire group alone. In desperation, she grabbed her amber and waved it in front of Theo's dazed face.

"Do I have your permission?" Lark asked.

"Huh?" He blinked up at her.

"I can help you, do I have your permission?"

"Uh sure."

It wasn't exactly the most definite response, but Lark took it. She gripped her crystal and reached out with one hand. She swallowed her long-held dislike of Theo as a person and her hesitation to get physically close to a male she wasn't related to as she gently rested her fingertips on his forehead. The amber in her hand grew warm and the life-affirming energy flowed through her and into her team leader. The contact lasted for only a moment before she shut it off and backed away, quickly stowing her crystal.

"What did you do?" Theo asked. He got to his feet and looked around in surprise. "I nearly went into burnout, but you stopped it."

"Just used an old home remedy," Lark said.

"Can you do that for the rest of them?"

Lark shook her head. "I can't without their permission. I might be able to do something once they wake up, but I'm no Healer."

For a moment, Theo's face darkened in anger. He muttered something under his breath about *bleeding heart semantics* that had Lark bristling. Theo said, "At any rate, you helped me out. Now we have to get this bunch back to Shadowmoor and let them know what we found here. Are you all right to drive?"

"Yes, I am," Lark said with as much conviction as she could muster.

Theo looked at her with a long gaze that made Lark uncomfortable. He only said, "All right, get us back home."

"Yes sir," Lark said.

The site of destruction fell behind them, but the knowledge Lark carried with her sat heavily in her gut. The Border that kept them safe and unnoticed was failing. Their world was dying?

THEY ARRIVED BACK at Shadowmoor as evening fell. Theo was sequestered in an emergency meeting while the fledglings were ushered into the Wellness Center where they were fussed over by Healer Andrews. Lark dutifully submitted to an examination even though she felt fine, if stressed and tired.

She changed out of her dusty travelling clothes and into one of the center's nightshirts. Lark tried to relax in the unaccustomed luxury of a private room, but couldn't lie still. She paced and considered escaping to go see Violet when a knock at the window startled her. The room was on the top floor of the building. She had no idea who or what could be outside. Puzzled, Lark opened the window and peered outside to nothing other than empty darkness.

"Step back."

Lark's body reacted instinctively to the command. She threw herself onto the bed as a dark swoosh heralded Violet's arrival. Like a giant bat, she swooped in through the window and landed on both feet. Immediately she sank down next to Lark.

"You are unhurt?" Violet asked. Her eyes were wide and she looked upset.

"I'm fine," Lark said. She couldn't stop the smile. "Green Trees and Blue Sky but it's good to see you."

Violet relaxed a fraction. "I should skewer whoever thought it acceptable to endanger you like that."

"It's no big deal," Lark said. "We're just a bunch of fledglings, nobody of importance."

Violet leaned forward. She cupped Lark's cheeks and smoothed back the forelock that always fell across Lark's brow. Her eyes bored into Lark's. "You are important to *me*," she breathed. "These past few days have been interminable."

"I missed you too," Lark said before she could stop herself. Violet was very close. Lark knew she shouldn't, but she liked having Violet's hands on her. Her body woke up with a hot, humming feeling that filled her like fire. The urge to reach out to Violet, pull her into an embrace was almost overwhelming. Lark couldn't help but lean into Violet's hold. The moment stretched out. The only sound was their breathing. Lark's entire being focused on Violet's lips, full and soft and tempting like nothing else Lark ever encountered. Her eyes started to drift closed.

Suddenly Violet drew back and stood. Lark was left cold and aching. She trembled with the need to move, to do something. Indecision held her still.

"Now that I know you are unhurt, I will take my leave," Violet said in a clipped voice that didn't quite ring true. She clutched at her skirts with trembling fingers.

"Uh, sure," Lark said. She couldn't think of anything else to say. Violet was at the window again when Lark broke out of her frozen spell. "Wait. How did you get here in the first place?"

Violet looked back over one shoulder. Her lips twitched into a slight smile that resonated through Lark like sunlight. Violet said, "I am used to scaling sheer rock cliffs with a basket on my back. It was no mean feat to climb the tree next to this building and avail myself of the roof."

"Huh," Lark said, quite impressed. In a flash of swirling skirts, Violet was gone. Lark stood. She swayed dumbly for a while before she shut the window.

Alone once more, Lark fell into her bed with her thoughts in a blur and a tingling warmth in her belly. Lark was almost afraid to close her eyes. When she finally gave into exhaustion, she dreamed.

Lark wandered through endless corn fields, her vision obscured by the laden stalks. She was searching for something, frantic with the need to find it. A clearing opened up in front of her. Lark stumbled into it, glad to breathe easily once more. She immediately knew she'd found what she was looking for.

In the middle of the clearing, Violet stood like a tower of darkness. She had her back to Lark, but when she turned, her face was alight with the smile Lark loved to see.

"I've been waiting for you," Violet said in a low voice. Lark's knees got weak at the tone. It was inviting, tempting and predatory all in one. "Come to me," Violet purred and held her arms out.

She didn't feel herself move but at once she was against Violet. Lark didn't hesitate before she folded herself into Violet's arms. She felt Violet's heart beating against her chest, she melted into the firmness of her body. Lark traced one finger over Violet's lips, exploring the softness before she leaned forward, hungry to taste them. Violet smiled, then parted her lips. Lark's eyes fluttered closed…

LARK GASPED AND wrenched herself fully awake. She threw off her bedcovers and swung her feet over the side of the bed. Dawn was still a few hours away, but Lark was terrified to let herself go back to sleep in case she invited another dream. Her legs trembled. A slick warmth swelled between her thighs and her heart pounded. Lark's body was on edge, primed and hungry. Lark held her head in her hands for a long moment as the primeval hunger battled with her self-control. She was in complete disbelief about what she saw and nearly did in her dream. A deep twinge between her legs invited Lark to take care of herself, but she couldn't give in.

An early morning bath would be the best remedy to her restless mood. Lark tied her tails up into a jolly bunch before she picked up her discarded travel clothes. She wrinkled her nose at them. A trip to the laundry was in order. Lark helped herself to a towel and a fresh nightshirt from the linen closet before she slipped out of the Wellness Center. Her wand pressed into her back and the contact comforted her. Above her an old, tired moon hung low over the trees. The last stars decorated the sky. Her breath steamed into the cold pre-dawn air as Lark hustled across the dark compound to the laundry shed.

She heard sloshing from the inside and as she entered, she steeled herself to meet one of the other residents of the compound. Lark stopped in her tracks. Violet stood in front of one of the washers. She sang a sweet but melancholy song to herself. A black, silken garment and a towel were draped over the bench beside her and her long boots were propped up against the side of the washing barrel. She hadn't seen Lark standing frozen in the doorway because she in the process of pulling her nightgown over her head.

The rising hem revealed long legs clad in knee-length drawers, not dissimilar to the ones Lark favored, save for the fact they were slightly longer and richly trimmed in lace. The nightgown came off completely and Lark's brain stopped all functions at the sight of Violet's bare back. The line of her body was long and sleek, her delicate shoulders and finely muscled arms tantalizing. Even without the restrictive garments, her body was slender and supple.

The nightgown went into the washing barrel and Violet was tugging at the drawstring at the waist of her drawers when Lark managed to break out of her brain-stall. Her body jolted into action.

Lark turned around so fast she collided with the door. She stammered, "Oh Green Trees, sorry about that, Violet." She heard Violet squeak and Lark pressed an arm over her eyes. She gestured behind herself in what she hoped was a friendly and innocent way. "I should have knocked but I thought it was just one of the fellows in here."

"I am glad *you* weren't one of the fellows." Violet's voice sounded muffled and Lark guessed she had grabbed up the towel or something and was hiding in it. "As I would not have allowed someone who precipitated such a breach of my modesty to live, and the murder of one of your members would not help the already strained relations between our peoples."

Uncomfortably, Lark wondered what the penalty for her own breach would be. None came except for a sudden exclamation and muttered oath.

"Limor's left buttock! Lark, could you give me a hand, please?"

"Sure thing, if you're decent," Lark said.

"Yes, it's safe to turn around." Instead of anger, the tone was rich with amusement.

"Okay then, what happened?"

Violet stood in front of her washing barrel, wrapped in a dressing gown of fine black silk. She looked most annoyed. Lark fought a fresh wave of tingling warmth at the sight of the deep valley of milky skin revealed by the slight gap at the front of the robe. Lark couldn't help but notice the hard nipples tenting the fabric. She swallowed hard. She could not be caught staring. Lark forced her attention to the washer.

Violet said, "I dropped my bracelet. It fell out of my pocket." Violet paused. She looked at Lark for a moment before she said, "I was wondering if you would consent to helping me out. I know you can levitate things, and I don't want to take a chance with my hand and the paddles in there. I mean, if it isn't too much trouble, I'm sure I could dredge it out with a stick just as easily."

"That's okay, I'd love to help you out. It's no problem at all," Lark said. She swelled with pride. She twitched her wand over her shoulder into her hands. It was the first time Violet had actually asked for her to use her wand. She had to do it properly. Lark gathered her energy and concentrated on the contents of the washer. They undulated gently with the movements of the spring-driven paddles. Even though it was possible to clean clothes with wands, most Wanderers were loathe to use their small reserves of energy for mundane tasks unless absolutely necessary. Lark did her best to ignore the lacy garments floating about while she located the bracelet. It was a simple string of polished garnets. With practiced ease, Lark lifted the bracelet out of the sudsy water. She got a kick of joy at the sudden brightening of

Violet's face as it surfaced.

"Thank you," Violet said. She held out her hands with a wondering look on her face. Lark set the bracelet down with the softest touch she could. Abruptly, Violet thrust the ring of stones at Lark. She said, "It is yours."

"Oh no, I couldn't take something like that. You can make it up to me by, uh," Lark stammered to a halt, extremely aware of those long fingers that drifted over the jewels with such grace and tenderness. Before she could stop the thought, Lark wondered what it would feel like if Violet touched her like that. She wet her bottom lip and said, "by helping me out sometime."

"I insist," Violet said. "I never wear bracelets as they interfere with my cuffs. I found the stones along the shore near my convent and polished them myself—do not worry, they carry no taint of Ringsworn enchantment. While making this item was enjoyable, I've only kept it out of habit." Her gaze faltered. Her fingers curled over the deep red gems. Her arm dropped to her side. "Actually, please forget this incident. It was inappropriate. I apologize."

"No, don't be sorry," Lark said. Before she could change her mind, she reached out and folded her hands over Violet's. A sparkling thrill raced through her at the contact, homing in on the last place Lark wanted it. She nearly groaned as a stab of heat pierced down through her belly. "I'd be honored to accept your gift. Thank you."

"It is nothing," Violet said. She bowed her head and slipped the bracelet over Lark's fingers. She guided the sleek stones to her wrist. Only then did she remove her hand from Lark's arm.

Lark held her hand up to the lantern. She liked the way the light pooled within the stones. She gazed past them to where Violet stood with her dark eyes resting on Lark.

"Beautiful," Lark breathed. Suddenly angry with herself at the lapse, Lark turned around to hide her scowl. In as calm a voice as she could manage, she said, "Would you mind giving me a bit of privacy? I just need to throw a few things in the wash and then I'm heading for the baths."

"Actually, I'm going that way myself," Violet said. "I will wait for you outside the door."

Lark's shoulders tensed. She wished she had brought a dressing gown or something like that. She hadn't counted on meeting anyone, and certainly not the woman she'd just dreamed about in a very intimate way.

Lark selected a washing barrel and started the water flowing. She dumped in a scoop of soap powder and gave the crank a few turns. She stifled the breath of desire with fierce determination and concentrated on her laundry. She took off her nightshirt and underclothes, which joined the rest of her discarded clothing in the barrel. As Violet had done, Lark left her boots by the washer. Lark wrapped her towel around her body and scooped up her fresh nightshirt. She ducked back outside and hissed in a breath as the cold air hit her bare skin.

"Let's go before either of us freezes," Lark said. She broke into a fast trot with Violet beside her.

They were halfway across the clearing when Violet grabbed her arm. "Go left. Cook Brown is coming. Duck down here."

"Oh manure," Lark breathed. She allowed herself to be pulled off course and behind a row of bushes. She'd forgotten how early the cook got up in order to start his daily baking. With another tug on her arm, Lark followed Violet. They ran bent over, dodging branches as they fought their way through the under-brush. Violet's dressing gown flapped about her ankles, revealing a flash of white skin. Both of them were tousled and covered in branches and loose leaves by the time they reached the baths.

Lark yanked the door open and ushered Violet inside. They collapsed in a pile of bush-remnants. The entrance hall ran the length of the room with the individual baths located behind numbered doors. All of them showed "vacant" signs, which Lark was grateful for.

"That wild chase certainly didn't protect my dignity," Lark said. She used the nightshirt to whack leaves from her towel onto the floor. She shouldn't have looked, but the image of Violet's bare legs flashing through the slit of her robe was burned into her mind.

A low chuckle broke through her roiling thoughts. Lark looked up. Violet had one slender hand pressed to her mouth. Her shoulders shook and she burst out laughing. The sound of her mirth filled the room. It was the first time Lark heard Violet laugh. The sound resonated from Lark's heart to the tips of her toes.

Lark put on an annoyed air. "I'm glad *someone* is amused at this predicament. If one more branch gets stuck in my towel, I'm going to have to marry that bush over there."

"That would be a shame," Violet said through her chuckles. "However, I'm certain any inappropriate branches will soon float off with the judicious application of hot water, which is what I plan to do."

"Me too," Lark said. She let loose with a grin. Violet's amusement was contagious.

"I have always loved a hot bath," Violet said. Her face was thoughtful as she pulled the jeweled combs from her mass of braids. "Winter was so long by the sea. The only time I was ever warm in my convent was in the bath. It was my favorite thing to do."

"I know the feeling. Nothing beats a hot bath on a cold day," Lark said.

"Indeed." Violet's smile faded. "Sometimes I worry about Sister Perpetua all alone there. But with me gone, she's free to go elsewhere. Who knows, maybe she'll find herself with devotees returning to those walls once they no longer hold my curse within them. She can start over, build a new order in the temple of Limor."

Lark forgot she was only wearing a towel. She faced Violet squarely. "But that's your home. Aren't you planning to go back there when you're done here?"

"No."

The empty look in Violet's eyes chilled Lark. The snap of a towel brought her back to the present.

Violet said, "Get yourself and your bush into the bath before you catch a chill."

"Yes ma'am," Lark said. She flipped the sign on the door of the bathing stall nearest her and ducked inside. The changing area was small, with a basket for her clothes. She dropped her towel and stepped into the inner room where the squat wooden bath waited for her. She pulled the chain to start the cascade of water into the tub from the common heater overhead.

Lark picked up a bucket and doused herself from head to foot. Over the noise of the waterfall, she heard Violet splashing away and humming to herself in the cubicle next to her. Lark drew in a breath. She closed her eyes as the vision of suds coursing over moonlight-pale skin invaded her mind. She could picture as clear as day the soapy waves skimming down Violet's curves and slender legs. Lark bit her lip as a rush of heat filled her. She couldn't fight the arousal that woke with her dream and simmered ever since. The characteristic splash of water spilling over the sides of the tub told Lark when Violet lowered her body into the bath.

"Mmm...that feels so good." The words hung in the air. They carried the same sultry note from her dream.

Lark considered clapping her hands over her ears. Her heart pounded and a buzzing feeling sawed away at her. She knelt on the wooden floor with the last of the hot water running down over her body. Lark's breath came faster. She couldn't help but listen to Violet's soft sounds of enjoyment, almost drowned out by the water falling into the bathtub. Lark shifted against the insistent heat between her legs. The feeling was relentless, and her throbbing womanhood demanded she do something about it or suffer the lingering aftereffects for who knows how long. Lark leaned her head back against the wall. On the other side, Violet was lying in her own bath. Did she have her eyes closed in pleasure? Was she stretched out with her fingers stroking her body under the water?

Lark trailed a hand down over her breast. She bit her lip to stop the moan as she brushed her fingers over her own nipple. She brought both hands up to cup herself fully. Was Violet soft like that? Did she ever tease herself like Lark was? Lark could only wonder as the idea filled her body with a wonderful rush of heat.

Fantasies were free. Of course she would never act of them, but Lark was desperate for release. She had to decide which way to go and soon. One hand drifted down over her belly. Lark had already passed the point of no return. The noise from the bath provided a cover for her actions. Lark delved her fingers farther down. She sought the secret place between her legs and spread her knees slightly. A slick heat greeted her. Lark wasted no time finding the source of her pleasure. Panting breaths filled the small enclosure. She trembled with need, every bit of her on fire with just the idea of Violet close to her.

For an instant, Lark allowed herself to imagine the fingers on herself were Violet's, the tugging at her nipple, cherry-hued lips. When the peak claimed her, Lark had to bite back the cry that

welled up in her throat. She shuddered against the spasms that
gripped and shook her without mercy before she sagged back
against the side of the tub.

The relief was welcome, but Lark felt empty. She sank into
the hot water of the bath and buried her face in her arms. She
wished she never let herself dream about what she could not
have. She betrayed the trust Violet had in her, violated her with
her wayward thoughts. The garnet bracelet burned against her
skin.

Lark washed as quickly as possible and pulled her nightshirt
on over her half-dried skin. After the briefest of farewells, she
escaped from the bathhouse and hurried across the compound.

Chapter Eleven

LARK DIDN'T RECOVER quickly from her revelation and subsequent bathing experience and spent the day in a funk that not even Alice's prodding and Murray's best tambourine solo could pull her out of. She sleepwalked through her morning training session, earning more than one sharp reprimand from Guardian Snell that did nothing to improve her mood. Mind elsewhere, she washed the dinner dishes as usual. She half-listened to Alice chatting when a commotion caught her interest.

The black barge swooped down and hovered unsteadily over the landing platform, encased in the shimmering rainbow-colored shields of a number of Guardians working in tandem. Shouts rang through the compound. Several cloaked Guardians raced across the clearing, faces grim and wands ready. As the barge landed and the Guardians in it collapsed, a group, headed by Rosalie, surrounded the last man who was keeping a black bundle afloat with his wand. His keening voice cut through the air. Lark flinched from the pain in it.

The crowd swelled. Shields snapped into place and the procession vanished into the council house. The last one in was Violet who walked with her head high and face set. She passed close enough that Lark could see the fear in her eyes, how her hands shook as she clenched them around each other. The Guardians outside cast multiple shields over the entire building, sealing it completely.

"What do you think they've—" Alice began but Lark cut her off.

"Cover for me here," she said. Lark dropped her sponge and yanked down her sleeves. Her garnet bracelet clicked with her movements.

"But I want to—"

"Do it!" Lark snapped. She was taken aback at the hurt look on Alice's face, but this was more important than a few bruised feelings. Lark heard a meek, "Okay," at her back as she whirled and dashed through the compound to the girls' dormitory. She didn't stop until she raced up the narrow stars to the loft and slammed the door behind her. She needed privacy. With trembling fingers, Lark shook out her pink scrying crystal and breathed it into life. She concentrated on the large one in the meeting room. Its solid, smooth presence welcomed her.

The meeting room flared into existence in the crystal before her. Nobody appeared to notice the extra member in the room. The entire gathering clustered around the large table. Most of the Guardians were standing. They took turns shielding the item on the table.

Violet sat, silent and with her head bowed as if she was resting. Only the white knuckles of her clenched hands gave the indication she was not at all at rest. Rosalie stood to one side of her. She idly swung her wand in one hand. It was the first time Lark had seen both of them together and she was struck by how utterly different they were. Her heart gave a strange jolt. Lark forced her attention to what was happening at the table.

Head Guardian Williams leaned forward to address one of the Patrollers, a woman with curly brown hair tied back in a sensible ponytail. When she turned, Lark saw she had a long scar from just under her left eye to her chin, which bisected her lower lip. She had eyes like river-water. At once Lark knew the Patroller was Rosalie's mother.

"Helen, what is this?" Williams asked.

"It's definitely Ringsworn-made, looks like a belt buckle," she said. "We found it in an Outsider's home on the north side of the river, in Eastbrook, that's in the suburbs outside Compton. We've been tracking it for a while and we only just got out before the Outsider's law enforcement came. It took seven of our people just to get it here. Three of them are in bad shape because if it."

"Are you telling me an Outsider had it?" Williams asked, his eyebrows raised with an incredulous look.

"That's right."

"Are you quite sure? I can't imagine any of them would be able to comprehend anything like this, let alone use it."

"Artifacts don't care who they use." Helen slammed her hands on the table. "But enough talking. We have to get rid of it now. Every second that cursed thing is here is another second we're closer to all of us dying from it. It's turned itself on and it's lashing out at anything that comes near it."

"I understand," Williams said. "And I am aware of the urgency of this task. However the proper wards need to be put in place and for that, we need more information."

"We don't have any. The woman who had it wasn't talking. She was dead," Helen said in a tight voice. She pointed a finger at Violet. "Get that Ringsworn to do her thing already. We've agreed to enough of her demands, now let's see her earn them."

In her loft, Lark bristled. Couldn't they see how much Violet had already sacrificed for them?

"Is that true?" Williams asked. "Did this artifact take a life?"

"Sure looked like it," another Guardian spoke up. Lark recognized him. He was an affable fellow named Pierce who often played his fiddle for them when he passed through. His face was nearly grey under his tanned skin. He paused and swallowed hard before he said, "She — she was on her back, surrounded by all sorts of containers. Pizza, burgers, boxes that had whole cakes in them, that sort of thing. Just piles and piles of it. And her — guts." He continued in a querulous voice, "Looks like she clawed them out. Sorry —" Pierce left the table and hurried off in the direction of the water closet, hand over his mouth.

"Now you see why we need to get this thing done now?" Helen said. She glanced behind herself at the team of Guardians who were shielding the artifact. Their faces were streaked with sweat. "We're running out of time here."

"You seem to have found an edacitas knot," Violet said.

"Yeah, and?" Helen crossed her arms over her chest. "I don't care what it is, just get rid of it and finish these damned storms."

Violet raised her head. "This artifact is not the cause of the storms. While it is powerful in its own way, and may cause some local turbulence, it is not a Bloodring. It allows the bearer to consume great amounts of food without consequence. However, as I have said before, in the absence of proper training, the bearer does not use it. The artifact uses the bearer. It was for the best the holder of this artifact died when she did, before her never ending hunger spurred her appetite for more than just 'pizza and burgers'."

"You mean, like she'd eat people?" Rosalie asked in a shocked voice.

"Among other things," Violet said. "But, eventually, yes."

"Your people made that? Like, on purpose?"

"This is not a standard Ringsworn item." Violet said in a tight voice. "The ones who made it, and those like it, disregarded the most basic tenets of our craft and worked outside our rules. Our rulers opposed them strongly, even before the Wanderers chose to involve themselves."

"And we all know how well *that* turned out," Helen sneered. "Your people might still be in the ring-making business if your rulers had been more than just strongly opposed."

"Mother, please," Rosalie said. She looked uncomfortable.

Violet didn't reply.

Helen said, "In any event, we're stuck with a bunch of these horrible things. So, what are you going to do about it?"

Williams held up a hand. He asked, "Miss Ironwrought, can you do as you have promised? As we have been led to believe by your people?"

"Yes." The word was soft, final. A cold shiver ran down Lark's back at the tone of her voice.

"What do you need?"

"Get everyone out of here who does not need to be," Violet said. "For safety, keep the outside shields up until the artifact is neutralized."

Williams looked around the room. "Jonas, Smith, and McEnna, you're shielding here. The rest of you, please inform the team outside you will be leaving."

"I'm staying," Helen said. "How do I know this isn't just some trick to get artifacts for herself?"

"She goes," Violet's tone was a low growl. "Or I get up and walk out of here. Never to return."

"I'm sorry, but it would be for the best if we comply," Williams said.

"Mother," Rosalie said again. "We have to trust Violet."

Helen narrowed her eyes, but she didn't say anything more. She turned and stalked out of the room with her daughter close behind her.

With only the small group left, the hum of the shields was like a subliminal bee in the ear. Lark shook her head. Her crystal started humming in synchrony. With a heavy feeling in her belly, Lark looked at the scene. Violet was on her feet, hands spread on either side of the artifact, face down as if listening to something. Her shoulders rose and fell as she took a few deep breaths. Then, after a long moment, she moved.

Violet's hand snaked out. Her fingers passed through the multiple layers of shields as if they weren't even there. She shook the item from its wrappings. Lark heard the shocked gasp of one of the Guardians echo through the room. In the flash before her fingers closed over it completely, Lark saw the artifact. It was a circular medallion-looking item made out of metal ropes that twined endlessly around each other. There was no stone on it. Even through the filter of the crystal, the sick, malevolent energy oozed through the air like a miasma. Violet lowered her head. She drew in a breath that Lark unconsciously echoed. She cradled the deadly artifact in both hands. Violet's fingers tightened and her eyes closed.

It was done.

There was no dramatic explosion, no great release of energy, nothing except Violet opened her hands and a fine dust rained down from them. She turned and addressed Williams. "The artifact has been neutralized. There is no more need for shielding."

The shields flickered out. The instant the last resonance faded, she turned and walked out. Or at least she tried. Violet's legs buckled after three steps and she collapsed in a sea of black skirts. She waved off the offers of help from the Guardian nearest her. Instead she heaved herself upright using the table as a support.

"Is she all right?" the Guardian whispered to Williams.

"I am fine," Violet said the words through clenched teeth. She got to her feet, back straight and shoulders down. Her face was paler than usual, but she looked composed. Using her fine-tuned awareness of Violet's body, Lark clearly noticed the tremor, the short, shallow breaths that swelled her breasts against the confines of her bodice. "I will retire for the night, if nothing else is required of me."

"That's fine, you may go." Williams said. He nodded to the assembled group. "Good work, all of you. Dismissed."

Only Violet didn't respond. She stalked out of the room in a swirl of petticoats. Lark was just about to snuff her own crystal when Williams turned his head. His eyes fixed on her through the scrying crystal. Lark instinctively kicked herself backwards away from the crystal. The seat of her trousers skidded over the floor of the loft.

"Miss Greenpool, please see me immediately."

The tone brooked no disagreement. Lark shambled down the stairs and out of the dorm. Her heart pounded and a cold sweat broke out all over herself. She walked into the council-house and entered the now-silent and dark meeting room. Head up and unrepentant, she faced Ulric Williams, the top-ranking member of the Guardians, who had his arms crossed over his chest and looked at her with a set face.

Lark didn't know if she should attempt to explain or apologize. She stood with her hands shoved into her pockets. Guiltily, she dragged them out and clasped them behind herself in a more formal pose. She itched to go check on Violet. It seemed like she was teetering on the edge of something dangerous. Worry gnawed at Lark.

Indicating the crystal behind himself, Williams said, "This was a cunning idea, however there is a reason the events that take place in this room are confidential. I am going to relocate this item to the lounge. I trust the events of this night will remain in strictest confidence, and I do not expect any more attempts such as this one will take place in the future. If these guidelines are followed, I also see no reason to report this incident to anyone else."

"Yes sir," Lark said. A rush of relief weakened her knees.

"You are an adult and nearly a full-fledged Guardian," Williams said. "And as such, able to make decisions for yourself. Knowing that, I would like to ask you to see that our esteemed guest is not in any difficulty. It seems that of everyone here, only you have managed to form a favorable rapport with her. I fear for the safety of anyone else I could send on this errand. However, do not hesitate to summon assistance should you feel the situation requires it."

Startled enough that she could only gape, Lark stood there for a moment.

"Yes sir," she said. "May I go now?"

"Of course." He paused. "You were going to her no matter what I said, weren't you?" He said the words softly enough that Lark didn't have to answer. She didn't need to. They both knew it was true. The probing depth of the Head Guardian's eyes told Lark he had seen through her. Without another word, she made her escape, practically running through the compound.

She didn't stop until she knocked on the door to Violet's cottage.

"Are you all right? Please open the door, it's Lark." There was no answer. Lark pressed her ear to the rough wood. A dull thump filtered through. Alarmed and desperate to act, she tried the door. It was unlocked. With a grateful prayer that she didn't have to add lock picking to the list of illicit things she did that day, Lark eased the door open. She called out, "Violet, I'm coming in."

She scanned the room, but Violet was nowhere in sight. The door to the lavatory was ajar. She peeked in and her heart froze at the sight that met her eyes.

Violet was down on her knees on the tiles. She held a towel to her face that was stained through with crimson. Her shoulders shook. Her skin was so pale it was almost grey. The floor and commode were awash in vomit and blood. Lark threw herself down beside Violet and took her around the shoulders. She didn't care about the sickly warmth that seeped into the knees of her trousers.

"Violet, I'm here, it's going to be all right."

A pale hand reached out and pushed weakly at Lark. Violet shook her head. She pulled the towel away and attempted to speak before a violent spasm shook her. She coughed out a bloody stream, spattering droplets over her sleeves and front. Violet dragged in a shaking breath. She sagged heavily against the base of the sink. "Please go. I don't want you to see this."

"Hey, don't worry about me," Lark said. She reached up and grabbed another towel, which she used to dab at the hanging threads streaming from Violet's lips. The coughed-up blood coated her mouth red in an obscene parody of the way she used to paint her lips. In a matter-of-fact tone, Lark said, "I've birthed goats and butchered hogs. This here isn't going to beat that, not by a long shot. And you're in no condition to be left alone. Come on, can you try and stand? I want you off these cold tiles."

Violet allowed herself to be levered up. She gripped Lark's arms almost painfully tight. Lark held herself still and let Violet set the pace. Finally, Violet stood, her long skirts sodden with blood. She stumbled and Lark caught her in an instinctive embrace. The tremors that gripped Violet's slender frame echoed through Lark's body.

A few careful steps into the room, Lark helped Violet to sit on her bed, propped up against the pillows, before she raced back to the water closet for more towels. One of them she soaked in the warm water from the washstand's pitcher and returned to Violet's side with it in her hands. With only concern for Violet on her mind, Lark sank down onto the bed and carefully wiped Violet's face.

"Have you neutralized anything like that knot thing before?" Lark asked.

Violet's eyes widened. "How?"

"I saw what you did. There was a scrying crystal in the room and I used it—not out of simple curiosity. I was worried about you. Believe me, I'm not telling anyone what I saw. I would never betray your trust."

"I'm glad." Violet drew in a shaky breath.

"Are you going to be okay?"

"I will recover shortly, I just have to get this out," Violet gasped. She doubled over as a new wave of coughing gripped her. Lark was ready and pressed the damp towel into her hands. Lark grabbed the basin from the washstand and held it for Violet. Lark rubbed one hand up and down her back and murmured soft words of comfort. She noticed the blood was darker and came out in clotted clumps. Lark wondered if that was a good sign or not. Violet raised her head and reached out. She gripped Lark's hand. Haunted eyes sought Lark's. Violet said, "To answer your question, yes, I have done this a number of times before, but never with an artifact so strong or so evil. Never with one that had taken a life."

"What you did in there was a miracle," Lark said.

Violet released her grip on Lark to lean over and spit a mouthful of red chunks into the basin.

"It was not," Violet whispered. She dragged one long cuff over her chin. "For Rings and other artifacts with their own energy, I drain them and make them useless. But that is not my true power and curse." She lay back against the pillows and closed her eyes. Her chest heaved. After a number of labored breaths, she spoke again, "I do not use Rings, not wands or crystals either. I use people."

"It's okay, don't try to talk," Lark said.

Violet opened her eyes. She reached out to grab at Lark's hand once more.

"Listen to me, Lark. Anything I do, any energy I use, I must take from others. Living beings. Every item you've made, everything you have a strong bond, a 'mine' feeling, is a key to your life energy. If I have that object, I can use that connection to draw energy from you." She paused and put one hand over her mouth. Lark braced herself for another attack, but it seemed to subside and Violet bowed her dark head before she spoke again. "The more strongly bound an object is to one person, the deeper resources of energy I am able to access. Unfortunately, the source must suffer the effects. Taking too much energy at once can have fatal consequences. I am limited to only what the vessels can provide." She raised her head and looked at Lark directly, her eyes bright and urgent. "Do you see why it is dangerous for you to be around me? What if I forget myself, reach out for something and find you there? What if I drain more than you can provide? It only takes a thought."

"You would never hurt me," Lark said. "I know that."

"Do you?" The words were spat at her with such venom that a jolt of pain stabbed Lark in the chest. Speaking so much at once triggered another spell and Violet bent over, clutching her towel to her face. After the coughing had subsided, she slumped back, desperate breaths high and shallow in her chest, much too fast.

"I can't breathe," she gasped. She clutched at the delicate lace at the front of her bodice, tearing it in her frantic efforts. Her lips were a sick, bluish color. Perspiration gathered in the hollow of her collarbones.

Lark was on her feet in an instant. She said, "I'm getting Healer Andrews."

"No. Wands can do nothing for me." Violet said. Her shoulders heaved with the effort to drag air into her lungs. She lurched to her feet and clawed at her clothing. "Get this off me."

Immediately, Lark grabbed the back of Violet's bodice and tore it open in a spray of tiny buttons. Violet pulled at the laces at her sides. The rich black skirt and frothy petticoats spilled onto the floor. Lark stared, confused at the laced corset in front of her.

"Untie the knot at my waist," Violet gasped. Her head drooped. "Quickly."

"You'll be all right soon as can be," Lark said. She yanked at the laces with trembling fingers and the knot slipped free. With a practiced jerk, Violet unhooked the fasteners at the front and the garment fell to the floor.

Free of the constricting corset, Violet dredged in a shuddering breath. She clapped a hand over her mouth and staggered into
the little lavatory, where she bent over the commode one more
time. Lark kept a watchful eye on Violet's back as she whirled the
discarded clothing over the privacy screen. She grabbed her wand
and did a lightning fast cleansing sweep of them as well as the
blood-speckled sheets. Her heart ached for what Violet was going
through. For the first time she understood how dangerous the
mission was. A thought stole Lark's breath, leaving her shaken
and cold. What if Violet never meant to return to her home
because she knew the cost of success was her life? Tears stung at
her eyes and Lark swallowed them down. She vowed to find a
way so that inevitability would not happen.

Lark worked quickly. She gathered up the soiled towels and
put them in a rain bucket she located behind the door. Almost as
an afterthought, she crouched down and swept up the scattered
buttons and set them and the garment they came from on the window seat.

Lark didn't know how much blood a person could lose and
still function. For an instant, she wished she had her family Almanac handy so she could look it up. She'd just finished putting the
room into order when Violet reappeared. She leaned heavily on
the lavatory doorframe and looked like a nightmare, but the calm,
even breaths put Lark at ease. It appeared the worst was over.
Violet took a tottering step toward Lark, who met her halfway.
She gathered Violet up in her arms and simply held her.

"You're going to be okay," Lark murmured. She drew in a
reverent breath as Violet nestled against her.

Lark's heart thundered, her entire body trembled with the
wave of emotion sparked by the woman in her embrace, but Lark
ruthlessly fought it down. It was not the time for such things. She
concentrated on guiding Violet over to the bed. Lark eased her
down to the pillows as gently as she could. Lark would not think
of the resilient softness of the body pressed against hers, separated by the thinnest muslin. She would not allow herself to
understand the completion she felt at the trusting way Violet
leaned against her.

Lark straightened up quickly and raked her hair back. She
said, "You're looking a sight better, I have to say. How about a bit
of tea?"

With a nod, Violet hitched herself higher on her pillows and accepted the mug. She sipped at it slowly, quiet and withdrawn in the wake of the earlier excitement. While Violet drank her tea, Lark dampened a fresh towel and came over to Violet's side. She hesitated for a moment before she perched on the side of the bed and held the offering out for Violet to take. The cream-colored muslin undershift clung to Violet's body, sweat-damp and nearly translucent. It was thinner and more delicate then anything Lark had ever seen before. Her face got warm. Lark forced her gaze to wander over the inside of the cottage, away from temptation.

"How about I get your nightdress?" Lark jumped to her feet.

"Yes, please. And my waist-pocket too."

Happy to comply, soon Lark was back at Violet's side. She watched with interest as Violet delved into one of the pair of delicately embroidered pockets and took out a slim, brightly colored paper box. Violet popped two small tablets from a sheet of them and swallowed them with a gulp of tea.

Perhaps sensing Lark's fascinated look, Violet got the ghost of a smile on her lips and said, "Outsider alchemy. These treat headaches and other pain."

"That's right clever," Lark said. "Where did you get something like that?"

Violet stuffed the box back into her pocket and said, "Where do you think the disappearing Ringsworn families are going? We only have a single city left to us in the Protected Isles. Those who have left need to return from time to time, to keep their abilities. Sometimes they take lodging in my convent and share what small resources they have."

"How about that?" Lark said. At once she was saddened by the loss of a people she never knew. Aware of how close they were, she stood once more. "It seems like you're all right, praise Summer Rain. Anyway, I don't want to impose any more, I should be—"

"Would you stay? Just for a short time," Violet asked. She looked more vulnerable than Lark had ever seen her.

Lark couldn't refuse, but she had to be calm and act normal. Violet had been through enough injury that day without Lark adding insult to it.

With what she hoped was a carefree nod, Lark twitched her wand into her hand. She said, "How about you get yourself comfortable and I'll clean up in there? It'll only take two shakes of a duck's tail."

Lark ducked into the disaster area of the water closet and swept the walls and floor clean. Her sure movements sent everything in a tight spiral down the drain. She caught a glimpse of herself in the mirror over the little hand-washing faucet and was startled at the streaks of dried blood on her hands, face and clothing. With a few splashes of cool water and a pass of her wand, Lark took care of herself. Satisfied, she returned to the main room and was relieved to see Violet, changed into her nightdress, sitting up in her bed with the black tablecloth pulled over her lap. In the candlelight, she looked quite calm, if still a bit weak.

"Thank you," Violet said. Under the blankets, she drew her knees up to her chest. "That must have taken a lot out of you, all that cleaning. From what I have observed, Wanderers do not usually choose to expend their energy that way."

Lark shrugged and sprawled down on the window seat. She kicked her legs out and crossed her ankles, projecting confidence she didn't feel. Lark said, "I'm a sturdy country-gal, stuff like that's my specialty."

"Indeed," Violet replied with an arch of one brow. She pulled the blankets around herself and curled up like a sleepy kitten. She settled against the pillows and asked in a soft voice, "Would you stay until I am sleeping?"

"Sure will, if that's your wish," Lark said. She tried to ignore the thudding of her heart, the rush of protectiveness that was tempered by something else she desperately did not want to feel. She folded her hands behind her head and leaned back in her seat. "Want to hear a funny story?" Lark asked.

"Okay." The casual word sounded odd but good coming from Violet.

Lark launched into a dramatic retelling of her disastrous entrance to the outpost that had Violet stifling her giggles into a pillow and Lark breathed much easier at her recovery. Guiltily, Lark picked up the damaged bodice and dug out her needle and spool of thread. While she sewed the buttons back on, Lark talked about a number of funny things that happened to her. Being rather thoughtless and accident-prone, Lark had quite a few stories to tell.

After a while, Lark ran out of stories and the room fell into a comfortable silence. Violet's eyes drifted closed somewhere along the line and Lark sat still, content to just exist in that moment in time with the mended garment on her lap. The bodice in her hands was lined and the stiff material had conformed to the contours of Violet's body, bearing small creases here and there. The garment was a style Lark had never seen before and seemed quite old. Lark wondered if Violet made it herself or if she came across it another way. Unconsciously, Lark stroked her hands down over the garment.

Her gaze softened as Violet's breaths deepened. Lark put aside the bodice and leaned back in the window seat. She reached behind herself to tuck a cushion a bit more securely into the small of her back. Far from being disgusted by that evening's events, Lark felt more physically close to Violet than she ever had. After all, she had Violet's blood and who knows what else all over herself until a few minutes ago, not to mention the fact that she'd practically ripped Violet's dress off. Her lips twitched into a crooked grin in spite of herself. That certainly was a new experience.

Even though an arm's length and a half separated them, Lark was hyperaware of the rise and fall of Violet's chest, the small shifts she made as she snuggled deeper into the blankets. Her face was relaxed and soft in repose. Violet was always so strong and mysterious, so independent and angry. So different from what she was at that moment. Lark was certain only a few people, if any, had ever been allowed to see that side of her. She was honored and humbled by that knowledge. Lark finally admitted to herself that she wanted nothing more than to hold Violet in her arms, kiss her like a man kissed a woman. And she didn't want to stop at kissing.

It would never happen. Lark would live her life and die untouched. She couldn't bear the thought of giving herself to any fellow, and certainly no woman would want her, least of all Violet.

Lark leaned forward, her body folded around the sharp pain that hit her right in the gut. She buried her face in her hands and let out a long breath. Being so close to Violet, walking that razor-edge where one slip would end everything would be torture. She couldn't do it. Lark raised her head and gazed at Violet, lying defenseless in slumber. She was their last hope in a battle against a force of nature that would destroy everything and everyone in Lark's world. If she found out, there was no doubt she would be disgusted and shocked. If Violet left in anger, the chances of winning that battle were close to nothing.

There was only one choice. Lark didn't have the strength to fight her newly-awakened desire. She would fail in her control and invite untold disaster. Tears welled up in her eyes and Lark impatiently scrubbed a cuff over her face. The only answer was for Lark to step away, end all contact and put a stop to the temptations that threatened to derail the most important alliance in their history. There would be no more clandestine meetings in the pantry shed, no fun evening chats in Violet's cottage, and absolutely no more hugs, accidental or otherwise.

Lark went to the side of the bed. She looked down at Violet one more time, trying to burn the image into her mind. Lark wished she could stay there in that moment of peace for all eternity. Reluctantly, Lark snuffed the candle. In the darkness, she reached out and her hand unerringly found Violet's brow. With a feather-light touch, she smoothed the silken strands back. In slumber, Violet moved under Lark's hand, pressing into her palm. Lark squeezed her eyes shut at the rush of desire born from the simple touch.

She wrenched herself away and banged her elbow against the door as she stumbled outside with the rain bucket of soiled towels swinging from one arm. Lark didn't feel the chill bite of the night air, she didn't see the glittering sprawl of stars overhead. She walked on numb legs to the clothes washing shed.

Lark slumped down onto the bench that ran the length of the room. She leaned her head back against the wall. She listened to the sloshing of the washer and tried to ignore the deep ache in her chest along with the feeling that she had made a terrible mistake.

Chapter Twelve

LARK MANAGED TO avoid everyone until the next morning. After she took the towels off the line and folded them, she left them on the windowsill of Violet's cottage at a time when she knew Violet was in her morning meeting. Lark turned from the cottage and walked away without looking back.

From that day, she changed her routine to rising as late as possible, often missing breakfast entirely and proceeding directly to her morning lectures. She only moved around in full daylight and traded her turns washing the supper dishes with anyone who would take her up on the offer. Because of that, Lark spent most of her free time mucking out the chicken barn, cleaning and maintaining their septic system, as well as doing just about every other chore nobody else wanted to do. She stayed far away from the baths and snuck into the Wellness Center to avail herself of the shower there when she got too grubby to stand herself.

Lark joined every social activity going, making sure she was surrounded at all times with a clot of giggling, chatting obstacles that stood between her and the dark Ringsworn. A few times, Lark glanced across the meal hall to catch Violet's gaze on her. The first time, the confusion in her eyes stabbed Lark through the chest. The second time, the confusion was tempered by anger. Lark swallowed her regret and told herself it was for the best. The only thing she couldn't bring herself to do was take off the garnet bracelet.

Exactly one week to the day that Lark had decided to end her relationship with Violet, Lark sat on her bed in a rare moment of solitude. That day, she couldn't summon the energy to plaster on the fake smile and keep up her end of the banter-filled conversations the other fledglings liked to indulge in. She rested her hands on her knees and closed her eyes as a deep weariness came over her. Alice bounded into the room with a cheerful greeting that snapped Lark to annoyed attention.

"Lark, are you going?" Alice asked.

"I've already been to the privy if that's what you want to

know," Lark said. She found the book she tossed impatiently onto the bedspread earlier, which happened to be *Amelia Strawberry and the Clue in the Pyramid*, and flipped through it. She wished Alice would go away.

"I mean to the social," Alice said.

"Social? Here? I didn't notice anything."

"They've been decorating the practice hall since yesterday. Coaches have been dropping off musicians and guests all day. Cook Brown's had everyone hauling around jugs of ale and barrels of beer since lunch. How did you not notice all that?"

Lark shrugged. She set the book aside and stretched out on her bed with her hands behind her head. "I'm not interested in that sort of thing."

"Honestly it's not really my thing either," Alice said. "I'm only going to show up to grab some food and see if I can swipe a bottle of something. A bunch of us are getting together for a bonfire. Come and join in. I'm sure it'll be a lot better than any old social."

"No thanks," Lark said.

"Are you okay?" Alice asked in a quiet voice. "You've been a bit...odd recently."

A flash of anger flared through Lark. She swallowed it and put on a fake smile. As cheerfully as she could, she said, "I'm fine, Alice. Maybe a bit tired, but don't worry about me."

"All right," Alice said, but she didn't sound convinced. She ducked into her own cubby and rustled around.

Lark stared at the ceiling until she heard Alice leave. In the silence, Lark was left alone with her thoughts. She couldn't forget the feeling of Violet in her arms, how their bodies had melted together. It was the last time Lark felt whole.

She rolled over as an ache deep in her gut flared into life. Lark wished she could take her unwanted feelings and turn them to dust like Violet had done to the artifact. She was a Guardian, she shouldn't waste her energy pining over something she could never have. Lark's stomach growled, protesting the fact she'd skipped both breakfast and lunch. Lark sat up too quickly and the room tilted. She grabbed at the bedcovers to right herself. She rubbed at her belly and got to her feet. No matter how much her heart suffered, her stomach was still alive and well.

Lark slung her wand over her shoulder before she left the

dormitory. She felt like a burglar picking her way across the compound. She hoped she didn't run into anybody who would insist she join the festivities. Lark breezed through the refreshments table and got a mug of punch and a sandwich before she ducked out the back door of the large hall. The lively fiddle music and talking voices faded behind her.

She found a secluded spot under a tree beside the practice hall. Lark folded her legs and sat down with her back against the tree trunk.

Through the bright windows, Lark watched the people on the dance floor, singles, groups, and couples. Rosalie had a serious-looking man hovering over her with his hands full of punch cups and cookies. He was unremarkable other than the fact he combed his hair back in a way that made it look like he had a shiny black helmet resting on his head. Lark's attention soon drifted.

One couple caught her eye. Jean and Medina swayed together at one side of the room. Medina had her eyes closed and her head rested on Jean's shoulder. Lark told Violet that wasn't normal. Lark wished with all her heart she never said that. It *was* normal. For Lark anyway.

Every moment sent a shaft of pain through her chest, but Lark couldn't take her attention from the social. She regretted turning her back on Violet, but she didn't know what else to do. She hoped Violet would move on, maybe make new friends who weren't cowardly and aberrant like Lark was.

Galled by the festivities and disgusted by her own actions, Lark poured out the rest of her punch and stalked off into the night. She headed back to the dormitory and stopped short at the sight of the bonfire, which crackled merrily between the buildings and was surrounded by a jovial group of fledglings plus a number of other junior staff members. Lark grimaced and tried to slip past it unnoticed, when a bright voice called out to her.

"Hey, you did decide to come after all," Alice said. "Come on over, I saved you a seat." She waved the bottle she was drinking out of as a greeting.

"Thanks," Lark said. She gave up on her idea of slinking off alone and hunkered down next to Alice, who immediately poured her a glass of strong cider. Lark was about to take a sip when the lively gathering went deathly quiet. Lark raised her head. Her entire body seized up. Violet stood in the shadows, the firelight flickered over her long skirts and caught the sparkle from her hair-combs. Her face was an impassive mask, but tension sizzled off her limbs.

Violet ignored the whispers and Alice's squawked exclamation of "Elvira!" and crossed the threshold between darkness and light. Hurriedly, a few people moved back to open up a spot. Without even acknowledging Lark, she sank down in a puff of sheer black over ruby silk. For an instant Lark considered leaving, but decided she was better off staying where she was. At least the others were there to provide, if nothing else, the illusion of protection.

"If I may be so bold as to invite myself to your festivities," Violet said. Her voice was low and as dark as the new moon. "I don't come empty-handed." With that, she produced a sizeable bottle of something labeled "Midnight Blood Wine" from the folds in her skirts.

"Hey, welcome to the party!" Alice fell over her feet and had to enlist the help of the people on either side of her to get herself upright again.

Violet opened the bottle and, to Lark's surprise, poured some into her own worn, red mug. Very deliberately, she raised the mug to her mouth and drained it in three measured swallows. Only after she set her empty mug down, did she offer the wine around. The assembled partygoers accepted happily and Violet poured generous glassfuls for anyone who wanted, but only sipped water herself. Lark did so as well. She had a feeling that night would not benefit from drunkenness. Around Lark, everyone talked and laughed and drank, but she could only think of the dark presence sitting across from her.

When the last of the wine was poured into a waiting glass, Violet stood. She looked over the gathering.

"Thank you for a lovely evening, but I must depart," Violet said.

Her announcement was met by a volley of farewells and thanks. Violet acknowledged them with a regal bow of her head. She turned her dark gaze on Lark, who froze. The rage simmering under the surface of Violet's impassive expression came to the surface. Her eyes flashed and her lip curled.

"Miss Greenpool," Violet said in a low growl. "Please see me to my room."

Lark stood. She had a feeling if she didn't walk out with Violet of her own volition she would be dragged bodily.

In silence, they crossed the grassy field. Violet opened the door to her cottage.

"Come inside for a moment," she said. It was an order, not a request.

Lark did as she was asked. She never thought she would see the inside of Violet's cottage again. Lark's heart pounded. Violet stood before her, her back to the closed door. She twisted her fingers together, face drawn and dangerous. She took a step toward Lark, who backed up automatically.

"Answer my question honestly," Violet said.

"Yes ma'am," Lark croaked.

"Why have you been avoiding me?" She barked the words out.

"I, uh." Lark stopped speaking and chewed her lip. How could she answer that? Her mind whirled. The back of her legs hit the window seat and Lark fell onto it. Violet loomed over her, not giving an inch. The quirk of humor on her lips, the flash of softness she sometimes let slip was gone, like it had never existed.

It was the end. Lark's eyes welled up with tears of shame. They might have been shards of glass for the pain they caused her as they spilled over. Desperate to squash the wave of emotion, she scuffed her sleeve over her face. The garnet bracelet rolled over her wrist, comforting and cool against her overheated skin.

"Tears will not save you." Violet hurled the words at Lark. "I am immune to them. And you have not answered my question. Do not make me repeat it, Wanderer."

"I'm sorry," Lark said. She didn't know what else to say and she was truly sorry—for everything. She gripped her hands together and tried to make them stop shaking. "I acted like a chicken-hearted kid. I ran away when I should have stayed right here."

"You are afraid of me." Violet stated that as a fact. "While I commend your sense of self-preservation, I believe I deserve at least the courtesy of an explanation. However, I already know why you left me. Your disgust at what I am, what you learned that night sent you running. I do not blame you. I am a monster."

Lark shook her head. She was afraid, but not of Violet. "I'm glad you let me help you and told me the truth about yourself. It didn't scare me then and it still doesn't. I ran for a different reason."

"Why then?" Violet snapped. She shook her head. "I was a fool to believe we could be friends."

"I really did want to be friends with you, but I can't anymore," Lark whispered. Violet's look of shocked pain spurred Lark to speak. "I can't be *just* friends with you. I want more than that. Violet, I want something a woman shouldn't. I want—I want more than your friendship. If I was a fellow I'd court you. I would do everything in my power to make you my lady. I swear on this Great Green Land I didn't ever plan to do anything to hurt you or disrespect you. I'm so sorry I had to be like this, feel this way when it's wrong, but I can't stop it and now I've wrecked everything."

After the storm of Lark's rushed babbling ended, Violet was silent. Lark wished she'd do something. Scream at her, throw her out, or laugh cruelly, mocking Lark's confession. Lark didn't expect what happened next.

In a rich swish of skirts, Violet sank to her knees in front of Lark and urged herself between Lark's spread knees. She reached out and placed her hands on either side of Lark's body. Violet leaned forward. They were so close, Lark felt the heat from her skin, heard the quick breath she took.

"You want to be more than friends," Violet said. "Close companions, perhaps in an intimate way?"

Lark could only nod. Shame burned on her cheeks.

"And you think I don't?"

Lark gaped. Violet was still looking up at her. The anger was gone, replaced with a searching expression. Lark's heart leapt. Violet wasn't going to lash out at her. Just the opposite, in fact. Her lips were parted, looking soft, inviting. She didn't move, just gazed at Lark, waiting. Lark's body burned, her breath came faster.

"You think I don't remember every time you touched me?" Each word rang through Lark like an arrow of light. Violet said, "Every time you made me laugh and every time you shared some tidbit of your life with me—I lived for those moments." Violet pressed forward until only the smallest distance separated them. For a moment, she dropped her gaze to Lark's mouth, which was hanging slightly open in shock, then back to meet Lark's eyes. She whispered, "I never thought you would feel the same. You aren't the only one who has been hiding, too well and needlessly it seems. Lark, what you want from me, I am willing to give. All you have to do is take it."

Violet hadn't rejected her.

Lark blinked rapidly. "What do you mean...take it?" Lark asked in a cracked voice. She couldn't afford any misunderstanding.

"Reach out to me," Violet said. "Touch me, if that is what you truly want. I will not refuse you."

Lark couldn't stop herself. She reached out as if to a butterfly poised on a leaf and took Violet's face in her hands. Violet's skin under her fingers released a feeling as if her insides turned to molten gold. Lark ran her thumb over the fullness of Violet's lower lip. Her heart thundered. She barely dared to breathe. Violet leaned into the caress, the shadow of a smile turned up her lips. Lark couldn't move.

Violet's deep eyes drifted closed. She whispered, "Take what we both want, Lark. Please."

That was enough to convince Lark to take the next step. She bent down and closed the distance between them.

The first brush of their lips was soft and hesitant. Lark drew in a breath of pure wonder at the shockwave of emotion unleashed by the contact. Where they met, a flame ignited and filled her entire body. Nothing had ever felt that good, or that right. Violet's hands came up and covered Lark's as their lips came together again. This time, the kiss was full and sweet. Violet moved against her. She responded to Lark's lips on hers with gentle pressure, which made Lark's brain explode into a dizzy storm of joy. Everything came alive at once. Lark's body thrummed with energy, her pulse pounded in the depths of her belly, her skin tingled with the need to be touched.

The feelings threatened to overwhelm Lark. She drew back from Violet with lingering reluctance. Lark gazed down at Violet. She could scarcely believe what had just happened. Lark pressed her fingertips to her own lips and let out a long, shuddering breath.

"That was...wow, that was unbelievable," Lark said. "Green Trees, I never thought it would be like that."

Violet rose and settled down next to Lark on the window

seat. She twined her long fingers around Lark's. Her usually moonlight-pale cheeks were flushed and she looked singularly lovely in the candlelight with her hair slightly tousled, her rosy lips wet from their kisses.

"We need to talk about this."

"Yeah, we do," Lark said. She blinked and tried to get her brain working again.

"Tomorrow," Violet said. She let go of Lark's hands, then reached out and drew Lark to her.

The kiss started out slowly, carefully. Lark's hands drifted to take Violet around the waist. Their bodies came together. Violet's lips against hers were soft. It wasn't enough. Lark drew her lips over Violet's, gently seeking more. She waited until she felt Violet respond to her before she increased the contact between them. A burning thrill took hold of Lark by the chest and she couldn't stop the urge to give herself to the kiss. Violet's breath quickened in time with her own.

Violet's hands moved up to Lark's shoulders. Her deft fingers stroked through Lark's hair. She cradled the back of Lark's head and wordlessly demanded a deeper kiss. With a moan of desire burning in her lungs, Lark consented. She opened her mouth. She couldn't hold back the need to taste Violet, the need to give her more. Lark's offer was accepted. Their tongues met with wet hunger.

A jolt ripped from her chest down through the pit of her belly. Lark pressed herself fully against Violet's body. She loved the feeling of Violet against her lips, within her mouth.

Under Lark's hands, Violet's body was hard, her waist small and tight, which only made Lark even more aware of the glorious softness pressed against her chest. Lark's heart thundered against her wraps. Her gut clenched, a gush of liquid need surged between her legs, called by the feeling of Violet in her arms. Her entire body was inflamed by the tiny sounds of pleasure Violet made in her throat. The lips against her own grew hungry and insistent. Lark was more than happy to comply. She lost herself in the embrace. She let her mouth claim Violet's and be claimed in turn. Lark rode the rush of arousal until she thought she would explode.

When they finally parted, both trembling and gasping for air, Lark leaned her forehead against Violet's, not willing to lose the contact so soon.

"You will not run away?" Violet asked, her voice was husky and low.

"Never again," Lark said. She straightened her back and rubbed a hand through her hair. "I'm sorry I left you all alone like that. You were right to be angry, it was the most hurtful and thoughtless—" Her words faded as Violet placed a finger on her lips.

"I forgive you," Violet said. She took Lark's face in her hands and brushed her thumbs over Lark's cheeks as if smoothing away tear-tracks. Her brow furrowed and she pressed her lips together. "I don't ever want to be the cause of your tears again," she said in a sorrowful voice that belied her earlier claim to immunity.

"It's okay," Lark said. "That wasn't your fault. You make me smile way more."

Violet dropped her hands with a slight smile of her own. "I trust you won't make any more unilateral decisions about our relationship?"

Lark shook her head. "Nope. At least, not on purpose."

"I'm gratified to hear that." With a reluctant glance at the sand-clock on the wall, Violet said, "As much as I don't want this evening to end, it's late and I have kept you long enough."

"You're right, it's past midnight." Lark jumped up and tucked her shirt back into her belt. "It's going to be like ploughing clay getting to sleep tonight," she said with a wry grin.

"Agreed," Violet said. Her eyes grew dark and sultry. She purred in a low voice, more to herself than Lark, "But I think you will manage to find a way."

Lark had her hand on the door to open it, but paused. A powerful force called her back. She couldn't leave without touching Violet one last time. Lark turned. She didn't even speak before Violet moved. Lark's back landed against the door as Violet surged up against her. The kiss was hard, desperate from the first instant, as if once Lark stepped through that door the spell would break and what had passed between them would vanish like frost at dawn.

Finally, she pulled herself from the intoxicating circle of Violet's arms.

They exchanged heated, whispered goodnights before Lark walked back to her dormitory. Her eyes were unfocused and a song of sweetness thrummed through her from her head to her toes. Instead of taking out her calming knot of turquoise and using it to lull her to sleep, Lark lay awake. A long time passed before she did sleep, preferring to run over the events of that evening in her mind. Her life changed the instant Violet's lips met hers. Lark crossed a bridge and she would never go back. The other fledglings trickled in, reeking of drink, giggling and fumbling around in the dark as they got ready for bed. Lark curled up and pretended to be asleep, idly stroking the garnet bracelet on her wrist.

THE NEXT MORNING, Lark was the first one up. She felt reborn.

Instead of her usual outfit of jaunty trousers and body-hugging top which stank of wood smoke and the cider Alice spilled on her at one point, Lark shook out a tunic and long skirt from her clothes box at the foot of her bed, both of a deep blue color. As soon as she was dressed, Lark wasted no time as she strode up and down the long room, whacking the groaning masses in the other beds.

"Up and at 'em kids!" she called out. She skipped the length of the room and threw open the windows. The clear autumn sunlight streamed in and invited a fresh wave of moaning. The girls who hadn't been at the drinking party the night before started their morning routines with a few pitying glances at the afflicted members.

"Why are you so cheerful?" Alice sat up in her bed. She looked a fright with her hair standing up in all directions. She grabbed up her blanket and peered underneath it with an expression of horror on her face. "And why am I wearing a potato sack?"

"Because you lost the dice game," Nora told her. She staggered over to the water closet and shut herself into it.

"Awww..." Alice groaned as she fell back into her mess of blankets. "I'm not going to get up today. Lark, just tell everybody I've temporarily died."

"No way am I letting you take the easy way out," Lark said. She stood at the front of the room with her hands on her hips. "You stay here and I stay with you. And you know what? I think

I'm in the mood to sing." Lark took a deep breath and was just about to launch into a lively tune when Alice's body hit the floor. Her bare feet scrambled around, making her potato sack ride up over her knee-length drawers.

"Okay, okay, I'm up!" She fell over one of the other fledglings, who was on her way to the row of washstands.

Even though she was the recipient of several nasty glares and a few rather sincere-sounding threats, Lark organized the groaning and complaining fledglings into a loose group on their way to the dining hall. En route she found a nearly-comatose Bethanie outside the junior staff house and led her over to their table. Lark distributed strong tea to her tablemates while teasing them with big bowls of oatmeal and muffins which nobody wanted. After a while, Murray stumbled to their table, where Alice and Nora slept on their breakfasts and Bethanie sipped gingerly at her mug of tea. He stopped in his tracks and looked Lark up and down.

"You're not dead," he said.

"Nope." Lark raised her head from her bowl, spoon in her mouth.

"All arms and legs still attached, no impaled objects that I can see," Murray said. He moved around to inspect the rest of Lark. She swatted him off. "Yup, definitely alive and unscathed."

"You know what that means," Alice said. She held out her hand.

"Uh huh," Murray said with a sigh. He dug a few coins from his pocket and passed them over.

Lark dropped her spoon in astonishment. "You had a bet going on whether Violet would kill me or not?"

"Murray wagered on that," Alice said.

"It makes sense," Murray said with his hands held out in appeal. "My Great Auntie Pacifica always told me to end arguments in a decisive way, and there's nothing more decisive than death."

"Uh huh," Alice said. "You too, girls, pay up."

Nora and Bethanie handed over their coins. Alice made a show of counting her newly-acquired wealth.

"What did the rest of you wager?" Lark asked. She folded her arms over her chest and frowned.

Bethanie answered, "I bet on missing limbs and Nora was sure you'd come back on a stake."

"Thanks for the vote of confidence," Lark said. She fixed Alice with a long look and got a sudden burst of nerves. "Alice, you didn't say anything. What did you wager?"

With a smirk, Alice turned back to her mug. "That would be telling."

Lark muttered and rummaged around in the muffin basket. She froze as heavy footsteps echoed through the room. They came to a halt directly behind her. Lark twisted in her seat and looked up at Violet who loomed over her. Even though she had her fists planted on her hips and a dark look on her face, the raw fury Lark had seen the night before wasn't there. In its place a wicked light danced in her eyes.

"You, Wanderer," Violet snapped. Around them, people edged their chairs away. Ignoring the reactions to her sudden appearance, Violet stamped her foot. The sharp retort sent the entire room into shocked silence. "In the library, *now*." She turned and stalked out of the hall in a liquid flurry of skirts.

Lark didn't miss the alarmed look that passed between her tablemates as she hastened to follow. Her own long skirts whipped about her legs until Lark grabbed them up and shoved them into her belt.

"No sense of organization, keeping the best books up on the highest shelves. Honestly," Violet said. "It is a shame and an embarrassment to be forced to deal with this level of incompetence."

As they went through the compound, Violet kept up a fierce monologue that lasted until the heavy oak door of the library closed behind them. Violet, still in predator-mode, backed Lark into one long aisle. At that time of the morning, the library was deserted. Surrounded by weighty tomes, Violet stood before Lark in silence. Her expression was no longer angry or even teasing. She looked unsure, vulnerable.

Violet didn't meet Lark's eyes. She said, "I'm sure you despise me for coercing you last night. I overstepped. I forced you to admit something you didn't want to and I took advantage of that." She raked a hand through her hair, her eyes on the floor. "I can promise not to do it again. I will not lose your friendship."

Lark couldn't speak. More than anything, she needed to touch Violet and reassure both of them. She reached out and trailed her fingertips over Violet's cheek. Lark could barely contain herself as she very gently stroked a thumb over Violet's cherry-kissed lips, just as she had done the previous night. A small gasp and flush met Lark's caress.

"I could never despise you," Lark said. She ached with the pain she saw in Violet's face. She hated how something so wonderful and pure was the cause of such self-doubt. Lark wanted nothing more than to banish that look from Violet's face forever. "I went to you of my own free will. Know this Violet, I stand by what I said. And what I did."

The transformation of Violet's expression to joy took Lark's breath away.

"What we did," Violet murmured. She took a step forward which closed the distance between them. "Am I correct in assuming we should not announce this new development?"

"Probably," Lark said. Her body ached for Violet's. Even though it was a semi-public area, she wrapped her arms around Violet's waist and pulled her close. Violet nestled against her. Lark lowered her head and murmured into Violet's hair, "The timing, as well as who we are. I guess it might be better to keep things quiet for a while."

Violet nodded with a heavy sigh.

"Not always," Lark said. She let one hand drift up and down Violet's taut back. "I don't want to keep this a secret forever. Just for now."

"I can live with that," Violet said.

The physical communication drew out as they lingered against each other. After what Lark felt was not nearly long enough, Violet broke the contact and drifted back a step. She clasped her hands in front of herself as she looked across the small distance that separated them. Her lips quirked up. "And am I also correct in the assumption that you have not done this before?"

Lark's cheeks burned. She said, "You're right about that." She rubbed a hand through her hair and gave Violet a grin and a shrug. "Crystalgazers aren't the most progressive folks around. It took me far too long to figure things out. I'm sorry to say I was a bit of a gosling for a while."

"That's nothing to be ashamed of. I was fortunate the Ringsworn do not suffer under the same backwards-thinking ways your people do," Violet said in an amused tone.

"But you were raised in a convent," Lark blurted out.

With the arch of one eyebrow, Violet said, "It is true I revere the goddess Limor, but I never joined the Sisterhood or took their vow of celibacy." She got that wicked gleam in her eye that never failed to send a thrill through Lark as she continued, "In addition to that, our halls of worship are receptacles of the long-held knowledge of my people. If nothing else, I've had the opportunity to study the ways of women. In theory anyway."

"They have those kinds of books in a convent? Green Trees." Lark muttered. Violet answered with nothing more than a mysterious look. "All right then," Lark said. She leaned one shoulder back against the bookshelf. "I spilled my secret, now it's your turn. How many times have you done this?"

"Once." The answer was quiet, Violet's eyes faraway. "It was more than ten years ago. A group of travelers lodged at my convent for a month, waiting for the winter freeze so they could pass over our border. I watched her from my tower and dreamed. The day they left I slipped down." Her lips turned up, the smile was heartbreaking. "I kissed her goodbye."

"You don't want to meet her again?" Lark asked. A shard of apprehension pierced her chest.

"No," Violet said. "Once was enough for her. You, on the other hand..." She didn't get to finish, the sound of the door creaking open interrupted them.

By the time the group of accountants entered, Lark was standing with a stack of books in her arms and Violet in front of her, with a look of satisfaction on her face.

"Those should be sufficient to keep me amused for this week, anyway," Violet said. She ignored the other people who skirted nervously around her. "Deliver my reading material to my cottage. You are dismissed."

"Yes, ma'am." Lark hid her laughter behind the stack of books on her way to the lending desk. She balanced her load on one knee while she hastily scribbled down the titles. She hoped nobody thought it odd that Violet's selection consisted of four cookbooks, the G to L volumes of their insect encyclopedia, a massive Outsider-made book called a road atlas, and a geometry textbook.

Just as she left the library with her load, Lark heard someone who sounded very much like Violet remarking in an airy way, "At least one of you is proving themselves useful."

Chapter Thirteen

FOR THE REST of the day, Lark was busy with lectures and practice and Violet with meetings so they weren't able to see each other, but Violet never left Lark's thoughts for a moment. Lark walked around with a huge grin on her face that nothing could eclipse. She daydreamed through lunch and didn't even mind when Alice swiped half of her pumpkin tart and pranked her by filling her tea mug with vinegar. She waved off questions about how she managed to survive the encounter with an enraged Violet the previous night. At dusk, she ended up on the big fallen tree where she gazed up at the darkening sky.

Lark thought back to the night she put her arms around Violet on that very log, and her body stirred in memory. Lark's mind drifted to where her path was leading and she caught her breath in alarm. She had very little idea exactly *what* she was supposed to do. Lark shifted on the rough bark and knit her brow.

She had no idea how to proceed. She had no rules to follow. The books Violet alluded to didn't exist in Lark's world. If they did, she would have certainly found them and devoured them. Lark winced. A worried pain started up in her gut. She wished she could talk to someone about her situation, maybe get some advice, but nobody could help her. The best Lark could expect was awkward platitudes, or worse, complete rejection.

Lark chewed on her knuckle, deep in thought. Then it hit her. There was someone she could talk to, if she only got her nerve up. Before she could convince herself otherwise, Lark jumped off the tree and hurried through the compound. Her long strides took her into the cluster of cottages. She stopped in front of one and knocked.

The door creaked open.

"Why if it isn't Lark," Medina exclaimed. She smiled and opened the door. "Come on in."

"Um, if it isn't a bad time."

"Not at all," Medina said. She ushered Lark into the cottage. Unlike Violet's, it had a sitting room with a low table surrounded by comfortable-looking armchairs. One of the armchairs held Lark's mentor, who looked up from the book she was reading.

"Mentor Elliott," Lark began. She twisted her fingers together.

"Jean," the older woman interrupted gently. "You're a Guardian now."

"All right. Jean," Lark repeated. She nervously licked her lips before she said in a rush, "I wanted to talk to you about Violet. And me. About something I realized about myself recently."

Jean studied Lark for a beat. She drew in a slow breath. "Sit down, child," she said in a soft voice.

Automatically, Lark whirled her wand off and propped it against the armchair opposite Jean before she sank down into it. Medina bustled around and set down a trio of mugs on the table, but nobody moved to pick one up.

"I'm not surprised to be having this discussion with you Lark," Jean said. "I know you've been spending a lot of time with Violet and I can see that's helped some things become clear for you. Of anyone here, she's the one who wouldn't judge you for being your true self. She can probably explain the things you've been wondering about better than any of us can."

Lark nearly fell out of her chair. Jean knew! Violet couldn't have told her, could she? Maybe it was Lark herself who had somehow given it away. Sweat popped out on her back and soaked into her wraps.

There was no way to go but forward. Now that her secret was out, Lark couldn't stop the words. She said, "I've always felt— different. From the time I was a youngun and it never got better. I tried to be like everyone else, really I did, but I just couldn't. Then I met Violet. I couldn't stay away from her, it's like we share some kind of connection."

With a soft nod, Jean said, "You and she have much in common."

"You're right, we do," Lark said. Her voice nearly gave out. Lark got a shy, fluttering feeling in her belly. She'd never spoken of such things so frankly. She hadn't been able to admit the truth even to herself until very recently. Lark picked up the mug of tea, more to occupy her hands than anything else. She said, "I should be happy, but I don't know what to do. I never learned how to be *myself*."

"It's all right to be confused at first," Jean said. "You were brought up one way and now you suddenly realized you're another. I promised myself if you came to me with questions, I would answer them honestly."

"You would do that for me?" Lark was breathless, but she had to know more.

Jean looked at her with understanding. "You're not the only one like yourself I've mentored. It isn't all that common, but I've had a few. I seem to attract students like you."

Lark's face got hot and she hurriedly gulped at her cool tea. Her hands shook as she placed the empty mug back on the table. Even though it took pretty much her whole life to come to terms with the direction her attraction faced, someone looking from the outside might be able to tell more easily, especially someone like Jean, who obviously had an insider's knowledge of the matter. Lark mentally kicked herself for being so blind.

"Okay, so now what?" Lark asked.

"You've admitted it to yourself, now you have to decide how much of this you want public."

"It's risky," Lark said. "I wanted to tell you — and Medina. I just knew you'd understand, and I'm glad I did. But this is all very new to me, and I don't think I want anyone else to know. At least not right now."

"That's natural. People might judge you once they know the truth, but it's important not to live a lie." Jean reached out a strong hand and patted Lark's knee. "You can do it, honey. If there's anything I can do to make this easier for you, just let me know. It's got to be a shock finding out you're not actually a Wanderer when all this time — Lark? You okay?"

"Fine," Lark croaked from where she was sprawled on the floor in an ungainly sprawl of skirts. "What did you just say?"

"You're not a Wanderer," Jean said. Her brow furrowed. "Wasn't that what you wanted to talk to me about?"

Lark shakily got to her feet and batted her skirts down. She rubbed a hand through her hair, then plopped back down into her chair. "Not exactly," she said. "But I'm not a Wanderer? You knew that?"

"I suspected for a while," Jean said. "The night of the hungry squall when you called the council-house from Pinecone Cottage proved it."

"Okay, so what in the Blue Sky am I?" Lark's breath caught in her throat. "I'm not a Ringsworn, am I?"

For a moment, she imagined herself clad in black, standing princely and proud next to Violet as they faced the world.

"As far as I know, no." Jean chuckled softly in her throat as if she understood. "You're something entirely different from most of us. Violet is actually a variation of that. You never feel drained or burned out, right?"

"Only once," Lark said. She shifted in her chair and glanced down at her wand.

"That's because your energy doesn't automatically come from within yourself like most of us," Jean said. "It comes from nature, from the ground under your feet, from the very air. Your wand is helpful and lets you focus, but you don't need a wand because you basically *are* one. I can't really say about crystals, they seem to be an exception."

"It's not a bad thing?"

"Not at all. It's just different. Your energy is long-lasting, sustainable, but not necessarily explosive."

Lark nodded. Jean's words rang true. Lark asked, "So it's okay if people know?"

Jean looked a bit uncomfortable. "It's a personal thing, and I'll leave it up to you to decide. Anyone who falls outside the norm can become a target for suspicion and mistrust. Guardians in particular aren't known for being open minded about non-standard abilities. I'd keep on as you were for the time being, but if you ever do want to explore your abilities, I can give you some training and of course, I promise my secrecy."

"Fair enough," Lark said.

"So what exactly did you come here to talk about?" Jean asked. "If it's not about Violet, then what?"

That was her chance to speak. Lark took a deep breath and went for it. "It is about Violet. I wanted to tell you I fancy her. And she fancies me right back. We, uh, talked about it."

"When did this happen?" Jean gaped at her.

"Last night," Lark said. Once the truth was out, Lark felt incredibly light. She hugged herself and let out a deep, happy sigh. "I can't explain the incredible feeling, how nice it is to be close to her. But I don't know what I should do. I want to treat her right, like a lady, but how? Am I the fellow? Should I do the courting? She's older than me so maybe it's the other way around. I just don't know." Lark huffed out a breath in frustration. She dropped her head into her hands.

"You've come to the right place for advice," Medina called out in her bright, lilting voice. She clapped Lark on the shoulder. "I think it's time you made Jean earn her Mentor's green."

Lark's head popped back up and she eagerly leaned forward.

"Okay. Here goes," Jean said without preamble. "There's no rule saying you and she have to fit into any kind of predetermined model. Just be yourself, take things slow, see where things head. Listen to Violet, find out what she wants and what she's willing to share with you. Let her know any expectations you have as well. As for the physical, well, just go with what feels right. Sorry for the vagueness, but I'm not really an expert on the subject."

"I beg to differ," Medina piped up. Jean became very interested in the thread hanging from the hem of her shirt and coughed into one closed fist.

"Thanks Jean. I feel better now," Lark said. She leaned back in her chair, deep in thought. "So I don't have limits, then."

"You do," Jean said. "But not like most people."

An idea that was at once both terrifying and audacious burst into Lark's mind. She summoned her courage and presented her idea to Jean, certain her mentor would refuse to assist. Against all odds, she accepted.

After the discussion, Lark rose from her chair. She was calm once more, her mind and body at rest. The next day would bring new discoveries and hopefully Lark's theory would be proven correct. They said their goodbyes and Lark confirmed the time they'd meet again the next morning.

As Lark was about to leave the cottage, Medina stood and pulled her cloak over her shoulders.

She said to Jean, "I just remembered we need more hand towels. I'll be back in five minutes."

"Take your time," Jean said.

Medina came up beside Lark and said, "If you don't mind, I'll walk a bit with you."

"That's fine," Lark replied.

They strolled into the still evening.

When they were about halfway back to the girls' dormitory,

Medina said, "There are three things you need to know about how to properly love a woman."

"What?" Lark choked and nearly tripped over her own feet.

Medina slung an arm around Lark's shoulders and pulled her close.

"One, don't go straight for the clit. Two, don't go in dry, and three, don't be afraid to use your tongue."

"My tongue? But I already—" Understanding dawned. Lark stopped in her tracks. "Green Trees," she whispered.

"You are on the verge of discovering the most wonderful, amazing thing in the entire world," Medina said. "Enjoy every moment and know this, it only gets better."

With that, Medina was off. She walked briskly through the darkness, serenaded by the shimmering song of late crickets.

Instead of returning to her dorm, Lark slipped through the quiet cluster of buildings and headed for the pantry shed. As she hoped, a tiny flickering light shone from the crack of the shed's door. Lark eased it open and found Violet sitting at the counter with two mugs and a basket in front of her. The source of the light was a cluster of candles on a silver dish, held in place by the melted wax of their predecessors.

"Good evening. I was hoping to meet you here," Violet said. Her gaze welcomed Lark and sent a shock of joy through her. "Would you care for some dried persimmons?"

"I'd love some," Lark said. She propped her wand next to the door and came over to sit beside Violet like she had so many times before.

Unlike any other time before that, she didn't feel the flash of unease, the need to stop herself from thinking or feeling too deeply. Lark relaxed into the comfortable rhythm as if it was just yesterday they sat side by side, sharing a midnight snack instead of an entire week of confusion and emptiness. Violet's lips turned up at the corners in reply as she passed over the basket of dried fruit. She reached down and placed a slender bottle on the counter. It was unlike the one she shared with the trainees the previous night and Lark was intrigued.

"How about a glass of wine instead of tea?" Violet asked. Her gaze held Lark's. She didn't wait for a reply before she reached for the corkscrew. "I heard your birthday will come in a month's time and I wish to celebrate with you."

Lark regarded Violet for a moment, puzzled. Why would she wish to celebrate something so far in advance? Unless she didn't plan to be around for it. Lark's soul chilled at the thought.

She dredged up a brave grin and held out her mug for Violet to fill with dark red wine. "That's right kind of you. We don't usually make a fuss of birthdays after the sixteenth one."

"Really?" Violet looked up from filling her own mug.

Lark nodded. "When we're little, our folks usually do something special every year, but once we're sixteen, we're adults. After that, we celebrate life milestones. They're more important than years."

"Such as?"

"You know," Lark said. Violet fixed her with a penetrating look that made her uneasy. "Stuff like getting married, having younguns and building your farm up. The barn-raising parties are the best."

"Indeed," Violet said. She rested her hand on the neck of the wine bottle. She let out a breath and shook herself. "Indulge me this one last time, then. Happy nineteenth."

"Thanks," Lark said. She clunked her cup with Violet's and gulped at the contents. A festive feeling swallowed her unease. The wine was fragrant with blackcurrant and something dark and heady that drew her appetite. Lark set her cup down and said, "Nobody knows my actual birthday. They just kind of calculated backwards when I was found."

"Be that as it may," Violet said as she looked into the depths of her own wine cup. "I wish I could see you through all of them."

Violet's posture spoke of infinite sadness.

"I told Jean about us," Lark said in a rush. "That's okay, I hope."

"Of course." Violet leaned forward. The sadness was replaced by a tiny quirk to her lips made her look like a mischievous sprite in the candles' glow. "I've always found Jean Elliott fair and open-minded. She's your mentor, isn't she?"

"Yup, since I was twelve years old. I did my apprenticeship with her too," Lark said, pleased that Jean had found favor in Violet's opinion.

"She's very proud of you," Violet said. "Jean has told me several amusing stories about your escapades over the years. A certain incident involving a pumpkin pie, a slingshot, and several frogs comes to mind."

Lark groaned dramatically. She flung her hands out and said, "That wasn't all my doing. I had accomplices who steered me wrong."

"Those are the best kind of accomplices," Violet said. She sipped delicately at her wine and Lark gulped hers. Lark smiled when Violet's hand crept into hers. She savored the silk of Violet's palm pressed to hers, naked skin on skin. The moment of intimacy was sullied by a guilty pang in Lark's chest. Violet had confessed to her, told Lark her secrets and trusted her enough to show her true self. Lark hadn't. Not yet. Intimacy was not only physical. Lark needed to take that step, however difficult it was for her. She had to do it that night. Lark shifted in discomfort and looked away from Violet.

"Violet, I need to tell you something," Lark said.

"What is it?" The note of unease caused Lark to look up into Violet's face. Violet worried at her lower lip. Hesitantly, she asked, "Is it about..." She waved one hand between them.

"No, it's not about us," Lark said. "It's about me. I'm—I'm not like most people."

Violet cocked her head in a silent question.

"I don't need a wand," Lark said. "I draw energy directly from everything around me. Which means I'm not actually a Wanderer. Jean told me earlier tonight."

"How do you feel about that?"

"Kind of confused, to be honest," Lark said. "I've never been a Crystalgazer. I barely qualify as a Guardian. And I just found out I'm not a Wanderer either. I don't know what I am."

Violet reached out and cupped Lark's face. She spoke softly, but with sincerity. "Labels and the groups we put ourselves into are not important. What matters is what we do, not names we assume for ourselves or what others call us." Her dark eyes held Lark's. She said, "I have never touched a Ring in my life except to destroy it. I lived apart from others for most of my life and have very little firsthand knowledge of my people. I've never felt like a proper Ringsworn either. And you know I don't fit into any particular group with regards to my abilities."

"At least that makes two of us," Lark said. "We can be on the 'none of the above' team."

"I like that," Violet said with a half-smile that never failed to send a bolt of pure light straight through Lark's chest every single time. "I have been called many things over the course of my life, and will certainly be called many more, but I do not let that define me and you shouldn't either. You are unique and beautiful and bold, Lark. And that's what I fell—" Violet faltered and a flush colored her cheeks, "felt was honorable and good about you."

Violet let go of Lark, who was left with the odd feeling she'd missed something.

Lark drained her cup and accepted a refill. The wine left her feeling warm and a bit buzzed, which helped her get out the next words.

"I have a proposal," Lark said. "I ran it by Jean and she said she'd help. I want to train with you, to work as a team. I'd be the source and you the catalyst. Together we would be—"

"Unstoppable," Violet breathed. "That power you have, it is present in my people as well. Sister Perpetua is one such as you, Lark. It is inaccurate to say I am not dangerous to you, but you are far safer than most."

"So you'll do it?"

"There are people who would not be pleased this has happened. That one such as I has access to this amount of power."

"Maybe. But I'm not one of them. And neither is Jean. She's on our side for this, and everything else too."

"In that case," Violet said. "I will try."

Lark let out her breath, filled with an equal measure of nervousness and joy.

"You are not afraid?" Violet's gaze was focused on her.

"Nope. I trust you."

"And I, you."

With a secret little smile that Lark ached to taste, Violet helped herself to a dried persimmon from the basket. She twisted off a small morsel and put it into her mouth. She trailed one finger over her lips, delicately licking off the lingering sweetness. Lark looked at her in surprise. Violet never licked her fingers. She preferred to use her delicately embroidered handkerchief, which currently sat ignored in her lap. Lark's mind went blank. She watched as Violet's tongue slowly tasted one long digit for much longer than Lark thought was necessary. The movement was soft, sensual. Lark wished with all her mind and body she was on the receiving end of that tongue. Violet's eyes met hers with a wicked light in them.

Lark croaked, "You're doing that on purpose."

"Yes I am. So you will think about kissing me," Violet said, her voice low. "Is it working?"

"Sure is," Lark said. "But there aren't many minutes of the day I'm not thinking about kissing you." She grimaced and clenched her fists on the rough material of her skirt. "Sorry, that was disrespectful."

"No, it wasn't." Violet said. "It's true, isn't it? And we have already accepted each other. Hiding the truth or being misleading would be disrespectful."

"That's good," Lark said. She got to her feet and drew close to Violet. She hoped Violet couldn't feel the pounding of her heart. "Then, may I kiss you?" Lark asked. Her voice was husky with desire.

"Please do," Violet whispered. She closed her eyes and lifted her chin, her parted lips and unguarded expression extending an invitation Lark was only too happy to accept.

Lark brought both hands up. She held Violet's face with a gentle touch. Her fingertips trembled with the desire she denied for so long. Lark trailed one thumb over Violet's lower lip, savoring the softness and strength. She wanted to burn every moment into her mind. Lark was still trying to convince herself it wasn't a dream, trying to make herself believe she wasn't going to open her eyes and find herself twisted up in her sheets, frustrated and aching and alone. Finally Lark couldn't stand it anymore. She leaned down to brush her lips with Violet's. The first contact was gentle, almost shy.

With Violet's face in her hands, Lark kept her kisses light and soft, memorizing the feeling of Violet against her, taking in her delicate scent, tasting the sweetness of persimmon and wine that lingered on her lips. Supple arms came around her waist and Violet kissed her back, hard.

Eager to meet Violet's urgent demand, Lark's movements became faster, the need within her spurring Lark to open her mouth and accept Violet's willing entry. The fact Lark was standing while Violet was still perched on the tall stool made the next step occur naturally, easily. Violet broke the kiss and bent to meet the skin of Lark's neck. Violet claimed her with a warm, wet caress of lips and tongue. The thrill of the first contact had Lark reeling. Her body flared into life and desire coursed through her.

"I like this, your home-people's costume," Violet said between kisses. She raised a hand to the front lacing of Lark's tunic. "And I'd like to undo it."

"Yes, please," Lark said. Her voice was breathy and hoarse.

She drew in a deep breath as Violet's slender fingers tugged at the laces. The front of her tunic fell open to reveal the leather cords of her crystal pouch and a line of her cotton wrap. Lips trailed down from Lark's neck until Violet placed a kiss at the very edge of the material that held her in its soft embrace.

"You are so beautiful," Violet breathed.

Before she could think about what she was doing, Lark took Violet's hands in hers and drew them against herself. At the first brush of Violet's palm meeting the swell of Lark's breast, Violet let out a sound of such pleasure that it resonated down to Lark's toes. The feeling of Violet cupping her was almost too much and a deep shiver started up in Lark's knees and radiated upward. A thrumming tension burgeoned between her legs. Lark didn't try to stop it. She wasn't sure how much more she could take and still remain in control of herself, but Lark was in heaven with Violet's hands on her.

Violet lowered her head and rested her cheek against Lark's chest. She let out a long breath and closed her eyes with a secret smile playing about her lips. That smile only made Lark hungry for more and she leaned forward to press herself more strongly into Violet's hold. She bit back a moan when Violet lazily trailed one thumb over the fabric of her wraps where her hard nipple lay underneath. The touch sent a hot tingle through her entire body. With one more lingering kiss on the fullness before her, Violet drew back and slowly pulled the laces of Lark's tunic tight once more.

"For the record," Violet said. "You have my permission to kiss me anytime you wish."

"Anytime?"

Violet looked up into Lark's eyes with a spark of humor dancing in her own. "Anytime within reason. Use your judgment and common sense."

"Will do," Lark said. She silently marveled at the ideas Violet's words called up.

"Maybe we should be getting back," Violet said when she finished righting Lark's clothing.

"Good idea," Lark said. She swallowed the billow of heat that rose from the depths of her belly. "I don't want to keep you out too late. Jean said we should meet her in the practice room directly after breakfast."

"I hope our venture is successful," Violet said with an uneasy expression. She rubbed a hand through her hair in a casual, almost rakish gesture that sent a warm glow through Lark's chest. Tidying the counter took only a moment. When everything was in order, Lark swung her wand back over her shoulder and followed Violet into the night. Lark made sure there was a prudent distance between them as they made their way slowly through the compound.

As if they'd planned it, they followed a meandering course on the edge of the clearing. Lark enjoyed the closeness and intimacy with Violet at her side even though they weren't even touching. One day, Lark promised herself, she would reach out and take Violet's hand in hers. One day she would be proud to declare to the entire world that she belonged to the woman who walked beside her. While Lark wasn't sure what Violet wanted, Lark would give Violet anything she asked for, whether it was forever or just for now.

The chill night air did nothing to quench the fire Violet lit within her. As she walked, Lark was extremely aware of her own need, each step sent a small tremor through her. Lark tilted her head back and scanned the sky, trying to take her mind off the warm fist of desire between her thighs. Her thoughts whirled. She had to speak.

"You are like starlight," Lark said. She waved one arm up at the sprawling vista of stars above them. "Not like moonlight, that belongs to everyone. Starlight is flickering, elusive, easily hidden. You are a single star in the sky, one that only I know how to find. The most beautiful one there is."

Silence fell after she finished and Lark got ready to blather on about something more mundane when Violet spoke. "That's the most beautiful thing anybody's ever said to me." She turned to face Lark. "And you are sunshine."

"Painful in large doses?" Lark joked.

With a quirk of her lips and a shake of her head, Violet said, "Warm. Nurturing. Loving. When I stand before you, I feel blessed with light. Like dawn has finally broken."

Lark felt her cheeks flare red. "And that, Miss Violet, is the most beautiful thing anybody's ever said to *me*."

The low chuckle that met her statement made Lark wish they were back inside the pantry shed so she could properly thank Violet for her words and show the sentiment behind them was returned in full. They faced each other in the darkness, a distance from the spilled lights from the cottages. Lark felt as if the rest of the world faded away, leaving them the only ones in all creation, two people alone under the calm eye of the stars. She could think of nothing other than how much she wanted to taste those beautiful lips once more. Against her better judgment, Lark took a step forward. Her heart gave a kick as Violet moved to meet her.

"Lark, my Sunshine," Violet whispered. She held her hands at her sides, fingers curled as if to stop from reaching out. "Go now. Go before I kiss you right here and now and cause a great scandal to shake this outpost."

The spell broke. Lark took a step back. Her cheeks were warm and she was glad at least one of them had a lick of sense.

"Can't have that," Lark said. She stuffed her hands into her pockets. They said a quick, chaste goodnight and Lark hurried off back towards the dorms.

THE NEXT MORNING, Lark scrambled to finish her chores. On her way to the practice hall, she was delayed by the arrival of a coach carrying the outpost's share of the monthly tithes from the main intake center. Under the direction of Outpost Head Weinberg, Lark and several others helped to unload the boxes and baskets.

She recognized her own parents' contribution of several bushels of apples plus a dozen jars of pickles. The apples were misshapen and wormy, but Lark knew they were the best of the lot. They included extra, as they always did in tacit support of both Lark and the Guardians in general. The storms wreaked havoc with crops and livestock and got worse with every season. Even at their compound, ham and mutton were a rare treat as nobody wanted to slaughter an animal when there were so many stillbirths and breeding stock struck barren.

Finally, Lark made her escape and went straight to the practice hall. It was their rest day so the hall was free to use. When she entered the main practice room, Violet and Jean were sitting on barrels, chatting with Medina who jumped up with a cheerful greeting. After the lovely incident with Violet unlacing her tunic, Lark was sorely tempted to put on her long tunic and heavy skirts again. But in light of their practice session, she decided to go with her usual trousers as they were easier to move about in. After all, if she got turned over and dumped on her head, they would save at least a bit of her dignity.

Lark's hurried apology for being late was met with a cool nod from her mentor.

"Are you going to have lunch in the meal hall?" Medina asked. "Or should I have Cook Brown make up a basket for you here?"

"We'll go with the basket, thanks," Jean said. With the answer, Violet relaxed almost imperceptibly. Lark was glad as well they would have a break from the crowded and raucous meal hall.

"All right then. I'll be back at noon," Medina said. She leaned down and gave Jean a long kiss full on the mouth that left Lark feeling hot and flustered. She didn't know where to look. Even when Lark lived in their home, she was never witness to such a display.

"Was that for our benefit?" Violet asked. Her lips quirked into a tiny smile as the couple parted. "If so, then I appreciate the demonstration. However, I assure you, Lark needs no instruction in that area."

Medina just answered with a wave. She breezed out and left Jean and Lark to glance uneasily at each other. Jean raked back her short grey hair with one hand, pink around the ears.

"Okay, let's get started," Jean said. She banged her staff down on the floorboards and cleared her throat. She leveled Violet with a calm gaze and said, "If you're going to work as a team, first we need to start with managing the energy transfer itself. We can practice with casting shields. That needs a deep, steady source, which is exactly what Lark can provide. After that we advance to anything the two of you can come up with. The sky's the limit."

"Not the sky," Violet breathed. "The farthest reaches of the cosmos."

Jean raised her eyebrows at the remark. "All right then. Lark, you know how Violet works. We need an anchor, something of yours. Oh, and I'd put your wand down if I were you. That's way too strong for what we want to do today."

Obligingly, Lark propped her wand against a bale of hay. She rummaged in one of her pockets and came up with a marble from her collection.

"Take your time, kids," Jean said. She stretched out her legs and looked relaxed. Nonetheless, she had her wand out and held it against her side.

Violet drew close to Lark, who felt a shock of electricity race through her at the first brush of Violet's fingers against her own. Her touch was cool and soft against Lark's palm.

"With your permission," Violet whispered. Lark nodded. She didn't dare to move as slender fingers closed over the glass sphere.

A deep well of energy awoke within her at the contact. It hummed up through the soles of her feet, resonating within her and streaming out from herself. With a jolt, Lark's knees buckled. In an instant, Jean was on her feet. Only Violet's sure grip on her elbow kept Lark upright. The contact broke off suddenly.

"We can stop," Violet said.

"I'm all right," Lark said. "I wasn't expecting that. But I'm good."

The hand left her arm. Violet stepped away and put down the marble. She looked at Lark. "You don't feel weak?"

"No, I feel good," Lark said.

Violet cupped her hands, a soft glow emanated from them. She glanced over to Jean. "What should I do with this?"

"Anything you want," Jean replied with a grin and a shrug.

Violet opened her fingers and the energy coalesced into a delicate silver rose. Lark caught her breath at the shimmering perfection of it. With a bow of her proud head, Violet passed the creation to Lark. As soon as she touched it, the rose became hundreds of tiny sparks. They floated away in a sparkling cloud and vanished in a breath.

"Showoff," Jean said with a snort. "All right now we've established this is not going to kill anyone, let's start working on the shields. This time, keep the connection and work as one."

"I've never cast a shield," Violet said. "I don't have any idea how to even go about it."

"Let Lark's experience guide you," Jean said. "She's a dab hand at shields."

"Are you ready?" Violet had her hand out, poised over the marble.

"Sure," Lark said. Her heart give a kick as Violet's eyes met hers.

Violet picked up the marble and the now-familiar feeling of the connection buzzed into place. Lark stood still. This time the contact didn't end. When Lark team-cast with other Guardians, they worked in tandem with a leader giving the orders. This time, there was no leader. They simply *were*. Lark didn't need to give an order. She focused on what needed to be done and felt the answer resonating through her from Violet.

With a nod and gesture from Jean, Violet held out one hand. A shimmering red bubble engulfed the two of them. The shield wavered once, then came back strong. The edges tingled with silver. They were both contributing to the bubble of energy that surrounded them with Lark's energy streaming through Violet and picking up her unique resonance. The shield held, strong and unwavering in the morning sunlight.

For all the oddness of the situation, for all the risk, Lark felt safe. Beside her, Violet's face was soft, her lips parted in wonder.

"Are you really all right?" she asked.

"Sure," Lark said.

"Amazing!" Jean leapt to her feet. She bent to study the shield. With a satisfied grunt she straightened up and raised her wand. A smallish bale of hay rose into the air. "All right, I'm sending you some interference. Violet, you might need to shore up the shield as we go. Lark, give us a holler if you feel your personal energy going. We're not trying to use you up. Slow and steady, like pulling a string through your fingers, okay? Get ready, folks!"

"You heard the woman," Lark said with a grin, her feet braced against the floor. "Let's see what you can do, Violet."

"What *we* can do."

Lark glowed, her eyes and heart were full of Violet as the bale of hay impacted with the shield and spun away from them.

The rest of the morning was spent mostly refining Violet's channeling technique using various items Lark had brought with her. While the marble was a good start, they had much more success with other things such as a small paper craft Lark had made a while ago. Violet refused to touch either crystals or wand and while Lark was certain she would be safe, she knew going slowly was better, if for no other reason than to quiet Violet's worries.

During a break, Lark left to fill their water jug from the pump behind the practice hall. After their busy morning, Lark was hot and dusty. Once the jug was full and capped, Lark cupped one hand under the spray and splashed her face. The cool water invigorated and refreshed her. Lark yanked out her shirt tail and dried off.

"That looks lovely." Violet's low voice startled Lark.

"Yeah, it's great. Cooled me right down."

"Actually, I'm a bit overheated myself."

Lark grinned and put one hand on the pump. She gestured with the other. "Be my guest."

To Lark's surprise, Violet bent down and splashed herself off as well. She straightened up and Lark gallantly offered her shirt. With a quirk of her lips, Violet sank down to her knees. Lark's breath hitched. She hadn't thought the innocent gesture could be so erotic. She swallowed hard and didn't breathe or move until Violet rose and stepped away from her.

"Thank you," Violet said.

"No problem," Lark said. Her entire body ached with the need to touch Violet, but she held herself still. They were in the middle of the compound, after all.

Lark asked, "What are your plans for the rest of the day?"

"Besides laundry, I have none. This is my day of rest as well."

"Good," Lark said. She chewed her lower lip for an instant before the memory of Violet's kisses drove all doubts from her mind. "Then how about meeting me in the woodshed after Jean lets us out of here?"

"Mmm, wonderful idea," Violet purred. "I'm assuming we're not simply going to collect some kindling, then?"

"I guess you could if you wanted to," Lark said. Desire thrummed through her. "But I was thinking we might find something else much nicer."

"Consider your invitation accepted," Violet said. "Now let's get back before Jean sends out a search party. Or gets bored and summons her bride for some distraction as well."

MEDINA SHOWED UP at noon with a generous basket of sandwiches and a large bottle of tea. She joined them for a leisurely picnic on the practice room's floor, surrounded by bales of hay and barrels.

Lark was glad she already told them about herself and Violet, because she couldn't stop sharing long, lingering glances over lunch, her mind and body charged from more than just the lesson. At one point, Violet leaned over and delicately fed Lark a morsel of fruitcake from her hand.

The gesture left Lark stunned and blushing while Jean and Medina exchanged knowing glances. At least Violet wasn't licking her fingers. Lark didn't think she could resist that, even with an audience.

After lunch, Jean enlisted Medina's help to see how well Violet's shields could fend off attacks from two sources at once. After some initial hesitation, Violet managed to do so, though she came perilously close to drawing from Lark's personal energy and backed off immediately. They finished with a battery of easy exercises that left Lark filled with satisfaction.

"Okay, that's all for today," Jean said. She gave them a nod. "Good work people."

"Thanks," Lark said. She felt like she was glowing.

Violet took her leave and swept from the room. Full of energy, Lark grabbed up a broom and started to sweep up the piles of loose hay they made during the practice session.

"What's this now?" Medina said. She came over and relieved Lark of her broom. She answered Lark's confused expression with a smile and a wink before twirling to begin her own cleanup. "You don't want to keep her waiting. Go on, we'll deal with this."

Her mouth flapped open, but Lark didn't argue. Quickly, she shouldered her wand and made a beeline for the door. She called back over her shoulder, "Thanks for the practice. Sorry about the mess, though."

Medina's answer of "pish posh" and Jean's chuckle faded as Lark pelted across the grounds. The morning's sunlight deteriorated to a surly overcast afternoon sky. Distant rumblings of thunder were carried on the breeze. She slowed her steps and wandered about in a casual way, just in case anyone took notice of her. Nobody did. At that hour, most people were taking naps or playing cards in one of the common rooms.

The wind picked up and Lark shivered in the sudden chill. She reached the woodshed and forgot the cold at once.

Violet slipped from the shadows as soon as Lark closed the door behind her. There was no need for words. Lark gathered Violet up in her arms and leaned back to rest against the stacked kindling. Their bodies molded together. Lark lowered her head. She brushed her lips over the silk of Violet's cheek. Lark was prepared to savor the moment and move slowly, but Violet apparently had other ideas.

Violet's long fingers twined in Lark's hair. She pulled them together in a firm kiss, welcoming Lark with a soft sound deep in her throat.

Desire led her to grow bold and Lark ran her hands up and down Violet's back. The buttons on the silken bodice rippled underneath her fingers. Lark recalled the night she ripped it open and discovered a hint of what lay beneath the confining garments. Drunk on the memory, her hands drifted lower and took Violet around the hips. She nearly lost herself when Violet moved with the touch and rocked herself against Lark's body, never breaking their kiss.

The kiss got deep and hungry. Lark opened her mouth to Violet. She couldn't stop the tremors of arousal that woke up within herself, particularly after a slender thigh pushed between her own, guided either by the suggestion in Lark's hands or Violet's own desire.

Violet pulled away first. She chuckled deep in her throat.

"While it was novel seeing you in a skirt," Violet said, "I think there are several benefits to trousers." As she spoke, she canted her hips forward, driving her thigh between Lark's once more. Lark gasped and a shudder rolled through her.

"Blue Sky, Violet," Lark gritted.

At once, Violet let up the pressure. "I apologize," she said and made a move to draw back. "I overstepped again."

"No way," Lark said. She bit her lip to stop the lascivious grin. She tightened her grip on Violet's hips and pulled their bodies together once more. Lark drew in a breath. The pleasure of having Violet between her legs overrode Lark's shyness. She said, "I like having you right here."

She had to stop talking when Violet's lips met hers once more. The kiss was wet and heavy and Lark felt like she was on top of the entire world.

Finally they broke apart and Lark sucked in a breath. She held herself very still, wanting to savor the moment for as long as possible. A thick heat gathered at the place where Violet pressed against her. It was more intimate than any embrace they'd shared until that moment. Lark gazed into Violet's deep eyes. Their breaths mingled. Lark couldn't speak. She wanted nothing more than to hold Violet to her, give everything she had to the woman in her arms. Not just now. Forever. Her heart was full of only one woman. Her whole universe was contained in Violet's eyes. The depth of her feelings both shocked and thrilled Lark.

Both of them were panting, the air of the small shed was heated and thick with their combined breaths. With each one, the inviting swells of Violet's breasts rose and fell. Lark bent her head and kissed a line from Violet's throat down. She was spurred on by the low hum of approval and she pressed her lips to the softness of Violet's breast, tasting the slightly salty musk of Violet's skin.

"Starlight," Lark murmured. She pulled herself away from the intoxicating fullness and brought one hand up to tease Violet's lips with her thumb. She sucked in a gasp of pleasure as Violet turned her head to kiss the inside of her wrist.

"You never took this off," Violet said. She buffed her lips over the bracelet.

"I couldn't," Lark said. Her voice was weak and breathless.

"That's how I knew I still held a place in your heart."

"You did from the first moment I saw you," Lark said.

"I did?" Violet paused in her torment of Lark's wrist and looked at her with searching eyes. She pouted in a completely uncharacteristic way that almost made Lark laugh out loud. Violet said, "I rather hoped to be menacing. I practiced that speech in my mind a hundred times on the coach ride over."

"I'm sure everyone else was shaking in their boots," Lark murmured.

Violet gave a satisfied *hmph* and snuggled closer to lean her head against Lark's shoulder.

The hand resting on Violet's hip drifted lower. Even through the layers of skirts and petticoats, Lark felt the wonderful roundness of Violet's rear. Lark drew in a breath. Her face felt hot. Her body was even hotter. She shook the fog of arousal from her mind and said, "You were amazing today. I can't believe it worked so well. Thank you for taking the risk."

"It is you who risked everything," Violet murmured. She gave the tender skin at the base of Lark's neck a soft nip before she said, "Know this—I will never use you for anything trivial, anything I cannot do myself or by other means."

"Of course," Lark said. She let out an involuntary groan as Violet's lips found a sensitive spot near her collar and lingered there. "I was thinking if you ever have to neutralize an artifact again, maybe I could help. Give you the energy to heal yourself. I hate the fact it takes so much from you."

Violet's soft movements stilled. "Perhaps." Her lips brushed over Lark's skin as she spoke. "If possible, I would keep you as far from those artifacts as I could. They are hungry and have a way of getting what they want."

An unpleasant shiver gripped her, but Lark suppressed it. She said, "Hopefully there won't be another one like that."

"There is no hope," Violet said. She looked up and the bleak expression on her face faded. "However I don't want to waste this time discussing dark things. I want to bathe in your light, my Sunshine. Kiss me."

Only too happy to comply, Lark met the insistent lips with her own. She welcomed the wordless communication until they were both trembling and panting into the wan darkness. The billow of raw passion swallowed her uncertainty and Lark took Violet's hand in her own and guided it as she had before to rest on the swell of her breast. However this time, she didn't stop there and let their entwined hands glide down to her waist.

In a quick, impatient motion, Lark yanked out her shirt. She gasped out, "Violet, please touch me." A thrill of nerves stopped her and Lark paused. She bit her lip before she quickly added, "Actually, you don't have to. I take it back."

She almost pulled away when a soft touch on her wrist stilled her.

Violet met Lark's heated gaze with her own. She rose up and

pressed her entire length against Lark, who drew a soft, deep breath when Violet got her thigh right where Lark wanted it.

"Why?" Violet whispered in her ear.

"Well, um, it's kind of personal, isn't it?" Lark stammered. "Asking you to do that and all."

"It is personal. Intimate. And I burn to touch you. With your permission?"

"Yes," Lark breathed the word.

Desire smoldered in Violet's eyes as she slipped her hands under Lark's top. Questing fingers tracing up from the bare skin at her waist stopped Lark's thoughts. A shockwave of heat was born with every inch of Violet's journey upwards. Lark's breath caught in her throat the instant Violet's fingers reached her wraps. Violet stilled her ascent and let out a long sigh of wonder.

"I have been dreaming of what you keep in here for a long time," she said. She lowered her head to Lark's neck and softly kissed her. Lark wanted to cry out as the touch of Violet's lips warred with the novel sensations of her nipples being stroked through nothing more than the thin layer of confining cloth. Violet let out a quiet hum. "And I am grateful you invited me to find out."

Lark was beyond words. Her eyes fluttered closed and her head lolled back and rested against the rough-cut wood at her back. Her body started to move, mirroring Violet's who was pushed up against her. The worry of getting a splinter was soon cancelled out by a gentle tug at her wraps.

"Tell me how to get this off you." Violet's words burned against Lark's skin.

"You've got the end there." Lark's voice sounded harsh and strained to her ears. "Just give a pull and it'll come oh—"

With a jolt through her chest, she felt the pressure around herself give way. The soft cotton fell to pool around her waist, still warm from her body. The fingers cupping her took on a new urgency. It was all Lark could do to keep from crying out as Violet's hands held her fullness, supporting her now the wraps were gone. Gentle thumbs found her and teased her nipples hard. Lark bit her lip.

"Good?" Violet asked. She drew back and studied Lark's face.

"Yes, that's so good," Lark said, her voice husky with desire.

"Please, keep doing that."

"Hold up your shirt," Violet said. "I want to see you."

A liquid surge of heat rippled through her. Lark had the hem of her top in her hands when a bright voice outside startled them both into stillness. The voice came again and the words rang through the woodshed: "Hey Lark? Are you around here? Laaaark!"

"Alice," they whispered in unison.

Violet quickly pulled away and ran her hands over her hair, smoothing the tousled strands. With a glance at the closed door, Violet turned back to give Lark one more quick kiss that did nothing to quench Lark's thirst for her.

Violet said, "Stay here until it's safe to leave. I'll see to our friend Alice."

Lark nodded. Violet whirled and slipped out of the woodshed. Alone again, Lark sank to the woodchip-strewn floor, very aware of her unbound breasts, the length of cotton coiled around her hips. Her legs shook. A sweet tension thrummed through her body and settled in the aching muscles of her thighs. She had never felt so alive, so ready to explode as she did at that moment.

"Why if it isn't Miss Chance." Violet's voice filtered into the shed. "I was just looking for Lark myself but she appears to have gone off to who knows where. I thought she'd be stacking kindling but evidently I was mistaken. However I did manage to find a good number of spiders to add to my collection."

"S-spiders? Uh, what kind, exactly?"

Lark pictured Alice's face and had to clap both hands over her mouth to keep the laugh from erupting.

"Large ones. With lots of juice."

"Seriously?" After a moment of silence, Alice said, "If you're not busy, how about giving me a hand looking for Lark? I wanted to see if she was going to take the dinner dishes with me or not."

"Very well. Where have you looked already?"

As their voices faded away, Lark let out a long breath. Her drawers were damp and sticking to her. She gingerly got to her feet and a shock of arousal pierced her belly with the movement. She took a few unsteady steps in the confines of the woodshed then crouched down in one corner to pull her shirt over her head with the intention of getting herself back in order.

Instead of dressing, Lark trailed her fingers down over one

breast and lingered on one achingly hard nipple. Frustrated heat once more filled her.

"Drought and flames," Lark muttered. She forced herself to concentrate on her wraps. Once she finished, she put her shirt back on and patted herself down, checking for anything else that needed fixing.

While she was shaken, it wasn't in a bad way. Not at all. Just the same, Lark didn't trust her legs to support herself yet and stayed in the woodshed. She breathed in the fragrant scent of freshly-cut kindling and calmed her mind. After a good amount of time had passed, Lark was ready to face the world again. She left the woodshed and made her way over to the big fallen tree where she hoisted herself up onto it and surveyed the compound.

She noticed a cheerfully bobbing shape coming across the clearing. Lark let out a shout of greeting and waved her arm. In response, Alice turned and waved back. Her long skirts kicked out around her legs as she trundled through the grass.

"Hey Lark, there you are," Alice said. She stood in front of the fallen tree and looked up at her. "Elvira was looking for you earlier. Is she mad at you again? Or still?"

A flash of anger spurred Lark. She heaved herself off the tree and landed firmly on her feet. "Alice, I'm not going to tell you again," she said with a note of steel in her tone she'd never used before. "Her name is Violet."

"Okay, sorry," Alice said. She took a step back with unease on her face. "Anyway, she asked me to give you the following message, ahem: get your worthless Wanderer backside over to the washing-house before she hunts you down and strings you up using nothing but your own entrails and feeds you to her spiders as a teatime snack."

"You've got a good memory, Alice. Okay, I'll head right over there," Lark said, impressed. She stuffed her hands into her pockets and fell into step with her friend. "Um, sorry for going off like that. But you never know who's listening and that nickname's not very flattering."

Alice looked properly contrite. She wrinkled her nose and said, "You're probably right. Anyway, so are you on dish duty tonight?"

"Yup. It's just me and you tonight."

"Good," Alice said, "Because I'm so tired of Great Auntie

Pacifica. At lunch Murray bored us all silly telling us about the time she accidentally won a pie-eating contest at some village's midsummer festival and then spent the prize money on beer and got the entire town drunk."

"Tall tales," Lark said with a snort. "If half of what he says is true about her, she's probably the craziest Wanderer who ever lived."

"Yeah, really. Anyway, I gotta go. I promised Bethanie I'd help her with the new bookshelf her supervisor got for their workroom."

"All right. See you at dinner," Lark said. She changed her trajectory and loped off toward the clothes washing shed. The door clacked closed behind her. Violet was already there, pulling bed sheets from one of the washing barrels.

"Hey," Lark said softly.

Violet turned to greet her with a smile.

"Good you're here, you can help me get these on the lines," Violet said and handed over an armful of freshly-laundered sheets. She gave Lark a long, lingering gaze full of desire. A rush of heat filled Lark and she swallowed hard. Violet said, "Only the fact that Alice is a good friend of yours saved her from becoming sausage filling earlier."

"I wasn't too happy with her timing myself," Lark said with a wry grin. "But she didn't do it on purpose."

"That's true," Violet said. The two of them headed out to the long array of clotheslines. The wind whipped around them, rustling through Violet's long skirts.

"Looks like another storm's coming," Lark said. The damp sheets in her arms chilled her in the sudden rush of cold wind. The electric tingle of unshed lightning filled the air. "Are you sure you want to put these out here?"

"You're right, I'll hang them on the drying rack in my cottage," Violet said. She focused on the ominous bulge of roiling black clouds on the horizon before she turned back to Lark and held out her hands. Lark obediently piled the sheets into them. Violet shifted her load and leaned close to Lark. She said, "While I wish to invite you back to my cottage, I wouldn't want tongues to wag when you leave hours later, thoroughly disheveled but well-satisfied."

Lark was still tongue-tied when Violet turned and headed

back toward the line of cottages. Flushed and warm, Lark hurried toward the relative safety of the girls' dormitory.

In the semi-privacy of the dormitory, Lark sprawled out on her bed with a happy but slightly frustrated sigh. She replayed the events in the woodshed, savoring the memory of Violet's lips and hands on her, the softness of her breasts, the resilience of her limbs. Medina was right. It really was the best thing in the world, but how long would it last? Lark wouldn't be a fledgling forever. Soon she'd get her Tracker's stripe and her days at Shadowmoor would be over. How could she be a Guardian and still have Violet in her life? If that was even what Violet wanted.

OVER THE NEXT several days, practice took precedence over pleasure, although they did manage to spend a good amount of time in each other's arms. The near-miss with Alice caused them to be more cautious and while Lark understood the need for prudence, she often lost herself in the memory of what happened in the woodshed, and what might have happened if Alice hadn't come along.

It was in that distracted frame of mind that Lark showed up at dinner. The air was heavy and already thunder rumbled through the outpost. The storms were becoming more frequent and more intense. That night's was threatening to be a big one. Lark wasn't particularly worried, her mind was elsewhere, not even on her meal, which that night was some kind of stew with a few hard rounds of bread for dipping.

Even though Lark barely tasted her food, she was acutely aware of Violet at her usual place at the head table. That night she was sandwiched between Head Guardian Williams and their grumpy driving instructor, Jane Snell. Lark didn't envy Violet's place and it took all of Lark's will to keep her eyes from drifting over to Violet. Absently, Lark stirred her cooling stew and wondered if they'd have a chance to meet up in the pantry shed that evening for a bit of practice and perhaps something more. She half-listened as Bethanie and Alice complained at great length about Murray cheating at some kind of card game they played earlier.

A kerfuffle at the door interrupted the buzz of mealtime conversation. Silence fell when a ragged man stumbled into the meal hall, shedding brambles and leaves from his torn and dirt-stained clothing. With hurried, jerky movements, he slammed the door behind himself. He turned and plastered his body against it, arms splayed wide as if trying desperately to shut something out.

Lark gaped. She knew him. The man was none other than Reuel Bucketsworth.

Instantly, all of the Guardians in the room were on their feet. They formed a typical defensive formation, shoulder-to-shoulder. One of the senior Trackers stepped forward, but before she could address the abrupt visitor, Reuel's bloodshot eyes fixed on Lark.

"Larkspur Greenpool," he cried out. His hands grabbed clumsily at the air as if he could pull her in like a fish on a line. "I implore you, protect me! I am in danger, he's coming for me. I beg you to help me!"

In a state of disbelief, Lark shouldered through the crowd. She crossed the room in a few decisive steps. She felt the weight of her wand across her back, but didn't move to take it. Lark squared her shoulders against the startled looks and murmurs from all around her.

"Praise the Great Blue Sky," Reuel said when Lark stopped in front of him. His body sagged. "Tell your people I need protection. He is coming!"

"Who's this coming after you now?" Lark asked in an acerbic tone.

"It doesn't matter who," Reuel said. His eyes darted around and his head swiveled as if expecting something to jump out at him any second. "It only matters that he's got a Bloodring."

Chapter Fourteen

FIVE MINUTES LATER, Lark reluctantly took her place at the large table in the council-house's meeting room. Head Guardian Williams was at the head, flanked by two, three-striped Patrollers, Mark Piers and Judy Miller. Two Trackers were at the door, their faces shadowed by their hoods.

Across from Lark was Reuel. While never healthy-looking, that evening he looked as if he would crumble to dust if anything tapped him. His arms and legs under his baggy clothes were bony and meatless, his face almost skeletal with puffy grey bags under his eyes. The veins stood out on the backs of his hands like colored worms. He slouched in his chair as if sitting straight was too much effort for him. Someone had gotten him a cup of cool tea, but he didn't drink, only clutched it in his shaking hands.

Williams looked from the trembling man to Lark. He clasped his hands together on the table.

"He came here for you specifically," Williams said. "Do you know this man?"

"Yes sir," Lark said. "His name is Reuel Bucketsworth and we're from the same village."

"Do you know why he sought you out here?"

"No sir."

Williams grunted to himself. "Mr. Bucketsworth," he said in his usual, commanding voice, "you came here asking for protection, which is something we, as Guardians, are in the position to give you. However, we need to know more details. State your case."

At the words, Reuel snapped into lurid animation. His clawing hands reached out, dragging at the cloak of the Patroller next to him. Piers shook him off with a word of warning.

"He is coming," Reuel hissed. He flailed around, his breathing got shallow and ragged. "He has *it*. He stole it. He took it!"

"I don't understand you." Williams shook his head dismissively.

Lark suppressed a pained grimace. With every passing second, she got a worse feeling. Reuel continued talking but made even less sense. His words tumbled out, nothing more than the incoherent mumblings of a disturbed person. He seemed convinced something awful was coming for him. Lark needed to get him lucid enough to express it, if for no other reason than to protect everyone at Shadowmoor if what Reuel was afraid of actually existed.

"Slow down. You're safe here," she said in a low, calm voice. "Reuel, breathe, okay? If you have an amethyst, take it out. Now." She tacked the last word on with a bit more command force. It seemed to work. Once Reuel had his stone in his hands, some of the mad tension left him.

"Who's coming for you?" Lark asked. She knew she was taking extreme liberties by questioning Reuel before her superiors, but the information he had took precedence over procedure.

"Owen Dooley."

The name was unfamiliar to Lark. She pressed on, "Okay, and he's got a Bloodring?"

Reuel shuddered and wiped the ragged hem of his potato-sack cape across his face. "Yes."

Williams stood. He put both hands flat on the tabletop and leaned over Reuel. "How did this Dooley fellow get a Bloodring?"

The question sent Reuel into a paroxysm of rage-filled twitching. He screeched, "He stole it from me, he stole my precious treasure, ripped it from me." Flecks of spittle lodged in the corners of his mouth. He turned beseeching eyes from one person to another. "I told him the Ring was special, it was not for sale, not like the bracelet, not like the buckle but he wouldn't listen. He came to me again and again asking for the Ring but I wouldn't sell it. Not that one. And then he threatened me with violence and he t-took it. After I searched so many years for it! I found it. The Ring is *mine*."

While Lark didn't know anything about a bracelet, the buckle was most likely the same one that killed an Outsider and nearly Violet as well. Her eyes narrowed in anger.

Williams asked in a thundering voice, "Are you saying it was you who dug up those cursed artifacts? After twenty years of war, after the Great Division, after you knew any person is expressly forbidden to touch them? And you *sold* them?"

"I had to sell some of them," Reuel said. His sunken chest rose and fell rapidly under his ratty cape. "I never intended to part with the Ring. The others clamored for owners and I needed money for sustenance and to run my shop. I needed to survive."

Williams' face twisted in distaste. "How did you find the artifacts? They were hidden under Locks nobody can open."

"Not nobody," Reuel said. His face stretched into a parody of a smile. "I am their Chosen One. They called to me, they wouldn't let me rest until I found them and brought them to the light once more. It was I who discovered that Keys can be coerced to open more than one Lock. It was I who left my home and my ungrateful, ignorant family to rescue these treasures from an eternity of isolation and hunger, hunger I feel in my bones still—"

Williams interrupted Reuel's impassioned babbling. "You realize tampering with Ringsworn artifacts is a very serious offense? One that will need to be severely dealt with?"

"Yes, oh yes," Reuel said. His eyes shone. "Yes, lock me up. Put me away in your deepest, most secure dungeon. I will go."

"That remains to be seen. Who did you sell the artifacts to?" Williams asked. "I know of no-one within our Protected Isles who would have anything at all to do with such foul, cursed things."

Reuel flinched. He curled into himself and mumbled something.

"Speak up, now."

"Outsiders. In Compton."

The assembled Guardians looked uneasily at each other. Lark was floored. She always thought it was some kind of fluke that an Outsider got a hold of the edacitas knot, but Reuel purposely sold artifacts to them. Unsuspecting, ignorant Outsiders who didn't have any idea what they touched, and of course no defense against them. Lark put a hand to her forehead.

"I had to go where nobody knew me, where I was safe to continue my search," Reuel cried out. He clasped his shaking hands in front of himself as if praying. "I needed money and the Outsiders were willing to give it to me in great amounts for the artifacts, but I didn't know! I never dreamed they would be able to use them."

Williams' expression was thunderous. He turned it onto Lark, who jumped. "Did you know he had these items?"

Lark hesitated before she said, "I saw him with one, years

ago. He should never have brought it into our village." She glared across the table at Reuel.

"Why didn't you report this?" Williams asked.

"What good would it have done?" Lark tried not to show the unease she felt. Cold sweat trickled down her back. "It never occurred to me he would actually find any more. Then he left and nobody had any idea where he'd gone."

"I was on a quest," Reuel said. "One of utmost importance. Neither wine, nor food could satisfy me. I could barely even sleep for their voices calling out to me. I had to find the artifacts and rescue them."

"What else did you 'rescue'?" Williams asked in a dangerous tone. "And who did you sell artifacts to?"

"I'm not telling you any more until you vow to protect me." Reuel closed his mouth with a snap.

"Very well." Williams put both hands down on the table and levered himself upright. He addressed the entire room. "We will continue this discussion in a more secure location. Our visitor will be taken to our lock-up facility of Hadley's End, and I want Miss Greenpool to accompany him."

Lark's mouth fell open. The word *no* thundered through her mind. She jumped out of her chair.

"Why me, sir?" Lark asked. She knew it wasn't her place to question the Head Guardian but she couldn't keep silent. "I told you everything I know. Is my word not good enough?"

"I believe you, fledgling, but this is a larger matter than just your word," Williams said. He glanced at Reuel, who was hunched over in his chair, shivering and looking like a tap could shatter him. Williams muttered, "At the very least, our guest may be more comfortable with a familiar face around."

Lark couldn't reply. Apparently Williams wasn't expecting one because he immediately turned to the two Trackers at the door and barked, "McIntyre and Robertson, escort our guest to the holding cell downstairs. And Piers, arrange a coach for transport. Preferably one of the enclosed ones. The air is always damned heavy after one of these storms passes. We will move out at dawn."

"Yes, sir."

Williams strode across the rich carpet and pushed open the double doors to the meeting room. He stepped into the hallway and said over his shoulder, "Miss Greenpool, you are to gather your belongings as you may not be returning here again. Do not be late to the platform tomorrow morning."

Through the fist of rage and panic in her throat, Lark gritted out, "Yes, sir."

He didn't acknowledge her as he swept off. In the wake of the Head Guardian, Lark stepped into the hallway and froze. Violet hovered in an alcove. Her dark red bodice and black skirt almost blended in with the dimly-lit wallpaper. There was no way she didn't hear Williams' parting words. Her face was white and she clenched her hands together. The expression of pain on her face cut Lark like a blade. A scuffle behind Lark made her whirl to see Reuel lunge in the grip of the two Trackers. His eyes were fixed on Violet's form.

"A maiden Ringsworn," Reuel said. His mouth hung open, saliva shone on his lower lip. Violet recoiled and turned away from him. Reuel didn't seem fazed by that. He said in a slimy-soft voice, "What an honor, an honor indeed. How lovely, a vision of power and grace. Ripe like a peach for my plucking. What a perfect addition to my collection."

Anger spurred Lark to act without thinking. She grabbed her wand and pointed it at Reuel. "Violet is a person and not an object. No matter what her background is, you will treat her with respect or you will answer to *me*."

Unlike the first time Lark pointed her wand at him, Reuel flinched. Apparently he learned his lesson that it wasn't just a harmless piece of wood.

"No, don't hurt me. I was only trying to—"

"Come on, Bucketsworth," one of the Trackers said with a sigh. They shoved Reuel through a door that led to a staircase. The door closed behind them and cut off Reuel's frantic whining.

Lark looked up and down the hallway. It was deserted except for herself and Violet, but that didn't mean they were free to speak. Lark shouldered her wand and took a single, measured step forward even though she really wanted to run across the hallway and throw herself into Violet's arms.

"Wait for me tonight," Lark whispered.

Violet answered with the barest of nods. It was enough. Lark turned and bolted from the council-house. Outside, the wind was sharp and the sky dark. Lark shivered and rubbed her arms as she hurried down the path that led to the dorms. Her breath came hard and fast and her mind whirled. She felt trapped. She tried to blame the tears that stung her eyes on grit kicked up by the wind.

Blindly, Lark stumbled into the girls' dorm and stood in the entrance hall amid cloaks hung on hooks and a few pairs of rainboots. She braced one hand against the wall and tried to summon the will to brave either the dormitory or the common room, both of which rang with laughter and lively voices. She couldn't. She needed someplace private to think. Bypassing both, Lark slipped up the stairs into the loft.

The one small window was shuttered. In the darkness, she sank down on the bare floorboards and hugged her knees to her chest. Her crystal pouch pressed into her sternum, but Lark didn't register the slight discomfort. It was dwarfed by the agony in her heart. She needed to do something, come up with a plan but she could only see the bleak future of being locked up at Hadley's End, away from Violet, unable to help her if the worst happened. Pattering feet on the stairs outside shook Lark out of her funk. The door swung open and Alice popped into the loft.

"There you are," Alice said. The square of light on the floor vanished as she closed the door behind herself. "What are you doing sitting here in the dark?"

"Just thinking," Lark said. Automatically, she shook her quartz into her hand. Light filled the narrow space. She let go and the crystal floated up to the ceiling.

"I always forget you have those." Alice looked up with a surprised expression that quickly vanished. She plopped down next to Lark and offered a mint, which Lark waved off. Alice popped the candy into her mouth and said around it, "Everyone's dying to know who that fellow is and what's going on."

"I can't tell you what went on in that room," Lark said. "You know that."

With her chin resting on one fist, Alice studied Lark. "Something bad happened in there, didn't it? You look like somebody's made soup in your best hat. Come on, Lark. I'm your friend. You can tell me. Maybe I can help."

"I doubt it."

"Maybe just talking about it will help. You know, process whatever's going on." Alice placed her hand over her heart, "I swear nothing you say leaves this room. Okay?"

Lark pressed her lips together for a moment before she made a decision. She took a deep breath and said, "That man, Reuel Bucketsworth, is from my village and he's the one who caused all the trouble. He got his hands on a Bloodring and some Outsider in Compton stole it from him. Reuel's terrified of the guy finding him. They're packing Reuel off to Hadley's End first thing tomorrow and Williams ordered me to go with him."

Alice's eyes and mouth went round. "No way," she said. "Why?"

"Maybe he thinks I know something or they want me to babysit Reuel."

"Do you want to go?"

"Of course not," Lark said more sharply than she intended. She rubbed an hand across her forehead. "I belong here. I don't want to delay my training and I can't leave—everyone." Lark caught herself before she nearly blurted out something she shouldn't.

"What are you going to do?"

Lark shrugged. Despair weighted heavily on her shoulders. She stretched out her legs and leaned back on her hands. Outside, the wind howled in the eaves. The storm was close. She furrowed her brow and scowled while she mulled her options. Alice stood and studied Lark's crystal. Her face was animated and Lark had to suppress a smile as Alice cautiously poked at it with a finger.

Alice sat back down and said, "It's not so great for you, but I bet that fellow's happy they're not throwing him out or dragging him to Compton to use him as bait to get the Bloodring. That's what I'd do if I got a hold of him."

"You're right," Lark said in a quiet voice. An idea burst into her head. She leapt to her feet, light and full of hope. "Alice, can you tell everyone I'm in the bath?"

"Sure thing." Alice looked up at her. "I'm not going to ask if you have a plan or not, but I just want to say good luck with it."

"Thanks, you're the best." Lark clapped a hand to Alice's shoulder and gave her a big grin. She stowed her crystal and gallantly held the door open for Alice. After she saw Alice back to their dorm room, Lark raced down the stairs. She grabbed her cloak from the peg on the wall and whirled it over her shoulders. At full speed, she burst from the dormitory into the darkness.

Already the forefront of the storm was on them. Rocks and

leaves pelted Lark as she fought her way across the compound. The air was thick with the smell of rain, however none fell yet. Lark was grateful for that as she hurried down the path that led to Violet's cottage. A thin line of light was visible from between the planks that covered the window and Lark was glad to see it, not sure what she'd do if Violet was still holed up in the council-house. She was about to knock when the door opened and Violet pulled her inside. She closed the door firmly and backed Lark up against it.

Her deep eyes searched Lark's face. "They're making you leave here." Her voice was bleak. "Sunshine, what are we going to do?"

The intimate nickname and the despair in Violet's voice caused a war of light and darkness inside Lark. She reached out and gathered Violet to her. With a deep sigh, Violet settled into the embrace. Her arms stole around Lark's waist and held her tightly. Lark wished she could freeze time and spend eternity in that moment. She let one hand trail up and down Violet's back. The other rested on the nape of her neck, cradling Violet against her. Violet nestled her face into the crook of Lark's shoulder. Lark closed her eyes. She could never give that up. She allowed herself to bask in their closeness for an instant longer before she let Violet go. Lark crossed the small room. She sat down on the window seat and looked up at Violet.

"It's going to be okay," Lark said with as much confidence as she could muster. "I won't let them split us up. I have a plan."

"I'm listening," Violet said. She perched on the bed and leaned close to Lark. Her eyes danced with excitement.

"I'm leaving here tonight," Lark told her. "And I'm taking Reuel Bucketsworth with me."

"Where are you going?"

"Outside," Lark said. She reached out and twined her fingers with Violet's. "But I can't do it alone. Will you go with me? We're going to get into a lot of trouble for this, obviously. What I'm suggesting is breaking a number of Wanderer laws."

Violet's lips quirked up. She gave a low, throaty laugh. "You forget, I am no Wanderer."

"No, you aren't," Lark said.

"And you can always say I coerced you."

"I'll take responsibility for my own actions."

Without hesitating for an instant, Violet said, "Very well. I would be honored to accompany you on this journey."

Lark let out a sigh as the tension she hadn't been aware of holding left her. "I'm honored to have you."

"So what is our next move?"

"We break Reuel out of the holding cell."

"How?"

Lark let a slow, sly smile spread over her face. "The door's got a Lock on it."

Violet arched an elegant brow in understanding and leveled Lark with a low, calm look. "When do we put this plan into action?"

Lark glanced behind herself even through the window was fully shuttered and the velvet curtains drawn. She said, "I want to wait a few hours and mobilize when the storm's at its peak. Everyone will be asleep or at least hunkered down inside and we'll be able to move about more freely. I'm not going to lie and say it won't be dangerous."

"That is fine. I have been hungering for some danger recently." With their hands still entwined, Violet leaned in closer to Lark. So close, Lark could feel the warmth of Violet's breath on her lips as she said, "Why don't you pass the hours until we must leave here with me? I don't think it would be prudent for you to be wandering around right now, attracting attention."

Violet's tone ignited a rush of raw fire.

"Good idea."

Violet tilted her head. Her gaze held Lark's. "And what shall we do here while we wait?"

"What do *you* want?" Lark's voice was low and husky.

"I want to feel you against me," Violet said. "Would you be agreeable to coming over here next to me?"

While her heart leapt at the thought of joining Violet on that big, comfortable-looking bed, Lark hesitated. She disentangled their fingers and rubbed a hand through her hair. "Are you sure? I, um, don't want to give you the wrong idea."

"You give me plenty of ideas," Violet purred. "Many of which are decidedly wrong."

Lark didn't need any more convincing. She stood and threw off her cloak and wand. She reached down to take off her boots but Violet stopped her.

"Don't mind those, it's not as if I will be sleeping in this bed tonight, or maybe ever again," Violet said. She edged back and opened up a spot for Lark to sprawl down on.

For the first time, Lark didn't sit chastely across from Violet, but laid down beside her, propped up on the pile of pillows. While she felt odd with her boots on the dark grey-shrouded bed, Lark soon forgot her consternation as Violet shifted closer and snuggled under Lark's outstretched arm. She placed one hand on the hollow in front of Lark's shoulder and rested her cheek on it. Her other hand was on Lark's belly, absently stroking up and down over the dappled green singlet. The caress which started at Lark's belt and ended at where her crystal pouch rested just under her breasts breathed life into a number of desires.

"Tonight. Two guards are stationed by the front entrance to the council-house. Male Trackers. I don't recall their names," Violet said. Her voice hummed through Lark's body. "They are on shift until dawn."

"Really? That's very useful information," Lark said. Her words were strained and breathless. Violet's hand on her and the soft weight of her body pressed against Lark's own was heady. She had trouble keeping her thoughts straight. Violet molded her body to Lark's. She chuckled as she did so, as if she was aware of the exquisite bliss and torment her closeness caused Lark.

"I make it a priority to keep informed of what is going on in that building," Violet said. "I have perfected the art of blending in to my surroundings, of giving off an aura that I don't care anything about their Guardian trivialities. They often speak as if I am not in the room."

"That's foolish of them."

"Yes, I agree. Have you ever seen the holding cell where they are keeping your village man?"

"No, I haven't," Lark said.

"Let me explain it then." Violet continued in her usual matter-of-fact tone, "You saw the door where they took your village man. There is a latch on the door at the top of the stairs, on the outside. There are no windows on the lower level and no other way out, so we will have to get him up and out the way we come in. Yannis Jordan is taking the first shift guarding him tonight. The holding room is small. He will probably be sitting opposite the cell, with his back to the south wall. There is an armchair with a table beside it, on the side away from the stairs where he most likely will station himself for the duration of his shift."

Rosalie's father. Lark got a cold shot in her gut. She was impressed with Violet's knowledge and calm attention to detail. Lark bent her head and pressed a kiss to Violet's temple in thanks.

Lark said, "So that's three guards to take out."

"How shall we do it?" Violet asked. "I have my blades, but I would rather not have to kill anyone. At least not tonight."

"I've got an idea," Lark said. "One that Wanderers won't be able to defend against and that Reuel Bucketsworth will."

"Excellent," Violet murmured.

"I just want to confirm one thing. Crystals have no effect on you?"

"That's right," Violet said. "I could probably destroy one if I had to, although it would be a pity. I rather like them."

"Don't worry, you won't have to. And that's good to know."

They lapsed into silence for a few minutes, and Lark was simply content to lie with Violet in her arms, thinking and plotting until Violet stirred and spoke.

"What will Outside be like, I wonder?"

"I've only seen pictures, but the buildings are bigger than anything here and all different kinds of shapes," Lark said. "The roads are wide and black and everyone is in a hurry."

"I imagine that's why," Violet said, her tone thoughtful, "they like 'fast food'."

Lark laughed and took up the hand that was resting on her middle. She pressed a quick kiss to the inside of Violet's wrist. Lark said, "Probably. I'll take the regular-speed version of food, though."

Outside, a hard wave of rain hit the cottage with a boom. Unconsciously, Lark pulled Violet closer to her as the roof shook under the assault. The cottage was smaller than the dorm where Lark was used to waiting out storms and the power of it was close and raw. The wind howling outside sounded almost human. The storm shutters rattled as if something outside was desperately trying to get in.

"Bad one tonight," Lark said.

"It will swallow us whole," Violet said. She hoisted herself up on her hands before she draped herself fully over Lark's body.

Her skirts painted the entire bed in a wash of black. "Is this all right?" she murmured.

"Yes, it is. Feel free to continue."

With the tiny quirk to her lips Lark loved, Violet reached out and trailed tender fingers down Lark's face, outlining her cheeks and lips before she surged up to claim Lark's mouth in a kiss that soon deepened. Almost losing Violet made Lark bold and she eagerly pushed into Violet's mouth. Violet met her with equal fervor.

The urge to go further took hold of her and Lark spread her legs. Violet breathed out a moan as she nestled between them. The position left Lark feeling exposed and vulnerable, but she soon forgot that. A deep, trembling heat filled her as their bodies molded together, their lips never parting. She took Violet around the waist, then her hands drifted to Violet's hips in a wordless plea. In response, Violet moved with her and pressed gently into the growing heat between Lark's thighs. The feeling was incredible, as if a glowing coal dropped deep into her belly. Lark's skin was alive with electricity, she burned with the desire to be touched. She needed Violet's hands on her more than she needed air.

Lark reached down and pulled out her shirt as she had in the woodshed that wonderful afternoon after their first training. She broke the kiss just long enough to gasp out, "You can also continue here."

"I would love to," Violet said in a low purr.

Quick as a cat, Violet's hand slipped under Lark's shirt. She tugged expertly at the wraps. They came loose and Lark arched her back to free the length of cotton. Violet pulled the cloth down to rest around Lark's middle. She couldn't see what Violet was doing, but Lark was intensely aware of Violet's fingers as she trailed them in a lazy circle around her fullness. Lark's breath hitched in her throat as Violet cupped her breast.

Violet studied Lark's face for a moment, then bent her head to kiss the taut nubs tenting up Lark's shirt, first one, then the other. Lark cradled Violet against her. Her belly clenched and her thighs ached with suppressed need. She was desperate to have nothing between herself and those maddeningly soft lips.

Lark arched her body once more and bit back a groan. "Violet," she said between heaving breaths, "if it's all right, I want you to um..." she trailed off.

"What do you want?" Violet's eyes flicked up to meet hers again. She gave Lark a wicked look and dropped another kiss to her covered nipple, which cause Lark to groan again. Violet said, "I am yours to command." The words jolted through Lark.

"I need to sit up," Lark said. Violet drew back and Lark was barely able to contain the wave of desire as she reached down and pulled her shirt up to her armpits then over her head in a single motion. Her crystal pouch went along with it, but she was unable to think of anything else than how much she ached for Violet's touch. Lark swallowed hard and said, "I want your kiss...there. On me."

"By the blessed goddess." The words were soft, reverent. Violet pressed Lark to lay back down and kissed a line of fire down Lark's neck. The embroidery on the front of Violet's bodice was slightly scratchy on her tight nipples and bare belly, but Lark loved it just the same.

Violet moved downwards, dragging her lips over Lark's skin until she reached the swell of Lark's breast. Lark had to stifle a cry of ecstasy as Violet's tongue traced a ring around one pebbled aureole. Violet cupped Lark's other breast with her hand, her thumb brushed over the nipple. Lark groaned and arched her back in response.

When Violet's mouth came down fully over her, Lark had to close her eyes. Her head went back into the pillows as a wave of fire hotter than any other she'd ever felt roared through her. She was grateful for the noise of the storm outside because she couldn't stop from crying out. Her hips rocked of their own accord. She was powerless against the force of pleasure gripping her. It was too much. Lark breathed in short gasps. A universe opened up behind her closed eyes, sparkles of light flashed in the darkness. She was a heartbeat away from yanking her trousers open and inviting Violet to finish what she started. But she couldn't. Lark didn't want it to happen like that.

"Please stop," Lark gasped.

"Why?"

"Oh Green Trees," Lark said. She looked down to where Violet hovered, lips inches from her slick, tender nipple. "This is going to end up somewhere I don't want it to. Not yet."

"I'm sorry," Violet said as she sat up. A flash of pain and

unease crossed her face.

"No, don't be sorry," Lark said. She rubbed one hand through her hair. "That was good. Too good, maybe."

Violet answered with a small half-smile. Lark couldn't help but lean forward and kiss Violet one more time, softly and tenderly before she stood up. She was very aware of her bare breasts exposed for all the world to see. A quick glance around the room revealed her shirts and crystal pouch draped over the wash-jug. As much as she felt out in the open, Lark didn't mind. She held herself still, allowing Violet to look her over from head to foot. For the first time, Lark understood the unbelievable feeling of baring her skin to someone she had so many feelings for; desire, protectiveness...and love. The word rang true in Lark's heart and mind. A great burst of understanding dawned on her. She loved Violet. Probably had for a while but it was the first time she actually put the word to it.

"Sweet Limor," Violet breathed from her position on the rumpled bed. She cast her eyes down. "Have mercy on my soul."

"It's all right, you can look as much as you want."

Lark was unsure about the figure she was casting, her wraps coiled about her hips, standing tall and free and shirtless but the heat she'd seen in Violet's brief gaze told her it was an agreeable one. Lark grabbed up her discarded clothing and strode over to the water closet. She left the door open on purpose. She wanted Violet to see her, if she was so inclined. She wanted Violet to know her, all of her, and she wasn't going to hold back.

In the small room, Lark splashed her face and shook out her long tails. Her earlier revelation still rang thought her. Lark's hands trembled. She felt like her body couldn't contain the amount of joy she felt at that moment. Her mind whirled. With the movements that were automatic from years of practice, Lark fixed her wraps, then pulled on her long-sleeved, black shirt and the green dappled one over it. She settled her crystal pouch and turned from the mirror. Outside, the storm howled and the keening wind shook the walls. Lark folded herself into a sitting position on the bed and guided Violet to her side once more. Violet curled up and lay her head on Lark's shoulder.

"My Sunshine. You are so beautiful, so giving of all of yourself," Violet breathed. She reached out and put a gentle hand on Lark's face, buffing a thumb over her lips in an echo of the motion she'd used earlier on Lark's breast. "I could very easily—" she broke off without finishing the thought, eyes dark and head down, withdrawing. Violet murmured, "But maybe I shouldn't. This is all new for you. You are so young."

"I'm not a child," Lark said. She took Violet's chin in one hand and brought her back to up meet her gaze. "I'm legally an adult. I'm a Guardian. I'm old enough to give my life to protect my home and my people. Why can't I share some intimacy with someone I—care for." Lark choked on the last words. She didn't mean to say that much.

"You care for me," Violet said softly.

"Sure do," Lark replied, purposely in a light tone. "And I really like being with you, Violet. You are really good to me, and I want to return the favor," Lark said. She fought a smile that threatened to break the mood as Violet's cheeks pinked in an uncharacteristic blush.

"I am not opposed to that," Violet said. She pressed her hands to her cheeks. A sharp gust of wind shook the cottage. Rain beat against the storm shutters and droplets sprayed onto the glass. Violet pulled herself from Lark's loose hold and sat up. She twisted to look at the sand clock over one shoulder. Violet said, "It seems the storm is peaking. The time to move has come."

Suddenly on full-alert, Lark got to her feet.

"Get anything together you want to take with you," Lark said. "We'll be moving fast, so pack as light as possible."

"I understand," Violet said. She stood and strapped her knife belt around her small waist. She tucked the belt under the hem of her bodice and settled her full skirts around the daggers before she picked up a few items from the dresser and slipped them into her pockets.

Lark was ready. She had never felt so alive, so strong and ready to do battle. She wondered how much was due to what she and Violet had just shared. Lark shouldered her wand and pulled her cloak over her shoulders. At the door, Violet put on her own cloak. It was the one made of light-sucking material she wore the day she arrived. Reality set in and Lark's heart pounded. Her skin tingled with anticipation and nerves. They were really going to defy the direct order of the leader of the Guardians, head off alone into the great Outside, stand together against anything that would threaten them.

Together as one.

Lark's heart gave a leap in her chest, and she knew she had to speak. "Violet, I want to tell you something. I—"

"Don't," Violet said. She shook her head, and reached out to press a finger to Lark's lips. "Don't say it Lark, my Sunshine. Please." She rose up and kissed Lark briefly on the lips, using the motion to pull Lark's hood over her head. She whispered, "There is no need for the burden of words. I will stand by you until the end."

Taken aback, Lark nevertheless felt a surge of confidence. She squared her shoulders. Her wand was snug and ready against her back, her crystals warm and safe under her shirt. She braced one hand on the door and looked back over her shoulder at Violet.

"Let's do this," Lark said. She cracked a wild grin.

Chapter Fifteen

THE STORM GRABBED her the second she stepped outside. Lark staggered under the onslaught. Instantly her cloak twisted around her legs and the freezing rain pounded on her back and shoulders. The thick material sloughed it off, but Lark knew it was only a matter of time before she was soaked through. Behind her, she felt Violet's presence. Lark glanced back, but could only make her out as the blacker-than-black hole in the storm.

The paths were rivers of mud so Lark strode across the grass to the council-house. She pressed herself against the wall of the council-house for a moment as she scanned the deserted compound. The rain continued to pour down and Lark shook the streams of rain from her hood. Nobody was out and thanks to the storm shutters, they were unobserved. She crouched down beside the front porch and put one hand into her shirt. She came back with her turquoise. Lark focused her concentration and the knobby stone started to glow in her hand. She'd forgotten about that. The outside world was blotted out and Lark was swept into a warm tent.

"I've got my cloak around us," Violet whispered into Lark's ear.

"Thanks," Lark said. This was going to work. They were a team.

Lark steeled herself and calmed her mind. She sent a shot of energy though the turquoise and it hummed in her fingers. Relaxing waves pulsed through the air. *Sleep.* She fed more power to the crystal and extended the soft, warm field of slumber past herself and Violet, filling the minds she sensed in the building. True to her word, Violet was unaffected by the crystal. In fact, the crystal's influence was blocked around her as if Violet was a pillar of stone. On the edge of her consciousness, a golden spark flared into life. The source was Reuel's amber, counteracting the turquoise.

After the waves of sleep settled, Lark waited for another agonizing minute, hardly daring to breathe. When she thought it was safe, she slipped from the warm confines of Violet's cloak and quickly let them both into the entrance hall. With one arm out in a silent command to wait, Lark stood still for a moment. Rainwater sluiced off their cloaks and pooled on the tiles. Gentle snoring broke the sudden quiet. The two guards slept soundly, one sprawled out on the floor and one propped up against the wall.

They crept down the stairs to the room where Reuel was sitting on the cot in the holding cell. Yannis Jordan was slouched in a chair across from the cell, just as Violet had predicted. He was also dead to the world with his chin resting on his chest. Reuel had his amber in his hands.

Lark was pleased to see that under his disreputable cloak, he was wearing a new outfit of sturdy trousers and coarsely-knit sweater that probably came from their storage shed. An empty bowl and basket sat on a tray next to him. Reuel perked up when Lark came into his field of view. He looked past her and in an instant, his wan, woebegone face changed. His mouth stretched, revealing yellowed teeth in a chilling approximation of a smile and he leapt to his feet, swaying slightly as his wasted body rebelled against the sudden movement.

Lark held a finger to her lips. She stepped back and let Violet come forward. Violet brushed back her cloak and extended one hand to the door of the holding cell. While Reuel tried to eat her alive with only his eyes, Violet grasped the Lock on the holding cell's door and it crumbled to dust. She stepped back, looking calm and Lark finally let her breath out. While she knew logically this Lock was not a malevolent one, Lark was still relieved to see for herself that Violet was unaffected by its destruction.

The door swung open. Reuel lurched out and his shambling steps sent him careening into the small table next to the sleeping Guardian, nearly tipping it over. With wide-eyed horror, Lark could only watch as the mug Yannis had been drinking from rolled across the tabletop. It reached the edge and dropped off. Lark flinched and steeled herself for a fight. The crash she expected didn't come and she cautiously opened her eyes. Violet crouched next to the table with her robe and skirts spilling out around her like a lake of ink. The mug was nestled in one white hand, inches from the floor.

Violet moved silently as a shadow as she rose and set the mug back down. With an impatient motion, she shook the drops of spilled tea from her fingers. She shot a glare at Reuel who seemed immune to its poison. As soon as her heart started beating again, Lark ushered them up the stairs and they hurried through the howling storm, bent over and heads down. Lark was relieved that Reuel came with them without any question or complaint. She had a feeling that was due mostly to Violet's presence.

The covered hangar area where the coaches were kept loomed up in front of them. Lark dashed in and went straight to a line of mid-sized coaches. A small, slim figure sprang out from one of the support pillars. Lark screeched to a halt in a flurry of long black cloak.

"Alice! What are you doing here?"

"I'm coming with you," Alice said. "to Compton."

"What? No, you're staying here," Lark said. "This isn't your fight."

Alice planted her feet and said, "One, this certainly is my fight and two, you've never been Outside." She threw her cloak open and Lark saw for the first time she was wearing a form-fitting pink shirt with striped sleeves and a picture of a cupcake on the front and slim, denim trousers. Alice crossed her arms over her chest. "I've been out there and I can help you. I know things about surviving there you don't and I can help you get around the city." She glanced over to where Reuel stood a small distance away. His arms hung limply by his sides. He swayed in the wind as if he was a scarecrow. Alice said, "Do you want to be dependent on *him* to guide you?"

"The girl has a point," Violet said softly to Lark. "I urge you to decide quickly before any of the guards wake up and sound the alarm."

Lark fixed Alice with a stern look. "Okay, you can come with us." She held up a hand to head off Alice's triumphant leap. "But I want you to know I'm in charge. This is going to be dangerous and if I tell you to run, you do it, all right?"

"Yeah, I guess I can agree to that," Alice said. "So let's go then."

Lark nodded and hurriedly untied the mooring line of the coach nearest her. It was a sturdy one, tapered at bow and stern for speed and would hold all four of them easily. It was divided into four sections by planks that could be used as benches in safe times or to hide under when it wasn't. Unfortunately, it didn't have a roof, but with Alice to cast a shield while Lark drove they didn't need one. Lark threw the rope into the coach and grabbed her wand. She stilled her mind and prepared to levitate it when Alice's shout interrupted her. Lark had time to only get out half of the oath she was aiming for when a whistling thud resounded through the hangar. Lark jumped back. The quivering shaft of an arrow stuck out from the pillar next to her.

Cloak streaming with rain, Williams strode into the hangar, flanked by several other Guardians. Yannis Jordan was in the lead, face red and dangerous-looking. Instead of a wand, Williams had a crossbow in his hands and it was aimed directly at Violet. Lark cursed the fact that the coach was between them. Even if she made a leap over it, she still wouldn't get to Violet in time.

"This has gone far enough," Williams said. His hands were steady on the weapon, his eyes cold. "While our energy doesn't affect you, I imagine, Miss Ironwrought, you are just as susceptible to steel as anyone else."

"Would you care to bet your life on that?" Violet said in a mocking tone. However, Lark didn't have to see her face to know she was only wearing the mask of bravado.

Lark cast about for something, anything to help and found her scrying crystal in her hand. If only Violet would look her way, Lark could toss it over and give her the means to defend herself. Beside her, Alice was frozen with one foot over the side of the coach, hands full of rope. The closest one to Violet was Reuel, and he just stood there with his mouth hanging open.

The crossbow didn't waver as Williams turned to address Lark. "Whatever that Ringsworn promised you, let me assure you it's all lies." His voice boomed over the storm's howls. "Or whatever she's blackmailing you with, all will be forgiven if you simply put down your wand and come back to us now."

With a shake of her head, Lark shoved her hood back. She glanced over to Violet, who had moved closer to Reuel. Behind her back, her long fingers curled around Reuel's homemade cloak.

Lark needed to distract him. She stepped forward and said in a loud, pompous voice, "Violet hasn't promised me anything and I trust her with my secrets. Head Guardian, you're about to make a huge mistake."

"I see," Williams' voice was hard. "Let this be on your head, then, young fledgling."

"Please—NO!" Lark's words ended in a shriek as Williams loosed the crossbow bolt.

In a shimmering silver arc, Violet's hand came up and she snatched the bolt out of the air. Beside her, Reuel's limp body slumped to the ground. She only held the missile for an instant before she flicked it back where it came from. Williams staggered back with the bolt protruding from his shoulder. He grabbed the shaft and fell to his knees. Around him, the other Guardians brandished their wands.

"You double-crossing traitor!" Yannis hollered. He whipped his wand back and released a burst of energy.

The crackle of the Guardian's attack was drowned out by Lark's agonized scream. Violet didn't have a chance to move before the blue beam hit her square in the chest. Lark's own chest seized with a fist of pain as if she was struck as well. Against the roaring storm, Violet stood still. Lark couldn't breathe. She waited for Violet to fall. She didn't.

A low chuckle started up. Lark felt it rising from the ground, burning up through her knees until it burst out into a bright, ringing gale of maniacal hate. Violet threw her head back and bared her teeth in a vicious snarl as she laughed into the howling wind. This was the monster Violet had warned her about, the demon she struggled so hard to hide.

"Did you think you could stop me with that? How wrong you are." Her tone was deep and feral. She held her hands out in front of herself and the cluster of Guardians looked at each other in alarm.

"Dammit, I told you to hold your fire," Williams shouted. He dropped the crossbow and drew his wand in his good hand. His face was dark with rage and something else—fear. "Shields up and don't let her get too close. At no time are you to take retaliatory action, understood?"

"Yes sir," the Guardians replied in unison.

Each Guardian snapped up a shield around themselves. Violet took a slow, measured step forward. The air hummed with energy. The group started to back away. Violet met every backwards step with a steady, forward one of her own. When she herded them to the edge of the hangar, Violet lowered her head and growled at Yannis, "I should thank you, Guardian Jordan. You have given me a sweet, powerful gift, one of such strength and deep roots as I have not tasted before." Her lip curled and she spat, "However it is rank and unrefined, like its giver."

The vibrations of every word thrummed through Lark as if they were connected. Violet shimmered with power, dangerous and magnificent. The air seemed to solidify into an icy black wall. A blue glow started up between Violet's splayed fingers and swiftly changed to her own silver shimmer.

"Say goodbye, Wanderer filth." The words were cold, mocking. Lark had never heard Violet use that tone before, no matter how angry she was. It was chilling. Lark knew what was coming next. She couldn't speak, couldn't move or even take her eyes from the scene.

Lark clenched her hands, steeling herself for the worst. Instead of a retaliating attack, Violet paused for the briefest of seconds before she made a sweeping motion with her hand and called up a wall of dizzying, almost-white flames. They bisected the hangar, cutting the group of Guardians off from the neat rows of waiting vessels, then circled around to contain the group. Violet dropped her hands and fell back a step.

That was the catalyst that unfroze Lark.

"We move out now. I've got Violet, you get Reuel," Lark snapped the order to Alice.

"Yes ma'am," Alice said.

Lark leapt into the front of the coach. Alice scrambled in behind her. Even before Alice had a chance to sit down, Lark sent a surge of energy through her wand and the coach shot forward. Alice let out a squeak and fell to the deck in a tumble of cloak and limbs. Sweat pricked at Lark's hairline with the effort it took to maneuver in such close quarters. She heard shouting from inside the fire barrier and saw a few flashes of energy, but nothing got through.

They passed Reuel's unconscious body and Alice used her wand to sweep him into the coach. She deposited him in the cargo space at the stern. Lark dipped the side just enough to scoop Violet up around the waist and pull her unceremoniously into the boat-like vessel. They landed in a tumble on the floor of the coach, which wavered for an instant before Lark righted it.

In Lark's arms, Violet trembled. Her entire form shimmered

with stolen energy.

"Alice," Lark called over her shoulder, "get ready to shield us."

The coach soared free of the hangar and burst into the storm. Wind buffeted the vessel and rain poured over them in stinging, icy needles before the glowing green of Alice's shield hummed into existence around them. The rain and wind stopped. Even so, Lark kept her body bent low over the plank in front of her.

"I have to get rid of this energy," Violet said. Her upper lip shone with sweat. "Let me give them a parting shot to remember us by."

"Do it," Lark said.

Violet bared her teeth and held out both hands. A shockwave of silver energy rippled out from her fingertips. Alice's shield didn't even slow it down. The wave hit the hangar. It shattered the supports and sent the roof crashing down on the group of Guardians. The one glance Lark spared over her shoulder told her that through luck or design, Violet left enough of the pillars intact that the roof was not flat on the ground. The coaches were left badly damaged and temporarily unusable, and while the Guardians were trapped under the timber, Lark was reasonably sure nobody was crushed.

Lark spared a second to give Violet a quick nod before she turned her attention to steering the coach through the howling storm. In the middle of the coach, Alice held her wand in both hands. Her shield wavered and flickered but didn't vanish.

"Keep it up Alice," Lark gritted her teeth as a blast of wind knocked them off course.

"Trying!" Alice shouted back. She rubbed a hand over her forehead. A bolt of lightning cracked quite close to them and Alice flinched. She recovered and shored up the shield with the stubborn strength she'd often shown in their practice sessions.

"Atta girl!" Lark said. "Just hang on a bit more. We're coming to the edge of the storm soon."

At Lark's side, Violet had her eyes screwed shut. She was completely still except for the rise and fall of her even breaths. The coach gave a deep lurch, which Lark struggled to correct. With the motion, Violet's eyes snapped open and she wrenched herself upright. She grabbed onto the plank in front of her and peered over the side with trepidation. Without thinking, Lark reached out and hugged Violet around the shoulders with her free arm.

"I hope you're not afraid of heights," Lark said. She sent the coach soaring over a looming outcrop of black rocks that jutted up from the surrounding forest.

"No, I quite like heights," Violet said. She gave Lark a wan smile that had the recipient feeling relieved and giddy. "It's hitting the ground I have an issue with."

"That's not going to happen today," Lark said. While she couldn't quite believe they were actually speeding toward the city in a stolen coach with a sprung fugitive in tow and the wreckage of the outpost behind them, Lark felt lighter than she had since Reuel came stumbling into Shadowmoor. She almost wanted to laugh.

After a few more agonizing minutes of battling to steer through the storm, the coach burst out of the wall of clouds and moonlight broke over their heads. The deadly chill left the air. The howling wind was replaced by the soft sounds of crickets. Overhead, the stars winked down on them from the clear blackness.

The shield vanished in a hiss of static and Alice collapsed onto the floor of the coach. She peered up at Violet.

Alice shook her head and said, "Holy crap, Violet, I didn't know you could do that, like explode things and whatnot." She pulled herself into a sitting position and crossed her legs. "I have to say, you have the evil laugh thing *down*. I nearly wet myself when you let loose with it — and I'm on your side."

Violet quirked her lips up in a pleased smile.

"He's not dead, is he?" Alice asked. She poked at the pile of rumpled clothing where Reuel lay.

"No, he will be fine after he regains his energy, although it may take a day or two," Violet said. "I regret having to use him like that."

"You didn't have a choice," Lark said.

"That's true." Violet's words were soft. Her fingers knit around each other for an instant before she folded her arms on the side of the coach and looked out over the moonlit countryside sprawling underneath them. She glanced back once over her shoulder and caught Lark's eye. Violet said, "This is truly the best way to travel. Your piloting skills are impressive."

Alice snorted. Violet looked at her with a question in her deep eyes.

Instead of answering, Alice cupped her hand over her mouth and said in a stage-whisper to Lark, "I guess I shouldn't tell her that you failed your driving test five times before Guardian Snell got fed up with retesting you and just threw your papers into the fire, should I?"

"No, you don't need to spill that," Lark said. "And just for the record, most of the times I failed on a technicality."

"Yeah, the technicality that gravity exists."

Violet covered her smile with one hand.

"I passed on the sixth try," Lark said. "An actual career coach-driver, who I've known since I was a youngun, tested me that time. Funny how my driving skills improved when there wasn't somebody constantly yelling insults at me and threatening to hurl my butt over the side."

With an arch of one brow, Violet said, "I can see how that might affect one's performance."

Lark pulled out her agate and consulted it. "We'll be arriving at the border of the city in half an hour or so. We'll land in the middle of it."

"Aye aye captain!" Alice sang out. She sprawled out and wrapped herself up in her cloak. "I'm beat from all that shielding. Mind if I take a nap?"

"No problem, I'll wake you up when we get there," Lark said. She slipped her agate back into her pouch and pretended to be busy looking at something over the side when she was actually calculating how long she should wait before letting her hand steal into Violet's.

In only a few minutes, Alice's light snores resonated through the hull and Lark was about to reach out for Violet when the cool fingers pressed into her palm. Violet scooted over until her shoulder brushed Lark's.

"Now that you've seen what I truly can do, and the damage I cause, are you not afraid?"

"Nope," Lark said. She tightened her fingers around Violet's. "Not for an instant. I respect you and your power. It's part of who you are and that's fine with me. I want you to know I'm okay with that. All of it, even the stuff I don't know yet."

Violet didn't say anything more, but Lark was intensely

aware of every breath along with her own happily racing heart.

The forest thinned and the Border loomed in front of them, invisible and intact, at least in that area. Lark felt the vibrations travel through the air. She hummed the matching note the way she practiced during training. The ancient energy parted enough to let them through and reformed behind them.

They left the embrace of the land and for a while, only the black expanse of the sea spread out underneath them. The wind carried the tang of brine and Lark felt like a speck of sand under the dazzling sprawl of stars overhead. Violet leaned against her, soft and relaxed as if dozing. Lark wrapped her cloak around them both, enjoying the closeness and warmth.

Once more, they flew overland. The glowing clusters of white and orange lights in the horizon slowly became larger. Violet sat up. Her face was alive with interest. She crossed her arms on the side of the coach and gazed out. Beneath them, the crisscross of black roads was studded with lights at regular intervals. Occasionally they passed over a farmhouse and barns larger than any Lark had ever seen in her life.

Lark reached over and gave Alice's foot a shake. Alice sat up and yawned.

"We're coming up to the city," Lark said. "I'm going to go in as high as I can and set us down in a straight drop so we won't be seen. Alice, use the mooring rope to make sure Reuel's not going to fall out. Violet, grab onto something so you're secure as well."

Nods met her announcement and Lark put the coach into a steep climb. The city lights blossomed beneath them as Lark pushed them both higher and farther. Violet clutched at the bench.

Lark, feeling brash, said, "It'll be over in a minute, but feel free to hang onto me if you like."

Long arms wrapped around her waist from behind, and Lark held back a gasp of surprise as Violet pressed against her back. A quick glance over at Alice assured Lark she was busy trussing up Reuel in the cargo area. As they ascended, the wooden beams creaked and groaned. Around them was nothing but silence and the air steadily grew colder. Lark was glad for the warm presence at her back. Sitting flat on the deck, Lark inched forward to wedge her knees under the plank in front of herself. She turned enough to put her non-wand arm around Violet and drew her close. Lark hoped she could pull off the casually disinterested expression she was fighting to maintain. At the stern, Alice had her hands wrapped around the ends of the rope and looked quite calm and ready.

They reached the apex of their flight.

"Hang on! Here we go!" Lark's voice sounded loud in the chill silence.

Violet hid her face in Lark's shirt. Lark put both arms around her, enfolding her in a tight embrace before she released control of the coach and let it drop. The gaping, artificial-light studded mass of buildings opened up beneath them. Wind whipped through cloaks and skirts. The ground hurtled toward them. When they were on level with the tallest of the buildings, Lark brandished her wand. She caught the coach just as they plunged into an alley and slowed it with a gentle touch. She set the coach down on the damp pavement amid weather-beaten metal boxes overflowing with trash. As soon as they stopped moving, Violet pulled away and sat up. Lark was cold where Violet had been.

For a moment, Lark held herself still and just looked around in awe. The city was different from the pictures she'd seen in training. It was larger and harsher that she imagined, with a deep, thrumming energy pulsing through it like the heartbeat of a sleeping colossus. The buildings were huge and loomed over them. The alley should have been suffocating, but Lark felt free. The darkness was split by lights everywhere. Shiny metal ground carts roared by on the road, each equipped with their own sets of multicolored lights.

Lark's heart thudded. She shouldered her wand and scrubbed her sweaty palms on her trousers.

They were Outside.

Chapter Sixteen

"IS EVERYONE ALL right?" Lark asked quietly.

"I'm fine," Violet said. She looked pale but composed in the orange glow of the lamps lining the street.

"No problems over here," Alice said. "Nice landing, by the way, except I think I left my dinner up in the air somewhere along the line."

Violet got to her feet and with a rich swish of skirts and cloak, she stepped over the side of the coach. Lark and Alice followed. Violet walked to the end of the alley and stood still for a moment, gazing up and down the road. Her form was outlined by the streetlights. When she turned back, her face was alight with wonder and excitement.

"Where shall we go now?" Violet asked.

Lark said, "We need to find a place to spend the night. Alice, any ideas?"

"How about a hotel?" Alice said. "We'll need money. I've got some, but it won't last long."

"I will sell my blades," Violet said immediately.

"No, you shouldn't do that," Lark said. Without thinking, she placed a hand on Violet's arm. "They're special to you."

"Nonsense. They should fetch a good price. I have read about such transactions and I would like to try my hand at it." Violet drew close to Lark and murmured, "And I have something much more special to me now."

Lark felt her cheeks warm. Violet looked so excited at the prospect that Lark didn't have the heart to deny her. "All right. We can do that tomorrow when the shops open."

"Excuse me," Alice said. She put her hands on her hips. "But aren't we in this pickle because of Ringsworn stuff floating around? Isn't it kind of defeating the purpose?"

"Don't worry, young Guardian," Violet said. "While they are Ringsworn-made, they are nothing more than what they seem."

"Okay then," Alice said. "Hang on a moment. I want to take a look around."

She popped out of the alley and Lark waited a bit for her to return. Soon, Alice came running back to them and ducked into the alley.

"Good news," Alice said breathlessly. "I know where we are. The main street is only a couple blocks from here. We're right in the middle of Compton and there's a hotel just down the road a ways. Good choice, Lark."

"Thanks," Lark said.

Alice looked over to where Reuel lay in the coach. Her mouth twisted into a grimace. "You two are going to have to carry him. We can't be too obvious about levitating stuff anymore."

Violet echoed Alice's look of distaste. "If we must," she said.

With some jostling and cringing, Lark and Violet slung an arm each over their shoulders and hoisted Reuel's unresponsive body between them. With her free hand, Lark levitated the coach up to the roof of a nearby building. It wasn't the best solution, but it would do for the time being. If any Outsider happened to find it, they would most likely mistake it for a boat and hopefully leave it alone.

Alice took the lead and directed them to a white-striped zone on the road that was controlled by a set of three lights. When Lark studied them in a module about the logistics of travelling Outside, she hadn't really understood how it all worked, and gratefully followed Alice.

The hotel was a tall building with a large glowing orange sign on it that said Holly's Hotel. It was only a block away from their landing site, but Lark was still sweating and breathless when they reached the wide concrete steps that led up to the entrance.

"Wait a moment," Lark said. She paused and caught her breath. "Here's the plan. Violet and I will pretend to be drunk so Alice, you're going to play the well-meaning friend and get us all a room. We'll stand behind you, so you do the talking."

"One room?"

"Yup. We have to stick together."

"Okay, but I'm not sharing a bed with him."

"Green Trees, I wouldn't make anyone do that," Lark said. She looked over at Violet and nodded. "Ready? Okay, start now."

With that, Lark let out a giggle and lurched forward. Violet played along and matched her shambling steps with Lark. En route, Violet sang a few warbling notes of a song, and even though she was being purposely bad, Lark was moved by the beauty of her voice. She quickly snapped back into character when the glass doors parted before them and they entered the lobby. The carpet under Lark's boots was worn and the air had a stale, musty scent to it.

Alice stepped up to the only person in the room, a heavyset woman of about fifty with stiff, red curls around her face and large gold hoops in her earlobes. She sat behind a long wooden counter and was absorbed in stroking her thumbs over a small rectangular object cradled in her hands. When she spotted Alice, she set aside the object and stood up. From where Lark stood, just inside the front door, she couldn't make out the name on the woman's nametag. Lark decided she must be Holly.

"What can I do ya for tonight, folks?" she spoke in a way Lark had never heard before, all harsh consonants, hitting the end of each word like a hammer to a nail.

"I'd like a room for the four of us," Alice said.

Holly stared at her for a moment. "Nice accent," she said. "Where you all from? You gals European?"

With a smoothness that impressed Lark, Alice said, "Yeah, we're here on vacation."

"Your English is real good," Holly said in a magnanimous way. "You guys okay with two double beds?"

Alice must have looked as dismayed as Lark felt at the prospect because Holly turned and quickly tapped her fingers on something Lark couldn't see on her desk.

Holly looked up once more and said, "How about I give you the family suite? It's got a sofa you can make up into a bed. There's linens and stuff in the closet."

"That's fine," Alice said. She looked over her shoulder to where Lark and Violet were trading hip-bumps via Reuel and snickering.

Holly pushed a piece of paper and pen across the counter. "Fill in this form, please."

Alice picked up the pen and scribbled a few things on the paper. She passed it back and Holly studied it. Apparently satisfied, she took the paper and started clicking away at a box-like contraption on the counter.

After a while, Alice handed over a bunch of paper bills,

which Holly took and counted.

"You gotta check out by ten. Drinks from the mini-bar and phone calls are extra," Holly said.

"Got it," Alice said.

"Oh, and breakfast is included. You can get it in the dining room on the second floor. Nothing too special, just cereal, toast, and boiled eggs, but you can bring it back to your room, if you want."

"Sure, sounds good."

Holly handed over a white card with a gold stripe across it. "You're in three-oh-two. Don't be too noisy, y'hear?"

"Don't worry, we're just gonna sleep," Alice said with a toothy grin that was a bit too wide.

"Elevator's over there," Holly said. She used a sausage-like finger to point across the dingy lobby.

"Thanks," Alice said. She darted over to a set of double, silver-colored doors and expertly pressed a button with a triangle on it. Lark was once more grateful Alice had invited herself along on their mission. When Lark passed in front of the desk, she was very aware of Holly studying them.

"Your friend okay?" Holly asked.

"He's fine," Lark said quickly. She pretended to stagger and giggled. She waved her free hand and said, "He just had a bit too much to drink."

"Uh huh. Well, if I gotta call an ambulance or he pukes on the floor, there's gonna be a surcharge."

"Don't worry," Lark said with a fake laugh. "We'll take care of him."

"Good. Enjoy your stay." Holly said. She returned to playing with her object and the four of them piled into the little swaying room their hostess called the elevator.

"Good job back there, Alice," Lark said. She shifted the burden on her shoulders. "Quick thinking with the European thing, whatever that is."

"I got that a lot when we came here before," Alice said. "Apparently people here think we're from some faraway land."

"At any rate," Violet said with a smirk, "you are fluent in the local dialect."

Alice laughed. Lark tried to, but with the dead weight of the man slung across her shoulders, she felt squashed and trapped and not in the jokiest of moods.

On the third floor, they found the room marked with the number 302. Lark waited impatiently while Alice fumbled with the card, which was apparently some kind of key. Finally the door opened and Lark staggered into the room, almost ready to fall down. As one, she and Violet let go of Reuel and his body slid down to rest in an ungainly pile on the floor. Lark bounced her shoulders and let out a long sigh of relief. Beside her, Violet shrugged off her cloak and hung it on the coat-rack by the door. Lark and Alice quickly followed suit.

The main room was larger than Lark expected. It was a beige-carpeted square, with two doors leading off it. It smelled like mildew and was decorated in a beige and brown theme, with a framed painting of a bland landscape on the wall. A small circular table and two worn armchairs sat in front of a large black rectangular object that was mounted on the wall. In a corner sat a squat white cold-box. When Lark peered inside, she discovered it was filled with bottles of different kinds of chilled beverages. A long sofa sat across from the black wall-object. Lark quickly mobilized her forces. They spread sheets over the sofa and Lark levitated Reuel onto it. Alice covered him with a blanket and stepped away with a satisfied look on her face.

Behind matching beige curtains, Lark found a set of sliding glass doors that led to a narrow balcony overlooking the street. Cautiously she slid one open and peered out. The hotel's sign cast orange light over the view. A waist-high metal can stood on the balcony and a few white and yellow paper tubes were scattered around it. Alice's voice called her back inside. Lark quickly shut the door and pulled the curtains closed.

"Lark? Would it be okay if I took a shower?" Alice poked her head out from the bathroom with a bunch of paper-covered things clutched in her hands. "This place has a nice set-up. Look at all the soaps we have."

"Go ahead. I'll stand guard until I can set up a perimeter," Lark said. "We'll sleep in shifts, like we do out on patrol."

"Okay," Alice said. "Anybody want to use the facilities before I take them over?"

"I'm fine," Lark said.

Violet nodded and made a regal *go ahead* gesture with one hand. Alice started to close the door, but paused halfway.

"I bet you'd be happy, Lark," she said. Lark looked at her in confusion and Alice clarified, "Remember the bonfire when it looked like Violet was ready to murder you? I bet you'd wake up in the best mood ever, and you did. Obviously you and Violet worked out whatever it was that was making you miserable. So you don't have to pretend like nothing's going on between you two. I'm not going to blab it, but I wanted to get that out in the open."

"You knew?" Lark asked. Her knees gave out and she collapsed onto one of the chairs. From her station looming over the table, Violet pressed a hand to her mouth.

"Come on Lark," Alice said with a mischievous grin. "We're been practically living in each other's armpits for almost a year now. I know you better than you think. I've never seen you light up the way you do whenever Violet comes into the room. And Violet never threatens to murder anyone else with as much vehemence as she does you. I wasn't sure until tonight, though. Friends don't hang onto each other like that. Just so you know, I think it's great." Alice paused and said in a somewhat resigned voice, "I'm probably going to regret asking this, but you two have disgustingly cute nicknames for each other, don't you?"

"They're not cute." Lark bit off the words in irritation. "They're fitting and meaningful, and no, I'm not going to tell you what they are."

"That's fine, some things are better kept between only two," Alice said. She shut the door before Lark could find the words to reply. As the sound of falling water started up from the bathroom, Lark got up and tried to cover her ruffled composure by exploring the bedroom. It had a window and a small closet with clacking wooden hangars. She stretched out on one of the beds and fiddled with the control board between them until she got the lights adjusted to a restful glow.

Violet came over and settled down beside Lark on the bed. Her skirts were a waterfall of black over the stiff, beige bedcover.

Lark turned to her with a smile. Violet's fingers stole around Lark's and squeezed her very gently.

"At least we don't have to worry about tiptoeing around Alice," Violet said.

"Yeah, that's a relief," Lark said. Violet's hand in hers woke something up inside Lark. It could be the leftover adrenaline of their flight, or even the longing to finish what they started in the cottage, but Lark was on fire with the need to touch Violet.

She glanced over her shoulder at the closed door, then met Violet's eyes. Lark caught her lower lip between her teeth as an undeniable urge welled up within herself. She guided Violet's hand to her waist and shifted closer until they were hip-to-hip on the bed. Lark's heart thundered in her ears. She was at once intensely aware of Violet's breaths, of the tightly reigned in but raw femininity of her body. Lark tilted her head and ghosted her lips over the silken skin of Violet's neck, skimming up to her velvety lobe. Under Lark's soft ministrations, Violet didn't move, but her breaths quickened. The hand on Lark's waist molded to her body. Violet's fingers dug ever so gently into Lark's skin. In response to Lark's soft kisses, Violet raised her chin with a soft moan. The sound only further weakened Lark's already crumbling self-control.

"What are you doing?" Violet asked in a strained whisper.

Lark dropped one more light kiss, her lips barely brushing Violet's skin. She murmured, "Exactly what you think I'm doing." Lark paused and drew back slightly. "Do you want to stop?"

"We should," Violet said. She drew in a long breath and placed both hands on Lark's hips. "But not yet."

Lark couldn't stop the rush of arousal that pounded through her body. She ached for Violet. She couldn't help but remember what happened back in Violet's cottage when Lark had come so close to crossing the line and surrendering herself completely. Lark reached out and very gently placed her hands on Violet's shoulders. Violet didn't protest. In fact, she seemed to know what was coming and practically purred with anticipation. Lark only had to give the smallest push for Violet to fall back onto the bed. Lark slung herself down on her side next to Violet and threw an arm around her waist.

"Oh," Violet let the word go in a sigh of longing. She arched her back and drew in a breath as Lark tightened her hold. Lark gave into her urge and brought her mouth down over Violet's. After a long, delicious moment, Lark released Violet's lips and moved to her neck. She was careful not to leave a mark but anything else was fair game. Under Lark's hungry lips and caressing tongue, Violet's breathing started to get hard and fast. Lark worked her way to the heavenly swell of Violet's breasts. She dropped an openmouthed kiss to the soft mounds that heaved with each breath like waves, hemmed in by the square neckline. She wanted more. Frustrated, Lark ran one hand up and down the front of Violet's bodice. The confining garments formed a barrier between her palm and the soft flesh she craved.

"One of these days," Lark said between heavy breaths, "I'm going to get this off you."

"You did once, I'm certain you can do it again." Violet wrapped her arms around Lark and hummed in her ear. "You tempt me, Sunshine. You make me want things I have never—" Violet froze. She looked toward the bedroom door, then back to meet Lark's eyes. "The water's stopped," she whispered.

"Time's up," Lark said, heavy-hearted. She quickly got to her feet and looked down in alarm. Somewhere along the line her overshirt got pulled up and her pocket belt twisted around. Violet was also similarly tousled. She put both hands to her hair and pulled out her jeweled combs to release her long braid. Escaping temptation, Lark strode back into the main room and parked herself at the balcony doors.

When the door opened to admit a cheerful and pink-cheeked Alice, a hastily-tucked-in-and-straightened Lark was gazing outside through a crack in the curtains as if she'd been that way the entire time. Violet was sitting at the table with her hands folded primly in her lap.

"Nice to see you two behaved," Alice said.

"Of course," Lark replied. She had to keep her eyes on the view outside. If she looked at Violet, she knew she'd either blush a million shades of red or burst out laughing.

Violet was next to use the facilities, and finally Lark stood outside the brilliant white shower stall and marveled at the twin taps that controlled how hot or cold the water was. She thought about stripping bare and blasting herself with freezing water so she could concentrate on shivering instead of squeezing her legs together in frustration at the memory of what Violet's lips could do to her.

The need for immediate vigilance won and instead, Lark stood at the sink and dug into the store of supplies the hotel provided. She sampled the stuff called toothpaste. She marveled at the amount of froth she created with her toothbrush and spewed out bubbles when she laughed at her reflection. She rinsed her mouth and decided she liked the minty aftertaste, quite different from the plain tooth-powder she was used to. For a moment, Lark wondered what it would be like to share a kiss with both of them breathing mint, or how it would feel for Violet to slowly lick a cold, tingling trail down her bare skin. Lark swallowed hard. It was going to be a long night.

Lark poked her head into the bedroom and found Alice lounging on one of the beds with Violet perched next to her, both of their heads were bent over a glossy colored book of some sort. Lark paused to admire the cute, homey scene for a moment.

Violet looked up and nodded in greeting. Lark didn't miss the flush that rose to her cheeks.

"I'll take the first watch," Lark said. "You two get as much sleep as you can and Alice, I'll wake you up for second watch."

"Sure," Alice said. She kicked off her shoes, rubber-soled laceups in a cheerful red canvas, and stretched out on the bed with her hands behind her head. She looked over at Violet, who looked ill-at-ease on the other side of the bed. "Are you okay to sleep in that? It looks pretty uncomfortable."

Alice reached out and poked Violet in the side. She jumped and let out an uncharacteristic squeak. Lark cringed and waited for Alice to become a pile of ash. She didn't expect what happened next.

Violet actually smiled. She waved Alice off as if she were a pesky but harmless insect. "It's not uncomfortable. I don't tight-lace and I appreciate the discipline," Violet said. "Let me assure you I am used to sleeping in a corset. When I started waist-training I only took it off for an hour a day."

"Wow, okay. I can see how you would need a lot of training and discipline to get used to that." Alice raised her eyebrows. She sat up and studied Violet with interest. "How big are you around? I bet I could get my hands around you."

"You are not correct, but welcome to try." Obligingly, Violet stood and took Alice's hands in hers. She guided Alice to take her about the waist. Her daggers gleamed in the lamplight.

Alice let out a low whistle. "I'm impressed. You're really cinched in there."

"She's pretty small out of it too," Lark said before she could think.

Both of them turned to stare at her. Alice with her mouth open and Violet with a knowing quirk to her lips. Alice held up both hands and moved back.

"Just so you don't think I'm making a move on your lady," Alice said.

"Even if you were," Violet said before Lark could speak, "I wouldn't be swayed. Not by you or anyone else."

The words unleashed a shot of heat in Lark's chest. Unconsciously, her hand went to her heart, which felt like it had stopped beating for an instant.

Alice laughed. "Yeah, I can tell," she said and sprawled back down.

Using the controls at the head of the bed, Alice switched off all but the smallest light over the doorway before she wrapped herself in her cloak and closed her eyes. Violet stood and claimed the other bed. Like Alice, she lay on top of the blankets. Her skirts dripped over the side and swept down to the floor. She tucked one arm under her head and let out a breath as she sank into repose. Lark ducked out of the room and grabbed her own Guardian cloak from the coat rack. She draped it over Violet's still form. She stirred and blinked up at Lark. Unable to help herself, Lark sat down on the side of the bed and smoothed back the hair from Violet's forehead.

"Don't want you to get cold," Lark muttered.

Violet closed her eyes and pressed against Lark's palm with a tiny smile. "Thank you."

Lark glanced over to where Alice was wrapped up in her cloak with her back to them. She bent down and swiftly pressed a kiss to Violet's temple before she stood and reluctantly backed out of the room. Lark eased the bedroom door closed. The lump on the sofa made snoring sounds but didn't otherwise move. In the darkened room, Lark drew her wand. She stood at the door and cast a Blind around it, which worked much like the Border did, causing anyone who came near to lose interest and move away. She followed up with a larger passive circle around the entire building. It took less energy to maintain than a shield and Lark would know if anything approached. On a more mundane note, she made sure the door was locked and the chain pulled.

Once she was satisfied their hideout was secure, Lark stationed herself in one of the armchairs with her wand propped up at her side, and idly flipped through the book Alice and Violet read earlier. It was a somewhat interesting account of various eating establishments around Compton, plus documentation of a local festival that appeared to be worshipping rainbows and odd costumes. Lark closed the book and leaned back in the chair. The room was still except for Reuel's snores and the faraway rumble of ground carts. Lark kicked out her feet and crossed her arms over her chest. A wave of sleepiness came over her and she hastily jerked upright. Lark stood and stretched her arms over her head.

She needed to get some fresh air. The room was warm and stuffy and not conductive to lookout duty. Lark shouldered her wand before she eased the sliding door open and stepped onto the balcony. At that hour, the street below was deserted. She watched, fascinated as the tri-colored light fixture at the intersection kept changing even though there was no traffic for it to direct. Wind rustled through her hair and Lark took a deep breath and raised her face to the sky. The air held so many different scents, the sky above glowed from the lights below, all but the brightest stars were invisible. Lark idly wondered how the Outsiders navigated and predicted the weather with all that light fogging up the heavens.

The sound of the door quietly sliding closed behind her brought Lark back to the present. She turned to see Violet standing with her hands clasped in front of her, hovering on the threshold.

"Hey," Lark said. She couldn't help the rush of heat to her face. She held out a hand. The tension vanished from Violet's stance. She crossed the small distance between them and stood at the railing, similarly looking out over the concrete landscape. Lark moved behind Violet and softly wrapped her arms around her waist. She couldn't help the sigh of longing as Violet melted into her.

"Couldn't sleep?" Lark asked. She nuzzled aside Violet's heavy braid and pressed a quick kiss to the side of her neck. "Did Alice try to snuggle?"

Violet answered with a chuckle low in her throat. "Alice stayed on her side admirably, she knows very well there is only one with whom I care to snuggle," Violet said. She folded her arms over Lark's, holding them together. "I did try to sleep, but it feels like a waste to spend a moment in slumber when this exciting new city is here in front of me. I feel free, born anew. It's so alien, but I'm not an outcast here, I'm not a dangerous thing to be hidden and controlled at all costs."

Lark tightened her hold in sympathy.

"I'm glad," Lark whispered. She pressed another kiss to the silken skin in front of herself. Violet tilted her head to expose more of her neck, which Lark took advantage of and showered her with affectionate kisses. Violet responded with a moan of pleasure that nearly kicked Lark's knees out. After a long, sweet moment, Violet slipped from Lark's hold and moved away. Her face was set.

"Before this—whatever this is between us—goes any further, I wish for you to know the truth." Her voice was distant and unemotional. "Why I was kept confined in a convent for most of my life. The true horror of my existence." She went silent and hugged her arms to her chest. Lark ached to reach out to her.

"Tell me, Starlight. I want to know. It won't change how I feel."

Violet took a deep breath. She spoke in a carefully detached monotone, "From the moment they understood my power, I was bequeathed to the Wraiths of Limor to be trained. Trained not to feel. To have no mercy. To be a weapon of last resort, death incarnate to our enemies. My purpose was to bring an end to the Wanderer people and victory to ours."

A sick feeling blossomed in Lark's gut. The bleak expression in Violet's eyes tore at her heart.

"I can only thank Heaven or Hell that the war ended when it did," Violet said. "before I was of age and could be unleashed to spread wanton destruction and unspeakable violence. Even when it became clear that we were losing, I was not summoned. Surrender was the merciful option over genocide and they took it." Violet brought her head up and met Lark's gaze. She said, "Whatever hellish destiny I was born into, it is not my intention to carry it out. I will not use my powers to harm innocent people. Believe that."

"I do," Lark told her. Even as she shivered under the weight of Violet's gaze, Lark felt only the deepest surge of love for her. Welcome or not, Lark knew without a doubt that she was fiercely and irrevocably in love with Violet and nothing she, nor anyone else, said or did could ever change that. Lark wanted to say too much, blurt out the unwelcome words. She squashed the urge and simply took Violet's hand in hers.

A tiny squeeze of the cold fingers wrapped in her own relieved Lark to no end. With their hands still clasped, Violet said, "My world was nothing more than the inside of the stone walls of the convent, the cliffs, and the icy Mother-ocean. But I had dreams. I dreamed one day I would get out of that place and *live*. I would meet people who weren't afraid of me. Who didn't cower away from me and my cursed powers. Who spoke of more than death and destiny and gods who turned their backs on us. I dreamed I would feel emotions without fear, and now I do." She raised Lark's hand to her lips and kissed her knuckles, softly, reverently. "I never dared to dream I would find you, Lark. You make me feel more than I ever dreamed I could."

Emotion choked her. Lark couldn't speak. She cupped Violet's cheek with her free hand and stroked her thumb gently over her lips. Violet leaned into her caress with a tiny smile. For a moment, Lark hovered on the edge of bending her head to give Violet a firm, deep kiss right there on a balcony where anybody could see them. Common sense returned and Lark drew back with an apologetic grimace. "Sorry, I can't keep my hands off you, it seems."

Violet raised her eyes. A sultry heat smoldered in their depths. "And I happen to like your hands on me," she said. She glanced back toward their room. "However, we probably shouldn't stay out here for too long. How about I take the second watch? Alice used a lot of energy shielding us. I'd rather she have as much uninterrupted sleep as possible."

"If you're sure you won't be tired," Lark said.

Violet shook her head. "Not at all. I feel like I've spent far too long sleepwalking through life. I don't wish to close my eyes for longer than I must."

"That's very kind of you," Lark said. "You can rest until my watch is over. I've got a few hours left."

"If you don't mind, I will stay up with you. If you have your Magic Squares cards with you, perhaps I can interest you in a game or two?"

Lark grinned. "Sure do. I didn't know Ringsworn played Magic Squares."

"We don't, however your mentor took it upon herself to teach me and I spent several entertaining afternoons trouncing various Guardians who needed to be brought down a peg or two. Apparently I have an affinity for the game."

Lark clapped a hand over her mouth to keep the laugh from bursting out. She held the curtain aside for Violet to go back into their room. Lark quietly closed and locked the doors behind herself before she dug into her pocket for the well-worn deck of cards. Violet settled down on the chair across from Lark and waited patiently while Lark shuffled.

Chapter Seventeen

"I WISH TO exchange goods for money." Without preamble, Violet addressed the young man at the front desk. The morning sunlight streaming through the gritty windows cast her hair into a blood-red halo. She loomed over the counter with a dangerous scowl. While Lark knew it was simply a front, the clerk didn't and he froze like a cornered chicken. Violet snapped, "Please inform me where I can do that."

The young man gulped. "Do you mean a pawn shop?" he asked in a pleasant, lilting way. His words were hesitant, as if he wasn't used to speaking the language. Lark was intrigued at finding a possible traveler like herself.

"Yes, if that is what you call it," Violet tapped her long fingers on the counter. Behind her, Lark stuffed her hands in her pockets and gave the terrified-looking clerk what she hoped was a reassuring smile.

"There is one just down the street from here," he said. His hands fumbled with a folded pack of paper that turned out to be a simplified street map of the greater Compton area. He drew two shaky circles on the map. "Here is the hotel, and Don's Pawns is here. Next to the bank. You can't miss it."

"Thank you, young sir," Violet said, with an elegant bow of her head. The clerk didn't reply, but he looked very relieved the conversation was over and returned the bow.

Lark took the map and together they exited from the hotel. She stood shoulder-to-shoulder with Violet on the broad sidewalk, getting her bearings. At the early hour, the majority of the shops lining the street were still closed, however the road was alive with purring ground-carts. The night before, the view was orange from the sign, but in the daylight, everything was an explosion of color. The street was filled with signs and bright flags. The ground-carts were in a dizzying variety of colors as well. Lark felt like a rainbow split open over the entire street. She got an inkling of why Alice was so excited about going Outside.

"Where to?" Violet asked in a much kinder tone than she

used on the unfortunate clerk.

"East through two intersections, then North."

"All right, let's go," Violet said. She started off with a spring and purpose in her step any Wanderer would be proud to claim.

As Lark walked beside Violet, she stole glances at her from time to time. She radiated strength and was striking in the golden sunlight. Violet's eyes were bright and her expression was open in wonder.

In the chill air, rank with the ground-carts' exhalations, Lark felt excited and alive. Something visceral within her responded to both the thrumming energy of the city as well as the very welcome presence of Violet at her side.

They reached the pawn shop where, instead of entering right away, Violet paused outside. She studied the wares offered in the barred window. The goods displayed were a number of time-keeping devices, interspersed with delicate gold chains and other jewelry, along with a few knives and other weapon-like objects. Each bore a small tag printed with the price. Lark noted with no small amount of pride that none of the items even came close to the skilled craftsmanship of Violet's daggers. Beyond the window display, the shop was crammed with objects ranging from musical instruments, to dolls in dusty glass cases.

Violet opened the front door, which released the clanging of a bell, and she strode into the cluttered shop with Lark close behind her. The worn flooring under their feet rang with their footsteps.

A man who Lark assumed was Don stood behind a squat cash-machine on an old-looking wooden counter that was flanked by more glassed-in showcases. He was bearded and husky and didn't look very welcoming. The sleeves of his plaid shirt were rolled up, displaying meaty forearms decorated with intricate designs. He had a skull on one side and whirling geometric forms on the other. Around his thick waist, he had a wide leather belt and the sleek handle of a handgun rose from the holster. Lark had never seen one in person, but she knew about Outsider weapons. Mentally, she went over defense strategies, should the man decide to use it on them. Guardians had a policy of non-exposure, but they were allowed to defend themselves when necessary. Lark was trained to use her powers in a subtle way, and additionally, Outsiders tended to disbelieve their own eyes and misremember events that couldn't be explained by their rigid worldview.

"What can I do you ladies for today?" he asked. He spoke in the same harsh, clipped accent Holly had.

"How much will you give me for this?" Violet asked. She placed the finely worked leather belt and its bounty of six sheathed daggers on the counter-top.

"May I?" Don asked with surprising gentility. He picked up the belt and held it up to his face. His eyes surveyed not only the proffered item, but also took in the appearance of the two women standing before him, his calculating gaze left Lark feeling rather bare. He put the belt down on the counter and crossed his meaty arms over his chest.

"I'll give ya fifty for the lot."

"Fifty? Only fifty of your measly dollars?" Violet spat and Lark instinctively backed up a step. Violet drew one razor-sharp dagger from its sheath and held it in her fingers. The lights of the shop played off the slim weapon. Violet said, "As you can see, each blade is made of the finest steel and mother-of-pearl, perfectly balanced and holds an excellent edge. It is fit for the waist of the fiercest of fighting ladies."

Don uncrossed his arms, leaned over the counter, and carefully placed both big hands flat on the worn wooden surface. He said, "Sixty, and that's my final offer."

Violet didn't reply. She flicked the dagger into the air. The blade caught the light as it spun in a tight arc over her head. She snatched it out of the air and slammed the blade into the counter, right between Don's thick fingers.

"Jesus Christ!" Don flung himself backwards and landed against the large cupboard that loomed behind the counter. A second dagger whipped through the air and buried itself in the cupboard door with a solid *thunk,* pinning Don by the collar. He twisted to look at the hilt protruding from the space between his shoulder and neck. Don looked back at them and said in a shaking voice, "The fuck's wrong with you, crazy bitch?"

"Watch your language," Lark spat. She wasn't familiar with the details of Outsider vernacular, but she certainly knew disrespectful words when she heard them. She lowered her head and said in a raw, threatening tone that brooked no dissent, "Do not insult my lady."

The words startled her, but Lark didn't take them back. At any rate, Don was preoccupied with what Violet was doing. Violet, face impassive, carefully drew another dagger. Her eyes never left the shopkeeper's.

"I believe you made a slight misjudgment," she said in a low growl that sent a thrill down Lark's spine. "Allow me to correct the misunderstanding. I am not here to be mocked or taken advantage of." Violet brought the dagger to her lips and ran her tongue delicately over the flat of the blade before she said, "I believe you can do better than *sixty*."

Don's hand twitched toward the weapon at his side, but flinched back as the dagger flashed through the air. It thudded home beside his hip. With a serpentine slithering sound, Don's gun belt fell around his feet.

"Okay, six hundred," he quavered. He reached up and tried to pull out the dagger holding him to the cupboard, but it was buried deeply and didn't budge. Violet's only answer was in the form of another dagger, which flew like a shooting star and landed snugly nestled in the juncture of his legs. "JESUS!" Don howled.

He performed a kind of hopping dance, as he tried to keep himself as far as possible from the blade, a hairsbreadth from a very sensitive area. Lark wondered who this Jesus person was that Don kept yelling for. If he was Don's assistant, he wasn't a very good one as he seemed to have escaped, leaving his boss in an unfortunate position.

"Six hundred is only slightly less insulting than your previous offers. Keep going." With a casual nonchalance, Violet pulled the dagger from the counter and polished it on her sleeve.

"Okay! Okay, you got me," Don said. Behind his beard, his face was red. "How about a grand?"

"What is a 'grand'?" Violet hissed. The dagger flicked to a ready position in her hand.

"A-a thousand dollars," Don said. Sweat streamed from his face.

The silence stretched out for a long, agonizing minute and Lark held her breath. She glanced from Violet, who held herself still with tension radiating from her posture to Don, who looked as if he was about to wet himself.

"Agreed," Violet said. She sheathed the dagger and stepped

away from the counter. "You may release yourself and prepare the payment. Understand this," she lowered her lashes and gave Don a blistering look through them that had Lark's breath catching in her throat at the intensity of it, "I do not regard double-crossing lightly and do not assume these blades are the only weapon I have with me today."

Sweating even more, Don gave up on the dagger and wiggled out of the plaid shirt that was pinned to the cupboard. He gingerly came back to the counter in a white undershirt that had seen better days. He dragged a handkerchief from his pocket and mopped at his forehead while he opened the cash-box. After counting out a pile of bills, he put them in an envelope and set it down on the counter. He took a printed notepad out from behind the counter and held a pen over it. Lark noticed without surprise that his hand was shaking. Violet seemed to have that effect on people.

"Who should I make the ticket out to?"

Violet leaned over the counter to study the paper. "Is that necessary?"

"Only if you want your stuff back," Don said. "Store policy is three months to pay back the amount plus service charges or it goes out on the floor for sale."

Violet regarded the man through narrowed eyes for a moment before she said, "Very well. Make it out to Violet Iron-wrought. No, that's *w-r-o-u-g-h-t.*"

Don muttered to himself as he filled out the form. He tore it from the pad and passed it and the envelope across the counter. Violet pocketed both with a refined elegance that impressed Lark. Don picked up the brace of daggers once more and held the soft leather belt reverently in his hands for a moment. One thumb ran over the delicately worked silver buckle, set with polished opals. He raised his head with a half-grin.

"Shit, lady, this really is worth a grand. More than that, actually. I, uh, I'm sorry I lowballed you there. No hard feelings?"

"Of course not," Violet said with a tiny quirk to her lips she got when she was having fun. "I do believe that is the practice of 'haggling' is it not?"

With that, Don let out a peal of laughter. He swiped at his forehead once more and waved toward the door. "G'wan you two. Git before you totally break me."

Not needing any more persuasion, Lark ushered Violet back to the street. Once they were back in neutral territory, Lark was euphoric and giddy. She jumped ahead of Violet and walked backwards with a big grin on her face.

"You were so great in there, I just can't help myself," Lark gushed. "I want to hug you right now — or do something else. I won't of course, but I still really wish I could."

At the flash of emotion in Violet's eyes, Lark stopped walking abruptly. Violet didn't. Just before they collided, Violet snaked a hand out and grabbed Lark by the back of her head to drag her into a firm kiss. Lark froze the instant their lips met, then closed her eyes and eagerly welcomed Violet's mouth. She couldn't believe she was kissing Violet right there in the middle of the sidewalk. Lark's knees nearly buckled. Too soon, Violet drew away and slowly licked her bottom lip.

"Did that satisfy your urge?" she asked.

"Kind of," Lark said. "Now I can't stop wishing we got two rooms."

Violet only chuckled and began walking again.

AT LARK'S KNOCK, the door swung open to reveal a relieved-looking Alice.

"I'm glad you're back," she said. She aimed a thumb over her shoulder. "He's been moving around a bit and I think he might be waking up."

"Okay, thanks for holding down the fort here," Lark said. She crossed the room and stood by Reuel's side. Under his papery eyelids, his eyes rolled and he rocked slightly back and forth on the sofa. She debated with herself for a moment before she reached out and tapped him on one shoulder. "Hey, Reuel, can you hear me?"

He took a deep, sudden breath and opened his eyes. He wrenched himself upright and looked around. "Where is this?" He flapped around in panic. "Where have you brought me?"

"Calm down," Lark said. She held her hands out to stop him from trying to get up. "Let me explain. We're Outside —"

"No!" Reuel howled. "You have brought me here to be killed! I demand you return me to safety at once! Take me back to Shadowmoor!"

"He doesn't take orders very well," Violet said. She moved to stand behind Lark, who wanted to scrub the look of avarice Reuel directed at Violet clean off his face.

"You," he said in an oily, breathy tone.

Violet answered in a scathing tone that could blister rock, "I am Violet Ironwrought. I don't know who you believe I am, but I assure you, you are nothing more than thieving scum to me."

She stood proud and tall, magnificent in her anger. Lark was secretly glad it wasn't directed at her.

Head down, Reuel crossed his arms over his sunken chest. He said, "I thought one of your lineage would welcome my efforts to rebuild the great legacy of the Ringsworn."

"Is that what you thought you were doing?" Violet's words were icy. She pressed her lips together and her hands worried at the silken layers of her skirt. Lark's heart ached at the bleak look on her face. Violet said, "You have no idea the hell we lived. It galls me to admit this, but in a way it was a blessing the Wanderers stepped in when they did."

"What do you mean?"

"I mean," Violet growled, "think about what it was like for us to live in the shadow of those horrible artifacts. Never knowing who possessed one, never knowing if a loved one would fall under the cursed spell. I may have been but a child, however I heard the stories. I saw the scarred remains of the families who were touched by the dark items, who fled in desperation to the thin protection provided by my convent. Toward the End Days, nowhere was safe. Those who chose to remain in our ancestral lands lived their days and nights in mortal fear. Do you think I want to return to that?" Violet asked. "Do you think *any* of us wants to? Answer me!"

Squirming, Reuel muttered something which ended in a squawk as Violet reached out and grabbed him by the collar and hauled him to his feet. The blanket that covered him fell in a heap, but neither of them took notice of it.

"I couldn't quite catch that." Her words were civil but her tone indicated she was on the verge of losing the thin veneer of control keeping her from lashing out. Worried, Lark took a step forward, not sure what she could do, but wanting to be ready in any case.

"I didn't think about that. I—I apologize."

Letting out a bark of cold laughter, Violet released her hold on him. She turned away and shook her head. Reuel crumpled to the floor, where he remained. While Lark ached to go to Violet and try to reassure her, she had a feeling that it would be better to give her a bit of space.

Reuel scanned the room and stopped, staring at the line of three cloaks by the door. He grabbed onto the table and pulled himself to his feet. Before Lark registered what he was doing, he was running his hands up and down the blacker-than-black cloak. A wheezing whine came from him.

"I have heard of this marvelous cloth," he said. "I never dreamed I would be able to touch it."

"Step away from there, Bucketsworth," Lark snapped the order. Reuel immediately slunk back toward them with a look of contrition on his grayish face.

He fell into one of the armchairs. Alice helpfully pushed the basket on the table toward him. Reuel ignored the leftover hard-boiled eggs and rolls in favor of glancing furtively towards the cloak rack.

"What did you do to me?" Reuel asked.

Violet rested her forehead in her palm for a moment with a look of regret. "I took your energy," she said. "I regret I wasn't able to ask permission. I channeled it out using your cape. It is made by you, isn't it?"

He nodded, making his jowls shake. His eyes shone and something like a smile stretched his lips. "My lady, you are most welcome to anything I can provide," he said. "Say the word and it is yours. Including myself."

Violet rolled her eyes.

"I'm glad you said that," Lark said in a super-cheerful voice. She sat down at the table across from Reuel and clasped her hands on top of it. "Because we need your help."

Reuel opened his mouth, then closed it and slouched down in his chair. He muttered, "I don't see what I can do for you."

"You're our link to the Bloodring," Lark said. Both Alice and Violet moved to flank her and Lark drew herself up. "We have the means to destroy it. All you have to do is lead us to it. What do you say, are you in?"

Reuel dropped his head into his hands. A long silence stretched out.

Violet leaned over the table. She said in a tight voice, "This is a chance for you to redeem yourself, right the wrongs you caused by your rash actions. Your only chance."

Reuel was silent. He heaved a long sigh. He raised his head and looked at each in turn before he said, "All right. I will cooperate. I will do anything in my power to help you find Owen and the Ring he stole from me. But...must it be destroyed? It is such an exquisite—"

"Yes. We can't let something like that stay free," Lark said, "and thank you for your help." She hesitated for a split second before she held out a hand to Reuel. He took it and gave her a weak shake before he let go and his hand fell limply into his lap.

"So were you guys successful?" Alice asked.

"Yes," Violet answered. "I was able to exchange my blades for what is known as 'a grand' of dollars."

"Sweet," Alice said. She held out one fist. Violet's lips quirked up before she met it with a gentle bump.

Reuel stared at them with his face ashen and his mouth hanging open. "I would have gladly paid you double," he cried out.

Violet turned her head and simply fixed him with a freezing stare. "No, thank you. Enough of our relics have passed through your grubby, undeserving hands."

"But I was only—"

"All right, this Owen fellow," Lark said in a no-nonsense way, cutting off Reuel's whining self-justification. "Where is he?"

Reuel said, "I know the location of the company where he works. Davis Consulting."

"That's a start," Lark said. She crossed her arms over her chest. "Give me more. For example, what exactly can he do with the Bloodring?"

Reuel's face went sullen. "I don't know. I never saw him use it," Reuel trailed off. He shook himself and said, "I don't know what any of the artifacts do. They do not choose to reveal their inner natures to me."

"Then you are simply a tool to be used and discarded," Violet said, with a derisive curl to her lip. "The artifacts know no loyalty."

"I know," Reuel said in a broken voice.

Violet turned on her heel and marched over to the cloak rack. She came back with her cloak draped over her arm. Reuel jumped violently when she held it out to him.

"It is yours," she said. "I have had enough of darkness."

"I am honored to accept your gift," Reuel said, his face a mask of surprise.

His fingers fondled the inky material in a way Lark didn't particularly like, but she didn't comment. Violet was full of contradictions, both fierce and forgiving at once. Her heart grew warm with emotion.

"So how do we get there?" Alice asked. "To that Owen guy's workplace."

Lark yanked the map from her pocket and smoothed it out on the table. She pushed it across the table towards Reuel and pointed. "This is our hotel here. Are you familiar with this area?"

Reuel studied the map for a moment. He nodded. "Yes. We can walk from here," Reuel said. He rolled up his sleeve and checked his watch. "Owen should be there now. When did you want to go?"

"No time like the present," Lark said. She whirled her own cloak over her shoulders and looked at each member of her motley team in turn. "Let's do this."

Chapter Eighteen

THE WALK TO Davis Consulting was silent. Lark was deep in thought, planning her strategy. While the easiest way to get the Ring would be to full-on ambush Owen, Lark wouldn't go that route. For one thing, it was too risky given the fact they didn't know what Owen was capable of, and for another, the Guardians didn't rule by force, but by reason. Conversation, consideration, and compromise were the three main tenets of their profession. Lark didn't want to lie either. She weighed how much she should tell with how much she should hide.

Owen's workplace was a five-story edifice that would look most forbidding if it was in Shadowmoor, but it was dwarfed by the mirrored glass buildings around it. More than anything, the dark pall that hung over it like a moldy miasma separated it from the rest. Bile rose up in her throat as they approached and Lark swallowed hard. She glanced around to see if the aura was affecting anyone else. Alice looked the way Lark felt, with her face twisted in disgust. Violet was pale but composed, her face unreadable. Reuel, on the other hand, jumped from one foot to the other as if he couldn't contain himself. His mouth was stretched into a lascivious grin.

The Bloodring was close. There was no doubt. Even the air was heavy with dark energy. Lark fought the nagging feeling she felt that energy somewhere before. It resonated within her core like she was coming home, but something was off about it. Underneath the surface, something rank and twisted lurked. Lark shook her head and focused on the physical world. The sick feeling subsided somewhat.

Reuel hurried them over to the entrance of the office building and looked back over his bony shoulder at Lark with an expectant expression on his face.

"This is it," he said. "Owen's company is on the top floor."

"Thank you," Lark said. "You're free to go."

"What?" Alice squawked. "What if he isn't telling us the truth?"

"He is," Lark said. She squared her shoulders and stepped through the doors.

The lobby was bare and populated by only a few rusty-looking potted plants. She marched over to the elevator. While they waited for the doors to open, Lark noticed Reuel slipping into the lobby behind them. He was sunk so far into his newly-gifted cloak that he seemed to be nothing more than a shadow. Lark put his lingering presence out of her mind when the elevator arrived and the three of them got on.

On the ride up, Violet surprised Lark by very gently taking her hand and giving it a quick squeeze while Alice pretended the numbered display over the doors was the most fascinating thing ever.

"Tread carefully," Violet said. She started to say something, then closed her eyes. A crease of pain marred her forehead. She shook her head. "It can't be," she said, more to herself than Lark.

A bell dinged and the doors slid open on the fifth floor. Violet let go of her immediately, but Lark still felt the warmth of her fingers.

At the head of her small entourage, Lark marched down the tiled hallway to the sign that declared itself Davis Consulting. Her boots rang against the floor and her cloak billowed after herself. She calmed both her expression and her breathing. None of her Guardian training had prepared her for the situation. In fact, most of it was geared to avoiding anything resembling it.

Davis Consulting was housed in a cramped room filled with desks. A number of people bustled around, not unlike the accounting room back at Shadowmoor. Lark stopped in front of a long desk that declared itself "reception" in blocky letters affixed to the front of it. Behind the desk sat a curly-haired young woman with round spectacles that gave her a cute, bookish air. She looked up at them, then blinked a few times.

"Uh, can I help you guys with anything?" she asked.

"I am Lark Greenpool," Lark declared with as much confidence as she could muster. She tossed one side of her cloak back over her shoulder, placed a hand on her hip and shook her trailing bangs out of her face. Lark focused on the young woman's nametag. "Honorable Miss Madison Lambert, I wish an audience with Mr. Owen Dooley."

"For fuck's sake," the young woman muttered. "Why does

my last day in this hellhole have to be weirdo day?"

"Excuse me?" Lark asked archly.

Madison fixed her with a blatantly fake smile and said, "Nothing. Okay, do you have an appointment?"

"No," Lark said. She glanced around, hoping for something to inspire her. Violet was as still as a statue beside her and Alice hovered behind her. Lark announced, "I don't have an appointment, but I wish to make one. As soon as possible. The matter I need to discuss with Mr. Dooley is of the utmost priority."

"Hang on," Madison said. She lifted a curved item from the desk and held it to her face, then pressed a few buttons on the contraption. She said, "Owen, there are some people here to see you. Something about utmost importance. No, I didn't ask for more details, do that yourself, sheesh." Madison paused. She listened for a while, then sighed in an annoyed way. She looked up at them again. "Three girls, kind of young like twenties. Probably European. What? Um, yeah, I guess I'd classify one of them as hot. One is kinda goth and one is...cute." Madison said the last word while looking at Alice and got two pink spots on her cheeks. Her attention went back to the device and she listened for a moment longer before she said, "Uh huh, okay. Sure." She replaced the hand-part and said, "You're in luck, Owen says he'll meet with you."

"Thank you," Lark said. She couldn't help the triumphant grin that broke through the sick feeling.

Madison stood up and said, "He'll see you in pod three. This way, please."

Obediently, Lark followed Madison out of the office. In the hallway, they passed a young man who was carrying a large paper cup with a lid. When he saw Madison, he held his free hand up in the air and made a "wee-oo wee-oo" kind of noise with his mouth.

"Emergency! 9-1-1 coming through," he said.

"Shut up Kevin," she said. "For that, my ambulance is never gonna pick up your sorry ass."

"Ooh, feisty," Kevin said in a drawl.

She replied by raising her middle finger at him in what Lark assumed was a rude gesture.

Pod three was a small room with a table in the middle and a large window that looked out over the street below. Cords of various thicknesses and colors lay over the tabletop like sleeping snakes. Lark was the first inside. She gestured for Alice to stand by the door before she sat down at the table. Violet followed.

A minute later, a man entered. He was small and mousy, with thick glasses and thin hair. He was in the standard business attire of suit and striped necktie, but he had a thick sweater vest on underneath it and a flannel undershirt peeked from the cuffs of his jacket. He had the same meatless, fragile look that Reuel did.

He also seemed to have a keen interest in Violet, focusing all of his attention on her. He rounded the table, never once breaking eye contact with her. Lark grimaced. He didn't even notice when Alice eased the door closed and stood with her back to it.

The waves of malevolent energy rolling off Owen buffeted Lark and told her without a doubt he was in possession of the Bloodring. Lark had never met him before, that she was certain, but the feeling of familiarity didn't die. She almost wanted to reach out and touch him. Lark tore her thoughts away from the urge and fixed Owen with the sternest, most authority-filled look she could muster.

"I'm Lark Greenpool and I'm here on behalf of the Guardians," Lark said. "I believe you have something of ours."

As if it took great effort, Owen turned his head and acknowledged Lark for the first time. Owen's face changed from avaricious to annoyed. He pushed his chair away from the table and made a move as if to rise, but Lark held a hand out. Owen fell back into his chair as if standing was too arduous.

His eyes bulged and he clutched at himself. "You're not taking it away. It's *mine* and it needs me. It wants me to have it."

"I'm not disputing that," Lark said. She spoke carefully. "I came here because there are some things you must know. That Ring is not from your world. It doesn't belong here and it's upset the balance between your world and ours. Countless lives are in danger, including yours. We have the ability to control artifacts like that, however you don't. We need you to hand over the Ring now, before anything worse happens."

"Bullshit," Owen spat. Lark froze, stunned. Owen let out a jeering laugh and swiveled his head around. "Okay, Bucketsworth, nice try. You can come out now, joke's up."

"This is not a joke," Lark said.

"Prove it," Owen said. He crossed his arms over his sunken

chest and reclined in his chair. "Prove you're not some college kid Bucketsworth bribed to come here and try to get his stuff back. Because it's not gonna work. *If*, and that's a big fucking *if*, you convince me, we'll talk. If not, I'm calling security on your asses."

Lark slowly stood. "Very well," she said. She ignored Alice's shocked gasp and reached into her shirt. She pulled her clear quartz crystal from it and held it in her hand for a moment. Owen snorted rudely, but wrenched himself upright with both hands clutching onto the arms of his chair when Lark set the crystal alight and floated it over the table.

Owen's mouth fell open slightly, then he scowled. "Nice magic trick. No deal."

He jumped up and snatched at the crystal.

"No!" Lark batted him away. The crystal fell to the table with a clunk. Owen's hand clamped onto her wrist and Lark was roughly jerked forward. The garnet beads pressed painfully into her skin.

"Let go of her," Alice shouted. She drew her wand and pointed it at Owen. Just as quickly, Violet threw herself in front of Alice.

"Don't," Violet said the word in a tight voice before she collapsed onto the floor.

Owen looked from Lark to Violet in rapid succession. Lark used that moment to wrench herself from his grasp. He took a step back and looked down at his hands. For the first time, Lark saw the Ring on his finger. It definitely hadn't been there a moment before. The Ring was blackened silver and held a large stone the color of clotted blood. The last piece clicked into place. Impossible as it was, at that moment Lark knew what—and *who* that Ring was.

"Arsehole of the goddess," came from the floor. Two white hands appeared on the table, followed by an unsteady-looking Violet rising to her feet. "Owen you little bitch," she growled.

"Who're you calling a bitch," Owen whined. His body crackled with energy, the air around him sparkled silver. "You wanna see who's a bitch, look in the mirror."

Violet just replied by making a beckoning motion with her finger.

Owen threw both hands out and energy gathered between his spread fingers. Before the attack, Lark lunged and grabbed her crystal, in the same motion she slid across the table and corralled Alice by the door. She knew what Violet planned to do—level the playing field. A volley of silver energy soared past her. Lark instinctively shielded Alice with her body and ducked down.

Violet took the full brunt of the attack without flinching. Her drained look vanished. She stood tall and insolent, with one hand propped on her hip.

"Is that the best you could do?" Violet asked. She tilted her head and smiled a cold, unpleasant smile. "Hit me again. Go on. I could do this all day."

"What the fuck?" Owen backed up until he collided with the wall.

Violet turned. "Go," she said to Lark, who obeyed without question.

Lark shoved the door open and pushed Alice out ahead of her. They stumbled into the hallway and came face-to-face with Reuel.

"What are you doing here?" Lark asked in astonishment.

"I had to know," Reuel said. He shrunk down into his cloak. "I had to see what happened to my precious treasure."

"You're going to see more than you like unless you get moving," Lark said. "Owen stole some of Violet's energy and she's in the process of getting it back."

"What?"

"That Ring, it's Violet's," Lark said. She swallowed hard.

A crash shook the building. Lark barely had time to whirl her wand out before the wall of the meeting room exploded into the hallway. Dust and chunks of plaster pelted the shield Lark threw up around herself and Reuel. A glance over her shoulder assured her Alice was safe in her own shield. Screams and shouts erupted from the office, and people spilled into the hallway. At the forefront, Madison directed people to the emergency stairwell.

Madison shouted over the din, "This is no fucking drill, everybody out, now!"

Owen emerged from the dust. His face was twisted into a maniacal grin. He grabbed at a fleeing office worker who screamed and collapsed onto the floor. Lark sucked in a breath. The way he went for people directly and not objects told Lark that Owen didn't know the finer points of the Ring's powers—or its weaknesses.

Without hesitation, Lark levitated a potted plant and pitched it at him. Owen batted it aside, laughing and jeering. His laugh cut off an instant later as the chair Violet threw impacted with the back of his head, sending him staggering to his knees.

Violet strode out of the wrecked meeting room. She shot Lark a triumphant look.

"What the fuck, Owen?" Madison asked from where she was helping a stunned worker to the stairwell.

Owen replied by blasting the ceiling. More rubble fell, completely blocking the stairwell. Lark stifled a curse. While the worker made it out, Madison was trapped with them. Lark swept up another plant and threw it at Owen. She didn't even try to hit him, she just wanted to distract him.

Owen blasted the plant just as Violet swooped and grabbed him around the neck. Silver energy flared all around her. Violet kicked his knees out from behind and shoved him flat against the floor. She flipped him over onto his back and her fingers closed around his throat. She bared her teeth in a fierce smile that sent a shaft of fear through Lark.

Violet's eyes were dark with hate. She moved slowly, deliberately, as she sank to her knees, pinning Owen to the floor and pressing him down in a mockingly intimate gesture. Owen batted helplessly at her hands and made an awful gargling noise. Silver bolts of energy sizzled around them, but Violet didn't stop. Lark couldn't look away. Her eyes filled with mad tears as she watched the woman she loved becoming a murderer.

"Oh my God," Madison said from her station in front of the rubble where the emergency stairwell used to be. "She's really going to kill him. I'm calling the police!"

Scuffing the sleeve of her shirt across her face, Lark could only stand there, her wand clutched in her shaking fingers. Her mind screamed for Violet to stop, but she couldn't speak. Owen's body started glowing, the now-familiar silver energy gathered around him.

Violet didn't let up. Owen's struggles got more frantic. His eyes bulged and his face turned a mottled purple. Only a few more heartbeats and it would be over. Lark couldn't turn away from the death-match. A thin scream interrupted the battle. It was Reuel. He twisted and cried out as he was dragged across the floor by an invisible force.

"Tra-a-a-ade," Owen croaked. He extended a hand and Reuel rose into the air, clutching at his throat.

Violet raised her head, a look of alarm on her face. The feral light in Violet's eyes flickered, her guard slipped for an instant. It was only a split-second of hesitation, but it was enough.

With a deafening bang, Violet was thrown into the wrecked office. Lark's vision went red with rage. She focused on where Reuel was twisting in mid-air and threw a shield around him. Within the glowing sphere, he tumbled to the floor and lay there, panting. Without another word, Lark sprinted into the office and threw herself to her knees beside Violet. She gathered Violet up in her arms, not caring who saw. Violet's eyes were closed, but she was breathing. Lark fought back the cry of relief when Violet groaned and pressed a hand to her head.

"The cops are coming," Madison said. "Owen, stay right there, okay?"

"I don't think so. They can arrest all you motherfuckers," Owen said. He staggered upright, rubbing at his throat. Bolts of energy from his hands raked the entire room. Alice shouted and dove behind one of the remaining desks as more of the ceiling crumbled and rained down. Lark bent protectively over Violet and threw a shield around them.

Reuel stirred and sat up. Owen reached out toward him. He clenched his fingers with a twist and Reuel's body was dragged across the floor to Owen's feet. Owen looked across the debris-strewn hallway that separated Lark from him. He said, "Tell you what, how about I just take this piece of shit with me and we'll call it even?" He reached down and grabbed Reuel by the collar.

Violet stirred in Lark's arms and opened her eyes. Lark banished her shield with a whisper of energy.

"Get me up," Violet whispered, struggling to rise. "We can't let him take Reuel away with him."

Even though it was against her better judgment, Lark put an arm around Violet's waist and eased them both off the floor. Just as Lark straightened to her full height, something square and heavy landed at her feet. Puzzled, Lark picked the worn Almanac up.

"Give it to Violet," Reuel gritted. "She knows what to do." His words choked off when Owen gave his collar a vicious wrench.

"No tricks or you can kiss this asshole goodbye!"

"Do it!" Reuel's weedy voice trickled back to them.

With a decisive snatch, Violet took the Almanac from Lark. Two things happened at the same time. Reuel's body hit the tile floor of the hallway and a silver shockwave exploded out from where Violet stood, the air around Owen filled with shrapnel. Owen barely managed to deflect Violet's attack, then he aimed a hand at the ceiling.

A deep shift in the air dropped through Lark's belly. The remaining ceiling rose in a shower of plaster and dust before it fell away in a graceful arc. The sky opened up above them. A shattering smash below began a symphony of horns honking and people shouting. A long, wailing siren pierced the air.

Wind whipped through the wreckage. Lark fought through the choking clouds, wand out and ready, but Owen and his unconscious cargo were already gone. Lark coughed on dust and spat out the vile taste of defeat that filled her mouth.

"Alice!" The sound of Violet's voice snapped Lark to attention. Violet swooped down on a pile of rubble, pulling at a bright pink piece of material. Her hands were white with plaster dust. Lark's gut clenched. She joined Violet just as Alice sat up.

"Ouchies," Alice said. She was pale and clutched at her arm.

"Let me help. I'm an EMT," Madison said. She rubbed at her dust-covered curls with a grimace. "Okay, from tomorrow I'll be an EMT."

"What does that mean?" Lark asked.

"It means I'm trained to take care of injured people," Madison said.

Lark backed up to let Madison through. She kept an eye on Madison, who got down next to Alice and prodded at her.

"Looks like you got a broken collarbone," Madison said. "I can patch you up so it doesn't jostle, but you need to go to a hospital. I think the police are outside and they can—"

"No hospitals," Alice said through gritted teeth.

Madison pressed her lips together. "Lark, do you think you could get the first aid kit for me? It should be under the reception desk."

"Sure thing," Lark said. She was grateful to be of use. "What does it look like?"

"White box, red cross."

"Got it." Lark didn't even try to be discreet. She levitated the jagged remnants of the office off the desk and hunkered down to peer under it. The little box was dusty and slightly dented, but the desk protected it from the worst of the damage.

"You're gonna be just fine," Madison said to Alice in a calm voice. She took the box Lark passed over and took out a number of bandages. Her movements were sure and her words gentle. Reassured that Alice was in good hands, Lark relaxed her guard and turned to Violet.

"Are you okay?" Lark asked softly. She took in the hunch of Violet's shoulders, the strain on her face.

"I'm sorry," Violet whispered. She shook her head and sat back on her heels. "I could have ended this but I wasn't strong enough. I had him, Lark. I had his life in my grasp and I couldn't finish him."

She looked down at her hands and Lark ached to reach out to her. Violet closed her eyes and then suddenly was on her feet. Without another word, she swept out to the hallway. Her hands clenched.

"Limor's barren quim!" Violet slammed her fist into the wall. She dropped her head into her hands. Her shoulders shook. Lark drew in a shocked breath. She never thought she'd see the day her strong, impassive Violet was brought to tears.

"Um, there's a kind of balcony out through that window," Madison said with a quick jerk of her head. "If you need a bit of privacy. It's gonna take a few more minutes before I get done here."

"Thanks," Lark said. She hesitantly approached Violet from behind. She reached out and touched Violet on the shoulder. "Let's go outside and get a bit of fresh air."

Violet swiped a sleeve over her face before she turned and nodded.

The balcony was narrow and gritty. A bright orange tarp covered a bulky object in the far corner. Eyes bleak and face drawn, Violet sank down to her knees on the bare concrete. Lark followed. In the distance, a rhythmic flapping sound started up. Something was coming through the air.

"I was trained for that moment," Violet said. "I spent my entire life preparing for it but when it really mattered I couldn't do it."

"You're not a killer."

"Yes, I am." Violet turned her hard gaze to Lark. Her face was set and white. The stony, blank expression was belied by the tracks of tears on her cheeks. "You don't understand. It is my birthright, my only reason for being. Because I failed in this one simple thing, I was imprisoned all my life for *nothing*."

A shock of pain took Lark's breath away. Violet closed her eyes, leaning forward again onto her clasped hands. Unable to stay still, Lark reached out. She wrapped her arms around Violet and pulled her close. Violet didn't fight her, instead she relaxed into the embrace. Lark stroked back the tousled and dusty hair from Violet's brow and pressed a kiss to the top of her head.

"It isn't failure to care," Lark said. "So you couldn't look a man in the eye and take his life with your bare hands. There aren't many people under this Blue Sky that can do that, and I doubt they've got any soul left. You told me I have a beautiful soul, but so do you. I don't know anyone braver or stronger than you. You left everything you knew to come here and help the people who wrecked your world. People who insult and mistrust you, who take your sacrifice for granted. You could so easily hate us all, but you don't." She gathered Violet closer. Lark couldn't remain silent any more. "And that's why I love you."

Violet tensed.

"I know what you can do," Lark said. A black pit opened up in her gut, which she tried to fill with words. "I know you are capable of a lot of things, many of them violent and final. The fact that you have the strength to stop yourself is one of the many reasons I fell in love with you. I know you don't want to hear it, but I needed to tell you."

"No, my Sunshine." Violet's words were hot against Lark's chest. Her hands clenched on Lark's dusty sleeve. Her voice dropped and Lark had to strain to hear what she said next. "I just didn't want you to regret it, because I won't say it back."

"That's all right, I wasn't expecting it," Lark said. Keeping her voice level took all the strength she had left.

"Um, guys?" Madison's head poked out of the window. "Sorry to interrupt your moment here, but the police are all over outside. Something tells me you don't want to be here when they come up."

Madison moved back and Violet got to her feet. She looked

shaky, but much better than a few minutes ago.

"You are correct in that assumption," Violet said. "Thank you for your assistance and please accept my apologies for destroying your workplace."

"Ah, don't worry about it, it's my last day anyway," Madison said with a grin. She held the blinds up in an invitation to re-enter the building. "It's not gonna break my heart if this place falls into rubble."

Lark turned to duck back through the window, but she felt a prickling sensation on the back of her neck. She twisted to peer down into the narrow alley below. Lark caught her breath as she nearly fell into silver-blue eyes that were trained on her. A woman was standing in the alley staring up at her with a singular interest. She was wearing some kind of black vest and her power-ful body was hung with equipment. Over short-cropped black hair, she had a jaunty hat on her head. She was strong in the way men are but still undeniably female, and Lark was captivated. She couldn't look away.

The woman below moved first, grabbing a black box from her shoulder and shouting into it.

Instinctively, Lark put a hand over her crystal pouch. Her agate grew warm and the words swelled in volume.

"Flora! Where the hell's the fucking fire department with their ladder truck? Don't tell me they got lost in this dinky little town. Shit."

The box squawked in reply. Violet's gentle touch on her arm broke the spell. With a glance over the railing, Violet took Lark's hand and guided her back into the building.

"Did you like what you saw?" she asked with an amused quirk to her lips.

The cold spell from Lark's blurted confession broke. She grinned back. "Yeah, I did."

Violet fixed her with a calculating look. She arched a brow and asked, "Do I have competition?"

"Huh?" Lark asked. She slapped herself on the forehead even as her cheeks burned. "Green Trees, no, not like that. I just thought I really want a hat like that."

"Come on, let's check on Alice," Violet said. She gave Lark another lingering look and fell into step with her. Back in the office, they met up with Alice, who was looking pale with one arm and her chest swaddled in white bandages.

"Are you okay to move?" Lark asked. "We need to get you to a safehouse."

"Yeah, I think so, but are you sure that's a good idea?"

"I'll scry them up at Shadowmoor," Lark said. "Work out a deal."

Overhead the flapping sound became louder and a mechanical flying machine appeared. It swooped low over them. Lark let out a cry of surprise and clutched at Violet, both of them stared until the bug-like thing roared away.

"Woah," Alice said. "I've never seen one of those things up close before." She fixed her attention on Lark again. "Anyway, we have to get out of here. Soon."

Madison watched them with a mystified look on her face. After Alice spoke, Madison shoved herself into the middle of the group. "And exactly how are you all going to do that? You can't go out the way you came in, that's for sure. Can you guys like, um, fly?"

"No, we can levitate things but we can't fly," Lark said. She gave up on even the pretense of following the Guardians' secrecy policy. After what Madison had seen that day, there was no point. "Is there any other way we can get down to ground level besides the stairs? I can't risk levitating anything with so many people around."

"Maybe you saw that thing on the balcony," Madison said. "It's a ladder for emergencies like a fire, and I guess whatever the hell happened today. How about I set it up for you? Don't worry, I'm the emergency response coordinator here, so it's kind of my job."

"Great, that'll do fine," Lark said.

Intrigued, she followed Madison and leaned her elbows on the windowsill. Lark watched in fascination as Madison lifted the orange tarp, revealing a sturdy machine with a chain-link ladder coiled inside it.

"So what exactly are you?" Madison asked. She turned the crank and the ladder slowly extended over the balcony railing. "Wizards or something?"

"No, we're just normal people," Lark said.

"Uh huh." Madison didn't look convinced. "Is Owen one of you?"

"Definitely not."

"Just so you know, I'm not going to tell anybody about you guys. Not like anybody'd believe me."

"Thanks," Lark said. "You're probably right."

Madison straightened up and dusted off her hands. "Okay, ladder's down." She climbed back in through the window and stuck her hand out to Lark. "Good luck." Lark hesitated for a moment, then she clasped Madison's hand in hers and gave it a firm shake.

When they reached the ground, Lark cast a Blind to get them through the milling crowd unnoticed. She looked around for the woman from the alley and saw her trying to direct people away from the wrecked building. Lark tried to fix the powerful aura of authority the woman exuded in her mind. She wanted to be like that, strong and bold and commanding.

Once they were a few streets away from the scene of the battle, Lark pulled them into an alley. It wasn't ideal, but at least it was semi-private.

"I need to contact Shadowmoor," Lark said. She looked down at herself and made a face. The battle in the office left all of them in no shape for an audience with the Guardians. Lark brandished her wand. She said, "Alice, Violet, stand over there and let me get the dust off you two."

"I can do myself," Alice said. She pulled out her wand with her uninjured left hand and flipped it into the air. She caught it with a flourish. Lark raised her eyebrows, impressed. Alice preened. "I practice both hands just in case."

"Good idea," Lark said. She turned to Violet and gave a courtly bow. "With your permission, my lady?" she asked.

Violet replied with a low curtsy, the cultured gesture was a stark contrast to her scruffy appearance. "You know you have it," she said in a quiet voice meant only for Lark's ears.

Lark swallowed the sappy grin. When they were presentable, Lark pulled out her scrying crystal and held it in her hands while she collected her thoughts.

"This is my doing," Lark said, "So I'll be the one who takes responsibility."

"Nuh uh," Alice said. She shook her head. "We're all in this together. We present a united front, got it?"

"All right," Lark said with a flash of gratitude and pride. She looked from Alice to Violet, both of them with calm, determined faces. "Let's do this," Lark said. She bent her head over her crystal, feeding it from the deep reservoir of energy that hummed beneath the sprawling city.

The crystal clouded for a moment, then cleared. An image formed and wavered. Lark breathed a sigh of relief when Jean Elliott's face and figure came into focus. She was sitting in the lounge with a mug of tea next to her, like she was waiting for Lark to call.

"Lark, is that you?" Jean asked in a sharp voice. The vision lurched as Jean fumbled with the lid of the box. "Whatever possessed you to go off like that?"

"They were going to split us up," Lark said. "I couldn't let that happen."

"That's life," Jean snapped. "Things don't go your way, you grow up and deal with it."

Lark felt her face flame hot and a dangerous look of her own surfaced. "Jean, you know it's not that simple. As a team, and only as a team, we've got a chance to stop this before it's too late. None of us are doing this for personal reasons. We are all adults and chose this course of action as the best one."

"All right," Jean said. She rubbed a hand through her short hair. "But you're going to have to convince the people in charge and not just me. How about I get Ulric, then."

"I'd appreciate that," Lark said. She was aware of Violet and Alice hovering behind her. Jean's face disappeared and as Lark waited, she tried to get her thoughts in order. She could only hope the Head Guardian would hear her out.

Soon Ulric Williams' face filled the crystal. "Convince me not to dismiss you from the Guardians," he said without preamble. "Who do you have with you?"

"Violet Ironwrought and Alisson Chance."

"And the Bucketsworth man?"

"We, um, got separated," Lark said. "But we have identified the Outsider who has the Bloodring and we're going to get it back. Head Guardian Williams, I assure you that we are your best bet. We can do this."

"I agree," Violet said. "And I refuse to consider another course of action. Remember, it was you who asked for my assistance. This is how I'm giving it. If you do not wish me to return to my convent you will not interfere."

Williams gave a long sigh. He crossed his arms over his chest. "What do you need?"

Lark nearly dropped her scrying crystal in surprise at the quick acceptance. She collected herself and said, "Promise us safe passage and lodgings as well as the freedom to act as we see fit. Guarantee that, and we'll destroy that Ring and return order to our world. After that, we will submit to the judgment of the Guardians."

"Agreed," Williams said, even though he didn't look pleased about bowing to the ultimatum. "I will spread the word you are not to be interfered with."

"Thank you, Head Guardian," Lark said in a breathless rush. "You won't regret your decision."

"Humph," he said before the crystal went dark.

"Nice one," Alice crowed. "I would be giving you a high-slap but, you know," she said and looked down to her bandages.

"Are you in pain?" Violet asked.

"A little," Alice said with an abbreviated shrug. "But I'll be okay."

"You didn't ask for clemency," Violet said, studying Lark. "With me, you hold all the cards, you could have used that as your leverage."

"It's not fair," Lark said. She stowed her crystal. "I'm not going to use you as a bargaining chip to get myself out of trouble."

"You could lose your position."

Lark brushed a finger over the back of Violet's hand while looking deep into her eyes. "As long as you're with me, I don't need anything else."

"Your romantic drivel is giving me a toothache," Violet said. Her brusque tone was softened by a quirk to her lips and a dancing light in her eyes.

"Me too," Alice said. She wrinkled her nose. "How about we get going, then?"

"Yes, the day's not getting any younger," Lark said. "Alice, do you know how we can get to the safehouse from here? You were there once before. Is it near here?"

"Yup," Alice said. "It's about a ten-minute walk, or we can take the eleven-bus and get off at the Ash Lane stop."

"Wow, you really do know your way around here," Lark said. "If you two are all right to walk, I think we should do that. I don't like the idea of us being stuck inside a ground-cart with a bunch of Outsiders right now."

"I'm all right, it's my arm that's busted, not my legs," Alice declared. Violet nodded her agreement.

Alice trotted off. Lark took a step to follow, but Violet saying her name stopped her. Lark looked back over her shoulder. Violet had her hands clasped in front of herself. She looked undecided about something.

"Lark, I—" Violet bit her lip and looked away. She quickly said, "It's nothing. Let's go."

In a swish of skirts and long strides, Violet strode after Alice. Lark followed, certain whatever Violet wanted to say wasn't *nothing*.

Chapter Nineteen

THE SAFEHOUSE WAS a tall and slim brick building, identical to the others in the long row. Nothing distinguished it from its neighbors except for the brass numbers nailed to the front door.

"Here we are, number 127," Alice said. She knocked and the door opened to reveal a ruddy, beaming woman about the same age as Lark's mother. She gave off the same bustling, welcoming air until she saw Violet, who pressed up to Lark's side.

"Who do we have here?"

Lark jumped in with a cheerfulness she had to fake, "I'm Lark Greenpool and this is Violet Ironwrought. And you already know Alice."

The woman's hand tightened on the door knob. For an instant, Lark's heart froze. A long moment passed where Lark was certain they wouldn't be allowed entry. Their hostess' face relaxed and she opened the door fully. She said, "Come in, come right on in. I apologize for being a bit abrupt, we don't often get visitors of such importance here very often. I'm Mrs. Merry Keeble, by the by. Pleased to meet you."

Violet bowed her head and swept into the bone-defying, impossibly low curtsy she'd used earlier on Lark, with none of the joking. She was graceful and elegant in her sincerity. Lark gazed at Violet's form in wonder, her breath caught in her throat.

Violet straightened up and said, "I am honored to be allowed entrance into your home. If there is anything I can do to assist you, do not hesitate to ask."

"Oh pshaw," Mrs. Keeble said. She pressed a hand to her generous bosom. "That's a very kind offer, but there's nothing really I can think of. At any rate, please come in and make yourself at home. You are among friends here."

Once they crossed the threshold and hung up their cloaks, Lark felt a great weight lift from her shoulders. Outside was more stressful than Lark imagined, crowded with people and machines, in addition to being the ersatz leader of their group.

Lark could temporarily let her guard down. They were in familiar territory. Safe in more than just name, the house was protected on multiple levels. Mrs. Keeble immediately started fussing over Alice.

"Alice, dear, whatever have you done to yourself? Honestly, I can't leave you alone for a moment before you're bumping and banging yourself."

Alice rolled her eyes and submitted to being ushered into the kitchen and perched on a stool. "Mrs. Keeble, never change," she said.

Mrs. Keeble tutted and drew her wand from her sleeve. "It's a good thing I'm a dab hand at patching you folks up. Now let me see here. Hold still please, Alice."

While she muttered to herself, a long, thin man who was the exact opposite of Mrs. Keeble slipped into the room. His expression was mild and didn't change when he saw exactly who the newcomers were. Wordlessly, he turned to the stove and began putting things into a skillet. Good smells filled the room. Lark's stomach threatened to growl. Surreptitiously, she pressed her hands to her belt.

"All right, all done," Mrs. Keeble said. She helped Alice unwind herself from the bandages. "How's that, dear?"

"Not bad," Alice said cheekily. She placed a hand on her newly-healed collarbone and rotated her shoulder. "Will I be able to play the fiddle?"

"Of course you will, bless."

"That's great," Alice said. Her eyes sparkled. "'Cause I couldn't before."

"Oh you!" Mrs. Keeble snapped the tea towel at Alice, who danced out of the way. Lark got a wave of emotion from the familiar scene, except her memory supplied her own mah snapping the towel. By that time, the man was dishing up platefuls of ham and grilled winter vegetables. He set a basket of rolls in the middle of the long table, plus several small jars of pickles and preserves. A jug of tea was already on the table, along with a collection of mugs.

"I'm sure you all want some supper after your journey. Dig in, we have plenty," Mrs. Keeble said. She gestured to the laden table. "Oh, and if you could all hand over your account books, I'll stamp them and settle your fare."

Lark and Alice obediently passed over their blue-covered books. Violet produced a black one with a gold embossed border that had Mrs. Keeble's eyes going wide before she whisked off with the books clutched in her plump hands.

"Mr. Keeble's the best cook," Alice declared. She dropped into a chair. After a moment, Lark followed suit, along with Violet. As one, they bowed their heads in a quick prayer that Lark felt more sincerely than usual, then dug into the meal. Violet initially hesitated over touching the utensils, but once she grasped her spoon, she ate with gusto, quite different from when she first came to Shadowmoor. They were enjoying some of Mr. Keeble's pumpkin pie, which Lark decided was second only to her own mah's when a gust of cold wind blew through the kitchen, followed closely by two black-cloaked figures.

"Rosalie," Lark breathed. The man behind her was the same one who was with her at the social. For a moment, Lark wondered if they were more than just patrol-partners. Feeling territorial and protective of her small group, Lark aimed a sharp look to the newcomers and squared her shoulders. She said, "I assume Head Guardian Williams sent you to check up on us."

Rosalie took off her cloak and handed it to the man with an offhand manner. He swept out of the kitchen with it. "In a way, yes," Rosalie said. She chewed her lip in an uncharacteristic display of uncertainty before she straightened up defiantly. "I volunteered to come out here and see if I could help. It's been so frustrating all these months, waiting for reports and never getting anywhere. You are on the forefront, and I want to go out there with you."

"That's very generous," Lark said. "Are you sure? It's going to be dangerous."

"That's what we've been training for," Rosalie said. She looked grim, but determined. "We're here at your disposal."

The half-formed plan floated into Lark's mind. "Thanks, I'll let you know the details soon enough."

Rosalie nodded briskly. The man came back into the room and they both sat down at the table. "Have you met Matt Fletcher?" Rosalie asked.

He bobbed his dome-head, all the while staring at Violet. "So you're the chosen one who's going to save us all?" he asked abruptly. "Ouch!" He reached under the table to rub his shin while glaring at Rosalie.

"Matt, don't be an ass, please," Rosalie muttered. She waved off Mr. Keeble's offer of food, instead, she clasped her hands on the table. "So you've seen it? The Bloodring."

Lark nodded slowly. She didn't want to think about what it meant. "Yes, I did."

Saving Lark from having to answer any more questions, Mrs. Keeble bustled in with an armful of bedding and a conflicted look on her face. "I was just about to show you to your rooms, but we only have room for four on the single ladies' floor and one is already occupied by a...guest."

"It's okay," Alice piped up. She threw Lark a mischievous glance that Lark didn't understand. "Put Violet in one of the family rooms. That's what you did when the bunch of us was here last."

"Oh...well..." Mrs. Keeble looked troubled. "It's just that regulations dictate those are not for single use. Yet, I absolutely can't allow a lady on the gentlemens' floor and there's simply not room enough for two in the singles' rooms."

"Lark will share with her," Alice said. She propped one elbow on the table and waved expansively, her face was just a little too innocent. "Won't you, Lark?"

Mrs. Keeble glanced from Lark, who was frozen half in delight and half in shock, to Violet, who regarded the scene with a stoic look and an upraised eyebrow. With a decisive nod, Mrs. Keeble said, "I suppose that's the best solution, if everyone is fine with that? All right then, you two can have the Rainbow Suite, that's the smallest family room. It's got two beds for you dears. Nightclothes and towels are in the closets of the washing-up rooms. Ask me or the mister if you need help with anything."

"Will do!" Alice answered on behalf of everyone.

That was the signal for everyone to get up and make their way to the stairs. On the way up, Alice bumped Lark's shoulder with hers and whispered, "You owe me one."

"More than one," Lark whispered back. Her face glowed with heat and she focused on Violet's slender waist and slim body in front of her, which was probably not the best thing to do to keep herself from blushing madly. Lark's heart thudded. What would happen if she and Violet were alone for more than a few minutes? What would that night bring? Lark was in agony to know, but at the same time she quailed at the idea. Her recent declaration opened up a chasm between them and Lark wasn't sure what to do about it.

The Rainbow Suite on the third floor was a smallish room with a window that overlooked the back yard of the safehouse which sported a birdfeeder and a nicely laid-out kitchen garden. The neatly made-up beds were side by side, separated by a small table. A dressing screen took up one corner, while a washstand took up another. Lark nervously eased herself down on one of the beds and Violet took the other. An awkward, uncomfortable silence fell between them.

The emotions Lark tried so hard to deny welled up inside of her. The words she said, the sentiment that was not necessarily welcome or even returned came back to her. They were stuck together, dependent on each other for the time being and Lark made things awkward and sullied. Maybe she'd ruined everything like a starry-eyed gosling.

She looked away, ashamed of the tears that stung her eyes. Lark stood and made a show of taking off her waist pocket and wand. She lay them both on the bed.

"I'm going downstairs for a bit," Lark said. "I remember Alice telling me about how they've got a library and I've got a hankering for a nice book right about now. Are you okay here?"

"Yes, I too would like some solitude," Violet answered. She turned away from Lark and peered out of the window. She held herself straight and tense.

"Okay, yeah, me too. Um, good to hear that," Lark stammered. She practically fell out of the room and down the stairs. The crushing weight in her chest got heavier with every step. She barely made it to the library before the tears came. She curled up in one of the overstuffed armchairs and buried her face in her arms. She tried not to make any noise, save for pathetic sniffling into her handkerchief.

A crash jolted Lark upright. She pressed her handkerchief to her mouth, mortified beyond belief. A grey-haired woman in leather pants and a jaunty jacket stood in the door with a look of surprise on her face.

"Aw hell," she muttered to herself and eased the door closed behind her. She righted the lamp she'd knocked over and leaned against the wall, one booted foot tapping uneasily on the floor. "I didn't mean to interrupt."

"No, it's okay," Lark said quickly. She scrubbed her face with the cuff of her sleeve and tried to calm her breaths while she surreptitiously studied the woman. For her age, she was whip-thin and held herself with confidence and strength. Lark hastily stuffed her damp handkerchief into her pocket and stood up. "I'm Lark Greenpool."

"Well, don't that beat all," the woman said. She strode into the room with energetic strides. She grabbed Lark's hand and gave her a hearty shake that left Lark mystified. "I've heard all about you from my great-nephew Murray."

"Great Auntie Pacifica," Lark gasped before she could help herself. "And I've heard all about you too!"

"Heh, and that's not even the best stuff," she said. "And none of that great auntie bit, okay? Fuck, that makes me feel old. 'Scuse my French. Hang around with Outsiders enough and you start cursing like one. So refreshing and direct, they are. Anyway, take the load off, no need to be all formal. I'm not a Guardian, just a normal Wanderer doing what we do best."

Lark sat back down and couldn't help the melancholy sigh that escaped from her.

"Maybe it's none of my business," Pacifica said, "This doesn't have anything to do with that fetching young Ringsworn I saw coming in practically on your arm now, does it? Sorry, I was having a smoke on the roof and I saw you and your gals arrive. I saw how close she was standing to you. I know the Ringsworn, and they don't let anybody get within an arm's length unless they really trust them, and sometimes not even then."

Lark considered brushing off the question, but her admiration for the older woman wouldn't let her. Lark covered her flushed and damp cheeks with her hands. "Yes, it has everything to do with Violet." She didn't elaborate. Pacifica seemed openminded, but Lark couldn't take any chances. Not for herself, but for Violet's reputation.

Pacifica dragged over a footstool and straddled it in a smooth motion. Her leather pants creaked and the chain hanging from her belt tinkled merrily. "Before you go clamming up on me," she said with a twinkle in her eye, "Let's just say I've had my own heart stomped on by more than my fair share of young ladies in my day." She chortled. "Not-so-young ones too. Come on now, stand on the shoulders of giants and see if I can be of any help."

After a moment where Lark wrestled with her thoughts, she said, "I told her I loved her."

"Huh," Pacifica said. She regarded Lark shrewdly. "And let me guess. She didn't say it back."

"That's right," Lark said. Her throat felt tight. She gulped and wondered if she should get her handkerchief out again.

"It's a tough thing to say. Not everyone can or will say the words, for lots of reasons."

Pacifica reached into her breast pocket and took out a battered paper pack. She took a white stick of rolled paper out of it and held it up. "Mind if I have a smoke? Don't worry, I'll open the window. Merry gets on my ass about that."

"Go ahead," Lark said automatically.

Pacifica went over to the window, opened it and lit the white stick with a flame from a metal box similar to the one Violet had. After taking a few puffs and releasing a cloud of noxious smoke, Pacifica waved her hand through it. "Filthy habit, I know. An ex got me hooked — ex boyfriend that one was. A lot of good times we had until I was the one to stomp on his heart." Pacifica got a wry grin at the memory. She held the stick in one hand, wedged between her fingers while she gazed outside. "Anyways, maybe she doesn't say the words, but if she feels it, she'll tell you in other ways. Keep a lookout."

Lark mulled over Pacifica's words as Violet slipped into the room. Violet glanced over to where Pacifica hung out the window, blowing a stream of smoke into the garden and backed up a step. She looked pale and her expression was carefully blank.

"I was just leaving," Pacifica said. She took out a small pouch and hurriedly disposed of the last embers of her smoke-stick. As she passed Lark, Pacifica gave her a light punch on the shoulder.

When the door shut behind her, Violet waited a moment, as if composing her thoughts. Lark waited in agony. She didn't know what to do. She felt young and stupid and awkward with no idea what to say, so ended up sitting in strained silence until Violet crossed the room and claimed the footstool Pacifica had vacated. Her long skirts whispered over the faded patterns in the carpet.

"Lark, I was wrong," Violet said. She looked so forlorn, Lark automatically reached out for her, but stopped a breath away from touching her.

"About what?"

"I mistakenly believed never speaking of something would make it untrue." Violet pulled her long braid over her shoulder and fiddled with the leather cord at the end.

"I shouldn't have said it. It was stupid of me. I wish I could take it back."

"No," Violet said. "I don't want you to take anything back."

She looked up and Lark fell into her dark gaze. It was as if no time had passed and they were still back at that breathless first moment when Lark understood Violet desired her as well. Nothing stood between them. Violet was just as inexperienced and confused as Lark, maybe more so.

"Really?"

"Yes. And I'm sorry," Violet said softly.

"No, it's me who should be sorry," Lark said. This time she did move, reaching out and clasping Violet's hands in hers. They were cold and Lark automatically chafed the chilled fingers with her own. "I blurted it out in the heat of the moment, and I bet I caught you off-guard."

"It was I who did wrong by making a unilateral decision, specifically when I'd asked you never to do such a thing again. I have to apologize for—" Violet stopped speaking. Her lips twitched. "We're doing it again. Apologizing too much."

"It's good to clear the air." Lark had to grin at that. "Violet, I don't want things to be strained between us. I was thinking all sorts of daft things before you came down to talk. That took more guts than I had. Thank you."

Violet's lips quirked up into a full, beautiful smile that held no bitterness. She drew Lark's hand to her lips and lightly pressed a kiss onto her knuckles. A wave of heat raced from the point of contact, straight to Lark's heart—with a slight detour down between her legs at the decidedly predatory look Violet speared her with. She rose to her feet in a single, graceful motion, their hands still intertwined. "Dance with me," Violet said.

"There's no music," Lark said. She got up anyway and let Violet lead her into the middle of the room, where they had the most space to move.

"I will sing to you," Violet said. She let go of Lark's hand and draped her arms over Lark's shoulders. Lark automatically placed her hands on Violet's waist.

Lark grinned. She couldn't help but say, "I can't dance."

"I will lead you."

"Can't argue with that." Lark pulled Violet closer and Violet sank into her arms. She rested her head on Lark's shoulder, the way Medina did to Jean at the social what seemed a lifetime ago. Overcome with emotion and more grateful than she could possibly say for the unquestioning, uncomplicated presence of Violet in her arms, Lark's chest grew tight. Violet made good on her promises and gently guided Lark in a slow circle about the room, while she sang an achingly sweet melody about loss and darkness falling over the sacred sea.

Violet paused in both song and motion, leaving them simply standing in each other's arms. Violet's breath was warm on Lark's neck. She murmured, "I apologize for the melancholy tune. The Wraiths of Limor favor such renditions as they feel it brings them closer to the goddess."

"I liked it," Lark said. She closed her eyes and pressed her face into Violet's hair. "It's beautiful. Thank you."

"You're welcome. For the record, so far that's only two," Violet said.

"Pardon?" Lark straightened and moved back enough to look into Violet's face. She wasn't angry. It seemed like she was waiting for something.

"Two of the three important and difficult things to say. I want to hear you say the last one to me, without reservation."

Lark understood. Her heart pounded. Her hands trembled on Violet's waist before she raised them to gently cup her face. Lark traced the tiny smile that curved Violet's lips up. With as much conviction as she could muster, she said, "I love you, Violet. I'm in love with you. I'm smitten, I've completely gone daisy for you. You get my topsoil in a twist, my goose is a-gander—"

Violet's lips meeting her own stopped the increasingly silly list. Lark's eyes fluttered shut and she dragged her hands through Violet's hair. Her back landed against the wall of books and only increased the heat of the kiss. Lark couldn't get enough. She sucked Violet's bottom lip into her mouth, let go, then latched on for a full, deep kiss. Violet's moan resonated through Lark's chest. She slipped her hands over Violet's strong shoulders, down her back to her waist once more.

All pretense of dancing was given up. Lark pressed herself

fully against Violet, holding them together. Even through the layers of skirts, Lark was extremely aware of Violet's body. Her deep breaths surged over them both, their legs pleated Violet's voluminous skirts, seeking contact. The heat between them grew like a fever. Lark couldn't help but drop her hands to Violet's backside and grind them together. Violet met her thrust, trembled, then drew back.

"We can't do this here," Violet said in a husky whisper full of longing.

"I know," Lark answered.

Lark's entire body ached from the loss when Violet stepped away from her. The throbbing between her legs was so strong, Lark was afraid it would never cease. Still, she didn't protest aloud. Once they were disentangled, Lark quickly raked her long bags back and shook out her tails.

"Thank you for the dance, my lady. It was very...nice," Lark said. She fanned herself and was rewarded by a mock-stern glare from Violet, complete with eyebrow raise.

"I wish to bathe tonight," she said abruptly. "As well as avail myself of the clothes washing facilities. Shall we ascend?"

"Sounds good," Lark said. She took a few deep breaths. Her legs were decidedly weak and her heart rate wasn't quite back to normal. Violet was the first out of the room with Lark following a bit slower in order to keep from stumbling on her gawky colt-legs. By the time Lark arrived at the third floor, Violet had already disappeared into one of the bathrooms.

Lark selected a neat, blue nightshirt from the closet and grabbed a towel. She bathed quickly and laundered her clothing. She hung everything up in one of the drying closets before she returned to the room. Violet wasn't back from her bath yet. Alone with her thoughts, Lark couldn't stay still. Both her mind and body were at a fever pitch. She padded on bare feet up and down the length of the room, absently twisting the end of one of her tails in her hands.

The door creaked open and Violet slipped into the room. Lark's heart gave a jolt in her chest. Violet's hair was damp and loose. She was wearing a pure white nightgown with delicate embroidery on the front, flanking the long row of pearl buttons on the yoke. The harsh lights of the hallway contrasted with the single lamp in their room. The lights behind Violet cast a glow around her slender body, highlighting the soft curves and smooth, long lines of her legs.

She looked beautiful, innocent and desirable all at once. Lark caught her breath. She never wanted anything more than to fall into Violet's arms and drown there. Lark glanced away and sat down on one of the beds. Her belly clenched with pent-up desire. She drew her legs up underneath herself and faced Violet once more. The air was heavy with unsaid words. Before anything else, they needed to talk. The door clicked closed. Violet turned briefly to flip the courtesy latch. When her dark eyes met Lark's once more, Lark couldn't be silent any longer.

"That Ring," Lark said. "It's yours, isn't it?"

Violet crossed the room. She hesitated briefly before she sank down onto the bed next to Lark. She said, "I hoped I would never have to face it, but yes, it is. That Ring was made against all wisdom and precedence. A Bloodring should never have been made from one so young, or one with powers such as I have. I was but a small child and it nearly killed me."

"They must have been desperate," Lark said.

Violet gazed across the small space that separated them. "It doesn't matter. They were wrong. That unholy creation can only cause suffering."

"How can we beat it?"

"The Ring is flawed," Violet said. Her hands absently worried at the pearl buttons at her breast. Lark did her best not to follow them. "I can't destroy it myself like the others, but it can be destroyed."

"How?" Lark asked. She leaned forward.

"It can be overloaded. Like me, the Ring can't keep a reserve of energy. We need to find Owen once more, persuade him to give into the Ring's hunger. If it takes in more energy than it can hold, the stone will crack, effectively killing the Ring."

Lark nodded. While she was grateful Violet wouldn't have to perform the same procedure she had with the knot, she got a burr of worry about the possible implications of the artifact's destruction. Violet's expression was so carefully blank, Lark feared there was something else Violet wasn't telling her.

At any rate, Lark had to focus on facts. They had come too far to turn back. Their world depended on it. The plan she mulled over came into focus. She said, "When Reuel wakes up, I bet he's going to scry me up. If he doesn't by morning, I'll call him. Find out where he is and meet up. I'll offer myself. Once the Ring gets me, it will have more power than it can handle."

Violet shook her head. "One is too risky. You can't supply enough at once. We'll need more people." She reached out and took Lark's hand. "I won't allow you to sacrifice yourself for this. You are too valuable, too pure, unique, and...dear to me."

Lark covered Violet's hand with hers. Her heart pounded in her chest. She shifted and scooted forward on the bed. Only a breath separated them. Lark said, "You're dear to me too. You're my world, Violet. I want to give you everything I am and everything I have." The words were rough and breathless, but Lark had to get them out. "Lie with me tonight."

Violet lowered her eyes. She looked uncertain.

"Sunshine," Violet said in a gentle voice. "I ache for you. I yearn for you with every heartbeat and every breath. I can't tell you how much I wish I could welcome the dawn in your arms, but I cannot. I mustn't. You deserve someone who can promise you a lifetime, someone who can give you a respectable name, a life, children..."

Lark gaped. After all that time, Violet still thought Lark would run off with some fellow. Lark nearly laughed out loud. She calmed herself and said, "Violet, look at me." Violet raised her head and met Lark's gaze without flinching. Lark said, "If you say no because it's not what you want, I'll abide by that. But if you refuse because you think I should save myself for some future person, that's not a decision for you to make. Know this, if for whatever reason our paths diverge and I end up with another, *she* will know I was yours first. And I want you to be mine. I'll ask you again. What's your answer?"

Violet pulled her hands from Lark's grasp and rose gracefully to her feet. She spun and went over to the other bed. With a quick motion, she whipped the quilt and sheets back, replacing them in a messy pile. The look she met Lark with when she turned around once more was dark with desire. Deliberately, Violet unwound the length of leather from around her wrist and deftly tied her hair back. Lark gulped. The promise and purpose of that simple action echoed through her. She shivered with nerves and anticipation.

Silently, Violet crossed the small space and knelt down on

the bed in front of Lark. She reached out and placed a hand flat on Lark's chest.

"Yes," Violet purred. She pressed very gently and Lark joyfully fell back, pulling Violet along with her. Their bodies settled against each other, bare legs twining together. Lark thought her heart would burst from all the emotions that flooded her at that moment. She looked up into Violet's face, framed by a few loose, wavy locks and suffused with such emotion, Lark felt it like a physical touch, straight into her chest.

Keep a lookout.

Lark reached up and held Violet's trailing hair back with both hands. She ached to taste her, her entire body burned with desire, but Lark wanted to savor the moment. She would never have another first time. Neither of them would.

"Lights on or off?" Violet asked in a low, breathy voice.

Lark didn't even think. She reached out and with a flick of her fingers, the switch across the room flipped off. Lark shook out her quartz and set it aglow before she slipped her crystal pouch off and placed it on the bedside table. The quartz hovered over them. The room filled with the gentle glow, which was softer and more intimate than the harsh yellow illumination from the lamp. Violet drew back and regarded her with an amused arch of her brow, just the way she always did. In that instant, Lark knew that no matter what step they took in their relationship, they would still be the same two people. It was comforting to her on the cusp of that large milestone.

Lark returned Violet's look with a quirk of her own. "Do you want to see what other magic I can do with my fingers?"

A low chuckle welcomed her words. "Most definitely," Violet said.

They came together slowly, carefully. The first kiss was gentle, but soon became deep. Never breaking the contact, Lark rolled over onto her back and drew Violet to lie on her. The feeling of their bodies pressed together drove her breaths into jagged gasps. She never imagined such softness as Violet's breasts on her own. Only two thin layers of cotton separated them. Violet drew her bare leg up between Lark's, gently pushing the hems of their nightclothes up until finally they were thigh-to-thigh. Another inch and Violet would have proof of how incredibly aroused Lark was. Overwhelmed, Lark had to abandon Violet's mouth. She bit her lip to keep the moan of longing from escaping.

"That's really good," Lark whispered.

Violet dropped her head and kissed the sensitive spot on the side of Lark's neck that never failed to shoot sparks through her. Even with Violet's full weight on her, Lark arched her back, nearly lifting them both off the mattress. She lowered her hands and gripped Violet's hips. The supple muscles tensed and relaxed under her hands with the waves of Violet moving against her.

With every breath, Violet gave herself to Lark, surrendered to her caress. Violet, who was so guarded and cold at first. The weight of the gift was not lost on Lark. She could only hope to be worthy of receiving it.

Lark couldn't resist any more. She stroked her hands up Violet's taut back until she reached her shoulders, then down again until she was agonizingly close to the full breasts that tormented her with their nearness. Violet's eyes fluttered shut. She let out the smallest sigh.

"Yes," she breathed. She grasped Lark's hands and moved them to cup her fully.

Lark never imagined such softness and warmth. She held Violet reverently, then brushed her thumbs over the hard nubs. Experimentally, Lark stroked a few quick circles. Even through the nightgown, Lark felt the areolas pebble and tense. She couldn't believe the feeling of power that came when Violet responded to the caress with quickened breaths and flushed cheeks.

"Your fingers really are magic," Violet said between soft whimpers.

While Lark was struggling with an answer for that, Violet lowered her head and captured Lark's mouth in a deep, hungry kiss. It lasted until Lark thought she would pass out from lack of air and dizzying tension rising in her womanhood.

Violet broke the kiss and abruptly stood. Lark swallowed the groan of longing and frustration that rose up in her throat, but what Violet did next took her breath away. Violet slowly opened the front of her nightdress, then reached down and lifted the hem. It rose up her legs, to her knees, up higher until Lark thought she would die from the pounding pulses of fire in both her chest and significantly lower. A flush rose to Violet's face and she glanced away when she pulled the hem up to her waist, revealing the soft patch of dark hair that hid her most secret place, then finally over her head. The gown fell softly into a pool at her feet.

Lark swallowed hard. She couldn't look away. Violet was perfect. She was a goddess, rising from the sea. Her skin was seafoam pale, soft and tempting like nothing Lark ever encountered before. Her graceful throat and leanly muscled arms contrasted with the gentle swells of her breasts, rosy-tipped and rising with each breath. Her slim waist and rounded hips called Lark's hands to hold her, the dark triangle at her thighs mesmerized her. Lark forced herself to raise her eyes.

Looking lovely with her pink cheeks, Violet met Lark's eyes once more. The sudden connection sent a shock of heat through Lark. She gasped aloud when Violet placed a hand on her own breast, then trailed her fingers down to suggestively tease one tight bud. Lark ached to do just that. She couldn't speak. She could barely think. She only knew that she belonged to Violet, and she hungered to touch her and worship her.

"Your turn," Violet said in a harsh whisper. "I want to see all of you."

Lark's mind went blank, then she scrambled to her knees and with shaking fingers, she tried to get her nightshirt open. Violet sank back down onto the rumpled sheets, her nakedness glowing in the gentle crystal-light. Her breath was warm and gentle on Lark's skin when she took over unbuttoning the nightshirt.

Violet paused and looked up again. "Are you all right with this?"

"Yeah, completely," Lark replied. Once the nightshirt was unbuttoned, she shrugged it off and tossed it carelessly onto the floor. Her action was rewarded by a look of stunned awe from Violet.

"Sunshine," she breathed. "Every time I see you, you are more beautiful than the last."

Lark's reply was to take Violet's face in hers and draw her into a full, heated kiss. Violet moaned into her mouth and Lark felt pulses of arousal pumping through her, spreading out from between her legs through her entire body. She rolled Violet into the crumpled bedspread and lay down fully on her. Their bodies met for the first time in a passionate press of breast to breast and intertwined legs.

Lark couldn't stop. She wanted more. She ripped her lips

from Violet's and latched onto her neck. Violet's hands stroked up and down her back, grabbing at her shoulders and holding her close. The harsh breaths that resounded in Lark's ears drove her to slip her thigh between Violet's. Heat and slick wetness welcomed her.

"Good?" Lark managed to gasp between heated kisses.

"Yes, Sunshine, I like you right there on me," Violet whispered. She canted her hips and thrust into Lark. The contact was dizzying. Lark whimpered with desire. She couldn't stop. Her hips jerked as she rode Violet's thigh. The rhythmic motion and the sensation of Violet under her was intoxicating.

Lark sucked in a breath. She was in heaven. Violet's movements got faster and harder, her breath came out in short gasps. Her breasts bounced with each pump. She threw her head back into the pillows.

"So close," Violet said. "I'm yours. Yes, Lark. More."

Lark never felt such completion, such intense responsibility in the trust Violet gave her when she yielded control of her entire being over to Lark. And she didn't want it to be over too soon.

"Not yet," Lark said. She drew back, breaking the contact with Violet's wet heat.

"Oh," Violet breathed. The body under Lark's was tense and trembling. "Please, Lark, touch me. I need you."

Unable to deny the request, Lark brought her hands up and cupped Violet's breasts, this time with nothing separating her fingers from the silken skin. The sensation thrilled her. Rock-hard nipples tightened under her touch. Lark raised her head and looked into Violet's face. She was flushed and panting, tousled against the pillows, her lips parted and wet. A jolt of fire speared Lark in the belly.

Lark bent her head and deliberately kissed her way down between the gentle swells of Violet's breasts. She let herself be guided to one rosy nipple. With a sigh of ecstasy, she kissed it before she circled the pebbled areola with her tongue and hungrily drew it into her mouth. She couldn't help but gently tweak the other with her fingers, remembering how wonderful it was when Violet did that to her.

With a stifled cry, Violet arched back at the first contact, then clutched Lark to her. She raked her hands through Lark's hair. Each rasping breath drove Violet deeper into her, and Lark accepted her hungrily. She switched sides and suckled hard for a moment more before she let go with a wet sound.

Lark gazed up into Violet's face. Her eyes were half-closed and she was breathing in short, high gasps. Lark had never seen her with her guard down that much, not even in tears. Lark's breath caught.

That moment would live in her memory forever. Lark swallowed hard. She knew what she wanted to do, what every single fiber of her being ached to do, but would Violet let her?

Suddenly nervous, Lark wet her lower lip. She didn't have the words to say what she wanted to do, but had never been more certain than in that moment. Lark said, "Violet, I want to do something. I want to, um, please you."

"Lark," Violet whispered. She trailed her fingers from Lark's cheeks to across her lips. "Do what you will. Just do it quickly, ah!" She gave a short cry and pressed one hand to her mouth when Lark, bolstered by Violet's words, slipped her body between Violet's legs.

Lark bent her head once more and swiped her tongue over Violet's taut nipple before she continued her journey down. Each inch was marked by a soft, breathy moan from Violet. Soon, Lark reached her destination and urged Violet's knees up to open her more. She did so willingly.

Lark settled down between Violet's thighs. She couldn't believe where she was. Violet was milky with desire, spread and waiting and absolutely beautiful. She waited for Lark and no one else. Lark hovered on the precipice in both awe and indecision.

"Goddess have mercy," Lark whispered the words before she realized what she was saying.

"You don't have to, you know."

"I know," Lark said. "I want to. Very much."

A low chuckle echoed in Lark's ears. Violet reached down and gently parted herself with her fingers. She drew her own wetness over the sleek, inner petals. Lark gulped with a rush of sudden hunger at the sight. She squeezed her legs together as a rush of heat flooded her own womanhood.

"Don't be shy, you have one too."

"I'm not shy, just enjoying the moment," Lark rasped.

Before she could change her mind, Lark reverently dropped a kiss to where Violet's fingers were a moment before. A low mur-

mur of pleasure welcomed her. Lark bent her head and swiped her tongue up the gorgeous furrow that was sleek with womanly dew. She closed her eyes and hummed in pure pleasure at the sensations that met her exploration.

A firm hand on the back of her head urged Lark to increase her efforts. She rested her hands on either side of Violet's most intimate place and pressed ever so softly as she gave herself to her glorious task. Each swipe of Lark's tongue, each pass of her lips brought a sound of appreciation from Violet. Her hips started to rock, her movements grew fast and urgent.

"Goddess, I'm close."

At the words, Lark latched on to the rigid bud, the center of her pleasure and sucked without abandon.

"Yes, yes! Sunshine, take me over," Violet said. She shivered and bucked her hips. The soft exhalation that met the first jerk of release lifted Lark into the stratosphere. Even as she urged Violet to come fully to climax, Lark couldn't take her eyes from Violet's face.

Violet was propped up on her elbows. Her face was deliciously flushed, her eyes hooded and sultry. Each breath came on the heels of a tiny note of pleasure that thrilled Lark and kicked up her own arousal.

A heartbeat later, Violet threw her head back. She lost herself to pleasure. Lark was hard-pressed to keep up, but she did. The final waves juddered through Violet and left her limp and gasping, sprawled out in an unladylike way on the bedspread. Lark sat up and very carefully drew Violet's splayed legs together. She had her eyes closed and breathed slowly and deeply.

When Lark settled down beside her, Violet opened her eyes and snuggled into Lark's arms. She pillowed her head against Lark's chest and let out a sigh of complete contentment. One hand idly rested on Lark's belly, Violet's thumb brushed over her skin.

"Sweet Limor, how did you do that? I thought the heavens opened up and took me."

Lark smiled as she pressed a kiss into Violet's hair. She said, "I read about it once and I wanted to try it."

Violet raised herself up on her hands and stared at Lark in incredulity, then much to Lark's surprise, she laughed, a full, throaty sound, and caught Lark's mouth in a full kiss. Violet didn't seem to mind that Lark's lips must still carry her essence.

When Violet drew back, her eyes were dark with desire.

"Now it's my duty and joy to please you. What do you want?" Violet asked.

Lark looked away. She felt her face heat up. Her mind was suffused with pleasure, her body tight and aching for release, her only thought what she longed for Violet to do.

"I want you to take my maidenhead," Lark said. She gazed into Violet's face, searching for revulsion. All she saw was a slow dawning of wonder. "Before you ask, yes I'm sure."

"Sunshine," Violet breathed. She flushed and looked uncomfortable. "I hope I don't hurt you. I'm not exactly sure —"

"I'll let you know if anything's not good," Lark said. Her heart, now that she'd spoken, pounded like a hummingbird's.

Violet took Lark by the shoulders and kissed her, softly and slowly. Lark opened her mouth to Violet's searching tongue, then replied with her own. They drank deeply of each other for a few sweet, achingly tense moments. Slowly, Lark eased over until she was on her back underneath Violet.

"Starlight," Lark whispered. "Please, now."

Violet paused with a look of indecision before she brushed her lips over Lark's once more and reached down. Slender fingers trailed down Lark's belly and met her thatch of curls.

"Yes," Lark whispered. She opened her legs to give Violet clear permission. Her breaths were shallow and fast. She wanted to hide her face, but she didn't want to take that moment from either of them. Lark arched back and raised her arms over her head. She couldn't stop the shockwave that rippled through her at the first brush of Violet's fingertips over her most sensitive area. Violet circled her throbbing pearl, causing Lark's hips to buck, then she dipped lower.

Violet drew in a breath. "By the goddess, Lark you're so ready for me."

"Yes, please take me, Violet," Lark urged. She felt Violet bending her leg and complied. She had to bite her lip hard to keep from crying out at the sensation of Violet slowly pushing into her. She lay still, trying to adjust, fighting just to keep breathing. The feeling of being filled was overwhelming. Lark wasn't sure if she wanted to laugh or cry. Lark didn't know how many fingers Violet had inside of her, but Lark was packed full. It wasn't unpleasant. Far from it. Lark's appetite for more fired up.

"You're all right?" Violet asked her.

"Uh huh," Lark replied. "Just, ugh, please do something. I'm so hot right now, I could go off anytime. I *need* to."

With a wicked little grin, Violet pulled out, then thrust deep again. Lark clutched at the pillow, at Violet's shoulders, at her own hair as the rhythm picked up. She couldn't help herself and rocked Violet deeper.

It wasn't long before the white light of climax crashed over Lark. She shuddered and gasped. She reached down and stilled Violet's hand between her legs, loving the way she held Violet within herself. After the last peak faded and Lark was drained and limp, Violet gently withdrew. She painted loving circles on Lark's womanhood with her wetness, causing a few more jolts. Finally, when Lark was fully sated, Violet took her hand off Lark and they snuggled together, bare as the day they were born, one in body and soul.

"Thank you," Violet whispered. "Are you all right?"

"Never better," Lark declared. She trailed her hand up and down Violet's back. "I think I waited all my life for you."

Violet replied with a soft kiss to the side of Lark's neck, which sent a thrill of pleasure through her.

Under Violet's soft, teasing lips, Lark pondered starting a little something more but a giant yawn interrupted her. "Sorry, I was going to try and keep you up until dawn, but you tuckered me out."

Violet laughed softly. "I'm about asleep too."

Violet slipped from Lark's embrace. She got up and soundlessly padded across the floor. Trying not to stare at Violet's perfect backside, Lark stretched out on the crumpled bedding and sighed happily. She had never been that exultant, that full of emotions and yet so drained at the same time. Something landing beside Lark startled her and she patted around until she found her discarded nightshirt. Violet perched on the side of the bed, buttoning up her nightgown.

"Do we have to?" Lark asked. She rolled over onto her back, not bothering to even try to hide anything. She smirked at the flush and intense look Violet gave her before she glanced away.

"Yes, we do," she said.

"All right, just because you insist," Lark said. She scooped up her crystal pouch and settled it between her breasts before she pulled on her nightshirt, purposely leaving it scandalously unbuttoned.

Violet laughed softly, shook her head, and stood.

"Excuse me for a moment," she said before she silently slipped from the room.

Lark burrowed under the comforter and wondered how she could entice Violet to spend the rest of the night in her bed. She was still mulling that when Violet returned with a warm, damp towel.

She lifted the bedclothes and very gently nudged Lark's legs apart.

"I don't want you to go to sleep wet," Violet said. "Do you want to do this yourself, or will you allow me the honor?"

When Lark realized what Violet was asking, her face got hot. She was on the verge of refusing, but then gave permission and allowed Violet to clean the evidence of their lovemaking from her thighs. Lark had to admit, she did feel better afterward. Lark sat up and twined her fingers with Violet's.

"Would you stay here tonight? With me?"

Violet's expression was tender in the soft light of the crystal.

"Yes. Now move over and give me a pillow. I hope you know I won't appreciate it if you steal the blanket."

"I won't," Lark said. Her heart felt like it was full to bursting with love. She made space for Violet to slip under the covers. Lark pulled Violet to her, who melted into the embrace like it was the most comfortable and natural thing in the world. Lark snuffed the crystal and sleepily tucked it back into her pouch before wrapping her arms around Violet once more and holding her close.

"Goodnight Sunshine."

"Night, Starlight." Lark couldn't stop smiling. She was deeply satisfied, more than a little tired, and completely at peace.

She was loved.

Chapter Twenty

STILL IN DARKNESS, Lark stirred and opened her eyes. Violet lay in slumber in her arms. She snuggled against Lark's chest with her arms wrapped around her, possessive even in sleep. Her face was nestled into the crook of Lark's neck. When Lark moved back to look at her, she saw Violet's face was peaceful, innocent, and soft. A wave of love swelled in her chest.

"Wake up Violet, my Starlight," Lark whispered.

"What is it?" Violet asked. She stretched, tousled, loose-limbed and almost glowing. Lark felt much the same way herself.

Released from Violet's embrace, Lark sat up and placed a hand on her chest. The warmth of her scrying crystal met her touch and she shook it out. Without thinking, Lark put an arm around Violet and drew her close. She pressed a kiss to her temple as if it were the most natural motion in the world. Violet closed her eyes and hummed in contentment.

"Someone's calling me, and I think I know who."

"Then you'd better answer." Violet twitched the covers back. "I'll leave."

"No, it's all right. Anything Reuel says to me he can certainly say to you."

Violet settled back into Lark's arms. In Lark's palm, the stone flared into life. Reuel's scrawny, ghostlike face was not a welcome addition to their bed, but Lark was relieved to see him nonetheless. He opened his mouth to say something, then gaped and cast his eyes down. His fishbelly-white skin flooded with blotches of red.

"I'm sorry, I shouldn't have scryed you up so early," he stammered. "I didn't know I would disturb the lovely Miss Ironwrought, and what an absolutely fetching nightgown."

Brusquely Lark waved him off. She agreed with him, but she certainly wasn't going to let him know that. She asked, "Where are you? Is Owen with you?"

"I'm fine, thanks for asking," Reuel said in a whiny voice. Sullenly, he said, "It took me a long time to triangulate my position, even with my best agate. For some reason, I keep getting knocked out in the middle of the action."

"I seem to remember you volunteered, at least the second time," Lark said.

"Details," Reuel said. "I am being held in a deserted storage facility near the harbor. Owen is becoming increasingly unstable. I believe using the Ring has done something to him. I have offered assistance, assuring him that Miss Ironwrought is the best and only one who can help him. After a fair amount of convincing on my part, he let me know he is open to another meeting."

"Good man," Lark said. He sketched out the location until Lark was certain she could find the place. They agreed to meet at sunrise. The crystal went dark and Lark stowed it with a heavy feeling in her chest. The end was coming. She didn't have the luxury of regret or second-thoughts. Whatever happened that day, she would have the previous night to keep forever.

They had to move, and quickly, but first Lark had to do something. She stood and held out her arms, joyfully gathering Violet up in them.

"Good morning," Lark murmured into Violet's hair. She dropped a series of kisses that ended in a long, sweet meeting of Violet's lips to hers.

"Are you all right?" Violet asked when they parted. "Last night, I didn't hurt you?"

"Nope," Lark replied with a wide grin.

Violet reached up and cupped Lark's face in her hands. She brought them together and touched foreheads. Her breath was fast. She was nervous.

"Lark I just wanted to say…" Violet trailed off. Abruptly, she let go of Lark and said, "Nothing."

It was the second *nothing* from Violet in that many days and Lark burned with curiosity at what exactly *nothing* was. At the same time, she wasn't sure if she really wanted to know. Violet turned and ducked behind the dressing screen, effectively ending the conversation.

Lark hurriedly yanked on her clothing and bounded up the stairs. She knocked on Rosalie and Alice's doors, then sent Rosalie to rouse Matt. In whispered tones, Lark told them to assemble in the kitchen and be ready to move out. Alice ran off to find their hosts and organize an early breakfast.

When Lark returned to their room, Violet emerged from behind the screen, still midway through dressing. She turned and presented her partially-laced corset to Lark.

"Would you do the honors? Pull slow and steady, with one last strong yank to cinch the waist."

Lark couldn't speak. Her voice drowned in emotion. The gesture was simple, but the intimacy resounded through her. She followed Violet's quiet instructions, paused to let her breathe, and finally knotted the laces in the tight curve of Violet's back. Lark couldn't help but wrap her arms around Violet from behind. She kissed the perfect pink curve of her ear and whispered into it, "Thank you, my Starlight."

Violet leaned into the caress. She lifted her chin and accepted Lark's kisses to her neck. Lark's chest burned. Her body remembered the exquisite torment of Violet's touch. She stroked up the hard front of the corset up to the unbelievable softness of Violet's breasts.

Violet's tiny gasp inflamed Lark more than she could believe.

"I have half a mind," Lark murmured, "to take you back to bed right this moment."

Violet's whispered response was interrupted by a soft knock. Instantly, Violet sprang from Lark's arms and slipped behind the dressing screen once more. The rustling of rich fabric filtered into the air.

Lark glanced at her reflection in the mirror of the washstand just to make sure nothing was out of place. "Who is it?" she asked.

"Just me, sweetheart," Mrs. Keeble's voice came through the door. Lark looked back over her shoulder.

"Hang on a moment," Lark said, stalling for time.

Violet eased out from behind the screen. Once more perfectly aligned and cinched securely with her heavy braid coiled around her head and neatly pinned up. She held herself with the grace of a queen. In response to Lark's unspoken question, she nodded.

Lark opened the door and their hostess bustled in. She had a length of thick, fawn-colored material in her arms, which turned out to be a long cloak. It had a line of embroidery around the hood and hem, spiraling vines and roses of impossible delicacy.

Mrs. Keeble held the cloak out to Violet. "I noticed you didn't have one, and well, it's chilly out there."

Violet regarded the offering, then raised her eyes to Mrs.

Keeble. "I can't accept this."

"You will," she said. Her chubby hands pressed the fabric firmly into Violet's arms. "It was my grandmother's, made for dressy events and such. She was a musician. She and my grandfather were among the elders who walked into the snow the winter of the Salt Famine."

Violet's face twitched. She bared her teeth in a fierce, feral grimace. Her fists clenched around the proffered cloak. "The Salt Famine is considered by certain members of the Ringsworn one of the most glorious victories of the war. It is also one of the most unjust, vicious and unnecessary actions taken against your people. I am not proud of that."

The words startled Lark. She learned about the war in school, although the actual events were not something she'd studied in much detail. Crystalgazers tended to gloss over the details and express relief it was over, while Wanderers were more guarded when it came to talking about it. Lark held herself very still. The war left deep scars on all sides.

Mrs. Keeble patted Violet's hand. At the touch, Violet jumped and relaxed her hold with an uncomfortable glance around. Mrs. Keeble said, "I didn't mean to bring that up to harm you. It's part of our history. I don't hold that against you. After all, you were but a youngun at the Great Division, and you're here now in our time of need. That's worth a lot in my books."

Violet traced the tiny, intricate border with one finger. "I would be honored to wear this into battle today. Thank you."

"All right, now let's get some breakfast into you all."

"YOU SURE YOU all got the right place?" The driver of the hired ground-cart twisted in his seat to address Lark. "There ain't nothing here 'cept warehouses. You folks into something shady here? 'Cause I don't want to get the rep for shady stuff."

"Nothing shady at all," Lark said. "Thank you for the ride."

The hired ground-cart pulled away. Lark paused and looked over the assembled members. Rosalie and Alice looked calm and ready, while Matt kept glancing at Violet, as if trying to figure her out. They were definitely at the right place. The same, unmistakable pall of the Bloodring was there, lingering like a noxious miasma.

"Are you all okay with this?" Lark asked. She met the eyes of each member in turn. "I'm asking you to make a significant sacrifice, put yourself under the power of a dangerous, uncontrollable artifact."

"Of course we are," Rosalie said. She stood proudly, every inch the consummate Guardian and pressed her hand to her sleeve, where her wand was tucked. "If that's what it takes to protect our world, then I'm all in."

Alice answered with a decisive nod that Matt copied.

"Let's go then," Lark said. The rest fell into step with her.

Lark threw open the double doors and strode into the gaping maw of the warehouse. The gritty floor was made of metal plates and here and there clots of wooden boxes lurked. She was sure their group made a striking picture, the five of them with their long cloaks sweeping over the floor, four black and one fawn. The oppressive feeling got stronger. Lark's gut twisted and for a moment, she felt like the hard-boiled egg she choked down at breakfast would come right back up.

At one end of the warehouse, Reuel and Owen waited. Owen was slouched into a moth-eaten and battered chair that looked like it was pulled from a rubbish heap. His head and limbs jerked from time to time, his face twisted with tics. Behind him, Reuel loomed with his cloak pulled tight around himself.

"He said you could help me," Owen's voice was rough and bubbly. He coughed and spat out a wad of clotted blood. Lark grimaced.

"That's right," Violet said. She stepped forward and regarded the hunched-over man. "You tried to control something that is uncontrollable and now you're paying the price. It's not too late. Let me show you how to harness the potential of the Ring." She held out a hand.

Owen curled up protectively. "I'm not giving it to you."

"And I don't want it." Violet took small, measured steps as she spoke. Her voice was low and hypnotic. Even Lark felt herself falling in thrall of it. "You feel it, its power, don't you? It's hungry, begging for you to feed it. I've brought you the best we have, the most powerful of our forces as tribute for the Ring. It is our honor to nourish it."

She threw off her cloak before she glanced back over her shoulder and nodded at the group. They followed suit with their cloaks fluttering to the floor before they formed a circle around Owen. As one, they drew their wands and each created a glowing ball of energy.

"Yesss," Owen said. He scrambled out of the chair and lurched toward the group. Lark backed up a step when he came near her. Her skin felt like it would burn if he touched her. She let her energy ball go and Owen snatched it like an animal snatching at a treat. He chuckled to himself while he collected the energy, ending up in the middle of a rough circle of Guardians. It was time.

"On my mark," Lark called out. She braced her stance and unleashed a wave of energy. It struck Owen and he staggered back a step, only to be buffeted on every side by different colored streams. The display would have been beautiful if it wasn't so deadly. In the middle of the storm, Owen shrieked and twisted. The Ring started to hiss and shoot off sparks. Lark felt its endless hunger, the craving for more and more energy even as it sucked down what they fed it.

Lark could barely contain her grim excitement. It was working.

"You tricked me," Owen said. He fell to his knees and clutched at his wrist. His eyes were wide and desperate.

"Take the Ring off," Lark said. "It's your only chance."

"Never!"

"All right, suit yourself."

Lark opened the floodgates. The others around her did too. The air was alive with their energy. The Ring sucked it all down greedily. A sizzling hum rose up from it.

With a hoarse yell, Owen collapsed onto the floor, limp and unconscious. Lark raised a hand and immediately everyone held their fire. Lark edged closer. She dropped to one knee and checked him for signs of life. He was breathing shallowly.

The Ring, on the other hand, took on a life of its own. It glowed and shot out more sparks. The last was so violent it rolled clear off Owen's finger and levitated. A high-pitched sound split the air as if the Ring was screaming in agony. It vibrated and great swatches of energy flew off it.

Violet was immediately beside Lark. She was pale, yet composed.

"It can't contain the energy, It's going to rupture," Violet said. "A shield will contain the blast. We'll do this as we have practiced."

"Got it," Lark said.

"You should stand back," Violet called out to the others.

"You heard her, stay back all." Lark didn't check to see if they followed her command, she trusted them. Out of the corner of her eye, she saw Reuel dragging Owen with him behind a pile of boxes. Lark turned her attention back to Violet.

Violet stood directly in front of the Ring. She closed her eyes and held out her hand. Lark knew what she had to do. She got behind Violet and wrapped her arms around her slender, strong body, wand ready. Violet's white hands covered hers, then stroked down to meet the smooth wood of her wand. Lark felt the sudden yank, the connection pulling energy through her. Everything she was, everything she had, opened to Violet's will. She was nothing more than a conduit and Violet was her direction. She gave herself up without hesitation.

A red and silver-sparking shield sprang up around the Ring. It hummed with their combined power, backed up by the endless stream from underneath the city. For the first time, Lark felt the power harnessed inside the cracked gem and twisted silver. It was huge, bigger than anything she'd felt before. There was no question that if it went off, there would be nothing but wasteland for miles.

"It's too big," Violet said with a note of desperation in her voice. "I can't contain it. I will bleed off as much of the blast as I can and buy you time, but I can't contain it." She struggled and tried to let go of the wand, but Lark held her. Violet spoke again, her voice panicked and cracking, "Get everybody out *now*."

Lark twisted around. She looked directly at Alice and said, "Run."

"You too! Lark save yourself, I beg you!" Violet cried out. She made a move to let go of the wand, but Lark covered her hands with her own.

"I'm not leaving you here," Lark said. "At least we can hold it back long enough for the rest to get away. I wish you could have met my folks, and I could've taken you around my village. Thanks for the good times." She paused, then whispered fiercely, "I love you and regret nothing."

Violet took a deep breath. A wan smile thawed her features.

"And I love you." She leaned back into Lark's arms. "My Sunshine."

The Ring cracked.

There was a split second of absolute silence before a white shockwave ripped through her. The pain was unbelievable but the shield held.

Everything happened in slow motion.

The white-hot explosion tore at their defenses.

Violet set up shield after shield in an endless dance as the inner ones burned away.

Each one cost them more than they had, but there was no way to stop.

Violet's unique spinning vortex directed the energy and bound it into dense shields faster than Lark could think.

Lark channeled all her energy, but it wasn't enough. They were going to fail. She tightened her hold on Violet and breathed a prayer of thanks for allowing her final moment to be with the woman she loved.

Something hit her, a bold streak of energy. Lark peered through the shimmering haze. Alice stood with Rosalie and Matt. All three added their last reserves to the shield. Lark's eyes teared up in gratitude. The shield held.

Her world narrowed down to nothing more than a white pinprick. Her body and mind and soul screamed in agony but she couldn't stop. The uncontrollable, destructive energy bent against the walls of the shield. The shrieking vortex resonated, the skin-peeling timbre changing as if it was being forged into something else.

The battering storm became pulsing waves of heat that resonated against the layers of shields, folding against them and filling the black void like a tide returning to the shore. The explosion peaked. In her arms, Violet's body shuddered with the final impact. She let go of Lark's wand and threw her hands up. The residual energy transformed into a wave of pure light. The roof of the warehouse directly over them evaporated in a white-hot dome of vaporized metal.

The waves broke over Lark, streaming back into her and returning her spent life force. Strength came back into her limbs.

The flow stopped. Lark breathed again. Her body filled with a golden warmth. She looked around, dazed, and saw the group of Wanderers doing the same. They were healthy and whole and in one piece. Violet channeled the energy back through herself, returning everyone's gift with her own.

"We did it," Lark crowed. There was no answer. Violet's body was heavy in her arms. Lark gasped as Violet's full weight fell against her. Lark lurched sideways and they dropped to the dirt floor in a crumpled heap. Lark pulled Violet to her and looked into her face. Her eyes were closed. Her skin was cold and white. "No," Lark whispered. She couldn't draw enough breath. "Please no."

Burnt debris rained down around her like black snow.

"No. You can't leave me. I just found you." Lark's voice was barely a whisper. It took everything she had to get the words out. "Violet, Starlight, wake up, please."

Silence met her pleas.

Lark angrily threw her wand aside like it was nothing more than a stick. She dragged at her neck and fumbled her pouch into her hand. She frantically shook her crystals out. They scattered in the dust. She grabbed the biggest one and dredged up every last reserve of energy she had, channeling it into the crystal in a desperate attempt to reach Violet, using all of her strength to drag breath back into her lifeless body.

The radiant pink energy from Lark's crystal showered down over both of them, raising a stinging cloud of dust and rippling through Violet's wide-flung skirts but had no other effect. She couldn't be gone. It wasn't possible.

Someone pulled at her arm but Lark tore herself from their grasp.

"She's gone. The backlash was too much for her. Lark, I'm so sorry." Alice's voice cracked.

Lark didn't want to hear it. She couldn't let herself believe it. She grabbed at her chest to try and contain the pain that ripped through her. Alice kept tugging at her.

"Get up. We have to get out of here before the Outsiders show up. I hear sirens and they're coming closer. Please."

"No!" Lark screamed and flung her hand out. A shield snapped up, throwing Alice backwards. Blinded by tears, Lark clutched Violet to her chest and grit her teeth to contain the sobs that wracked her. Violet saved their world. She should be returning to Shadowmoor a hero, not like this. She sacrificed herself for all of them. She was worth a hundred Guardians. She deserved to live.

Lark took a few shuddering breaths. She knew what she had to do.

My life for yours.

Lark slowly, reverently lay Violet down on the scuffed floor. She paused, on her knees with her back hunched as if bearing the weight of the heavens on her shoulders. Then she raised her face to the sky. She reached deep into herself, deeper than her heart, deeper than her soul. She grabbed her very life energy and willed it into her hands.

More.

Her shield flickered out, her energy directed within. A hot wind whipped around her. Pieces of debris stung her skin. A well of energy surged up within herself. Lark focused it all into her hand. The force of it crackled through her entire body. Her fingers were translucent from the glowing ball within them, not red but the purest white. The light was so bright it burned her eyes even through her lids.

She had never felt such power or such peace. At that moment, on the cusp of taking that step, Lark knew why she was put on the earth, why she was born with the power she had. She softly, reverently placed her hand flat on Violet's still chest. Then she let go.

The shock lasted an instant and an eternity.

White light burned away the world and Lark prepared to meet the darkness.

It didn't come.

Violet's body jolted and she dragged in a sharp breath. Then another. Her breaths came in ragged gasps, but they still came.

She was alive. They both were.

Trembling, Lark reached out a hand and brushed back a strand of hair from Violet's face. Her eyes fluttered open at the first touch. Violet turned to meet the caress and twined her long fingers around Lark's. Tears rained down Lark's face, this time of joy.

"What happened?" Violet asked, her voice hoarse and whispery.

Lark tried to reply, but speech failed her. The only thing she could do was drag Violet's hand to her lips. She pressed a kiss to the inside of Violet's wrist and thanked every power in the universe for the strong, steady pulse. Violet looked up into Lark's face with a worried expression.

"Curse me, I've caused you tears again."

Lark shook her head, sniffled pathetically and dredged up a grin.

"Is everyone all right?" Violet asked.

Lark quickly looked around. Alice sat on the ground, dusty and hugging her arms to her chest as if in pain while Rosalie and Matt stood a distance away with their wands out. Reuel hovered over Owen, who looked completely bewildered.

"Yes," Lark said. She brushed her thumb over Violet's lower lip. "The Ring is gone and everyone is fine. You did it, my Starlight."

"That's good." Violet closed her eyes. She whispered, "I died in your arms, didn't I?"

"Yes, you did," Lark said. She drew in a shaky breath and scrubbed a cuff over her face. "But only for a moment."

"You are a gift from the Goddess herself," Violet said. Her face relaxed into a wondrous smile.

"I don't know about that. How do you feel? All right?"

"Yes, I feel perfectly fine. I wish I could remember the intoxicating embrace of death," Violet said. She sat up and gathered her skirts about herself before she playfully flicked Lark's trailing forelock out of her face. She said in a cheery voice, "I'll just have to wait until I meet the grim reaper in all Her glory again. As all of us will someday."

"Not too soon, though," Lark said. She couldn't help but give into the wave of pure joy and grin. She wanted to sing and shout and dance. She didn't care who was watching. Violet was whole and alive, sitting in front of her with long strands of hair falling out of her braid and dust all over her cinched bodice and full skirts, more beautiful than Lark had ever seen her. Violet gazed deep into Lark's eyes, who flushed, suddenly shy. Lark said, "Um, I wanted to let you know my memory may be a bit fuzzy. You know, just so you know you don't have to take anything back—"

"No. I meant what I said."

Lark couldn't breathe. "You love me?" she asked in a whisper.

"With all my heart." Violet's eyes bored into hers. "You are brave, dashing, foolish and beautiful all at the same time. You complete me and I can't imagine living without you — even if you are too damned cheerful at times, I still love you."

Lark's face heated up. She felt like she would explode from emotion.

Violet's lips quirked up into a crooked grin, then she sobered. Violet said, "The words kept trying to come out, even as I fought to contain them. I thought if I never said them, if you thought what we had was merely youthful infatuation, moving on would be easier for you."

Had. The word chilled Lark.

"You knew you weren't meant to return from this mission."

"Yes," Violet said. "The Ring is part of me. To destroy it is to destroy myself. I knew I would have to meet it sooner or later, I couldn't outrun its shackle to my soul forever. It was my destiny to die with it."

"You're free now. What you do next is entirely up to you."

"That's true, I don't really know what I want. I never planned for this."

"You've got time to think about it. Hopefully I'm in the plans somewhere." Lark kept her voice light, but her feelings teetered on the edge of despair.

"Of course you are," Violet said. "I am not going to let someone like you go."

"Good," Lark said. She leaned forward and pressed her forehead to Violet's.

The distant siren was getting louder. They had to move.

Lark stood unsteadily and helped Violet to her feet. Violet accepted the assistance with grace. Her fingers lingered over Lark's for longer than necessary. Lark picked up her wand and slung it across her back. Before her, Violet took a deep breath. Her strength and poise returned, along with Lark's peace of mind. Alice trotted over with their cloaks and passed them over. Lark whirled hers on with the worried thought it might be the last time for her to lawfully wear the black cloak of the Guardians.

"This way," Rosalie said. Absently, almost automatically, she cast a Blind around the entire group as they left the warehouse and Owen behind them. She started off in a brisk trot. Her cloak whirled out behind her. "There's a shelter over there where we can call for a hired ground-cart."

Lark fell into step with her. "Thanks for coming with us. You really saved the day."

Rosalie just shook her head, but she was smiling and looked triumphant. "All in a days' work for us Guardians."

Lark's belly lurched. "Probably not me. With all the laws I broke, I'll be lucky if they only boot me out and don't toss my sorry carcass into the lockup at Hadley's End for the rest of my life."

"I wouldn't be so sure about that," Rosalie said in a mysterious way. She twirled her wand in her fingers before she slipped it into her sleeve. "By the way, rest assured that Matt and I will only be giving statements about the Ring itself, not necessarily anything personal about the members involved."

"All right," Lark said, mystified. She slowed her pace and Rosalie barreled ahead of her. The meaning of the words hit her. Rosalie and Matt would keep her and Violet a secret. Lark was both grateful and saddened. She wished for the day they could be public, just like any other couple.

They would, one day, Lark vowed. Rosalie gave her the freedom to choose that day. Lark promised herself it wouldn't be too far in the future. At any rate, it would be prudent to keep that volatile information under wraps for the time being. At least until Lark could be sure she wouldn't destroy Violet's reputation by being summarily dismissed from the Guardians.

The group of them filed into the small metal-walled shelter. It boasted a bench and a machine that appeared to sell drinks. One side was open and overlooked the harbor. The air was thick with brine and some kind of mechanical oil.

Lark did a quick headcount. Reuel was with them, still wrapped in his cloak like he wanted to disappear. Lark dug his Almanac out of her waist pocket and held it out. "I believe this belongs to you."

He took it with a sullen look and hugged it. He sidestepped away from the group and looked ready to bolt.

Rosalie quickly intercepted him with her wand drawn. "Not so fast. You need to come back with us."

"Leave me here," he begged in a pathetic voice.

"Do you really want that?" Lark asked. "To live in hiding for the rest of your life? If you go back of your own accord, it'll be a lot better for you. I, for one, am willing to testify on your behalf. Without your help, none of this would be possible."

"Me too." Alice said. She added, "For your info, even if you try and run, with the number of Guardians we've got right here, you'll never get away."

Reuel hung his head and looked defeated.

Lark pulled Alice aside and said in a low voice, "I thought the one stipulation I made was if I told you to run, you do it."

Alice gave her a cocky grin. "Sorry, I must have gotten some dust in my ears. Didn't hear you."

Lark shook her head. "Okay, I'll give you credit for not shirking in battle. You're going to make a fine Guardian. North Wind knows, you're one already."

"You know it," Alice said.

"I want to apologize for throwing you off with my shield," Lark said. "You're not injured, are you?"

"Body is fine, dignity slightly ruffled," Alice quipped. "Luckily my backside and my cloak cushioned me well enough."

"Glad to hear it." Lark said.

Alice clapped a hand on Lark's shoulder and cupped a hand over her mouth to stage-whisper, "I'm gonna go over and get something to drink. I think there's someone who you should be spending time with instead of me."

Lark exchanged a shy glance with Violet while Alice skipped over to the drinks machine and inspected it with an excited air. Lark reached out and squeezed Violet's hand. There was no use in hiding anymore, at least in present company. In front of anyone else was another story.

Lark turned back to Violet with a smile and gave her hand one more quick squeeze before she gazed out across the choppy, grey ocean. They were going home, but if she could follow through with her plan, it wouldn't be Lark's home for long.

Epilogue

One month later

POPLAR VALLEY HAD never been decorated so gaily. Wreaths hung from the trees that encircled the village hall. Inside, buckets full of poinsettias dotted the long room where a merry fire warmed the air.

The atmosphere in the village was jubilant, and for good reason. Once the Bloodring was destroyed, everything out-of-kilter went right again. The late harvest was a bumper one, with plenty of pumpkins and apples for winter. Chickens laid more eggs than anyone knew what to do with and the goats produced so much milk, the overworked farmers had to enlist the help of every person with free time around them just to keep up. Wells that went acid were pure once more and the violent storms never returned. The aftereffects rippled throughout the land until every corner was healed.

Most importantly, the Border was whole again. Multiple teams of Guardians inspected every last mile of it and reported it strong as ever. The Protected Isles were still under their ancient protection. They were safe once more.

That day was the first village meeting since the destruction of the Bloodring. Everyone wore smiles and their very best clothes. Lark didn't take in any of it. She shivered in the chill air outside the hall. She scanned each new arrival and with each she sighed more. A month passed since the destruction of the Bloodring. If she thought four weeks' time would end her notoriety, she was dead wrong.

Even once the hearing finished and Lark was pardoned, demands for her time never ceased. People came clamoring to hear her version of the events. Lark refused to speak of them after she gave her official statement. Others wanted to give her an embarrassing amount of gifts, which she either refused or passed on to her friends and colleagues.

Violet as well was pulled in every direction. She was away

from Shadowmoor for days at a time, inspecting the repairs to the first of two chosen temples and dealing with her own flocks of curious gawkers. With the spotlight on both of them, privacy was impossible. Lark shoved her hands in her pockets and kicked her feet out while she paced up and down the spotty grass. It had been a while since she wore a skirt, and she felt hampered by it. Lark was thoroughly frustrated. She thought that finally getting permission to bring Violet to her village's meeting, ostensibly as part of her work as a "Goodwill Ambassador," would give them some sorely needed time alone. Lark was wrong. Violet surprised Lark by slipping away with Dillah on a mysterious mission she refused to speak about.

Lark was left alone and bored. She comforted herself with her most precious recent memory, the look on Violet's face when Lark rose to her feet before the Guardian Council and whirled the black cloak with its brand-new silver stripe over her shoulders for the first time, only a week ago. That, at least, gave her hope their future wouldn't be spent apart from each other. The few times they actually managed to meet in secret, they whispered to each other, "Soon."

"Waiting for snow out here?"

"Huh?" Lark jumped. With a quick flash of annoyance, she whirled and faced Merton. She managed a grin. "Hey there, Mert. You're looking mighty spruced up, I daresay. Those new boots?"

"Yup, sure are," Merton said proudly. His round face flushed. "I'm aiming to ask Emily Millerhouse to the social next month."

"Good for you," Lark said without rancor. That time, her grin was genuine. "I told you someday you'd find yourself a nice village girl."

"Yeah well, since I couldn't have you."

"It wasn't in the stars from the start. I'm not really a 'get married and start a family' type of person."

"I should have known. When I asked your parents for their permission, your dah told me to 'have at' but don't come crying to him if you sent me packing and your mah just laughed herself off her chair."

Lark couldn't help the guffaw that exploded from her. She gave Merton a hearty wallop on one shoulder that sent him staggering. "How about I get you a nice big cup of punch after the meeting, for old times' sake?"

"Sounds good," Merton said. "Heading inside now? It's colder than a hare's ear at Solstice out here."

"Go ahead, I'll meet up later," Lark said. Her attention was focused on the little procession that just arrived. She barely heard Merton's farewell. A wagon pulled by a sturdy brown donkey rolled to a stop and a figure got out. Lark's mouth fell open. She had no idea what Violet and her mother were plotting, but she never dreamed it would involve Violet arriving at the village meeting in classic Crystalgazer finery.

Her hair was pulled back into her typical long braid, held with a circlet of silver wire that was spun through with pink and green crystals. She wore no other jewelry besides that. Her outfit was simple yet elegant. Instead of her usual dark colors and heavy layers, Violet was dressed from head to toe in flowing, fine green linen. Her tunic was belted about her natural, slim waist and her figure had the typical, graceful line of modestly bound breasts. Lark recognized it as one of the outfits left by her grandmother on her father's side, who was too small for the dresses to be of use to Lark, even if she had wanted them. Lark was glad her parents kept them. They looked made for Violet, the gentle lines and whimsical hint of ages past suited her. A soft, off-white shawl completed the look.

Violet stood in front of Lark with an almost shy look on her face.

"Wow," Lark said. She couldn't help but stare. Violet stepped closer to her. Lark gulped. She found her voice and said, "Wow, that's, oh my, nice. Very nice."

"Tell me what you really think, Lark," Violet said with a twitch at the corners of her lips.

"I think I want you to come home with me now, instead of tonight."

"I wish I were going back with you," Violet murmured. Her expression was resigned. "Your family very generously saved me from having to share your loft by offering Yarrow's spare room."

"He doesn't have a spare room," Lark said, mystified. "I bet Dusty's giving up his room. He's quite the gentleman. Sorry you have to deal with my bumpkin brother, though."

Violet studied her for a long moment with a quizzical expression on her face. "Yes," she said slowly. She reached out and very lightly brushed the back of Lark's hand with her fingers. "Soon, Sunshine." She reiterated what had become their unofficial motto.

"Come over here," Lark said. She led Violet to a little gazebo that was usually reserved for serving punch during their outdoor meetings. Away from the line of sight of anyone in the village hall, Lark said, "I have something to show you and something to ask you."

"The answer is yes."

Lark flushed happily at the eager note in Violet's response. "Now Miss Violet, wait until I've actually asked."

"Haven't I told you to drop the 'Miss'?" Violet asked archly. "My love, you're nervous."

Lark didn't know what to answer, so she just dug at her crystal pouch and withdrew a folded packet of paper. "Before they took Reuel Bucketsworth away to Hadley's End, I got to have a private audience with him. This is a list of all the artifacts Reuel sold. They're still out there, circulating around and causing mischief and I think someone should go out there and track them down."

Violet raised a brow. "And did you have anyone in mind?"

"Yeah, me," Lark said. She took a step forward and clasped both of Violet's hands in hers. The paper crinkled between their hands. "And you. What do you say? Since he's not going to be available for a good long time, Reuel gave me the keys and signed over the deed to his shop — the entire building actually. It's mine now. He said it was better than squatters getting into it. I was thinking, we can use it as a base of operations while we search and destroy. Now that I've got my Tracker's stripe, I can decide my own patrols and my own partner and there's nobody I want at my side more than you." Lark finished her rushed babble and paused. She said, "No need to answer right away, give it —"

"Yes," said Violet. "I will."

Lark let go with a grin. "Seriously?"

"Absolutely."

Lark's heart gave a great leap of joy. She didn't know who moved first, but all of a sudden Violet was in her arms. Their lips met in a swift, hungry kiss. Lark had to close her eyes and gave a moan at the soft, intoxicating pressure. She could never have that enough. Too quickly, Violet pulled away from her. She was breathing hard and her cheeks were deliciously flushed.

"Now I think we should go and join the meeting before someone comes out looking for us," Violet said.

"Good idea."

Euphoric and dazed, Lark stuffed the paper back into her pouch and followed Violet. She felt like her feet weren't touching the ground. On the edge of the clearing, Lark paused and looked up into the evening sky.

The world was no longer the safe and pleasant one she grew up in. It was wide open, full of danger and adventure. Lark wouldn't be a spectator in her own destiny and she wouldn't be alone. She had a star to guide her; one only she knew how to find. The most beautiful one in the sky.

THE BEGINNING

About the Author

Mildred Gail Digby has a BSc in geology, however Takarazuka, pachinko, and no laws against drinking beer outside lured her to teach in Japan. Her favorite thing to do is add lesbians to any situation and make a novel about it. She dreams one day of working as a professional beer taster and devotes a good deal of her time honing her skills in that area which, to an uninformed outsider, appears to be simply drinking a lot of beer.

She shares her non-angst-filled life with her wife of nearly ten years where the most excitement they have is deciding where to eat and forgetting where they parked their bicycles. Mildred is a sucker for oddball characters, opposites attract, and women getting what (and who) they want. She will squeeze a happy ending out of anything and still blushes when she writes love scenes.

Other Mildred Gail Digby titles to look for:

Uncovered

Lindsay Ryan spends her days hidden in the basement of a medical university's archives and her nights online as a pro mah-jong player. She is invisible, anonymous and most of all, safe. Lindsay lives only through the novels she devours every spare moment of her time.

Dr. Gwen Mukherjee invades Lindsay's sanctuary with coffee dates and conspiracy theories—both of which wreak havoc on Lindsay's solitary existence. Inexorably attracted to the odd but charismatic doctor, Lindsay can't keep her distance from Gwen. Neither does she want to. For the first time, Lindsay experiences romance outside the pages of a book.

When Gwen discovers a horrible truth about the town they live in, the unscrupulous company responsible will do anything to keep their secrets safe. And that includes setting Lindsay up as a wanted fugitive to use her as bait to trap Gwen.

Lindsay is thrown into the spotlight. Now, to have a future with Gwen, all she has to do is make it out alive.

ISBN 978-1-61929-430-1
eISBN 978-1-61929-431-8

Stay

Jade Mayflower sees ghosts, can curse with enough vitriol to strip paint, and drives like she's in an action movie. In short, she's not a typical Private Investigator. Which is just as well because Connie Mason isn't a typical client. She's a disembodied spirit who appears in Jade's office one night with a job: Find out what happened to her and who did it.

Jade takes the case, not only because Connie has one of the cutest butts Jade has ever seen and a cute personality to match, but also because of Jade's righteous sense of justice — the tusche is a nice bonus, though. With Connie as her vaporous partner, Jade investigates Connie's life and the truth begins to take shape. In spite of herself, Jade is drawn to the sweet, and sometimes spicy, young woman who has a habit of blushing adorably when Jade flirts with her — and who flirts right back.

Even as their friendship deepens into something much more than that, Connie is being called over to the other side and she can't resist forever. Time is running out as Jade races against the clock to solve a crime where she is falling in love with the victim.

ISBN 978-1-61929-422-9-6
eISBN 978-1-61929-423-3

Perfect Match: Book One

After a tragedy derailed her life, Dr. Megan Maier crawls back to the land of her birth to take a job in a private Jewish hospital. There, she meets Syler Terada, a pediatric surgeon with a brash attitude and a lack of respect for authority who incidentally rocks a tuxedo. She captivates Megan with one glance. Conservative culture and rules against fraternization can't stop Megan. However the secrets she's running from can. The weight of her guilt prevents Megan from making the promise of forever, even though that's the only thing Syler wants from her.

ISBN 978-1-61929-414-1
eISBN 978-1-61929-415-8

Perfect Match: Book Two

Dr. Megan Maier is on her way to happiness and professional success when a hurdle to both appears in the form of Charles Brockman, the son of the hospital's president who has decided that Megan is the perfect partner for him and proposes to her. Megan turns him down cold, certain nothing could make her even consider his offer. Nothing except for Megan's secrets. Incriminating documents go missing and Megan has to face the truth that the cost of protecting herself, and the victims of her shattered past, is betrayal of the woman she loves.

ISBN 978-1-61929-416-5
eISBN 978-1-61929-417-2

Phoenix

What would it take to make you ditch your career, your pride, and run from everything you believe in? In private investigator Ashe Devon's case, it's the fact that her client ended up dead while under her protection. Out of the P.I. business, Ashe is just trying to survive the daily grind of her boring, vanilla life when her former boss calls her out of retirement for one last job: protect a local DJ from a violent stalker. Ashe is fully prepared to turn down the case until she meets the client.

Mystral Galbraith, aka Phoenix, is unashamedly gay, just a tad awkward and musically brilliant. Ashe is instantly captivated by her and can't ignore the fierce young woman's plea for help. Neither can Ashe ignore the stirrings of long-forgotten emotions that set both her heart and her boxer briefs on fire. While Ashe struggles to keep her relationship with Mystral professional, the tension between them simmers just beneath the surface.

More than Ashe's pride is involved—failure could cost Mystral her life. But is Ashe the right person for the job? If she doesn't get her hormones under control, the undeniable pull between them could compromise her judgment and open the door for history to repeat its tragic lesson.

ISBN 978-1-61929-394-6
eISBN 978-1-61929-395-3

MORE REGAL CREST PUBLICATIONS

Brenda Adcock	Soiled Dove	978-1-935053-35-4
Brenda Adcock	The Sea Hawk	978-1-935053-10-1
Brenda Adcock	The Other Mrs. Champion	978-1-935053-46-0
Brenda Adcock	Picking Up the Pieces	978-1-61929-120-1
Brenda Adcock	The Game of Denial	978-1-61929-130-0
Brenda Adcock	In the Midnight Hour	978-1-61929-188-1
Brenda Adcock	Untouchable	978-1-61929-210-9
Brenda Adcock	The Heart of the Mountain	978-1-61929-330-4
Brenda Adcock	Gift of the Redeemer	978-1-61929-360-1
Brenda Adcock	Unresolved Conflicts	978-1-61929-374-8
Brenda Adcock	One Step At A Time	978-1-61929-408-0
K. Aten	The Fletcher	978-1-61929-356-4
K. Aten	Rules of the Road	978-1-61919-366-3
K. Aten	The Archer	978-1-61929-370-0
K. Aten	Waking the Dreamer	978-1-61929-382-3
K. Aten	The Sagittarius	978-1-61929-386-1
K. Aten	Running From Forever: Book One in the Blood Resonance Series	978-1-61929-398-4
K. Aten	The Sovereign of Psiere: Book One In the Mystery of the Makers series	978-1-61929-412-7
K. Aten	Burn It Down	978-1-61929-418-9
K. Aten	Embracing Forever: Book Two in the Blood Resonance Series	978-1-61929-424-0
K. Aten	Children of the Stars	978-1-61929-432-5
K. Aten	Remember Me, Synthetica	978-1-61929-442-4
Georgia Beers	Thy Neighbor's Wife	1-932300-15-5
Georgia Beers	Turning the Page	978-1-932300-71-0
Lynnette Beers	Just Beyond the Shining River	978-1-61929-352-6
Lynnette Beers	Saving Sam	978-1-61929-410-3
Tonie Chacon	Struck! A Titanic Love Story	978-1-61929-226-0
Sky Croft	Amazonia	978-1-61929-067-9
Sky Croft	Amazonia: An Impossible Choice	978-1-61929-179-9
Sky Croft	Mountain Rescue: The Ascent	978-1-61929-099-0
Sky Croft	Mountain Rescue: On the Edge	978-1-61929-205-5
Mildred Gail Digby	Phoenix	978-1-61929-394-6
Mildred Gail Digby	Perfect Match: Book One	978-1-61929-414-4
Mildred Gail Digby	Perfect Match: Book Two	978-1-61929-416-5
Mildred Gail Digby	Stay	978-1-61929-422-6
Mildred Gail Digby	Uncovered	978-1-61929-430-1
Cronin and Foster	Blue Collar Lesbian Erotica	978-1-935053-01-9
Cronin and Foster	Women in Uniform	978-1-935053-31-6
Cronin and Foster	Women in Sports	978-1-61929-278-9
Anna Furtado	The Heart's Desire	978-1-935053-81-1
Anna Furtado	The Heart's Strength	978-1-935053-82-8
Anna Furtado	The Heart's Longing	978-1-935053-83-5
Anna Furtado	Tremble and Burn	978-1-61929-354-0

Melissa Good	Eye of the Storm	1-932300-13-9
Melissa Good	Hurricane Watch	978-1-935053-00-2
Melissa Good	Moving Target	978-1-61929-150-8
Melissa Good	Red Sky At Morning	978-1-932300-80-2
Melissa Good	Storm Surge: Book One	978-1-935053-28-6
Melissa Good	Storm Surge: Book Two	978-1-935053-39-2
Melissa Good	Stormy Waters	978-1-61929-082-2
Melissa Good	Thicker Than Water	1-932300-24-4
Melissa Good	Terrors of the High Seas	1-932300-45-7
Melissa Good	Tropical Storm	978-1-932300-60-4
Melissa Good	Tropical Convergence	978-1-935053-18-7
Melissa Good	Winds of Change Book One	978-1-61929-194-2
Melissa Good	Winds of Change Book Two	978-1-61929-232-1
Melissa Good	Southern Stars	978-1-61929-348-9
K. E. Lane	And, Playing the Role of Herself	978-1-932300-72-7
Kate McLachlan	Christmas Crush	978-1-61929-195-9
Kate McLachlan	Hearts, Dead and Alive	978-1-61929-017-4
Kate McLachlan	Murder and the Hurdy Gurdy Girl	978-1-61929-125-6
Kate McLachlan	Rescue At Inspiration Point	978-1-61929-005-1
Kate McLachlan	Return Of An Impetuous Pilot	978-1-61929-152-2
Kate McLachlan	Rip Van Dyke	978-1-935053-29-3
Kate McLachlan	Ten Little Lesbians	978-1-61929-236-9
Kate McLachlan	Alias Mrs. Jones	978-1-61929-282-6
Lynne Norris	One Promise	978-1-932300-92-5
Lynne Norris	Sanctuary	978-1-61929-248-2
Lynne Norris	The Light of Day	978-1-61929-338-0
Schramm and Dunne	Love Is In the Air	978-1-61929-362-8
Rae Theodore	Leaving Normal: Adventures in Gender	
		978-1-61929-320-5
Rae Theodore	My Mother Says Drums Are for Boys: True	
	Stories for Gender Rebels	978-1-61929-378-6
Barbara Valletto	Pulse Points	978-1-61929-254-3
Barbara Valletto	Everlong	978-1-61929-266-6
Barbara Valletto	Limbo	978-1-61929-358-8
Barbara Valletto	Diver Blues	978-1-61929-384-7
Lisa Young	Out and Proud	978-1-61929-392-2

Be sure to check out our other imprints,
Blue Beacon Books, Mystic Books, Quest Books,
Troubadour Books, Yellow Rose Books,
and Young Adult Books.